TAKE HEED OF LOVING ME

Take Heed of Loving Me

By ELIZABETH GRAY VINING

J. B. LIPPINCOTT COMPANY

PHILADELPHIA & NEW YORK

1964

Copyright © 1963 by Elizabeth Gray Vining

THIRD PRINTING

Printed in the United States of America

Library of Congress Catalog Card Number: 63–20398

PROLOGUE

HE WAS A POET AND, SO THEY SAID, A LIBERTINE. He was to become at last a famous preacher, perhaps the greatest England has ever had, and so popular that people crowded to hear him, king, nobles, gentlefolk and commoners, hanging on his words if not changed by them—for how often do sermons change lives? But they crowded to hear him, standing with uplifted faces and uplifted hearts, listening, so said a linen-draper with a gift for words (and a love of angling), as if to an angel from a cloud. His life in those days—if it had not been so always— was saintly, for the preacher's life, he said, was the necessary other half of the sermon. "It is too soon," he said, "to ask when the clock strikes eleven, Is it a good sermon? for I have but half his sermon then; his own life is the other half; it is time enough to ask the Saturday after, whether the Sunday's preacher preach well or no; for he preaches on all the week, if he live well, to the edifying of others."

When he preached about sin, he preached as one who knew by experience the slipperiness of habitual sin; the merry sins; the laughing sins that become crying sins; the whispering sins that we rock in our hearts, tossing and tumbling them in our imaginations; the forgotten sins; the unconsidered, unconfessed, unrepentant sins and all the sins that we call small: enough lascivious glances to make up an adultery, enough covetous wishes for a robbery, enough angry words for a murder. He could preach most entertainingly about sin, which he

5

knew so well, but when he spoke of hell, it was not of a place of fire and brimstone but of the torment of torments, a horror beyond imagining, the everlasting absence of God, the being secluded eternally, eternally, eternally, from the sight of God.

He was to write, in a book of devotions, words that lived down the centuries and pealed out more than three hundred years later, so ringing with poetry and with truth that people sang them who had never heard of him, people read them who read nothing else that he wrote, and were eased of their separateness:

No man is an island, entire of itself; every man is a piece of the continent, a part of the main; if a clod be washed away by the sea, Europe is the less, as well as if a promontory were, as well as if a manor of thy friends or of thine own were; any man's death diminishes me, because I am involved in mankind; and therefore never send to know for whom the bell tolls; it tolls for thee.

Years before he became a preacher, he was a poet—though in this lifetime only two or three of his poems were published and those not his best. He made songs and sonnets about his love of God, lyrics and verse letters of his elegant flirtations with great ladies, tender and passionate and—so they have been called—metaphysical poems for Anne (whom he loved and married and brought to poverty and hardship, all but destroying himself as well) and then all those brilliant and witty, daring, indecent, rebellious and hilarious poems of his sinful youth.

His name was John Donne.

BOOK ONE 1597

"I am two fools, I know"

i

HE WAS GLAD TO BE GETTING BACK TO LONDON—and he was not. Divided as always, he thought wryly, shifting wearily in the small, hard saddle. Mind and heart pulled against each other like a badly matched team. Worse than that: divided within themselves, mind pulling two ways, heart pulling two other ways. And over all, consciousness like a fitful lantern flashing now here, now there, illumining this, casting that into darkness.

The voyage had been a failure both publicly and privately. He moved again to ease the place where the hired saddle galled his leg. The noble lords, Essex, Howard, Raleigh and the others, had neither met the Spanish fleet in battle nor captured the treasure ships returning laden from India. At this moment perhaps Essex was telling the Queen how Raleigh had disobeyed orders. Admiration for Essex and disappointment over Essex's lack of interest in him warred briefly in John's heart. And he himself, he thought, moving from the public to the private failure, was returning, patronless and without prospects, to a dwindling—dwindled—patrimony and rented rooms, to London who as ruthlessly rejected failures as she delighted in overturning those who climbed too high too swiftly.

His spirits rose nevertheless at the sight of the city's roofs and towers in the distance. There was no other place to compare with it, not Paris nor Rome nor Madrid, and he had seen them all. In spite of his flat purse and a wasted summer, he felt power in himself rising like a spring that could not be quenched. At twenty-four, he thought with characteristic arrogance, he knew enough law to be a judge, enough theology to be a priest, enough medicine to be a doctor. He had, furthermore, written enough poems to publish a book, if he were willing to offer it with abject flattery to some great lord, like Nashe or Shakespeare or Drayton, street singers warbling at the door for their supper. He was free of all the bondages, family, political, religious, amatory. Benita rose before his inner eyes with an indignant expression on her lovely face and was summarily thrust aside. Perhaps not entirely free of love, he corrected himself. At all events, praise God, free from the sea. He had left behind him the stinking, crowded ship, the unendurable tedium of flat, glassy water and empty sails, the sickness and terror of storm, the deadly rumors, jealousies, quarrels and maneuvers of ambitious young men seeking place and fame through military adventure. Had left behind, too, the strange, sudden flashes of beauty—Teneriffe rising black against the night sky like some great rock on which the sailing moon must shipwreck—and those moments of rare happiness when friends on the deck at midnight opened their thoughts to one another without reserve.

His hired mare stumbled and he pulled her up. Francis Woolley, riding just behind him, spoke and he turned over his shoulder to listen.

"I think you got the worse of the two nags. I'll change with you, if you like."

"No, thank you. It's not far now."

On the squelching road ahead where last night's frost, melting, had left the ground a treacherous ooze, a band of citizens approached, some walking, some on horseback, two to a horse. The guide that he and Francis had engaged at the posting inn at Guildford whipped up his horse and blew a blast on his horn, while the common folk edged off the road into the bushes and looked curiously at the gentry splashing them with mud as they galloped by.

Fleetingly John saw himself as they might be seeing him, a slender young man in dark military dress with the gleam of his rapier at his side, hurrying, arrogant, important, preceded by the noisy guide, followed by his elegant young friend and a servant with their cloak-bags. His lip curling a little in self-mockery, he allowed himself to look still more fashionable and important, and glancing at the citizens as he passed, he met the merry eyes of a young wife perched behind her stolid husband on a fat sorrel horse.

His expert eye, sweeping over the white coif under the tied-on hat, the bright blue gaze with its candid, though possibly unconscious, invitation, the red cheeks and childish mouth, the plump breasts under the tight blue bodice, summed her up easily: no more than twenty to her husband's thirty-five, a baby left behind with its granddam, life bubbling and brimming within her unsated body. Accustomed as he was to the signs that women gave him, he felt stirred a little, a very little, by the moment's encounter. His heart? His vanity? Or only his mood, lightened by such an overflow of life?

Well past the little group, where the road widened, he waited for Francis to come abreast with him. The boy's thin face, still pale from his recent illness, was kindled with mischief.

"I saw her!" he said. "Why you? Why always you? What is there in that dark, smoldering face of yours that draws all the women?"

John laughed. "I have the advantage of you in age," he said. "She was a good five years older than you."

Francis Woolley, fifteen and the veteran of these past months of storm and calm and smells, of fruitless pursuit of an elusive enemy and a few scattered bullets, of men's talk over wine and tobacco at night, still wore his pale gold, pale blue, etched and transparent look that made John think of the fair-haired English boys who St. Gregory said were "angels not Angles."

"Oh, I wasn't thinking so much of myself," replied Francis cheerfully. "After all, I came behind you. She didn't see me. And at Plymouth I was sick. But it was the same with the host's

11

daughter at the inn. Tom and John Egerton were there and Mr. Wotton—he's older than you—and yet the girl saw only you."

"One at a time is her rule," said John, losing interest.

Benita once more swam across his vision. He saw her smiling, her dark eyes half veiled by the thick black lashes, her red mouth, so slightly, so endearingly irregular, parted, so that the white teeth showed. He all but felt her sweet, warm breath, her hand on his neck touching the pulse in his throat, almost heard her whisper at his ear, and he wondered at the pain and tumult in his body that followed on the thought of her, only at the thought—and that not long or willingly entertained. Again he brushed her impatiently out of his mind and knew the effort to be useless. The five months that he had hoped would damp his fever, sponge it away, had done nothing.

The village of Southwark lay ahead, and beyond were London Bridge and the great bulk of St. Paul's soaring over all the massed roofs and lesser spires of London. The silver river curved away, and in the distance to the west he saw the towers of Whitehall and Westminster and wondered if the Queen was there. And Essex? Was he with her or was he withdrawn somewhere in the country under the cloud of his failure?

The thought of Essex pricked him with discomfort. Twice he had sailed with him, one of the small, envied band of gilded young men attached to his person, last year to Cadiz, this year to the Azores, and still he was no nearer to the secretaryship he wanted than he had been when Harry Wotton, his friend from Oxford days, had first introduced him to the Queen's favorite. Last year, after the raid on Cadiz, which had been a signal success, the Earl of Essex had knighted sixty-six of his followers, and John Donne not among them. Not unduly discouraged by that—for it was not his military prowess by which he hoped to recommend himself—he had gone again with Essex this year, hoping to attract attention by his varied store of knowledge, his zeal, his usefulness. Wotton himself, secure as one of four secretaries, had done his best for John, but it was not enough. Or John himself had not been enough. Essex had scarcely seemed to see him. Even Tom Egerton, eight years younger, had got closer than he had done. But Tom, of course, was the Lord Keeper's son. Even Essex, for all the Queen's love to him, looked for powerful friends.

Francis at his side broke into his thoughts. "We're almost there. I'll not have a better chance than now to thank you for staying behind with me at Plymouth. I hope you know how grateful I am."

"You have thanked me already, more than enough. I was glad to have a few days at Plymouth anyhow."

They had given him time to have his clothes put in order after the bedragglement of the voyage. Francis had had a sharp attack of some kind of inflammation of the lungs and someone had had to stand by to see that he was properly cared for. Once the fever had abated, there had been little to do for him and plenty of time to walk on the Hoe and talk to sailors, to write the verses that came tapping at his mind; his honest lines, rough perhaps, but written in the words and cadences that people actually used, not the bastard flowery language of "poetry," with images from the new science and from actual life, not worn clichés and tired ornaments from the classics. Time, also, to dally with the innkeeper's pretty daughter, who seemed, after the long months at sea, a very flower of English girlhood. He hoped he would never have to meet her again and be disillusioned.

The two Egertons, Francis's stepbrothers, should have been the ones to stay and care for him, but they had been in a dither to get home again, and Wotton, after doing some business in Plymouth for Essex, had had to go on to London for further orders. John had waited till Francis was strong enough for the trip home and then they had ridden together by easy stages. He was aware—though this was not the determining motive—that Francis Woolley was the stepson of the Lord Keeper of the Great Seal and that a man who had failed to attach himself to Essex might look far before he could find a better second choice than Sir Thomas Egerton.

"I'll tell my stepfather how kind you have been," said Francis eagerly. "But I've no doubt that he remembers you from Lincoln's Inn."

"I think it's hardly likely. He had ceased to be Lent Reader before I entered there."

There was a chance, of course. Sir Thomas had kept his interest in Lincoln's Inn long after he became Attorney General, and he used to return sometimes for the moots, to watch the future barristers argue against each other in mock cases. Though he might well take notice of a promising student, he might also consider that one who had left Lincoln's Inn after only three years to travel abroad and then to dangle after the Earl of Essex was lacking in serious purpose if not in ambition.

Ambition. It was as persistent an itch as lust, as devouring and, John felt austerely, as discreditable. Yet if one was aware of intellectual powers as surging and as undeniable as one's need of women or as one's ability to rouse and satisfy a woman's desire, how would one not seek outlets? Some weighty employment in the state. He had heard the phrase and it had jumped to him as iron filings leap to a magnet. Lacking a fortune, a great name (the name of Donne was respectable but bore no luster) or family backing (his father, who had been warden of the Worshipful Company of Ironmongers, had been dead these twenty years) one began by being secretary to some public figure of power and influence.

He would make an elegy of the band of citizens, he thought, but first he would finish the poems he had begun at Plymouth. Having been near death—or near enough for his purposes—in the storm at sea, he had composed in mocking verse his will, and as he rode along he amused himself by filling out the stanzas.

In the first he intended to leave his possessions to those who had too much before: his eyes to Argus, his tongue to fame; in the next one, to those who had an incapacity:

My truth to them who at the court do live; . . .
My silence to any who abroad have been.

14

He chuckled over that. He had been abroad himself often enough to know the difficulties of holding an audience for the tale of his travels, too often to attempt to tell, except in verse, of his recent adventures.

I give my reputation to those
Which were my friends; mine industry to foes;
To schoolmen I bequeath my doubtfulness;
My sickness to physicians, or excess;
To nature all that I in rhyme have writ;
  And to my company my wit.
  Thou, Love, by making me adore
Her who begot this love in me before,
Taught'st me to make, as though I gave, when I did but restore.

Not that he would ever show it to Benita. She was beautiful, she was desirable, but she could not understand the simplest and easiest English poetry.

They crossed London Bridge with only a glance for the heads of traitors on spikes over the south gate, and turned into Thames Street. The smells of the city, of the garbage and other filth in the narrow streets, assailed his nose as its noises, the street cries, the rumbling of coaches, the shouts and quarrels, assailed his ears. There was an intensification of the stench as they crossed the Fleet ditch and then a gradual sweetening of the air beside the great houses by the Strand.

At Essex House no flags were flying and the courtyard seen through the iron gates was empty except for a servant or two. Essex then was in the country, at Wanstead most likely, or perhaps, if all was going well, with the Queen at Nonsuch or Windsor. At the entrance to the Savoy he said good-by to Francis, who was going on to York House.

"I'd be grateful if you would mention me to the Lord Keeper," he added abruptly, as if the words were jerked out of him, and turned toward his lodging.

It was a convenient place to live, midway of the Strand, between Essex House, near one end, and York House at the other, but its great days were over. John of Gaunt's palace, where Chaucer had been a guest, was two hundred years gone, but its old chapel was now the parish church of St. Mary-le-Savoy, and Henry VII's hospital still dominated the crowded precinct, where between the Royal Printing Press, which ground out acts of Parliament and proclamations, and the Savoy prison for military offenders, which was actually one end of the original palace, a few private houses marched along the river bank.

Riding through the gate under the Tudor rose and portcullis, John made his way through the swarm of beggars and vagabonds, and doubtless thieves too, clamoring for alms at the hospital. Twice a day they were fed, and the crowd of unsavory characters attracted by the free bread and cheese was one of the drawbacks of living there, and the chief reason why it was comparatively inexpensive. As he passed the small stone chapel, set in the green of its graveyard and trees like a village church, he saw a youth and a girl with a self-conscious smirk of happiness on their blank young faces come out of the entrance hand in hand and scuttle away into the shadowy passageway leading to the river. Another runaway pair, married by one of the Savoy parsons, who were notorious for performing secret weddings. Young idiots, he thought, to fly in the face of vindictive social disapproval, but he spared them a moment's hope for happiness.

At the door of a tall brick and timber house near the Royal Press he dismounted, stiff-jointed after being so long on horseback, handed his reins to the guide, paid him and ordered his bags carried in. As if she had been waiting behind the door, his landlady, Mrs. Haines, came bustling out to welcome him.

Like her house, she had come down in the world. The widow of an only moderately successful man of law, she had managed to hold on to her house and eke out a living by renting rooms. By all the laws of compensation, her courage, resignation and industry should have ennobled her, but the struggle itself had perhaps taken too much of her strength: the need ever at her back like a panting hound had forced her into little subterfuges, little flatteries and hints, little whinings and importunities that diminished her dignity and repelled even those who most sympathized with her. She was fifty; her hair was black and glossy still, her eyes a light anxious blue, her cheeks bright with a network of fine veins, her lips soft, because there were no teeth behind them, and pressed together in folds.

Delighted to see John, who was her favorite among her lodgers, she smiled broadly and toothlessly, a baby's grin in her worn face.

"Eh, Mr. Donne, I thought I'd be seeing you any day now. I have your rooms all aired and ready. Be careful there, porter, how you put down those cloak-bags. They're not sacks of coal."

He had two rooms on the ground floor, with a door from the bedroom opening directly into the yard, so that he could come and go unnoticed by the rest of the house. The other room, which was his study, was built over an old vault that had been part of the palace, and it was damp all year 'round, bitterly cold in winter. But it had a window looking out on the Thames and all the life that flowed there, and it had shelves for his books, those rows and rows of leather-bound and gilded volumes for which so much of his patrimony had been spent. It was to this room that he went as soon as he had paid the boy who carried in his bags, and after him pattered his landlady.

It was already dark and he lit the candle, the same one that he had left half burned and guttered with wax in the iron candlestick five months before.

"What's the news, dame?" he asked absently, lifting the candle to see if there were any gaps on the shelves.

"Oh, I've got on very well, though I've missed you sorely. My young men have been good to me, as they always are. Mr. Philpots—he's got a better post now as clerk in the Record Office—he has such a care for me and insists on giving me a groat over the rent we agreed upon. And Mr. Gooch brought me a bottle of canary from the Mermaid. It's threepence more a bottle there, but it's better."

"I have a piece of fur for you in my bag," said John, coming

17

up to the mark. "A sailor had it in Plymouth. He'd got it at a Baltic port. Sealskin—from Muscovy."

"Oh, now that's kind of you. You didn't have to do that. It will be a real comfort to me now that the weather's getting colder. I'll have Tilly unpack your bags for you and you can give it to her for me. That French man of yours, Pierre, will be here tomorrow. He comes every morning to see if you're back. Would you like some supper now? Some cold mutton and a salad?"

She bustled away. He thought he had left a couple of bottles of sack in the cabinet in the study, but when he looked for them, they were not there. The maid, Tilly, a sociable slattern, came in, ostensibly to unpack for him. He gave her the seal-skin wrap for Mrs. Haines and a bauble for herself, which made her grin with delight.

"Leave the rest. Pierre can do it tomorrow. Go and see to my supper, and I'll have beer with it. I've got no wine left."

She made no answer to that and there was no change in her expression as she turned on her run-down heels and slip-slopped off. He shrugged his shoulders in the way that he had picked up in France, and turned back to his books. They were all there, the poets, Dante, Aretino, Ovid, Persius, Juvenal, Horace, Virgil, the philosophers, the chroniclers, the statesmen, the Fathers, the theologians. How many hours, days, weeks, he had spent combing through Luther and Calvin and Servetus, Bellarmine and Beza, making up his mind about what he could believe, about what religion essentially was, about schism, about the old religion of his mother, of his brother Henry, of his forefathers, about the new religion of the Queen and the law. He had, as he sometimes liked to say, deprecatingly, "an immoderate, hydroptic desire for learning," but it was more than learning that he had pursued through all these tomes: it was a place to stand.

Tilly returned with a can of hot water and he splashed re-freshingly in the basin in the bedroom.

There was always something a little flat about coming home, he admitted, drying his hands. After the effort and expectation of the journey, the elation at the sight of Whitehall and St. Paul's and the Thames, the somewhat forced good fellowship with Mrs. Haines, the satisfaction in his books, the comfort of hot water, the prospect of food: what? This flat feeling. Was it loneliness?

His mother, safe in Catholic Malines with her third husband, would have been little comfort to him if she had been here; their differing views and the sorrow they had shared had separated them—and besides, Mr. Rainsford, his stepfather, was a deadly tiresome man. His sister Anne was in Hawstead with that lily-livered Jackanapes, her husband, William Lyly, who spelt his name, since his year in Paris, Lillé. Lillé indeed. And Henry, his almost-twin, only ten months younger, his gentle, gay companion at Hart Hall and then at Trinity, was dead. The thought of Henry, even after four years, was an aching hollow in the center of his being, an accusation and a burden of guilt that he could never argue quite away. Henry, harboring at Thavies Inn the seminary priest whom he, John, had turned away from his room at Lincoln's Inn, Henry, coughing and laughing and swearing in prison in the Clink, Henry suddenly dead of gaol fever: these were the memories that did not fade.

Tilly brought his supper on a tray and set it on the table in the study. Mrs. Haines followed to see that everything was right, and stayed to talk.

"I hear you took no prizes at all?"

"A ship and two frigates—but not enough even to pay for the expedition. The plate ships escaped us. They slipped into Agra while we were on the north side of the island. By the time we got into Agra Road the ships were standing high in the water. They'd taken all the cargo off, and they had got a garrison of fifteen hundred Spanish soldiers. Our supplies were too short to risk an attack. What are people saying here?"

"Oh, the Queen reproached my lord of Essex, it's said, but the people in general can see no wrong in him. When he came along the Strand with all his household trooping after him in their orange livery, everybody was out to cheer him. But he's in Wanstead now, they say."

"We had the worst storms I've ever experienced. Even some of the mariners thought it not amiss to pray. I heard one cry out, 'God help us!' "

"Nobody here complained of those storms," said Mrs. Haines sharply. "We knew the Spanish fleet had eluded you and was bearing down on England. It was the storm that scattered them, while you were chasing the plate ships in and out of the Azores."

"I daresay. But the whole expedition was doomed from the beginning. The weather was bad enough, but worse than that, a pack of Essex's enemies had been made into a council to hamper him."

Mrs. Haines had had all she wanted about the Islands Voyage. Her question had been directed primarily to the possibility of prize money and prompted by her own needs. She lowered her voice.

"I've had a serious misfortune, Mr. Donne."

"I'm sorry, dame. What went wrong?"

"I haven't told the other gentlemen, but I can tell you, because you belong to the old religion too."

"No. I don't. I've told you, dame. Not for several years now."

"Well, you understand about it. I've been going to Mass to Father Benedict all summer and nobody took any notice of it. I came to think they'd forgotten about their laws and I felt easy. Then last Sunday the pursuivants came and we were all taken up and fined."

"Oh, oh, I *am* sorry. How much?"

"A hundred marks. I had to sell my bed curtains and my best ewer. D'you think you could . . ." Her voice trailed away.

"Would fifty marks help?"

Her eyes filled with tears and the soft lips worked convulsively. "You're always so kind, Mr. Donne."

He got up from his meal to get her the money. It was not the first time that he had paid the fine, or helped to pay it, of some vulnerable, unhappy, obstinate person who still could summon courage to defy the law for the sake of worshiping in the old communion. In some half-acknowledged way he felt that he did it for Henry.

"St. Mary-le-Savoy is near, dame," he said gently, "and the Queen's church is the church of our country. It's right, I am sure, to accept the religion of one's country. After all, it is the same God and the same Lord Jesus."

She shook her head. "They say the liturgy in *English* at St. Mary's," she said disdainfully, finding an outward reason for an inner compulsion. "But it's not a question of country, Mr. Donne. You were brought up different yourself."

He swallowed the last of his beer and, leaving the rest of his supper unfinished, washed his hands in the pewter basin that Tilly had set on a stool beside the table.

"I am going out for a while," he said.

ii

IT WAS A SHORT WALK TO LINCOLN'S INN and to the room in the old building that once he had shared with Christopher Brooke, his friend since, two fifteen-year-olds, heady with freedom and the pursuit of learning, they had first met at Trinity College, Cambridge.

"Jack! At last! I've been expecting you every day. Come in, man, sit down and tell me all the news."

Christopher's clear gray eyes and white teeth shone in the candlelight out of his shadowed, long, thin face; his pleasure and affection were warm in his voice and handclasp. He put another fagot of wood on the fire, which flared up and lit the corners of the room. John sat down in the armchair while his host took a flagon of sack and two cups from the cupboard.

"News," John said. "London's passion for news never diminishes. Wherever you go, whomever you meet, the greeting is the same. 'What news?' What news have *you*? You have all my news already."

"Your verse letters. Yes, I got them. I think they are the best thing you have done so far. I took them to our friend Ben, to beguile his weary hours in prison. Did you know he has been in the Marshalsea?"

"Jonson? No! What for?"

"For a play he wrote—or wrote part of—called *The Isle of Dogs*. Nashe wrote the rest but he snaked out of it to Yarmouth. All the actors in the wretched play were dumped in gaol and all the theaters closed, not only the Swan, where *The Isle of Dogs* was put on, but all the others too. There was talk of tearing them all down, but the Curtain and the Rose have already opened again. After all, the Queen likes plays herself."

"I can't imagine our classical-minded Ben writing anything objectionable. What was wrong with the play?"

"It was seditious and slanderous, according to the Privy Council. I did not see it myself, but I'm told that it mentioned food shortages and high prices and the Council feared that it might stir up the poor to express some dissatisfaction with the government."

"My God. I suppose the poor wouldn't notice the high prices if Jonson didn't inform them. Can't anything be done to get him out?"

"I think he was released a day or so ago, in point of fact. But two months in the Marshalsea are no joke."

"I take it he had money enough to pay the fees?"

"He had plenty of friends to borrow from."

"What"—the writer's question rose irrepressibly—"What did he think of my verses?"

"He was delighted with them, especially 'The Calm.' He said those lines about the stillness—how was it?—'in one place lay Feathers and dust, today and yesterday'—were as fine as anything written in these times."

John was pleased. "There literally wasn't a breath of air," he said reminiscently. "And the heat! You can't imagine it. Pitch oozing from the cracks between the planks and the deck hot as coals. We tried to cool off with a swim, but we climbed out of the water, parboiled, to fry on the deck!"

"And after all the misery what did you get from it of those things that pushed you into going? Money, fame, 'the thirst Of honor or fair death'?"

"Not a thing. Not one thing."

"You think too much of death anyhow. What sort of death is *fair*?"

"A clean, swift death in battle, surely. Certainly not death by plague or gaol fever."

"One is just as dead. Well, let it pass. What about release from 'the queasy pain Of being beloved and loving'?" Christopher's smile was easy but his eyes had a searching look as he leaned over to refill John's cup. He had, John recognized, some disturbing thought, some other question behind the one he asked. He could read Christopher like a favorite book. Their friendship had been a lasting one, begun at Trinity College, during John's sojourn there, strengthened here in Lincoln's Inn, where they shared a room for more than two years.

"That too," he answered slowly, swirling the wine around in his cup and looking at Christopher under his arched eyebrows. "I thought we wound it up and tied it off last spring before I left. I went away stuffed full of virtue—but now I am in a fever till I can go to her. What news in that quarter?"

"You had better stay away from Stilwell House."

"Why? I have a message from Harry Wotton to his lordship that gives an excellent excuse to call there."

"Wotton has been all over London and the suburbs these last ten days. He has had ample opportunity to deliver his message himself."

"This is a copy of a poem. His modesty would scarcely let him plant that on his lordship unasked."

"I hope it's more discreet than some of yours."

John was silent. Whatever had been behind that searching look of Christopher's was about to make itself known; it was there, crouched like a cat, lashing its tail, waiting. He set his cup down and spoke warily.

"Which of mine?"

"That elegy on your mistress going to bed, for instance, and the other one entitled 'Jealousy.' They've come into Stilwell's hands and he is raging. Not surprisingly."

"But he can't know——"

"He suspects."

"He can't possibly know with any certainty that they are mine or suppose that they refer to his wife. How did he get them? They're not in print—and even my lady has not seen them."

24

"They are in manuscript—lavishly. You've given them to friends—and friends give copies to other friends."

John was disturbed but not convinced. "But they are only literary exercises, not to be taken personally. Anyone who knows his Ovid—and everybody reads Ovid—can recognize their inspiration."

"People dip into the *Metamorphoses* for good stories, but few read the *Amores* or the *Ars Amatoria*. And I don't remember anything in the *Amores* about an invalid husband, pampered and swollen and snorting in a basket chair."

"Oh, that." The relief that he felt revealed to him the intensity of the anxiety that he had not admitted. "That was pure invention. He certainly can't apply that to himself."

"I'm not sure that *pure* is the word! But you can't have forgotten his withered foot and his limp? He seems to have felt that the shoe fitted only too well. And he can't have liked your flaunting of the fact that you 'usurp his own bed' or the intimacies you describe in the other one. I'm afraid you've gone too far this time. For God's sake, Jack, be careful!"

"But he's got no reason to imagine that I was writing about his wife. We've been most cautious. And why should he assume that the verses are mine? They're not signed."

"Your style is unmistakable. And no doubt some officious fool has made all clear. A good many people, for all your caution and your silence, guessed who it was you loved. You know London. Who withholds any news here?"

John looked at him unseeing. What had he done to Benita with his verses, his—he saw it now—appallingly careless verses? Had he made her life unendurable?

Christopher leaned over and put a hand on his knee. "Forgive me, Jack. I don't say all this to make you wretched. Only out of friendship. You are I and I you—you wrote it in 'The Storm,' and so I feel also. You said that it is the preeminence of friendship to impute excellence, but I think it must warn of danger as well. You have been out of the country for five months. Stay away from Stilwell House now. Lie low till the storm blows over."

Anger, fed by remorse and damaged pride, rose in a bitter tide and found its outlet through a small crack. "Who thinks he knows whom I love?" he said fiercely. "There is nothing in the elegies to show who it might be, or if it is somebody real at all. May a curse wither him, whoever guesses or thinks or dreams he knows who my mistress is. Damn him, damn him, damn him. May he plan treason and believe he performed it. And confess and die. May he——"

"Calm yourself," said Christopher dryly. "Put it in a poem."

John glared at him, hating at that moment his friend as he hated himself. Benita, his gentle, dove-like love, how could he have so harmed her? How could he contrive now to see her and to find out what damage had actually been done, to explain the unexplainable, to ask her forgiveness? Tomorrow. He would go boldly to the house tomorrow, bearing Wotton's poem, that neat little poem, so correct, so flowery, so smoothly musical, so insipid. So safe.

A log flared up in sparks and broke, sending a wave of heat from the fiery golden coals. The flagon was empty. Silence lay over the two men for long minutes, healing, quieting. In its depths there had been communication between them, sympathy offered and accepted, advice offered and not accepted, rejection assimilated, confidence withheld, and understanding exchanged.

Christopher rose to put another log on the fire, but John stopped him. "No, don't. I must go. It's late."

"Why don't you sleep here? There's plenty of room and it's a dark night to go groping through the streets."

"I'll find a link-boy. I had better be in my own bed and get an early start tomorrow. I've much to do."

"Jack," said Christopher persuasively, leaning against the chimney piece, "why don't you come back here and finish your studies? The law is an honorable profession and offers opportunity for advancement. You have no feeling now against taking the oath, have you?"

"None at all. It was my mother's decision that kept me from

it at Oxford—and prevented my getting a degree. I was, after all, only fifteen then and much under her thumb."

"Then why not come back and take up the law where you left off?"

"For a simple reason—and one that no one ever thinks of—money. Have you the least idea that Lincoln's Inn is one of the most expensive places in England in which to spend seven years learning a trade?"

"I'd no idea that you were pressed. When you were here you spent money as if there was no end to it."

"I thought there *was* no end. My father left us each a small fortune—and then Henry's share was divided between my sister and myself. It should have been more than enough. But travel and expensive books eat it up fast."

"And gifts to friends and needy people! You do yourself little justice. I have only the allowance that my mother makes me, but it is a generous one and much more than I need for myself. I could lend you almost half——"

"No. But it's good of you. Lincoln's Inn had its place in my life, but that time is past and one cannot go back. I doubt if I should be happy here now."

"It was Henry's death, I think, that took you away, not the lure of travel."

"Perhaps," said John, his dark face wearing its most closed look and the glow fading from his eyes. "But don't disturb yourself about me. I have hopes."

iii

HIS CANDLE BURNED LATE. When the old one flickered in its pool of wax, ready to go out, he lit a new one. The room was damp and cold, and sneaking drafts made the yellow glow waver on the pages over which he bent. From time to time he rubbed his eyes to sharpen the edges of the letters, which seemed to grow vague, as if a film had spread across them. But still he stayed up, shivering even with a blanket across his shoulders, studying what he had written, trying to read it, not in the mood in which he had composed it, but coldly, as a bystander might see it or a wronged husband.

He kept his verses crammed untidily in the drawer in his table, first drafts, fair copies, extra copies, notes for poems still unwritten, all thrown together, higgledy-piggledy, along with blank sheets of paper and some odd pencils. Scrabbling through them in search of the two that Lord Stilwell was purported to have found so offensive, he was struck by a fresh idea and pulled out a piece of paper to jot down notes. "Put it in a poem," Christopher had said, and he scribbled further evils to call down on anyone who speculated about the identity of his mistress.

> *May he be scorned by one whom all else scorn, . . .*
> *Madness his sorrow, gout his cramp . . .*
>
> *And may he feel no touch*
> *Of conscience, but of reputation*

28

Too many syllables; he scratched out "reputation" and substituted "fame."

And may he feel no touch
Of conscience, but of fame, and be
Anguished not that 'twas sin, but that 'twas she . . .

But this, he thought, flinging down the pencil and crumpling the paper in his hand, came a little too close to home. Was he not himself anguished indeed, not that it was sin, but that it was found out—or like to be? He smoothed the paper out again and thrust it to the bottom of the pile in the drawer.

The word "Jealousy" jumped at him from the top of a page and he took it out and shut the drawer slowly, reluctant to read again what had been conceived so lightly, so carelessly, and had now become a monster. It was one of those forms that he called "elegies" in rhymed couplets of iambic pentameter. He had never intended it to be taken literally. He had started with the simple situation and galloped off from there, enlarging, exaggerating, distorting, until, he would have sworn, there was nothing recognizable left of the original elements.

He remembered perfectly the writing of it, and what had occasioned it. It had been in the spring, late April or early May. There had been dancing at Southampton House and he and Benita had gone to walk in the garden, where the air was mild and damp and fragrant—away from the city's reek of dung and garlic—with some flower that he, caring nothing for the minutiae of nature, could not name. Others had walked there too, and there was talking back and forth. It was no secret meeting. Lord Stilwell had not been there, for his lame foot made such parties burdensome to him, but there were many others eager to attend on Lady Stilwell. She and John had seized the chance to be together, alone in the midst of company. She had worn, he remembered, something apricot-colored, with silver embroidery, and her farthingale was so wide that he had had to lean towards her to hear what she was saying in her low voice.

29

"He is jealous of you."

Her smile had been conventional, for the benefit of the others walking there, but her eyes, those great, melting Spanish eyes of hers, had betrayed anxiety.

"My lord is?"

"Yes."

"Does he say so?"

"He keeps bringing your name into conversation and looks sharply at me to see if I change color or look vexed. You know how cold and penetrating his icy blue eyes can be. I am afraid of blue eyes. They are like swords, cold and sharp as steel. That is one reason why I fell in love with you—your brown eyes."

Letting pass the opportunity to discuss his eyes, he had pursued the question of Lord Stilwell.

"You are sure it's jealousy? We have a great friendship, he and I, based on our common interest in letters and philosophy. He might well speak of me without any sinister purpose."

"No. I know him. He watches me like a hawk."

"And so would I, dear love, if I were your husband."

They had turned at the yew hedge and started back through a pleached alley of apple trees, where they had a moment's privacy. The sun had come through the blossoms and young leaves in splotches like golden coins.

She had stopped in the walk and turned to him. He had been startled by the naked anger in her eyes. "I am his slave! I would sooner I were dead—or he were."

To quiet her he had taken her plump white hand in his long, thin one and kissed each finger separately, lingeringly. Her eyes had filled with tears and he had seized her in his arms and kissed her lips. For a moment—how long?—they had been oblivious of everything, time, place, other people, and then he had felt her muscles stiffen and her hand come up against his shoulder to push him away. As he released her, he had seen the gold linked bracelet on her wrist and smiled at the memories it evoked. She had lent the bracelet to him and he had lost it; it had cost him twelve gold angels to have another made for her—and both of them some anxiety lest his lordship should notice its absence and ask for it. He had written a poem about it afterwards, full of puns on angels.

"You must not come again," she had said tragically. "Or send me notes. I think he guesses you have corrupted my maid."

Another couple had entered the alley behind them and they had walked on, hearing the music in the hall grow louder as they drew nearer.

"Perhaps he is kind. Perhaps he gives us warning. I will not come to Stilwell House, but we can meet elsewhere . . ."

He had taken home a troubled heart. His love for Benita had kept him for months strung taut as a wire between two posts with something like rapture at one end and self-disgust at the other. The times they had been together—he could count them on the fingers of one hand or less than two hands—had had a beauty and a poignancy that he had not found elsewhere. Perhaps the very fact of the secrecy and the danger had given them an added intensity, as well as the ease and beauty of their surroundings, which had had no part in any other stolen love he had enjoyed, and Benita's own passion and her skill—he must admit it—in lovemaking. He had had nothing to teach her. ("Nature's lay idiot," he had written to a girl now almost forgotten, "I taught thee to love." But Benita had taught him.)

At the other end of it: he liked Lord Stilwell. Their minds marched together well. He did not want Stilwell to know that he had seduced his wife. He had told himself, and would have liked to believe it, that if my lord could not satisfy his beautiful wife, younger than himself and more ardent, surely that left others free to try; but he could not rid himself of the knowledge that it was a shabby act to betray a friend, for friends of a sort they were, or the deep, if disregarded, conviction, ground into him by all the preceptors of his boyhood, that adultery was sin.

Weary of his thoughts, he had wished that he were in truth the figure he presented to the world, a devotee of love who recognized no difficulties but those of circumstance. And

31

thinking of this, he had—as many times before—filtered his emotions through verse to free them of their smart, as sea water is purged of salt by trickling through stones and gravel underground. He had written his experience into verse as if he were the cynic he would have liked to be. Out of three or four things said between them—"He's jealous," "I would sooner I were dead—or he were," "Perhaps he's kind," "We can meet elsewhere"—by adapting, exaggerating, extending them, he had built a structure, entirely new, that had made him smile, writing about it in a poem to show privately to two or three of his friends.

He reread the elegy now, aghast at the thought that Stilwell might see himself in it, that anyone might associate with it the name of Lady Stilwell.

"Fond woman that would'st have thy husband die."

What could Stilwell—or anyone—think of that? And of the picture of the deathbed, the dying man swollen with poison, vomiting, deafened by the cries of his kinsmen "Begging with few feigned tears great legacies"? His own preoccupation with death, he realized, and its physical aspects had carried him away. But how could Lord Stilwell know what images of death obsessed John's mind, of the dissolution and decay, the worms, the oblivion, so that write it he must, whether it was fitting or not?

He read on, sickened: the lovers scoffing at the husband's deformity, laughing at him to his face under the cloak of riddles, kissing and playing in his house, usurping his bed. He had ended the poem by saying that as traitors to a king go to other lands to revile their sovereign or to counterfeit his coin, so they without fear could "play in another's house," where they could scorn his household policies and his spies.

Only two lines in the whole thing were true—and those in the context could hardly sweeten the others:

> O give him many thanks, he is courteous,
> That in suspecting kindly warneth us.

Who could have given this poem to Lord Stilwell? Had he, John, an enemy who hoped in this way to ruin him? Or was it an enemy of his lordship's, trying to poison his peace? Or a rival, seeking to clear John out of the field? He tried to remember whom he had given copies to. Certainly to Christopher and Samuel Brooke—but they were safe. He had exchanged poems with Wotton, but not this one, he was sure. Not Jonson. He knew him only slightly and had given him no poems at all; it was Christopher who had passed along the two verse letters to him. But it was impossible to trace it to anyone. One copied and gave to another. He had almost as little control over a poem in manuscript as over one printed outright in a book.

But there was worse. He opened the drawer and rummaged through it again until he found that other one, the elegy on his mistress going to bed.

There was nothing in this, nothing at all, to suggest that it referred to any particular lady, and of course it had not. He had written it one night after a group of them—the two Brookes, Wotton, Jonson, one or two others,—had sat late at the Belle Sauvage, drinking canary and talking about poetry. Priding themselves on their knowledge of life and their modernity, they had ridiculed the outworn Petrarchan convention of love and the poets who still paid their tired, pretty tribute to it: the angelic mistress, the body as mere temporal clothing for the soul, the lover's religious devotion. He had come home and dashed off his elegy, inspired somewhat by *Amores I, 5,* and more by the talk still ringing in his ears. All of the old pious and reverent and romantic trappings he had flung out of the window, addressing himself to the real, the factual and the shocking, if readers were willing to be shocked. "Come, Madam, come," he had begun, and set the tone with those impatient and imperious words. . . . "Off with that girdle . . ."

Love, the poem made clear, was no more than physical passion. His mistress was no goddess but a warm-blooded woman. Instead of garlands of roses he sprinkled his lines with sexual puns and exuberant indecencies. Though he used the conventional poet's conventional comparison of his mistress's beauties with the riches of the Indies, he parodied it with anatomical explorations. Yet there emerged from it a beauty and an excitement, which came more from his own feeling about the new explorations and discoveries than from the experience of presiding over a mistress's disrobing:

"O my America! My new-found land!"

But that anyone should attach a name to the lady in the poem! A husband believe that his wife was being thus—and in detail—described and dishonored! He sat there at his desk in the candlelight, damning himself for a reckless fool.

There was nothing of Benita in it, though he had written it since he and Benita had become lovers. He was, in practice, far more Petrarchan than Ovidian in his relation to her. Though he used with her a mixture of formality and impudence which, he had long ago discovered, was almost irresistible to gently bred ladies, he was aware of the chasms between them, was often unsure of his standing with her, and he had been unhappy enough over the whole affair to hope, when he went to sea, that the voyage might wash it out altogether.

It was Christopher who had taken him in the beginning to Stilwell House. Christopher's father, twice Lord Mayor of York and a man of some family and substance, had been a distant cousin of Philip Gregory Nigel Charles Amersham, fourth Baron Stilwell, whose family seat was in one of the Yorkshire dales. Christopher had introduced his friend Donne at Christmastime, when a great concourse of people had gathered to drink Yule punch and to watch the Lord Admiral's company of players perform a very pretty interlude. Lord Stilwell had taken a fancy to John. A tall, gaunt, somber-looking man in his late forties, with wintry blue eyes under grizzled brows, he was lame, but only slightly so, and one forgot it unless he had to move quickly. He had a look of the country, as if his skin had known wind and rain and sun, and his clothes, though neat enough and new enough, seemed made for rougher usage than clothes got in London. But his disability kept him from enjoying the sort of country activities that his body appeared to be built for, and his interests were chiefly those of the study. They had talked of poetry a little and John had later given him a satire of his own, on which he had never made any comment

34

at all. His delight was in the reports of voyages and discoveries that came almost every day to London. Here John could match his ardors and they had talked of the Indies, East and West, of Africa and America, of maps and compasses and hemispheres.

Lady Stilwell had come, after they had talked long in the embrasure of a window, to remind her husband of his duty to his other guests, and had stayed behind with John, as if she were as surprised by him as he was by her. He had already, in his mind, constructed a picture of what Lord Stilwell's wife would be: a comfortable matron, forty-five or so, brisk, red-faced and kind. The beautiful young woman—young but in no way girlish—who looked up into his face all but took his breath away. She was foreign, he saw at once, and Spanish, he decided in the next instant. The dark hair and velvet black eyes, with whites like milk, the ivory skin, the rich red lips, not quite symmetrical, the rounded body and warm, deep voice with an entrancing hint of accent, all combined to be exotic and captivating. He had seen such a lady once in Madrid, aristocratic and unattainable, veiled in black lace and guarded by a middle-aged female dragon. He had gone with his lute to sing outside her window one night, fool that he was, and had remembered her ever since. All his imaginings about her, kept fresh and untouched by reality, he had hung upon Lady Stilwell.

"I brought a heart into the room," he wrote afterwards, "But from the room I carried none with me."

He had gone to the house soon again, to take his lordship a quaint map of Venice—and to talk with his lady. She was indeed Spanish, he learned. She had come with her father in the train of the Spanish ambassador. Later he could put together the whole story. Falling in love with London and coveting the freedom that married women enjoyed there, she had determined to stay on when her father returned to Madrid. The only opportunity that offered—or at least the only one that her father would consider—was this more than forty-year-old Yorkshireman, a widower and lame, but rich and possessed of a good title. So Maria Benita de las Vegas Moria had remained in England, childless mistress of a great house in Holborn, growing more beautiful every year, obstinately refusing even to visit that other place which her husband owned, in distant and savage Yorkshire.

"Whoever loves," John had written exuberantly, "if he do not propose The right true end of love, he's one that goes To sea for nothing but to make him sick."

He became skillful in the art of writing notes with both a surface and an inner meaning, and had quickly learned how vulnerable a phlegmatic, middle-aged maid could be to a combination of gold and charm—his gold and Pierre's charm. The right true end had not proved as difficult to achieve as he had feared it might be, for Benita knew how to smooth the way and Stilwell House was large, with many doors and passages.

The affair had soon come to absorb all his thought and energies with its danger and sweetness and fire, its occasional rapture and frequent disappointments. After Benita's revelation at Southampton House and the cathartic effect of the elegy he wrote next day, he had resolved to take the warning and to cut the affair off cleanly. But they had met at other houses; Benita was everywhere; unless he turned hermit and sat at home, he could not, it seemed, escape her, and the language of nods and smiles, the dialogue of foot against foot beneath the dinner table spoken under the eyes of all, kept him in a turmoil. When the opportunity to go to sea with Essex presented itself, he seized it eagerly, seeing in it not only the chance of money and honor—and possibly death—but a hope of freeing himself from this love.

Before he departed he had gone openly to Stilwell House to say farewell, bearing a gift and a poem. This was his answer to suspicion, a breezy boldness and the implication that there was nothing between Benita and himself to which his lordship could reasonably take exception, that it was all spread out in the open for him to see.

It would—might—have been successful but for those other

poems. Or perhaps the gift, his portrait, had been too vivid a reminder.

It had been painted by a cavernously thin, grimy, ardent young artist who had turned up one day in the Savoy, hungry and nearly despairing, lacking everything but the fever to paint. John had provided food and money for paint and canvas, and had sat for his portrait wearing an enormous black hat and the lace collar he had bought in Malines. They had talked of poetry and painting but without any meeting of minds, for the young man had been wholly serious and rather fierce about his work, incapable—and indeed ignorant of the very possibility—of irony. What John remembered most keenly about those sessions was the change that came over the young man's face as he worked, a look of deep, oblivious happiness. When the picture was finished, John had laughed a little at it and had paid him generously for it, but though he plainly needed the money, he had pocketed it without a smile and had barely glanced at the finished picture as he handed it over to John. His joy had been all in the doing; the money and the finished work were dross.

John had wondered at first what to do with the painting; he certainly did not want to look at himself every time he came into the room, nor did he wish to have a painting forever standing on the floor with its face to the bookcase. It was not a bad portrait, nor yet quite a good one. The young man had copied painstakingly all that he saw on the surface. The lace might have served as a pattern for a lace-maker, and the hat, the arched eyebrows, the dark, glowing eyes in the long face, the line of the moustache, itself no more than a pair of eyebrows on the upper lip, showed only half of the man that was John Donne, the half that went out in company, the "light squib of mirth" at a party. With the mouth the young artist had failed entirely; sensual John's mouth was, but not uncontrolled. Still, the picture had life in it and it was well enough painted, perhaps, to bring the young artist further orders if people saw it.

So he had given it to the Stilwells, with verses to the effect that it might look like him then but would no longer resemble him when he came home from the war, burned brown by the sun, with blue powder stains on his skin, his body reduced to a sack of bones.

Frowning a little now, he tried to remember whether there had been anything in this poem to alarm his lordship, and found it on a scrap of paper in his drawer.

Here take my picture; though I bid farewell,
Thine, in my heart, where my soul dwells, shall dwell.

Conventional, no more. The only other mention of love came after the description of himself after his battered return:

"If rival fools tax thee to have loved a man
So foul and coarse, as Oh, I may seem then . . .

No, Stilwell could scarcely have taken that amiss. It must have been those other poems. He clasped his hands behind his head and tilted his chair back, addressing a letter to his lordship in his mind.

Noble lord: For the time that I have had the honor to enjoy your lordship's unmerited favor, I have ever entertained the most profound admiration for the brilliance and subtlety of your lordship's mind, but I wish to tell you now that you are in error. Not perhaps so much in error as I hope to make you think you are, but enough to free my lady and me from the black toils of your unworthy—though I fear justified—suspicion. Seek the inspiration of my humble muse in the peaks and clouds of Latin poetry—not under your own roof. But do you know your Ovid?

He let the chair's front legs down with a thud.

What was his lordship enraged about? The supposed picture of himself snorting in a basket chair mocked to his face by his wife and her lover? By a description that he took to be one of his wife undressing for any fool to read and identify? If this were it, perhaps he could be set at ease by rereading Ovid and by some explanation, if he would listen, of the way poems were written. Or was he outraged by the infidelity itself? Did he merely suspect or did he know? Did he really suppose that in fashionable London an old man could keep a young wife faithful?

As the second candle guttered low, he parted the curtains and looked out of the window. The first morning gray had come and the river gleamed pale out of the mist that curled up between the trees that bordered Lambeth Marsh on the opposite side. As he watched, a boat containing a single oarsman and a gentleman with his cloak wound around him moved swiftly past, evidently hastening to shoot the Bridge while the tide was right, and from the other direction toiling slowly came a flat boat laden with firewood. Another day had come. He had been back in London less than twenty-four hours and already he was embroiled.

iv

```
┌┐┌┐┌┐┌┐┌┐┌┐┌┐┌┐┌┐┌┐┌┐┌┐┌┐┌┐┌┐┌┐┌┐┌┐┌┐┌┐┌┐┌┐
```

PIERRE WAS BACK. He had, during John's absence, given two or three other gentlemen a trial but had found them wanting. Whatever it was in John that had fastened Pierre to him in Paris three years earlier kept him tied securely still. Born a peasant, with a peasant's short, thick body, round head and broad face, bright black eyes and sly smile, he had long left the soil behind him. His knowledge of the world was extensive and tolerant; his passion was for clothes. He knew cut and fabric and trimming, had a discerning eye for color, took a consuming interest in all the changes in style, and with all this he had a quiet and dependable taste. His own appearance was so neat that he did his master, attending him on the street, as much credit as two or three other servants might. John sometimes wondered what it was that held Pierre to him, since it was certainly not his clothes, which were for the most part plain and dark. Pierre had, moreover, many other things to do for him besides attending to his wardrobe and he did them well, being a competent and even tender nurse in time of sickness and having a knack of getting around a cook and serving up the best that any house afforded. John wondered but never came to a conclusion, not thinking once of simple affection.

"I walked through the Royal Exchange only yesterday, just to see what they had," said Pierre, brushing John's black and gray striped wool trunks carefully, "and there was an aubergine-colored satin——"

John shook his head.

40

"It was so dark it was almost black, sir, except where the light fell on it. I think you would like it."

They spoke in French, for Pierre had little English and did not enjoy using what he had, while John liked to keep up his French, which was nearly as good as his Spanish. Languages, he well knew, were one important key to state employment.

"You really need a new suit, sir. Shall I bring you a piece of the aubergine satin to examine?"

"Velvet, Pierre. Black velvet. It's warmer."

While he was being buttoned, tied and buckled into his shirt, his doublet, his trunks, his hose, he answered questions about the only aspect of the Islands Voyage that had the slightest interest for Pierre.

"All those young gallants that went along in their bright clothes," said Pierre. "I wondered about them. There were jokes in the plays here."

"Those young, silken, painted fools. Oh, their clothes melted early, while we were still at Plymouth waiting for a breeze. Many of them deserted then and returned to London. The rest of us waited for the wind to rise and did nothing but eat while we waited. There was nothing else to do. Ply-mouth it was in very truth."

He made the pun in English and Pierre smiled perfunctorily.

"I hope you'll be content to stay home now," he said with all the moralizing primness of an old nurse to her charge, "barring, of course, Paris. Your cloak, sir. Will you wear the wide-brimmed hat?"

"No, no, not that. Give me something small and circumspect. No feathers."

"This is all that's left, sir. You've only the three."

It was a velvet flat cap, rather lawyerish and entirely appropriate, John thought sourly, for his mission. He put it on his head straight and then with a flip of his hand tilted it very slightly, while Pierre held the looking glass.

"Mr. Brooke," John said, "would not approve."

"No, sir. Mr. Brooke is a very sober gentleman. But I am always surprised, when he isn't wearing his gown, to see what bright colors he fancies."

41

"Not of my cap, nor of what I propose to do."

Stay away from Stilwell House? On the contrary, he would go directly there this first morning in London. Boldness—to the point of impudence, if necessary—was ever the best defense.

His cloak swirling around him as he turned, he went into the study and took the *Amores* off the shelf. It was a fine edition, published in Bologna in 1471, which he had picked up in Florence on the Ponte Vecchio. He stood with the volume in his hands, feeling again for an instant the Italian sun hot on his head and the smell of the Arno in his nostrils, grieving a little at the sacrifice he contemplated, perhaps a useless sacrifice.

"Your gloves, sir."

"Carry this book for me. Come, let's go."

The morning was clear and windy. Dust and bits of paper scurried along the Strand. Men wearing large hats had the brims blown down in their faces. A dignified justice in velvet came along, followed by ten or twelve blue-coats, all hurried into short, quick steps by the gusts of wind at their backs.

With Pierre closely on his heels, John walked east along the Strand, keeping the wall where he could, yielding it where he must to other men older than himself, scattering apprentices and beardless youths into the muddy kennel. Now and then a whiff of tobacco smoke from one whom he passed or of perfume from another mingled with the ordinary smells of garbage and urine and river mud that characterized the London atmosphere. With an observant eye he watched an overdressed young idiot in front of him, his absorbent mind blotting up details for future use: the differences of height to which he raised his feathered hat, determined, evidently, by the glossiness of the silk or the amount of gold lace worn by the recipient of the salute, the eagerness with which he now and then skipped all the way across the street to bow and fawn and grin before some courtier on his way to Whitehall.

Essex House was quiet, nobody coming or going. From the Angel Inn came a sudden outburst of laughter and John thought for a moment of stopping in for a glass of wine to fortify himself against the wind and the meeting with Lord

Stilwell, but feared to meet friends and be delayed. Beyond St. Clement Danes he turned into the lane that offered a short cut, through Lincoln's Inn Fields, to Holborn and Stilwell House. Some children with their hair blowing about their faces were playing on the grass and swinging from low branches of trees, but except for them and a few delivery boys with their baskets nobody was about.

Lord Stilwell's town house sat behind its brick wall in the open country beyond Gray's Inn, separated from Hatton House to the west by fields and orchards. Taking his book from Pierre and slipping without comment into his servant's hand a three-cornered missive containing the single word, "When?" John marched up the marble steps to the great front door under the Stilwell arms.

He found Lord Stilwell and his lady walking in the long gallery attended by Stilwell's page, a pert lad with a freckled face, and one of the young girls who had been sent by their parents to acquire address and polish under the guidance of Lady Stilwell. A silly custom, John thought it. No doubt the girl's own parents were busy polishing other girls from other houses, all of whom might better be under the eyes of their own mothers. Bachelor-like, he had firm educational theories, which, perhaps, were based on knowledge of a specialized sort not available to most mothers of young girls.

"Ah, Mr. Donne!" exclaimed Lord Stilwell with an appearance of cordiality that took John aback, so little had he expected it. "You are welcome indeed. We are alone today and very dull and mumpish. You must tell us all the news about the voyage."

Benita's beauty was under a cloud. Her eyes looked swollen and her mouth drooped. When she summoned a smile for John, the effort was obvious.

"You look well, Mr. Donne," she said with an attempt at archness. "No powder stains? No beard? No sunburn? Did you really go to sea, I wonder?"

"What else, my lady, could have kept me so long away from Stilwell House and you? I am come, my lord," he turned to his host, "for the purpose of reporting on the voyage and to bring you a small gift. There was no place in the Azores to buy souvenirs and, as you know, we did not touch on Spain or take any of the plate ships, and so I offer instead a small treasure that I captured in Florence some time ago. It is not worthy—but you will make it so by your acceptance of it."

Lord Stilwell shot him a stiff glance from under his eyebrows and, taking the volume in his hands, he examined the binding before opening it to the title page.

"Ovid," he said, his neutral voice revealing nothing.

"The *Amores* and the *Ars Amatoria*. I am sure you know the *Metamorphoses* well, but I thought perhaps you might find in this some slight pleasure." Would this gambit, he wondered, serve?

"You think I need instruction in the art of loving?" said Lord Stilwell, frowning.

"If you will excuse me, gentlemen," interposed Benita, "I will leave you now. We shall meet again later, Mr. Donne."

A faint light flickered in her eyes. It had been one of their small jokes, who were "Jack" and "Benita" when they were alone together, to emphasize the formal address in company.

He bowed and accompanied her to the door, hoping for a whispered word, but she gave him only a long glance that he could not read and turned away, saying to the girl, "Come, Sibyl."

By the time he returned to his lordship he had found an answer to the gibe.

"No possibility of *need,* my lord. On the contrary, I thought you might enjoy the pleasures of recognition—as Her Majesty the Queen might enjoy reading a book on statecraft. It is the *Amores,* not the *Ars Amatoria,* that I thought might interest you, if you were not familiar with it." As he spoke it seemed to him that he must be insane, to have come here, disregarding Christopher's advice, bringing a book his lordship no doubt possessed, exposing himself and Benita to God knew what of confrontation or vituperation, exposure and mortification. He was almost incredulous when Lord Stilwell said pleasantly enough:

"No, I've not read it. Shall we walk? Give me your arm. My foot is troubling me today."

"I am sorry, my lord. You carry your disability so lightly that one entirely forgets there is any difficulty at all."

Again that look, stiff and sharp, quickly withdrawn. But Stilwell took the proffered arm and they strolled the length of the gallery and back again under the portraits of the Stilwell ancestors. On the other side of the long, narrow room, leaded windows gave on the bare trees and gravel walks, the stretches of green grass of Lincoln's Inn Fields, the red brick chapel of Lincoln's Inn visible through the trees. The page trailed along behind them, bored, scuffling his feet and making hideous faces at their backs.

"This is your own copy that you have given me, I fear— and a fine one too. Won't you feel the loss of it?"

"I know it by heart, my lord. Too well, I am afraid. It gets into my own writing—a peacock among my own poor sparrows."

"You have written many poems, Mr. Donne? You are a poet as well as"—he paused, and John wondered if he was going to say "a lover"—"a philosopher," he finished.

"A poetaster, I am afraid. A mere stainer of paper."

"I thought those lines about your picture very witty."

"My poor verse is rough, but at least partly by intention. I am one of those who follow Ovid rather than Petrarch, abjuring 'poetic' images and worn-out ornaments which put the reader to sleep, to seek instead something fresh and strong that will startle him into attention."

"You gave me a copy some time ago of a poem of yours—a Satire,' I think you called it. Something about hating the city."

" 'I thank God I do hate perfectly all this town,' " murmured John. "But that is not true, of course," he went on, grasping at the opportunity thus presented. "In actuality, I love London. I could not live anywhere else."

"Then why say you hate it?"

"It is the poet's privilege, my lord, to take on other characters, speaking as if he were their very selves, thought their thoughts, entertained their feelings, however uncongenial such ideas and sentiments might be to him in his own person. As you are of course aware, my lord, Ovid writes as many different men in love——"

45

"Indeed. An actor-like person, playing all parts until he must scarcely know who he is himself. I remember your satire quite well: I thought the language most unpoetic—indeed, coarse. I must say, Mr. Donne, I fail to see what place words like 'out-spew,' for instance, or 'kitchen-stuff' or 'excrement' have in poetry, which is surely intended to please the ear and the mind? Or is the purpose of this—as you said—to startle the reader into attention?"

John had given him the poem months ago and he had never made any reference to it at all. Yet it was as fresh in his mind now as if he had read it yesterday. He must have been studying it recently, comparing perhaps its phrases with those in the other poems that roused his anger, to see if the same hand had written both. But he was not certain yet. His cold blue eyes revealed nothing, not anger nor hatred nor judgment.

"I believe the language of every day to be as appropriate to poetry as—indeed more than—formal, stilted poesies used in conventional verse—and only there."

"Upon my word, I don't use such terms as those I mentioned in my ordinary conversation!"

"No, my lord, this was rougher than most, perhaps, for it is a satire modeled on Persius, who was noted for his harshness. It is a new form in English, and I can claim to be something of an innovator."

"I believe Mr. Wenlock has written satires too?"

"Edward Wenlock?" John stiffened at the name as involuntarily as a dog's hackles rise at the approach of another dog. That bacon-brains. He was a parasite on Henry Wotton, a buoyant young man dripping with money that came from his father's speculations in building rows of tenements in the fast-growing suburbs.

"If he does write satires," said John unguardedly, "they are no more than imitations of mine—or perhaps of Hall's. He neither eats nor drinks nor spits but by imitation!"

His lordship smiled bleakly. "If you will forgive my candor," he said, "I like better the sort of poetry written when I was young. It was musical, there was beauty in it, and one could

46

understand it. There was nothing of today's affectation of praising women for vices instead of virtues."

Feeling himself again on dangerous ground, John said nothing, his mind raking through the drawer of his table. But Lord Stilwell went on in a reminiscent tone:

"I remember one by John Heywood—perhaps you know it?

> *"In life she is Diana chaste,*
> *In troth Penelopy.*
> *In word and eke in deed steadfast*
> *—What will you more we say?"*

What more indeed, thought John sardonically.

"Now that is the kind of love poem that appeals to me—and the kind of woman to address."

"That was written by my grandfather. He would be honored, could he know of your lordship's approval of his Muse."

"Your mother's father?"

"Yes, my lord. He died some fifteen years ago in Malines, but I remember him well. The object of the poem, or so I have often been told, was my grandmother."

"It was, no doubt, a simple thing. No one would praise it today, but I think we have tossed aside values that in my youth were held dear and that we would be the better for now."

They seemed to be on firm ground now, the superiority of former times. There was no vanity more pitiful, John thought, than that of old men exclaiming against the present day and praising the time when they were young. They betrayed themselves, for if the times were changed for the worse, who was it but they who had changed them?

His eyes kept straying to the door in hope of seeing Benita return. All was well, he thought. He had accomplished what he came for; his lordship was at least confused and seemed disposed to postpone judgment. The minutes dragged on and Benita did not appear. When a silence fell that neither he nor his lordship seemed to wish to fill, he pulled himself together and began to take his leave.

"I am sorry that Lady Stilwell is not here," said his lordship.

"Boy, go find your mistress and beg her to attend us. She will wish to see you, Mr. Donne, to say good-by."

As the page scurried off, Stilwell turned to John with a look that erased the half-hour of pleasant talk and fastened a clammy grip of apprehension on John's heart. "We have little time left in London. We leave on Monday for Yorkshire."

"Yorkshire, my lord?" By sheer effort he kept from stammering, but he could hear the quaver in his own voice. "To visit your estates there?"

"To live there. I have long been homesick for the dales—and I find that the London air does not agree with my wife."

As he made his stunned way out, preceded down the stairs by a footman, John saw what in his excitement he had not noticed coming in: that the hall was bare of its arras and that rolls of what must be tapestry, tied in burlap, lay on the floor against one wall, preparatory to being carted north.

At the front door he spoke to the footman, whom he had seen at the house often enough to know by name. "Shall you like Yorkshire, Ned?"

"Not I, sir. I could never leave London. I hope to find another place. If you should know of any, would you be so kind as to speak for me?"

"I'll keep you in mind."

"Thank you, sir. It's all very sudden and upsetting."

But John had no desire to gossip with the footman. He nodded abruptly and went out, joined on the steps by Pierre.

The sun had vanished behind piled-up purple clouds. The wind bit savagely now, and he held his cloak tight across his chest and lowered his head.

When they were out of sight of the house among the trees of Lincoln's Inn Fields, Pierre came up abreast. "I have a note for you, sir."

In his turmoil of spirit he had not thought to ask for one. He took it eagerly and sought shelter against the wall of one of the buildings to open it and read it. Like his note to her, it contained but one word:

"Tonight."

V

‎ㄷ┌ㄴ┌ㄴ┌ㄴ┌ㄴ┌ㄴ┌ㄴ┌ㄴ┌ㄴ┌ㄴ┌ㄴ┌ㄴ┌ㄴ┌ㄴ┌ㄴ┌ㄱ

THE WIND HAD FALLEN, the tumbling clouds blown themselves away; the moon, almost full, was white on roofs, gleamy on bits of ice where puddles had frozen, pale gold on a small painted door in the angle of a wing on the eastern side of Stilwell House.

The shadow of the wall covered John as he walked the short space from the postern, which had been unlocked for him, to the moonlit door. His hat pulled down over his face and his cloak wrapped around him, he knocked softly. The door opened immediately and he stepped inside, thankful to be out of the flood of moonlight.

Benita's maid was waiting there with a candle in her hand. Its light threw into relief the crag of her nose, the tent-openings of her heavy-lidded, small black eyes, the jut of her chin, and outlined each wiry black hair on her upper lip. Without any change of expression she turned, drawing her head shawl closer around her face, and led him along a narrow passageway and up a small circular stone staircase. A slit in the wall half-way up let in white moonlight that mingled with the yellow candlelight no better than oil and water mix. The upstairs corridor was wide and floored with broad planks of polished oak; at the end of it the door was open on a small, square room ruddy with firelight and dark with the towering bulk of a curtained bed.

49

"My lady will come when she can," the maid whispered. "Thank you, sir."

The gold coin disappeared into her draperies as she withdrew backward, closing the door with one hand, holding the candle with the other close to the narrowing crack until at length it was shut out.

John cast a quick glance about the room. The walls being covered with linen-fold paneling, there was no arras to come down. The Turkey rugs, so soft and silky to bare feet, were gone, but heavy velvet curtains were still drawn across the windows. Where the crimson bed curtains, elaborately encrusted with gold lace, were parted, linen sheets turned down over white blankets glimmered palely. The room was warmed by the burning apple logs that Benita loved, and fragrant with spiced rose leaves in a bowl on the table. In one corner on a slender stand of polished wood, the silver ewer had been filled with warm water, and fresh towels were folded beside the basin.

It was, except for the rugs, just as it had been before. John hung his hat and cloak on pegs against the wall, added his jerkin and doublet; in his trunk-hose and white linen shirt he sat down on a stool before the fire to wait. The great house within its thick walls was covered with silence like a heavy quilt spread over and tucked in at all the corners. Outside were the trees and the wind and the fields, the night owls and prowling cats, belated travelers or, it might be, thieves and murderers on Holborn Road. London itself and its bursting suburbs, with all their waking and sleeping life, were close at hand. But no sound from any of it seeped inside this house; he could hear only the rustle of the fire, the intermittent, fastidious gnawing of a mouse in the wainscoting and an occasional crack from the settling, breathing house itself, seeming as loud as a pistol shot and almost as startling. He kept his ear alert for the whisper of light footfalls in the corridor outside, but though twice he thought he heard her and jumped up to open the door, she did not come.

He put fresh logs on the fire from the wood box and sat bent forward into its warmth, his elbows on his knees, his head buried in his hands. This other fire, the love that he had foolishly imagined in the spring he could quench, burned more fiercely than ever, fueled by danger and the threat of separation. "For every hour that thou wilt spare me now, I will allow, Usurious God of Love, twenty to thee . . ."

He was dozing when the door faintly creaked, but he sprang up, knocking the stool over with a crash, in time to take her in his arms while the door was still open behind her. She wore a night robe of some soft, silky stuff and underneath it was only her small, warm, fragrant self, released from all the daily barricade of whalebone, brocade and metal embroidery. He picked her up in his arms, feeling the slender bones beneath the softness, and carried her to the bed.

"Jack! Shut the door. What was that dreadful noise? I thought it must wake the house."

He went to the door and listened for a moment at the crack before he noiselessly eased the latch into place. There was no sound of distant doors being opened questioningly, no shout for sleeping servants. He turned back, quaking with laughter. "I upset the stool!"

She sat gathered together in a bundle on the bed, the high collar of her robe around her ears, its skirts folded across her bare shins, her hands clasped about her knees. Her eyes were enormous in her shadowed face, her expression tragic.

"Why do you laugh? I can see nothing laughable in my situation."

He was flown with happiness. Even the fact that she said "my" instead of "our" situation—though he noticed it—did not damp his high spirits.

"I laugh for joy, my sweet, because after all these months and several kinds of danger, we are together at last. Whatever happens, we have tonight."

She warded him off with outstretched hand.

"I thought I should never get away. I could hear him banging about in his room long after the time when he is usually asleep. And twice he came into mine to see if I was—he said—safe and well."

He sat beside her on the bed and gathered her into his arms, rocking her gently as a mother soothes her child, his cheek against the dark cloud of her hair.

"But now here you are and here I am. Let's not waste a moment—or a thought—on him."

She struggled out of his grasp to face him, her eyes black and wild, her mouth shaped to spit out words.

"Do you realize, Jack, what will happen to me? I am going to be dragged away to that hideous, horrible, God-forsaken place of his in the north. The packing has begun already. I shall be a prisoner—an exile. I can't bear it. I shall go mad."

Sobered, he released her and leaned back against the massive carved bedpost, the curtains falling into place around him, so that they two were shut together in this little room, knee against knee, eyes searching eyes, as if they hung on one string, yet separated by God knew what chasm of feeling.

"Was it those wretched poems of mine," he ventured, "that set him off?"

"What poems? You never show me any of your poems—except that one with your picture."

"You would not like them." Nor would she. Her taste, if it could be dignified by such a term, was for the sugar comfits and tinkling bells of poetry. But it was not her taste he loved, nor her mind, if she by stretch of generosity could be granted a mind, nor her soul, but her body, her gracious body, where love itself dwelt. Let us love now and talk later, he wanted to cry, but he knew better. Holding his ardor in check, he must patiently remove the layers of fear, resentment, guilt, that wrapped her round, must lift them off as carefully and tenderly as if he were taking off girdle and gown, before her ardor could leap to meet his own.

"Christopher told me that someone had shown your husband some verses I wrote that angered him," he said conversationally from his place against the bedpost. "I have been desperately afraid that I had unwittingly brought trouble on you—on us."

52

"I know nothing about that. He is very angry and he has said dreadful things to me and I will never forgive him. And now he says he will not trust me in London and so we will go away to this place where I shall die."

"Perhaps when he cools off he will change his mind. If it was those poems, he may read them again and see them differently."

"Your poems! Do you care about nothing but your poems? I tell you I am dying and you talk about your poems! They had nothing to do with it——"

"I care about you. It is only as they might have injured you that I think of them."

"You care for nothing! I do not know why I am here now—at such a risk. I would not give a fig for all your poems—if they are all like one that I have seen."

"I said you would not like them. But which was that?"

> *"I can love her and her and you and you,*
> *I can love any, so she be not true."*

He could not read the look she flung at him as she said the lines; there was a taunt in it, he thought, a hint of triumph, of wounded feelings perhaps, perhaps not. But he did not stay to analyze it; he was off after a glint of danger: he had not given her the verses from which she quoted.

"Where did you get that?"

"Mr. Edward Wenlock showed it to me."

"Wenlock?" John knew him slightly—and only because he was everywhere; he would have been negligible if he were not so rich, a busybody if he were not so idle. "How did he get hold of it?"

"What difference does it make? I told you, you care nothing at all about me or what happens to me."

"My precious idiot, I wrote that before I knew you. It was dashed off out of mere gamesomeness, to please Christopher and some others that gather to read verse. I love you, Benita. If I have thought I loved before, it was only for form—and perhaps it is destiny's punishment of me now that when I love in truth I should suffer. I have found you—and you at once are snatched away. Do you think I am not torn?"

He felt a pathos in her searching look and in the way her eyes fell before his and her mouth lost its tautness. "I think you do suffer," she said, her voice falling so low that he could barely hear her. "We must comfort each other."

She opened her arms to him and they clasped each other close for a long, silent moment, his heart beating fast under the pressure of her soft breasts. She raised her head from his shoulder and their lips met.

"The fire is dying down," she murmured, her breath mingling with his, "take off that scratchy linen shirt."

2 Early as it was, the church was open. He entered and walked up the narrow nave, parting the icy darkness before him like a curtain, stumbling a little on the unevenness of a floor tomb. What light there was came through the paler parts of the painted window above the altar.

It was months since he had been in a church. He did not count the compulsory Sunday services on shipboard, and in Plymouth he had stayed late in bed on Sunday morning, though the landlord hinted that he was required by law to see that his guests attended divine service. It was not to a service that he had come now, on impulse, on his way home from Stilwell House. He came to feel himself within consecrated walls; if he could, to pray.

Gradually he became accustomed to the cold and ceased to shiver. The dark he liked. The less light there was in a church, he thought, the better it was for prayer.

He said a Pater Noster, but the words passed across the tumult of his mind like soldiers marching by a theater. Benita in his arms, Benita asleep with her head in the hollow of his shoulder, Benita crying and clinging to him when the maid came to warn them of the dawn.

"Our bodies will be parted but not our souls," he had tried to comfort her, feeling the falseness in it even while he was saying the words, for it was her body that held him. "We can

54

love still in our thoughts and dreams"—she stirred and he felt her impatience—"and in letters and gifts."

"It's well enough for you—you'll be in London."

If she included him in her grief for London, she did not say so. It was a miserable parting, with nothing to ennoble it. Their last farewells were hurried and trivial. Crossing the yard between the painted door and the postern, he had heard a cock crow in the distance and had wondered if it cried of betrayal or merely proclaimed a new day.

He summoned home his thoughts and tried to frame a prayer for Benita. But what should he ask? That Lord Stilwell would change his mind and stay in London? That Yorkshire would not seem so desolate to her when she got there? That she might be endowed with patience and fortitude?

He had much better pray for himself, for it was he who was in need. He had not dared to ask forgiveness for his sin while he was still enjoying it. Now that it was snatched from him, should he not offer up a contrite and thankful heart, and pray that he be not bound and tangled in thought of her or weakened by longing for what he could no more possess? Pray now —and quickly—for resolution to banish the intruding, the insinuating, thought that they still might meet again before the departure on Monday.

How could he send a letter to Yorkshire without her husband's learning of its arrival? Whom could he entrust with a gift? What sort of gift would please her?

It was lighter now. The colors of the carved and painted ceiling overhead, where sacred symbols mingled with the Lancastrian arms, began to reveal themselves.

"Since she must go and I must mourn . . ." The lines of a farewell elegy began to form themselves in his mind. "I saw the golden fruit, 'tis rapt away . . ."

The verger came in and made a noise with a broom. John got stiffly to his feet and went out. The day was well under way. Beggars with rags and matted hair were crowding around the alms door of the hospital. The precinct was full of people going about their business half asleep and sullen or wearing that bright, complacent look of the superior folk who like to get up early. The rhythmic slide and thump of presses told of some proclamation or gazette about to issue from the Royal Printing Press. On the river, gulls squawked over a drift of garbage and wherries moved swiftly back and forth.

John let himself into his rooms with his key, took off his cloak and jerkin and put on his heavy dressing gown, sat down at his study table and began to write. A pleasant conceit came to him.

> *Oh Love, that fire and darkness should be mixed.*
> *Or to thy triumphs so strange torments fixed!*
> *Is it because thou, thyself, art blind, that we*
> *Thy martyrs must not more each other see?*

He was still at it when Pierre came in bringing his morning cup of ale and a piece of toasted bread dripping with butter. He thanked him absently and motioned to him to set them on the table to one side.

"That's all now, Pierre."

But the man kept fussing about, straightening books on the shelves, taking out a volume now and then to blow the dust noisily from it. John tried to blot him out with the strength of his concentration, but gave up the effort at length, throwing down his pencil and taking up his cup of ale.

"Well, Pierre, what is it?"

The man lowered his eyes and a smile played around the corners of his mouth. "It's something I learned at Stilwell House, sir, from Mrs. Ferrier."

Benita's Abigail. John smiled within himself, amused as always by the formality that the servants observed among themselves.

"Yesterday I thought I would not tell you. But this morning it seemed to me that you ought to know."

"Anything with that preface is certain to be unpleasant. Keep it to yourself. I don't like backstairs gossip."

"No, sir."

56

John finished his breakfast and Pierre took away the plate and cup, closing the door behind him with ostentatious care.

In the somewhat oppressive silence that followed, John attempted to return to his poem. "And, dearest friend, since we must part, good night . . ." No. Something "night."

Something something, "burdens well born are light."

Pierre and Mrs. Haines were having a conversation in the bedroom. He found himself straining his ears. Was Pierre telling the dame what he had refused to hear?

"Drown night with flooding day . . ." No. "With hope of day. Burdens well born are light."

That was a fine piece of complacency. He bears a burden well for whom it is not very heavy to begin with. Easy enough for him, in London, mourning for his love—yet welcoming, if he be honest, his freedom—to talk of bearing burdens, but what of Benita? Forlorn in exile, with no company but his blue-eyed lordship, Benita, who was made for passion and tenderness, her health, her youth, her beauty eclipsed by her woe.

He had not heard Mrs. Haines's voice for some time now. By the thumpings and bangings in the bedroom, he surmised that Pierre was throwing the furniture about to convey the information that he was still there, pregnant with news.

"Pierre!"

"Yes, sir." He stood in the open door, expectant.

"Was it something about me? What you heard at Stilwell House?"

"No, sir. About Mr. Edward Wenlock."

"What?"

"His lordship was extremely annoyed, sir, to meet Mr. Wenlock very early one morning, just opening the door into the east staircase, preparatory to slipping away. His lordship had heard a noise and got out of bed to investigate. He looked in her ladyship's room first, of course."

vi

On Wednesday—not Monday as planned, for it is not a simple thing to uproot a baronial household, and there were inevitable delays—the Stilwells jolted out of London in their huge, uncomfortable coach and headed north. The following Sunday John went to Court.

All through the week he had stayed shut up in his rooms, writing. Sheets of paper drifted onto the floor like snowflakes; Pierre picked them up and was sworn at for his pains. Torn bits followed, half-sheets, quarter-sheets, inch-square pieces, according to the intensity of feeling with which they had been rejected, and Pierre was scowled at for not clearing them away. At the end of it John had a poem about a ghost (himself) beginning, "When by thy scorn, O murderess, I am dead"; two stanzas of ingenious pattern on the theme, "I am two fools, I know, For loving and for saying so In whining poetry"; a song, "Send home my long-strayed eyes to me, Which oh too long have dwelt on thee"; and finally a resolute "Farewell to Love," all of which he thrust into the drawer of his table; and putting verse as well as love behind him, he decided to seek his fortune seriously. Going to Court was the first step, for it was there that any great man who might be needing a young man to assist him could be met. If Lord Essex were there, he might, even though he himself had no employment for John, introduce him with a favorable word to someone else.

To Pierre's grief he would not wait for his new clothes to be finished. His old ones were cleaned and mended; he had new pumps of fine black leather; he came fresh from the barber's chair, where he was shaved, his hair cut, washed and dried with warm towels, his moustache—all five hairs of it—shaped, his ears filled with the barber's news, most of which he took to be invention—though there was one item, offered as an afterthought while the barber brushed his coat, that had the sound of truth. The Queen had created Lord Howard Earl of Nottingham, for, the barber said, accepting John's coin, his capture of Cadiz. But that last John did not believe; the Queen knew as did everyone else that thanks were due to Essex for Cadiz. Or was she rejecting Essex altogether? "God be with you, gentleman," said the barber, and John nodded, frowning because Essex was out of favor.

Pierre at his heels, he went to the Savoy Steps and chose among the boatmen clamoring there one whose boat had clean cushions on the seats. He might have had a place in a wherry for less cost than a pair of oars, but he would not pare pennies on his way to Court.

"Greenwich," he told the boatman, for the Queen was holding Court today in the little palace where she had been born.

It was a sad, gray, moist morning. On the lead-colored, greasy river sailed a swan, arching her neck in disdain for the rabble among whom she moved. It was easy enough to make solemn, stately poems about stately silver swans, but there was a black kite wheeling overhead watching for carrion: what could you do with that? John thought about it a moment, then lost interest, for it was people he cared about, not nature. As they passed the Bankside theaters he looked to see if flags were flying and, seeing none, concluded that the theaters must still be closed. One had to be careful what one wrote; Hall was taking a risk, publishing his satires. The bells of St. Saviour's in Southwark, honey-rich in tone, pealed out on the heavy air just before, the tide being right, they shot through one of the arches of London Bridge. For a moment the noise of rushing water echoing from the dank stone piers and from the mass of masonry overhead roared in his ears. Splashed a little by the tumbling water, he wondered if this time he would be overturned, but the next moment they were out in the light again, moving on broad, quiet waters.

On the left the Tower loomed up, massive, threatening. He disliked being reminded of the prisoners inside, eating their hearts out with hope deferred, falling ill and dying or being led out some cold morning to be beheaded. What hideous things went on behind stone walls while people in their very shadow went, oblivious, about their ordinary affairs, feeling petty irritations over trivial mishaps.

In the Pool, tall-masted ships rode at anchor, some of them having the look of foreign countries. Passing under one, he heard a parrot squawk and a monkey gibber, shrank aside when a sailor with rings in his ears spat into the water too near his shoulder. Wapping, with its wharves and crowding shops with nautical signs—ship-builders, sail-makers, ship-chandlers —and its Execution Dock, where the shrunken body of some poor devil of a deserter swayed and creaked, disappeared behind them as the river made its great loop around the marshes of the Isle of Dogs. The turrets of Greenwich Palace rose on the hill on the right.

Boats crowded about Greenwich Wharf, hired oars like his own, wherries, tilt boats, noblemen's barges, and people went streaming up the hill to Greenwich Palace.

John had been to Court often enough to know the procedure, but not enough to feel easy in it—or did anyone ever feel easy in the presence of royalty? Even those most accustomed, he had noticed, those who were close to the Queen and even some who were old enough to remember her father, always had a look of tension, an air of suppressed excitement when they approached her. He had himself no thought of attracting the attention of the Queen, only of meeting again the Earl of Essex or Tom Egerton, who had promised to recommend him to his father, the Lord Keeper.

Perhaps he had been, as Christopher had charged, foolish to leave Lincoln's Inn. He conceded the point, mounting the steps to the Palace. The law would have been a safe profession, though certainly not one that roused his ardor or absorbed his mind. But he *had* left it, drawn—by what? The pursuit of learning for its own sake, travel, adventure, the hope of attaching himself to some great lord who would waft him on to a secure niche near the heart of things, the Privy Council perhaps or an embassy abroad. Or had he been duped by his patrimony, which seemed at the time so large, into imagining himself one of those fortunate youths who take a few years at an Inn of Court as a final flourish to their education, the gilt on its gingerbread? In any case, here he was now, twenty-four years old, his fortune spent, approaching the Presence Chamber at Greenwich with the sanguine idea that he could find there, just by looking, a patron or an employer. It was not what his sober father, who had so carefully amassed the lost fortune, would have approved. He had been reckless, prodigal, overconfident; but even admitting all that, he was aware, deep within himself, of a force, a strength, awaiting its outlet; he felt that destiny held something for him, and he stretched out his hand for it in the only way he knew.

Looking over the shoulder of a shorter man in the doorway, he hoped that he would find some of his friends there, for it was important not to seem alone and unknown; hoped, too, that he could steer clear of clinging and obscure acquaintances, for it was important also not to be fastened to someone even more insignificant than oneself.

He entered the Presence Chamber at last with what he trusted was a suitable combination of confidence and modesty, and found himself seized upon by an eager nonentity with gaudy, shabby clothes and a painted face.

"Mr. Donne! My fondest hopes are realized!"

But not mine, thought John. It was a chance acquaintance met on the ship returning from Spain in '95 who held him now, spinning compliments around him like a spider's web.

"My dear sir! I have had the honor of seeing one of your poems lately and I have longed to talk with you about it. 'The Flea'! What an ingenious conceit! So clever! So daring!"

61

John strode doggedly into the room, this thing, firmly fastened, hastening with short steps to keep up with him.

"I have been longing to ask you—I trust your judgment wholly—whom do you conceive to be the best linguist?"

"Calepine's Dictionary," said John sourly. "Eleven languages in one volume."

"No, no, dear sir. What *man,* I mean."

"Beza, then."

For all John knew, the Calvinist theologian spoke only French and Latin, but he flung out the name to his tormentor as a man tosses a stick hopefully too far for a dog to find it.

The vast chamber, hung with gold-embroidered tapestry, roofed with Spanish chestnut, lit partly by the gray light through the windows and partly by candles in sconces on the walls, held a great company of men and women, brilliantly dressed, who moved about like actors in a play, preening themselves, bowing, curtseying, talking, posturing, always keeping an eye on the door through which the Queen would come. Courts were theaters, he thought, where some men played the part of princes, others of slaves. Those who were armed with honesty were like naked red Indians against the Spanish armies. He shivered, feeling the chill of his own honesty—for whatever else he was, ambitious, lustful, proud, he was honest.

He found himself a place under a window to stand and watch. The rich colors and shapes of the tapestries depicted the seven deadly sins. What, he asked himself, could be more appropriate for the place? Certainly all were here—pride, envy, sloth, gluttony, avarice, anger and lust, wearing their best clothes and outdoing one another. The young men looked as fresh and sweet, he thought acidly, in their white plumes, high collars and bulging trunks, their fine leather boots artificially wrinkled about the knee, as the fields they had doubtless sold to buy their finery, and he wondered how many of these slashed doublets and jewel-sewn sleeves would be in the Cheapside second-hand shops next week. Wondered, too, where all these bright young men had come from, all virile and glowing—from tennis or hawking or football—or the stews?

Tall enough to see over the heads of many of the company, he raked the crowd for Lord Essex, for the Lord Keeper, for Tom and John Egerton, for Francis Woolley, Henry Wotton or George Gerrard, but he found none of them.

Sir Walter Raleigh went past, walking with his brother-in-law, Mr. Throckmorton, and John swept off his hat and bowed. The great captain gave him little more than a nod in response; openly in rivalry with Essex, he was now, it appeared, on the high end of the seesaw, and John was but one obscure, would-be follower of Essex.

"Jack! At last! Where have you been keeping yourself?"

The voice and the hand on his arm caught him unaware. He turned to find beside him one of the men he most wanted to see, a handsome, elegantly dressed figure, breathing confidence and well-being. Harry Wotton was his friend from his days at Oxford, though Wotton was a good six years older than he. They had traveled together for a time on the Continent and had been on both the Cadiz and the Islands Voyages in Essex's train, though Wotton, as secretary, had been very much closer to the hero. Younger son of a well-to-do country gentleman of Bocton Malherbe, in Kent, he had two brothers knighted by Essex, one of whom married a sister of the Earl of Northumberland, and a niece who married Sir Edmund Bacon: useful connections flowered all around him. He had written a little poetry and one play.

"Oh, I've been right here in London since I returned from Plymouth. The real question is, where have you been?"

"In Wanstead with his lordship."

Of his two closest friends, John loved Christopher and admired—even envied—Harry Wotton. He had the things John valued: a discerning mind, a winning personality, the favor of Essex, opportunities to distinguish himself. He was—or seemed to be—moving in the direction John would have liked to follow, toward a success not merely worldly but one that would demand his full capacities and give him in return honor and a secure place in the shifting, struggling world. He lowered his voice to ask:

63

"How is it with my lord?"

"The Queen is displeased and he sulks. What have you been doing?"

"Defacing clean paper with ink marks."

"Good. What have you written?"

"A nasty little piece about an apparition, I being dead and a ghost——"

"Your nasty little pieces have suddenly become the fashion—did you know it? At least three people have asked me if I have seen 'The Flea.'"

"I hope you've not. My verses are like to get me into trouble." He shot a glance at Harry to see if that brought any spark of recognition to his keen brown eyes, but he saw in them only calm affection. "I've written a 'Valediction to Love' and now I think I should do a 'Valediction to Poetry' as well."

"Whose valediction—yours or an imagined character's?"

"Mine."

"To love? I don't believe it."

"True, nevertheless. I am finished with pursuing things that only damage me. The act of love is short, it leaves men sad and dull—unlike the animals, which are gay and frolicsome afterwards—it diminishes our span of life by one day for each time performed. It is good only for raising posterity—and that I can't support till I find employment. Not to mention the trifling circumstance of its being forbidden fruit."

"I am sure there is none of the forbidden fruit left, for we eat daily of it. Shall I see your verses? Why don't you print a book?"

"It's not in shape to print. It's rough. I do not intend to be smooth, of course, but as it stands, it is even rougher than I intend. Besides, I am looking for weightier employment than anyone would offer an acknowledged poet. I write only to amuse myself—and my friends, of course."

"Lord Essex has made no sign to you?"

"No slightest sign. I came here looking for someone to serve—since there seems to be no hope of my lord, and Tom Egerton, who promised to speak for me to his father, appears to

64

have vanished off the earth—but I think everyone here is too busy jostling for place himself to notice me."

"It is difficult for a gentleman. If you were a milkmaid, now, you could stand in the market place on hiring day and declare yourself."

"Even for that advantage I could not endure the insipidity of the country!"

"I don't know just what you do," Wotton went on, paying no attention to John's thrust in a long-continued argument between them on the attractions of city life versus country life, "lacking a powerful father or some cousinship to the Queen."

Wotton himself, John reflected, had powerful connections and his solid country background; he had inherited—it was another strength—the right religion for the times.

"When you see my lord of Essex, commend me to him——"

"Stay. The Queen!"

A door swung open and a procession emerged: gentlemen, barons, earls, knights of the Garter, all bareheaded, followed by the Lord Keeper carrying the seals in a red silk purse and flanked by a gentleman with the scepter and another with the sword of state. It was the Lord Keeper who seized John's attention and held it.

He had seen Sir Thomas Egerton at Lincoln's Inn several years before, when he had come in black gown and square cap to a moot, when the would-be lawyers argued against one another in a mock trial. Now in his robes of office, with his gold chain, the royal seals in his hands, walking before Her Majesty, he was a person of immense dignity and seriousness. It would take all of a man's mind and energy to serve this man; he would like to try it.

For the Queen, John, doffing his hat and going down on one knee as she passed, felt still a trace of the dislike and distrust with which his mother had infected all her children. He had to remind himself that Elizabeth had once been considered beautiful. Her wrinkled skin, hooked nose, thin lips disclosing blackened teeth, her bright, dry, red wig gave her a witchlike look, though there was undeniable majesty in her erect, stately walk. Below her bosom, bare and still—rather horribly —plump, gleamed white satin sewn with pearls; a marchioness carried the long train of her black and silver mantle.

The great hall was taut with excitement. Everybody there seemed to be spreading out his devotion to the Queen's grace as a peacock spreads its tail and thinking better of himself because he was there breathing this exalted air in which royalty moved and breathed. A shout rang out, sharp and clear, "Long live Queen Elizabeth!" and those closest could hear her reply, "I thank you, my good people."

A courtier in white velvet, wearing a heavy gold chain, brought up and introduced to the Queen, one by one, gentlemen of distinction, and she moved about greeting others, speaking to ambassadors in their own tongues. I should have told the pest, thought John, that Her Majesty was the greatest linguist of all; fortunes have been made by pleasing compliments that reached their targets. Now and then the Queen raised someone to his feet with a motion of her hand. To a Bohemian nobleman she pulled off her glove and gave him her small, long-fingered hand to kiss. A country gentleman with yellow stockings and a green taffeta cloak she greeted as an old friend. The ladies of the Court, all in white, followed her, and the gentlemen pensioners guarded her with their gilt axes.

In the ante-chapel at the far end of the hall she stopped to receive petitions, but there were only a few, so far as John could tell, craning his neck to see, and what they were he had no idea. But her graciousness was like a garment over those who knelt and mumbled.

Moved, in spite of his prejudice, by the nearness of the Queen's majesty and by the love and reverence that welled up in all those around him, John followed along into the chapel for divine service. He was glad to have Wotton beside him, kneeling there at the back of the chapel while music flowed over them and one of the Queen's chaplains conducted what John considered to be a short and perfunctory service. The

66

Queen, it was known, did not like sermons. At its close she returned in stately procession to dinner.

The setting up of the table in the hall was like a scene on a stage or perhaps some slow, intricate dance or masque. Men kneeling laid the fine white cloth and set out the foot-high silver salt cellars, the plate, the mounts of bread. To a fanfare of trumpets and the rattle of kettle-drums, scarlet-clad yeomen of the guard, bareheaded, marched in bearing twenty-four enormous silver dishes piled with viands, each dish being received by a gentleman of the Court and placed reverently on the table. After the Lady Taster, with a long ceremonial knife, had given each yeoman a taste of the dish that he had brought —their mouths opening for it like baby birds—the maids of honor came forward and filled silver plates with food to carry into the Queen's inner apartment, where with only three or four attendants she would dine in private.

The closing of the door behind Her Majesty was the signal for a general onslaught on the table. All resemblance to a stately drama ended abruptly; the sacred dance became a mob scene. Lords, bishops, ambassadors, gentlemen, ladies and hangers-on crowded around the twenty-four dishes, reaching, pushing, snatching, gobbling. The sound of voices rising higher and higher in conversation, like the wind in a nightmare, drowned out the music. John found himself with a chicken leg in one hand and a trencher of white bread in the other. Harry had got swept off in the crowd; the pest whom he had shaken off, pounced, now triumphantly revenant, upon him once more.

"Sir, are you acquainted with Sir Robert Drury over there?"

John looked in time to see a big man with a big nose thrust a patty into his mouth and jump backward, leaning forward, to avoid its sudden spurt of juice. He felt only a mild interest in Sir Robert, who was the patron of his sister's Frenchified husband.

"Did you notice the Queen's smile for the Bohemian baron? That will keep three embassies working late tonight to determine its meaning——"

John dropped his chicken bone on the rushes and wiped his fingers on his handkerchief, looking over the crowd for Francis Woolley or Tom Egerton.

"I beg you to excuse me, sir. I see a friend over there and must go to speak with him."

The table behind him was a ruin, as if a war had passed over it, looted, defiled, crumbs and spots on the white cloth, the twenty-four empty dishes pulled out of their orderly positions, crowded together at one end, sprawling apart at the other, one stately saltcellar lying drunkenly on its side, not enough left of the food to feed even one hungry beggar. The guests were turning away, chatting in groups, drifting toward the door. The Archbishop of Canterbury, very expansive, in an aura of holy state, was surrounded by ladies, one of whom turned as John passed, exclaiming:

"Why, Mr. Donne! I thought you were at the Azores—or in Yorkshire!"

She was beguilingly pretty still, with those extravagant black lashes and the mouth for which "rosebud," however trite, was the only word. But she had a brittle, artificial way about her now, no longer young and uncertain, ingenuously anxious to please, as she had been when he called her—it was an endearment—"nature's lay idiot," and without intending to or realizing till too late what he was doing had destroyed the very things in her that had drawn him to her. This vivacity was new and not learned from him, nor the little claw of malice that he deplored in a woman. Bowing now and murmuring a compliment, he threw a reminder of their outworn love into his faintly mocking smile and had the satisfaction—briefly felt and swiftly followed by wholesome shame—of seeing a flood of color mount toward the roots of her hair.

Tom Egerton, the elder son of the Lord Keeper, pounced on him as he turned away. The dark, eager, energetic boy who had slept beside John on the voyage and talked late about his longing for a military career looked the very figure of a young soldier, in spite of new, pale-colored clothes.

68

"Jack! Here you are! I've been trying to catch your eye. My father wishes to speak with you. Will you come with me?"

Assuming agreement, he hurried away, with John on his heels, longing to ask about Lord Essex but getting no opportunity as they darted around one group of people, plunged by a narrow opening through another. At the far end of the hall, near the ante-chapel, he opened a door into a small room where the Lord Keeper sat talking with two or three other gentlemen.

Sir Thomas Egerton rose and extended his hand to John. When he straightened up from his bow and put on his hat again, he saw that he and the Lord Keeper were of the same height; he found gray eyes, level with his own, searching, it seemed, his very thoughts.

"I remember you now, Mr. Donne. You argued very ingeniously in one of the moots, two or three years since. I thought that there was more literature and philosophy in your discourse than law"—his eyes unexpectedly twinkled—"but I took note of your eloquence."

"You are very kind, my lord Keeper. I wish now that I had been more diligent in the law."

"No matter. You are diligent in kindness. I asked you to come here that I might thank you for your care of my stepson Francis Woolley. What he and my sons have told me of you makes me wish to speak with you more fully than it is possible now. Would you be good enough to call on me at York House? Tomorrow morning I shall be at home and at leisure."

vii

SIR THOMAS EGERTON was prepared to set the young man at his ease, but he found that it was not necessary. Not that Mr. Donne was self-assertive or overconfident; on the contrary, his manner was an admirable combination of deference and composure.

He had him sit down where the light from the window fell on his face. The young man cast a glance at the view of Whitehall Palace and commented on it; he sent a more lingering look around the walls of the library, withdrawing it evidently with some difficulty from the books there.

"You are a great reader, Mr. Donne?"

"I find books a means to learning as well as a perennial pleasure. The greater part of my patrimony has been spent on books, but my collection is nothing at all in comparison to what I see here."

His eyes were large, dark and glowing under finely arched brows. His face was long and oval, his nose straight, his lips full; he wore a fashionable and, to Sir Thomas, a silly and affected thread of moustache. His brow was wide, his hair dark and thick and cut short. Tall and slender, he wore his quiet, well-made clothes well; his hands were still, no meaningless gestures, no fidgeting. His appearance would be an asset in any man's household.

Sir Thomas had not stopped with the enthusiastic account given him by his stepson or the more casual but still favorable reports of his own sons; he had made inquiries at Lincoln's

Inn and of Lord Essex, who praised Donne's intelligence and his remarkable command of languages and regretted that, since he already had four secretaries and Mr. Donne had no interest in a military career, there was no place for him in his own entourage.

"Your father, I believe, was an ironmonger?"

"He rose to be warden of the Company of Ironmongers, sir. He died when I was three years old."

"Your mother remarried?"

"Twice, sir. Her present husband, Mr. Rainsford, is almost a stranger to me, but I was very fond of my first stepfather, Dr. Philip Comminges. As he was surgeon at St. Bartholomew's Hospital, we moved from the house in Bread Street where I was born, which had a large garden, to another in the precinct of St. Bartholomew."

"I remember Dr. Comminges well. He was famous in his time. Your mother is still living?"

"Yes, sir, but in Malines. I last saw her two or three years ago. She was Elizabeth Heywood, the daughter of the poet and playwright John Heywood."

Sir Thomas knew about "merry John Heywood" too. "I have seen some of his interludes performed. Didn't he come under some sort of cloud?"

"He was accused of denying the royal supremacy in King Henry's time. He had been a singer and a player on the virginals to the King when he was prince, but that did not save my grandfather from being condemned to death over the religious issue. But he quite cheerfully recanted at Paul's Cross and escaped to Louvain. He came back to favor, briefly, during Queen Mary's reign, and there is a tradition in our family that he was called to her deathbed to divert her mind with his pleasantries. After her death he returned to Louvain and died there."

"You inherit your talent for writing poetry from him, perhaps?"

The young man looked startled.

"Never mind. It's no crime to write verse. My sons have only praise for yours."

"There is a Spanish proverb, my lord, to the effect that he who cannot make one sonnet is a fool and he is mad who makes two. I write only for my own amusement and that of my friends. I have no intention of publishing my verse. My mother's grandfather, if I may revert to my family, was William Rastell the jurist."

"Ah, yes. A very distinguished man. So the law as well as poetry is in your blood."

"And my mother's great-grandmother was a sister of Sir Thomas More, the Lord Chancellor."

A distinguished line, but determined Romanists every one of them. The young man had an honest pride in them; he did not gloss over the fact that they belonged to a proscribed religion.

"Have you brothers and sisters?"

"There were six of us, but only my elder sister and I are left. She is married to Mr. William Lyly, who has been called a witty atheist—though I question the wit."

"But not the atheism?" Better atheism, these days, than Roman Catholicism. He leaned forward, his elbows on the arms of his chair, to launch the inevitable, the crucial, question. "And your own religion, Mr. Donne?"

It was what both had been waiting for. It lay between them like a body that they, two doctors, were to examine. In the beginning Sir Thomas would have said that, once satisfied of the young man's other qualifications, he would make the answer to this question the determining factor in his decision. Now, so far had he come along the road to liking the young man, he found himself actually wondering if some way could be found out of the dilemma, should Donne prove to be a recusant. It would cut Donne out of further advancement, but would it be fatal to him, the Lord Keeper, so established, so secure in his own position, to have in his employ one who belonged to the forbidden religion? It hinged perhaps on whether he was a fanatical adherent, in touch with priests abroad, or merely a passive one. Surprised to find himself entertaining, even momentarily, such a question, he cleared his throat loudly and waited for the young man's answer.

Mr. Donne spoke slowly, not alarmed, not defensive, but as if he were recounting interesting facts about someone else.

"I was reared in the old religion, sir. Both of my mother's brothers were Jesuits, one of them, Jasper Heywood, at one time holding the Chair of Moral Theology at Dillingen in Bavaria. He had been page of honor to the Queen when she was Princess Elizabeth—we have had some slight touch with the Court."

"Are you in contact with him now?"

"No, my lord Keeper. Though I saw him in Rome when I was there three years ago."

Sir Thomas digested this, reluctantly, in silence.

"When I first remember him, as a very small child, he was here on a mission to England from Rome and he lived with considerable pomp. But the next thing I knew, he was imprisoned in the Clink. I used to go with my mother to visit him and to take him food. It gave me a horror of prisons. He was offered a bishopric in the English church if he would change his religion, but he refused."

Jesuits. Fanatics. The merry John Heywood might recant but not, evidently, the rest of them. Sir Thomas was silent, oddly disappointed, still more oddly wishing that the young man had seen fit to conceal some of these damaging facts.

"He was arraigned at Westminister Hall with five other priests and all were condemned. The other five were executed, but my uncle, for some reason or other, was pardoned, and he returned to Rome. By that time I had gone to Oxford."

"Your college?"

"Hart Hall, where, as you know, most of the Catholic boys are sent. My brother Henry was with me. We were rather too young, eleven and twelve, but our mother wished us to have as much of the university as possible before the age when we should be required either to take or to refuse the oath of supremacy."

"And did you take it?"

"No, my lord. The decision was my mother's—and those who were advising her. We were removed from Oxford and sent for a time to Trinity College, Cambridge. It is for that reason that I have no university degree, for all my studies."

"A pity, that. Though I understand from my lord of Essex that you have acquired considerable learning. Am I to infer that you submitted to your mother's decision rather than concurred in it?"

"I did not begin to think seriously about the question until I was at Lincoln's Inn. I was aware, of course, from an early age that no avenues of advancement are open to those of the Catholic faith, but I was contented with my studies and my friends and I drifted. My brother Henry's death four years ago pulled me up sharp. He was a more devout and a kinder person than I am. He was at Thavies Inn; he harbored a man named Harington, a priest from the seminary at Rheims, was caught and consigned to the Clink first and then Newgate, where he died of gaol fever."

"That was very difficult for you, if you had been close."

"We were devoted to each other."

Sir Thomas felt the young man's pain. He wondered why he thought it necessary to reveal so much, even while he respected the honesty that prompted it. As if he read the Lord Keeper's mind, Mr. Donne said:

"I fear I am burdening you with many unnecessary circumstances of my life, which is an obscure and unimportant one. But, sir, if I were to say to you, 'I am an Anglican,' and you employed me on that understanding, and you heard later of my brother's death, or if my uncle Jasper should come again to London and make himself conspicuous, you might think that I had been disingenuous with you."

"And are you an Anglican?"

"I do not know. I am not a Roman Catholic."

It had taken a long time to get that out of him. Sir Thomas was ready to drop the subject now, but he saw that Mr. Donne was not yet through with it. He felt a sudden pity for youth and its desire to have everything clear, to omit no stage of changing opinion. It was important to this young man, exactly what he thought and believed. Sir Thomas himself, at fifty-six, was thankful to leave his soul in the care of his chaplain, whose business it was, and to get on with more immediately interesting things.

"After my brother's death I shut myself up in order to find out exactly where I stood in this question of religion. I saw very clearly that if I was to find any honorable outlet for my ambition—and I am ambitious, sir—I would have to leave the religion of my family and adopt the religion of my country. But there is something very unattractive about abandoning one's religion simply to increase one's material prospects. So I set out to make a thorough study of both religions, to see what I honestly believed. I read the best modern authorities on both sides."

"Humph. That was very thorough. What did you read?"

"Cardinal Bellarmine of the Roman cause—the third volume of his *Disputationes* was just out—and Theodore Beza for the Calvinist point of view."

"And you settled your doubts that way?"

"I came to the conclusion that it is better to doubt wisely than to be indifferent or wrong. I think it is better to find one's own truth than to depend on outward authorities that contradict each other. If you would be willing to glance at this, it might explain where I stand."

"Humph. What is it?"

"I call it a 'Satire,' sir, but it sums up the conclusions that I reached."

"Thank you. Put it on the table, if you will be so good. I'll read it later."

"I would rather have you see that than some others of my verses. But in case they should come to your eyes, sir, I should say that I am indeed a sinner—but not guilty of all the sins I brag of."

"I see." He had audacity, this young man, and under his quiet manner a certain lurking gaiety. The Lord Keeper, for whom life had always been a matter of gravity, felt again drawn to him. "There is one other question I wanted to ask you. Why did you leave Lincoln's Inn?"

75

"The seven years looked very long, sir. And I had inherited my brother's share of my father's property. I went abroad to see the world and to study languages."

"You speak French fluently, I understand. And Spanish?"

"I am at home in both. In Italian and German I know enough to get about—and to read whatever I wish."

"You are ambitious, you say. What line does your ambition take?"

"I should like to serve the state in some useful way."

"Some little office, like an ambassadorship or membership in the Privy Council, I take it?"

He greeted the heavy irony with a gleam in his eyes. "To be your secretary would content me now, my lord."

After he had gone—with no definite answer—the Lord Keeper sat on at his desk, drumming with his fingers and going back over the interview. Which of them, after all, had controlled it? The young man had been almost blatantly honest; yet there was nothing unskilled in the way he had managed to say all that he wished to say and in doing so to forestall and explain any criticism or question that might arise. He was perceptive, daring, original. He had purpose. In his loyalty to his family Sir Thomas saw a quality that might be a strength to them both if they were associated.

He took up the satire intending only to glance at it, but he found himself reading it carefully, pausing here and there to reread where the sense at first eluded him, noting with approval the clear, flowing Italian hand in which it was written, a valuable skill in any secretary. The young man bade his soul, courageous in worldly ways, given to worldly loves and lusts, have the courage to seek true religion. Like all the other sinners from St. Augustine down, he wrote of his sins with zest. Sir Thomas found the verse unpoetic, for though it was written in rhymed couplets, it employed words and rhythms of daily speech, but it was fresh and vigorous.

> *Seek true religion, O where? Mirreus,*
> *Thinking her unhoused here, and fled from us,*

> *Seeks her at Rome, there, because he doth know*
> *That she was there a thousand years ago;*
> *He loves her rags so, as we here obey*
> *The state-cloth where the prince sat yesterday.*

That might appear to dispose of the Roman church as out-worn. He read on, to find that Calvinism, embraced by an-other hypothetical character, named Crants, was described in even less complimentary terms.

> *Crants to such brave loves will not be enthralled,*
> *But loves her only who at Geneva's called*
> *Religion, plain, simple, sullen, young,*
> *Contemptuous yet unhandsome; as among*
> *Lecherous humors, there is one that judges*
> *No wenches wholesome but coarse country drudges.*

Hmm. Well, Sir Thomas himself deplored the way some of the young nobles about the Court, the Earl of Essex in par-ticular, were rushing pell mell after certain Puritan preachers. But what had young Donne to say about the Queen's religion, which was after all the crux of the matter?

> *Graius stays still at home here, and because*
> *Some preachers, vile ambitious bawds, and laws*
> *Still new, like fashions, bid him think that she*
> *Which dwells with us, is only perfect, he*
> *Embraceth her, whom his godfathers will*
> *Tender to him, being tender; as wards still*
> *Take such wives as their guardians offer, or*
> *Pay values. . . .*

Now that would not do at all. "Some preachers, vile ambi-tious bawds." Sir Thomas threw the paper down. There were, unquestionably, unworthy men among the clergy, self-servers; the vicar in his father's manor at Ridley had wavered from King Edward's Protestant religion to Queen Mary's fierce Catholicism and back to Protestantism with Queen Elizabeth, all within a matter of a dozen years, and he was not alone in his gyrations; but these were offensive words the young man used.

Angrily Sir Thomas picked the paper up again and read on, not greatly appeased to find the satirist despising alike those who considered all religions bad and those who held them all to be good.

> ... *Careless Phrygius doth abhor*
> *All, because all cannot be good; as one,*
> *Knowing some women whores, dares marry none.*
> *Gracchus loves all as one and thinks that so*
> *As women do in divers countries go*
> *In divers habits, yet are still one kind,*
> *So doth, so is religion; and this blind-*
> *Ness too much light breeds. But unmoved thou*
> *Of force must one, and forced but one allow;*
> *And the right ...*

Still not satisfactory. Nor were his figures edifying, as if religion were a wife to be chosen by a man who had known many mistresses. No, no, he could not employ this man. His eye, continuing, came on words that moved him in spite of himself.

> ... *Doubt wisely; in strange way,*
> *To stand inquiring right, is not to stray;*
> *To sleep, or run wrong, is. On a huge hill*
> *Cragged and steep, Truth stands, and he that will*
> *Reach her, about must and about must go.*

Plain and rough though it was, that had the ring of authentic poetry. Down the page a little he came on another line that arrested him: "Keep the truth which thou hast found ..."

Only a Protestant, whether a conscious one or not, could write that. He finished the poem and read the last couplet twice:

> *So perish souls which more choose men's unjust*
> *Power from God claimed, than God himself to trust.*

78

He laid it aside, rose and walked to the window.

Stripped of that intolerable, that unfortunate, line, what the poem was saying was essentially that man should seek God Himself rather than man-made churches that claimed to have power from God. It was unorthodox and impolitic, but it revealed a man who at bottom was perhaps more genuinely religious than most young men of his age. For his part, Sir Thomas would much prefer him to have a conventional, correct, religious surface, no matter what lay beneath it. Still, it was evident that the young man was, as he had said, no longer a Roman Catholic.

The attraction that he had felt toward young Donne returned. He had a subtle and supple mind, even a brilliant one, above all an honest one; a mind, perhaps, that liked to plague itself. He had called his poem a "Satire"; it was doubtless to be considered somewhat as an exaggeration. Poetry and law were, after all, not a bad combination: fire and imagination added to justice and order.

The young man's parentage was respectable on one side, distinguished on the other. He might go far, with the advantages that come from working under a Lord Keeper—who was certain to be Lord Chancellor soon—and the opportunities of being known in the right places that such a position would give him.

Sir Thomas thought, as he seldom did, of his own birth: the natural son of a distinguished father. His mother he did not remember at all; she had died, he was told. But had she? Was she some poor, pretty little country girl who was robbed of her child, paid and turned away? He had grown up at Ridley, in Cheshire, mothered more or less by the housekeeper, alternately swept out of sight and brought forward to entertain his father's friends with his quaint observations. Brasenose College when he was fifteen, Lincoln's Inn for seven years, and he was off. Called to the bar at thirty-two, Solicitor General before he was forty, Lent Reader to Lincoln's Inn, Attorney General, Master of the Rolls, Keeper of the Seal. Who had helped him? His father, his own intelligence and determination, the Queen's favor, two fortunate marriages?

At any rate, here he was, established in York House on the Strand, with more business on his hands than he could cope with unassisted. He had two secretaries who were no more than scriveners, well-bred rabbits both of them. His sons were still only boys, one set on a military career with the Earl of Essex, the other gone back to Cambridge. He needed someone to stand between him and the incredible number of people who came begging around any public figure, asking for jobs, houses, favors, money, introductions, advice. All of them took time, for all must be seen, answered, assisted or put off, without offending them if possible, for one never knew who would rise and who would sink, and who might someday be in a position to return a favor fourfold. He needed an able man, a man he could trust, a man whom he could enjoy having constantly at his side.

Hearing a rustle behind him, he turned from the window and, at sight of the little figure standing there, smiled one of his rare smiles. Red-gold curls, hazel eyes, dimples, weedy little-girl's body: it was twelve-year-old Anne More, his wife's favorite niece, who came sometimes to visit them.

She dropped a curtsey when she caught his eye. "My aunt says, sir, when you are at leisure, would you come to her in her closet. She wishes to ask your advice about something."

"I'll come now. Shall we go together?"

He took a handful of her curls, affectionately, and shook her head gently. Her hair was silky and springy and he liked to touch it. She was the nearest thing he had to a daughter of his own and he loved her. With any luck, he thought, they might have her six or seven years still before she must be handed over to some irreproachable young man. Perhaps his own son John, he sometimes thought. Her father, Sir George More, Sheriff of Surrey and Sussex, aimed high, he knew, but even he could scarcely object to the son of the Lord Chancellor and doubtless by that time a baron.

She took his arm and hung on it. "Uncle, who was that who just left?"

"My new secretary, Mr. Donne. What do you think of him?"

But she suddenly turned shy, blushed and would not answer.

80

BOOK TWO 1600-1602

"Love's mysteries in souls do grow
And yet the body is his book."

VIII

ON THE FIFTH OF JUNE, 1600, all at York House were stirring early; the steward, the cooks, the serving men, the gentlemen ushers and the secretaries. The youngest scullion's dirty face already was streaked with tears, and the stable boys were quarreling about the best way to care for so many horses.

It had rained a little in the night and now the sun shone on wet grass and shattered roses in the garden, on the stones and brick and marble of the towering house. John, coming along the Strand from his lodging in the Savoy, with the sun at his back, found the gate already open and a little cluster of idlers gathered to wait for whatever there might be to watch. He stopped to speak to the porter.

"Everything is ready, Snoseman?"

"As ready as may be, sir. A bad day, I say."

John nodded and crossed the courtyard to the house.

He had supervised the preparation of the great hall the day before, but he stopped nevertheless to look it over once more. In the center stood the long table covered with a rare Oriental rug, with armchairs drawn up to it, where the eighteen Commissioners were to sit. Around three walls were the benches for the spectators, those two hundred representatives of all professions and qualities who had been invited to come and witness the humiliation of the Earl of Essex. John had written the letters summoning them from London and from their country places. He doubted if a single one would miss the chance to be present at the downfall of one with whom, two years ago, even a year ago, they would have been proud to be seen walking. He thought of that morning in March, nearly two years earlier, when Essex, newly appointed Lord Lieutenant of Ireland, had departed from London to go to put down Tyrone's rebellion. The whole nation had been on fire with enthusiasm; following in his train as he rode out were some of the greatest nobles in the realm and pressing close on both sides the common people crying out, "God bless your lordship! God save your honor!" Some of them followed him till evening, just to look at him. It had been a fine morning with clear skies, but later there had been a thunder shower—untimely in March—with showers of hail, an ill omen, for those who believed in omens.

He left the hall and went to the great dining room. Mr. Jewell, the steward, stood in the middle of a goemetry of tables looking troubled; his eyebrows seemed to have been raised and to have stuck there under the furrows on his forehead and over his darting, anxious eyes. There would be well over two hundred guests for dinner, and supper, too, if the session went on long. The great men's servants would go to nearby taverns, but their stewards and secretaries must be fed here.

"We have dined two or three hundred before—and well," said Jewell, "but there was time to prepare. This has been so sudden."

"It's not a banquet, you know. It's only something to stay their stomachs between sessions."

Mr. Jewell lowered his voice. "I don't suppose that *he'll* want much to eat, under the circumstances, but I've ordered a squab for him in his old room and a salad and some malmsey."

For nearly six months, up until the end of March, the Earl of Essex had had a room in York House, kept a prisoner there by the Queen's orders after his failure in Ireland. He had had one of the guest rooms except when he fell ill and the Queen had commanded the Lord Keeper to yield his own bedchamber to him. John, remembering her solicitude, comforted himself with the thought that she could not be intending now really to ruin Essex but only by this public humiliation to make him feel the power of her displeasure. He shrugged away the memory of those six months—York House crowded with Essex and his retinue, the Lord Keeper worried and harried, Lady Essex, defiant and tragic, arriving every morning at seven and staying till six in the evening, until suddenly her visits were stopped and the shadow of the Queen's wrath hung over them all. John himself, having lived at York House for nearly a year more like a son than a secretary, had returned to his lodgings at Mother Haines's in order to free his room for the visitors, but he had been there every day, all day, a part of the bustle and apprehension. The strain and worry of it all weighed heavily on Lady Egerton and might well have been the cause of her death. At any rate in January, in the midst of it all, she had gone to sleep one night and not waked in the morning. She was a gentle lady; John missed her for himself, but his heart was torn for Sir Thomas, who had been prostrated by the blow, so much so, indeed, that at length the Queen had felt it necessary to send word to him to remind him that the public service must be preferred before the private grief.

John went up the wide stairs to the corner chamber with the view of the river which was Sir Thomas's and had, for a few weeks, been the Earl of Essex's. His servant was just finishing dressing the Lord Keeper. He wore his state robes today and a tall-crowned hat with a stiff feather. He looked somber and in his hooded eyes John read his sorrow and his distaste for the day's work ahead.

"John," he said, dismissing the servant with a nod, "I know you have everything well in train. I depend on you." He put his hand, somewhat heavily, on John's shoulder. "You serve me as a king—not a subject—should be served."

John flushed at the praise. He had come to love the Lord Keeper as well as to respect his dignity, his integrity, his seriousness. He valued the praise and knew within himself that it was deserved; that in all the things with which the Lord Keeper entrusted him, whether small details of arrangements or larger undertakings, such as his recent mission to

Amsterdam over the treaty with the United Provinces, he had done his work skillfully, unobtrusively, dependably.

"You are the third young man in whose career I have taken a watchful interest," said Sir Thomas. "You are just beginning—Mr. Bacon is progressing—but my lord of Essex——" He sighed heavily and did not finish the sentence. "But if he takes this well," he added, "his troubles may be at an end. Shall we go to the chapel?"

They walked along the paneled gallery under some ill-done portraits of Egerton ancestors and one lovely one of Lady Egerton when she was Lady Woolley, with Francis, small and angelic, leaning against her knee with a dove in his hand.

Sir Thomas walked slowly, as if he were in no hurry to get into the day. "I warned his lordship—as you know. You copied the letter. I told him plainly that by his course of action he was doing for his enemies what they could never do for themselves, and exposing his friends to shame and contempt."

John remembered it well, remembered also Essex's indignant reply. That had been even before Ireland. Essex and the Queen had quarreled—the Lord Keeper had come home one day fairly trembling from having seen the Queen box Essex's ears—and patched it up and quarreled again, like two young lovers, though Essex was past thirty and the Queen more than twice his age.

"Perhaps things will be better after today," John ventured.

"It's been a bad year, John, altogether. Tom's death in Ireland last August, then my lord of Essex's troubles, and the loss of my dear wife. I feel like an old rock battered by waves and wind. Well, we'll go to morning prayers."

The service was said every morning at seven by the chaplain whether anybody was there or not. This morning John Egerton and Francis Woolley were waiting outside the chapel door, Francis looking taller and thinner in the new dignity of his Oxford degree. The sun came through the colored glass in the windows; Dr. King stood before the altar, which looked to John bare and cold without a cross, and began:

"'The hour cometh and now is, when the true worshippers

86

shall worship the Father in spirit and in truth, for the Father seeketh such to worship him.' "

On his knees, John was thinking of the five of them who had been together on the Islands Voyage: Tom was dead, killed in the war in Ireland; Wotton, who had been in Ireland as well, was lying low in Bocton Hall; and here were John and Francis and himself praying together in the chapel before they should have to go and hear Essex, who had stood so high above them all, accused and censured. Tom had been Sir Thomas before he died. One of the Queen's complaints against Essex was the number of knights he had made in Ireland contrary to her command. She would have liked to unknight them all but that Cecil or someone else had convinced her that their ladies would buzz like angry bees.

" 'The grace of our Lord Jesus Christ, and the love of God . . .' "

Even before the final words were pronounced, the noises rising from house and stable had reached the chapel, and what would probably be the last quiet moment of the day was over. The Lord Keeper took himself to the garden chamber and the three young men went to greet and to guide the arriving guests.

The benches in the hall were already filling up. As the Commissioners came, the Lord Treasurer, the Lord Admiral, the Archbishop of Canterbury, the Lord Chief Justice and the rest, they were led to the garden chamber to wait, in order to make an entrance all together exactly on the hour. Those who had been summoned as audience lost no time in finding themselves places in the hall where they could best see and hear. Sir George More of Loseley House, the Lord Keeper's brother-in-law, emerged from the small dining room wiping his beard with his handkerchief.

"Ah, Mr. Donne," he said, kindly condescending, "a busy day for you, no doubt."

He was a short, red-haired, red-bearded man, pompously affable, all the more pompous, John knew, because at sixty he was still subject to his father, who kept a firm hand on the reins at Loseley.

The noise grew as the gentlemen continued to pour in, their horses and servants filling the courtyard and stables. Some were expansive and genial, moving from their places to greet others, as if to display the range of their acquaintance, the vastness of their condescension. Some held themselves aloof. Some looked eagerly about them as if they had come to a play. But all, John thought sourly, appeared pleased with themselves for being there rather than saddened because a great man had stumbled on disaster—a fate, he would have liked to remind them, that walked at every man's back at Court.

Just on the verge of eight o'clock a last arrival, a country knight, came hustling in, and settled down thankfully in an empty bench at the front. John sent a footman to whisper to him that those places were being held for Her Majesty's learned Counsel, and, laughing overloud to cover embarrassment, the knight must climb over the knees of many men, apologizing as he went, to squeeze into the end of a bench at the back.

He had barely time to sit down, breathing hard, before the lawyers, Attorney General Coke, Solicitor General Fleming, Sergeant Yelverton, Mr. Francis Bacon, the Queen's Counsel, who had been born in York House when his father was Lord Keeper, filed in and took the places reserved for them. The clock began to strike and on the first stroke silence settled on the assembly. On the last stroke the Commissioners made their appearance, not marching in procession but ambling in clots, talking together. With a murmur of whispers and a scraping of chairs they took their seats around the table, the Lord Keeper at the head, an empty place at the foot. All the company, who had stood up to welcome the Commissioners, now sat down as they sat, with a great rustling and creaking of wood and fabric, a nodding of plumes. John, standing by the door, saw Essex approach, preceded by a guard.

He came from a small waiting room near the hall. Hatless, his fair hair curling on his forehead, he was soberly but handsomely dressed in black damask with a ruff of exquisitely sheer linen. He gave no sign of recognizing John as he passed, walking as usual, not gracefully, with his head thrust forward. He moved to the empty place at the far end of the table, where, at a sign from the Lord Keeper, he knelt down on the rushes. No one of the company there rose or took off his hat at the Earl's entrance or showed him any sort of courtesy, not even that of a glance of respect or sympathy.

"Thy glory, O Israel, is slain upon thy high places. How are the mighty fallen." The familiar words rang in John's ears. And all these people, he thought savagely, who had once been delighted to sweep off their hats to Essex, sitting there now, in smug judgment, wondering no doubt what advantage there might be for them in the day's proceedings.

Among the Commissioners, several had been especially close to the Earl; the Archbishop of Canterbury, for whom Essex was known to have a filial respect; the Lord Admiral, who had served with him on two expeditions against Spain; Sir William Knollys, his uncle. As if the Queen—or her secretary and Essex's enemy, Robert Cecil, who sat there now making no effort to conceal his satisfaction—had confronted him with his own closest friends, to make the people think that if they were against him, surely he must be wrong.

The Lord Keeper rose, cleared his throat and, in commendably few words, declared the cause of the meeting, which everyone already knew, and directed the Queen's Sergeant to open the case against the Earl.

Mr. Yelverton began with a prepared speech on the subject of Her Majesty's princely care and provision for the wars of Ireland and her gracious dealings with the Earl of Essex; he went on in this vein at some length before he came to the point, which was that this meeting today represented great clemency on Her Majesty's part, since it was by her mercy and favor held privately and not in the court of the Star Chamber.

Attorney General Coke spoke next, condemning the Earl's conduct under three heads, *quomodo ingressus, quomodo progressus* and *quomodo regressus,* amplifying each one with rich and bitter rhetoric. The charges were serious, that he had disobeyed Her Majesty's orders in a number of ways, all detailed at length, from making three-score knights to entering into a secret conference with Tyrone.

"The fifth and last, his return to England, contrary to Her Majesty's express commandment in writing, under the seal of her privy signet, charging him upon his duty not to return until he heard further from her, was intolerably presumptuous. It was also exceedingly dangerous, for he left his army in such a manner that if God's providence had not been the greater, the ruin and loss of the whole kingdom had ensued thereupon."

Sickened, John listened to the accusing words pelting like blows on the bowed shoulders of the man whom he had so much admired and so ardently wished to serve. If God's providence, he thought, had not moved on his own behalf, attaching him three years before to the Lord Keeper, he might now be one of Essex's followers, faced with the choice between disaster, if he remained loyal to Essex, or self-contempt, if he abandoned him in his misfortune and disgrace. Young Tom Egerton was dead in Ireland, but Harry Wotton, who had returned from Ireland with Essex, had found it prudent to depart quietly to Bocton and busy himself there.

"To conclude," thundered the Attorney General, "I find that the ingress was proud and ambitious, the progress disobedient and contemptuous and the regress notorious and dangerous."

John was thankful when, the tirade ended at last, the Archbishop obtained permission for the Earl to stand. It was the first sign of mercy, and it was followed, after Mr. Bacon's charges, by the suggestion that a stool be brought and Essex be allowed to sit.

After more than three hours of speeches there was a pause for dinner, and the resources of the great house were drawn upon to make all comfortable. The Earl of Essex was led back to his small chamber and a guard posted at the door. John, after some hesitation, went to try, if he could, to speak to him—not knowing what he could say but wishing to show him at least some small respect—but was told that there were strict orders that nobody was to be admitted.

The hearing began again after dinner. This time there was

some delay in gathering people together; some were loth to break off conversations begun in the dining room; some came straggling from the houses of office; a few had quietly gone, leaving empty spaces on the benches.

The Earl, permitted to speak in his own defense, read a prepared statement filled with meekness and penitence. " 'I have laid aside all thought,' " he began, " 'of justifying myself in any of my actions. The inward sorrow and affliction in my soul for the great offense against Her Majesty is more than any outward cross or punishment that can befall me.' "

Abandoning the written words, he spoke with such passion of his loyalty and affection for Her Majesty that his own eyes filled with tears and more than one of his hearers wiped their cheeks. He would have been well served, John thought, if he had stopped there, but he went on to answer Coke's charges, growing more and more indignant at the memory of them until the Lord Keeper interrupted, to warn him:

"My lord, this is not the course that will do you good. This extenuation of your offense will only lessen Her Majesty's readiness to pardon."

Cecil, speaking, for all his known dislike of Essex, with more courtesy than the others, acquitted his lordship of disloyalty but condemned his "circles of errors, which were all bound up in the unhappy knot of his disobedient return." Judge Walmsley compared Essex's coming home and leaving the army to a shepherd's leaving his flock to the care of his dog.

The accusations being now complete, the Lord Keeper rose to deliver the speech of censure. He paid tribute to Her Majesty's clemency and mercy, recapitulated everything that had already been said and concluded:

"If this cause had been heard in the Star Chamber, my sentence must have been as great a fine as ever was set upon any man's head in that court, and perpetual imprisonment in that place, which belongeth to a man of his quality, the Tower. But now that we are in another place, and in a course of favor, my censure is, that he is not to execute the office of a Councillor, nor to execute the office of Earl Marshal of England nor of

Master of the Ordnance; and to return to his own house, there to continue a prisoner as before, till it shall please Her Majesty to release both this and all the rest."

Here it might have ended but that each one of the Commissioners must in turn rise to deliver his own personal condemnation. John, hearing the leisurely periods, the spreading phrases, seeing the cruelty covered by the expanding self-satisfaction in their voices, felt disgust rising within him like a nausea. The Queen had loved this man, showered him with her favors, with rich gifts, with honors. His mother's feeling about the illegitimate daughter of Henry VIII, excommunicated by the true church, returned to John and he recoiled from the thought of her Court, where envy, jealousy and all forms of cruelty and dishonesty were unleashed, where people rose by stepping on the fallen and in time fell themselves, to be trampled underfoot in their turn.

Suddenly feeling that he could endure no more of it, he stepped out of the room and made his way to the terrace. The air after the fetid atmosphere of the hall was sweet and fresh. With the light breeze in his face, he walked across the terrace and took the path to the enclosed garden.

Lady Egerton had loved the garden at York House. After her death, though the gardeners labored as usual, something went out of it; a less sensitive taste filled the beds with gaudier flowers, faded blooms were left on stalks, the paths were less carefully raked. At the end of it, farthest from the terrace and out of sight from the house because of the thick branches of a yew, was a little bower that Lady Egerton had made; overarched with climbing yellow roses was a wooden seat from which one could see the river and its darting life. During the months of his imprisonment Essex had won at length the privilege of walking in the garden, and on fine days he could be seen pacing up and down the paths. If he disappeared into the bower, someone would be sent to watch him. After Lady Essex had been permitted to join him, she came every day from Walsingham House, where she was staying with her father. Women suffered, John thought, all women, but perhaps

92

Lady Essex more than most, having been Sir Philip Sidney's wife and widow before she married Essex.

Knowing that the speeches in the hall would go on for several hours yet and that he would not be missed, John made for the seat in the bower, only to find someone there before him, a girl. She rose at his approach and turned to face him. For a moment, taken by surprise, he did not recognize her.

"Mr. Donne! Have I changed so much?"

As soon as she spoke, he knew her—little Anne More, Lady Egerton's niece.

"You have indeed, Mistress Anne, but it is nearly a year since I last saw you. You've grown into a young lady, a beautiful young lady."

She smiled, dimples appearing in both cheeks, her clear eyes, not gray nor brown nor green but something of all three, shining. "I saw you at my Aunt Egerton's funeral, but I think you did not see me. I always see you, Mr. Donne, if I don't see anybody else at all."

He saw her now. In another girl what she had said would have been accompanied with arch looks and provocative, but she spoke honestly, as if she but mentioned a fact of her life but not of his. She had flowered, as girls do flower, suddenly. Her red-gold hair was a cloud around her face; her innocent eyes, small, straight nose, mouth a little wide with mobile and sensitive lips and white teeth had a new clarity; her lithe young body, fastened into a stiff, gold-encrusted dress, showed a hint of white breast below the square neckline. She was lovely as a flower and fresh as dew. Twelve or thirteen when he had first come to York House, she must be—he counted—sixteen now, or nearly that. No child; a woman; but she had no arts.

"Did you come this morning with your father?"

"Yes. He will go back tomorrow but I am to stay on, to comfort my uncle and preside over his house for him."

"And do you think you can do that?"

"I do it at Loseley for my father and my grandfather."

"It will be good for my Lord Keeper to have you here. He has been very lonely. He needs feminine companionship—perhaps more than most men, for all of his life is occupied with serious and heavy affairs."

"I know. What is happening in the hall now? Why aren't you there?"

"I came to get a breath of fresh air, because I could endure it no longer. They are one by one, all eighteen of them, denouncing my lord of Essex; even the Archbishop, who loves him, and Sir William Knollys, his uncle, cannot forgo the opportunity to grind their heels into a fallen favorite. They are drunk on their own eloquence and it will go on for hours."

"Shan't we sit down?"

She spread out her skirts and settled herself on the bench, motioning to him to sit beside her. The sun was warm. He took off his hat and dropped it on the grass, rubbing his forehead where the tight band had bitten into it. A breath of a breeze lifted his hair. From a bush nearby came the chirping song of a bird. A summer-afternoon stillness stole over them; even the cries of boatmen on the river seemed to withdraw into distance and unreality; they might have been sitting on the bank of a stream in some timeless summer land.

The girl beside him said nothing; her small hands lay loosely clasped and still in her lap. He took one of them gently in his own but made no effort to draw her closer. Their eyes met. He lost himself. The thongs of convention fell away; to lift his eyes, to lower them, to speak of the weather, to make compliments, to stand, to bow, had no meaning. Everything dissolved but the moment and the participating figure beside him. They were two and—caught in this timelessness of silence and sun— they were one. Their very souls hovering above their motionless bodies might have fused into one.

He did not know how long they sat there, held in an ecstasy, or what brought them back again to the garden—the silence of a bird, perhaps, or the falling of a shadow. It was no sound that recalled them, no movement of hers or of his, but he was aware again of the river, where boats moved, leaving wakes behind them, and voices spoke, of the woodenness of the bench on which they sat. Now she stirred and slipped her moist hand

94

out of his to lay it for a moment, light as a petal's touch, against his cheek.

"I must go," she said, and before he could protest or rise to follow her, she had vanished from the arbor. He saw her bright hair among the roses and the gold of her gown shimmering on the path. He stood looking after her till she crossed the terrace and disappeared into the house, then turned slowly to retrieve his hat.

He was not the same man when he went back to the hall to find that the turn had come around to the young Earl of Derby who, though he spoke without the harsh assurance of the others or their command of rhetoric, still managed to convey in his stammering words a powerful mixture of condemnation and satisfied envy. The Earl of Essex sat on his stool, motionless, while a long, late ray of sunshine, falling through the many-paned window, touched his shoulder. Nothing had changed, yet all was changed.

2 John lay long awake that night, reliving the strange interview in the garden, questioning, analyzing, probing, seeking the meaning. His distress over Essex, his physical weariness—for he had worked incessantly during the last five days preparing for the session—his revulsion from the cruelty and self-seeking of the Court life toward which he had been bending all his energies and ambitions: had all this painful emotion and bodily weakness combined to crack the shell with which he daily protected his inmost self? In the garden—which had seemed not like a London garden but some country bank beside a stream—something more had happened. Was it the scene, the moment? Or was it the girl? What had removed her shell? How long had their souls, out of their quiet bodies, hung there in the air between them? What held them together? Not sex. Her hand in his was all their contact. Refined by love, he thought, they had spoken a silent language of the soul, understood the control of loneliness, penetrated truth.

"Love's mysteries in souls do grow." It was a line for a poem. But what of the body? The body the book in which the

95

mysteries were written. In his other loves he had read the book first, hoping for information therefrom. But truth—it must be that truth began with the soul—yet could not end there. On the verge of revelation, he fell into sleep.

In the morning he wrote down in verse what he remembered of his thoughts the night before. It was not yesterday's event exactly as it happened; it was the essence of it, distorted as words always must distort what cannot be expressed, yet somewhere near the truth he had experienced. He ended it with the quatrain:

> *And if some lover, such as we,*
> *Have heard this dialogue of one,*
> *Let him still mark us, he shall see*
> *Small change, when we're to bodies gone.*

ix

It was Midsummer Eve and the long, pale twilight made it unnecessary, late as it was, to light a candle. John sat in the little room in York House that was known as his closet, ostensibly writing a letter but actually waiting for the return of the gay party that had gone to the wedding of Anne Russell and Lord Herbert in the Blackfriars. If they did not linger too long, he might have a glimpse of Anne More before he went to his lodgings.

It had come to this—and so soon. In a matter of three weeks his life was reorganized around a single purpose: to see Anne, alone if possible; if not, then in company or merely in the distance.

Once, only, they had been alone together. She had come here, to his closet, where, his work finished, he had been indulging himself with a book on the warm June afternoon. It had been cooler indoors than out; Sir Thomas was sleeping. John had not heard a sound but he had felt a presence and looked up from his book to see her standing there in the doorway in her green dress, her red curls moist on her white forehead, her lips parted, her eyes wide.

"What are you reading?" she had said, a little breathlessly.

He had jumped up, knocking the book on to the floor, and, inviting her in, had offered her his chair, a little troubled because it was warm with his sitting, yet there was no other in the room. He perched on the cool stone window sill himself, after retrieving the book and putting it in her hands.

"You read a great deal, don't you?" she murmured. "Are you never idle?"

"I read something—but not so much to avoid idleness as to enjoy it."

"Should I like this book?"

"Why don't you look at it and see for yourself if you think you would?"

He thought to tease her, for it was in Italian, but to his surprise she opened it at random and read a page or more without looking up.

"You know Italian?"

"I can read it, though I don't speak it very well. My father me taught. He visited Rome and Venice when he was young and brought back many books. But I have never seen this one. It is a strange poem, isn't it? What is it meant to be?"

"A man—Dante Alighieri was his name—dreamed of hell and wrote his vision in poetry. He writes well enough for me to love him—and yet he angers me too. He attacks Celestine and throws him into Purgatory only because he withdrew from the papacy. If he will punish retiredness thus, what hell can his wit devise for ambition?"

"Are you ambitious?"

"I acknowledge all sins except dishonesty."

"Don't brag."

"Of my sins or of my one virtue?"

"Both. Neither. But I think you have another virtue—humility."

"I am oftener accused of arrogance."

He spoke lazily, paying scant attention to what he said. Just to see her sitting there in his chair, shy yet determined, looking like a flower, making conversation, flooded him with happiness. He longed to put his arms around her, yet feared to move lest she take flight. He felt as if a wild bird had perched on his hand.

"I am amazed that you can read Italian," he said, helping her

98

with the conversation, tempted though he was to watch her struggle. "You have been curiously educated, for a girl."

"I like to study. I think I am my father's favorite. My mother died when I was six, and the baby did too. He would have been the eighth child. My eldest brother is at Oxford. He and my father do not agree very well."

"Are your sisters living?"

"Yes, all four of them. Three are married and the youngest is only twelve. My grandfather lives with us—or rather we live with him. He thinks it pure waste to educate a girl, and that is perhaps why my father has had so many tutors for me. My father gets along no better with his father than he does with his son." She laughed. "But I haven't come here to talk about my father's temper. John, I hear you are a poet. Will you show me some of your poems?"

"Who says I am a poet?"

"John Egerton—and my cousin Francis."

"Most of my poems are not fit for your eyes."

"Oh, fie. And you claim to be honest! I have seen a verse letter that you wrote about the storm on the Islands Voyage, and I thought it was beautiful."

On an impulse he took out of his drawer the lines he had written the morning after the day of Essex's scolding, and laid them silently before her. Scarcely breathing, he stood by her shoulder as she read.

> *Where like a pillow on a bed*
> *A pregnant bank swelled up to rest*
> *The violet's reclining head,*
> *Sat we two, one another's best.*
>
> ... ...
>
> *As 'twixt two equal armies, Fate*
> *Suspends uncertain victory,*
> *Our souls—which to advance their state*
> *Were gone out—hung 'twixt her and me.*
> *And whilst our souls negotiate there,*
> *We like sepulchral statues lay;*

99

> *All day, the same our postures were,*
> *And we said nothing all the day. . . .*

Rereading his poem with her, almost through her eyes, he found it new, as if someone else had written it, and more moving than he had known.

> *When love, with one another so*
> *Interanimates two souls,*
> *That abler soul, which thence doth flow*
> *Defects of loneliness controls.*
> *We then, who are this new soul, know*
> *Of what we are composed and made,*
> *For th' atomies of which we grow*
> *Are souls, whom no change can invade.*
> *But O alas! so long, so far,*
> *Our bodies why do we forbear?*
> *They are ours, though they are not we; we are*
> *Th' intelligences, they the spheres. . . .*

Her hand trembled as she turned the pages over and came to the last one. At the end—

> *And if some lover, such as we,*
> *Have heard this dialogue of one,*
> *Let him still mark us, he shall see*
> *Small change, when we're to bodies gone.*

—she looked up at him, her eyes filled with tears.

"But that's just the way I felt too," she whispered.

She had not come to his closet again, though nearly every time he looked toward the door he hoped to see her standing there.

But every day he had seen her at meals. He and Dr. King were not relegated to some lower table as secretary and chaplain often were in great houses, but sat with Sir Thomas. When there were distinguished guests, indeed, the Lord Keeper liked to have John there to help carry the conversation. On ordinary days he could speak openly to Anne and she could answer him.

Now and then he would slip in an Italian phrase and her eyes would shine as she capped it. In the midst of company, in mundane talk that all could hear, they spoke the secret language of their love. It was a game he knew well, but never had he played it with a partner of such innocence and grace. All that he had ever done before, he thought, was but a rustic game; any beauty whom he had known and thought he loved was but a dream of Anne.

At other times, twice or thrice, he had been dragged out of his closet by John Egerton or Francis Woolley, once by Anne herself, to join the company of young people in music or games. The dowager Countess of Derby, with her two younger daughters, was visiting York House. John thought that there was a match in the planning between John Egerton and Lady Frances Stanley, the second daughter. With Donne there were six for madrigals and they needed both his lute and his dependable baritone. Once the Lord Keeper and Lady Derby joined them. One of the songs that they sang was a cynical little trifle of his own which some unknown tune-maker had set to music: "Go and catch a falling star, Get with child a mandrake root." "Ben Jonson's song," said Francis, who suggested it. John did not correct him, but he soon saw that Anne guessed its true authorship, for at the lines, "And find What wind Serves to advance an honest mind," she shot him a quick look, and when it came to "And swear No where Lives a woman true and fair," she pursed up her lips in mock disapproval and shook her head. He returned a blandly questioning glance that obviously did not deceive her, and the little passage that took place in the midst of unseeing eyes deepened Anne's color and struck at John's heart a small delicious blow. Their intimacy, which had so little to feed it, grew on such small things.

Even the chance of a glimpse of Anne on the stairs, in a corridor or walking in the garden with her basket and shears, was enough to send John on unnecessary errands or to cause him in the morning to take the longer way around to his closet through the front door and up the great staircase, rather than his usual short cut by a side door and a circular stair in the tower. The hope of seeing her come back from the wedding flushed with pleasure and lovely in her fine clothes was enough to keep him here long into the twilight, scratching away at a letter to Wotton, who was still at home in Kent waiting for his lordship's trouble to blow over:

"I answer your letter because I remember I had a promise from you for many letters."

He knew that Wotton would like to know in detail all that had happened in regard to the Earl of Essex, but dared not write anything but generalities, since letters went through many hands and no one knew who along the way might read and tell. There was not, in any case, much to say at present. Essex was at home, given freedom but denied access to the Court. His friends hoped that the Queen was only continuing his punishment a little longer before forgiving and restoring him. Yet did she know, John wondered but did not write, the danger of pressing too far the humiliation of one of Essex's reckless pride—or was she deceived by his protestations of meek devotion?

I am glad of your friendship for many causes and amongst the rest you shall give me leave to make this use of it, that we may some time speak together privately of the course of these worldly things that are governed with too much instability.

He heard a sound of voices and stopped to listen: were they coming at last? But it was only some noisy fellows in the Strand coming from a tavern. He took up his pen again.

I am no courtier, for without having lived there desirously I cannot have sinned enough to have deserved that reprobate name. I may sometimes come thither and be no courier as well as they may sometimes go to chapel and yet are no Christians.

He attended Sir Thomas on Star Chamber days. He carried messages. He played cards with other young men in the great hall while they waited for the Privy Council to break up and their masters to emerge. He heard the gossip. He exchanged banter now and then with one of the Queen's maids of honor. He was in the audience when the players came.

The Court is not great but full of jollity and revels and plays and as merry as if it were not sick. My lord of Essex and his train are no more missed here than the angels which were cast down from heaven nor (for anything I see) likelier to return.

Through the door, carefully left open, he heard a stir down-stairs and hastily winding up his letter with "Always and all ways yours," he folded it and slipped it under a book before hastening down the stairs. The Lord Keeper and Lady Derby, with their attendants, had just come into the hall.

"Oh, are you still here, John! The young people are in the garden. You had better join them and hear about the wedding."

Lady Derby, who was surprisingly ill-favored in appearance, with her little brown monkey face, to have produced three beautiful daughters—and yet engaging, too, with her quick black eyes and humorous mouth—yawned widely behind a thin, veiny hand. "I suppose they will sit up all night talking it over, but I am exhausted. I am no Puritan—as you know, my lord—but I think wedding festivities have been carried beyond all bounds of extravagance. The thought of two more daughters of my own to marry off and two more fashionable weddings ahead fairly prostrates me."

"There is much to be said for clandestine weddings," said Sir Thomas unexpectedly. "But it was the presence of Her Majesty that made this one today particularly protracted and elaborate."

"But of course anyone who could induce Her Majesty to come would spare no pains to achieve it! Be thankful, Mr. Donne, that you have no worries. All the responsibility and the expenses fall upon the bride's family."

"Then they have the remedy in their own hands, my lady!"

"Oh poof! You can scarcely expect common sense and stern restraint of parents in a high state of emotion and competition, can you?"

Laughing, John went in search of the party that had returned from the wedding. He found them in the garden, the three girls squeezed together on a bench, their satins and jewels pale in the twilight, John Egerton and Francis Woolley sitting on the grass. They all hailed him with pleasure. John's eyes, flying to Anne, saw the bright color speak in her cheeks—almost, he told himself, as if her body thought.

Lady Derby's two daughters, Lady Frances and Lady Elizabeth Stanley, a little older than Anne and a little younger, looked almost like twins, with the same dark hair, creamy skin and high, slender, aristocratic noses. Frances was the prettier now but Elizabeth, thought John, habitual assessor of the qualities of ladies, would someday be the beauty of the family. Her quicker mind and warm heart would inform physical with spiritual loveliness, once a lingering childish plumpness and vagueness were refined away. She was immensely excited now by having been at such a great affair. Anne, John saw, was relaxed and dreamy, glowing with some inner fire.

"Tell me everything!" he said, sitting down beside Woolley on the grass and clasping his arms around his knees. "Did you all get love knots?"

The Stanleys had pinned on their bosom little ribbon bows of blue and yellow satin; Anne opened her hand to show a peach-colored favor clasped inside.

"They fell on the bride, right in the church," said Egerton with mock disapproval, "and tore them off her."

"Not just us," objected Lady Elizabeth. "Everybody did. Men too. She wore a white dress with love knots in different colors all over it. Right after the ceremony was over, the bridemaids started it and then the rest of us who were near enough plucked some for ourselves. After all, that is what they are for! My sister—Lady Strange, you know—had enough for everybody at her wedding. But she did not wear them—she threw them."

"I got one too," said Francis Woolley, displaying a tuft of violet silk. "I sent plate worth far more—why should I not have this?"

"A mazer bowl of muscatel was passed around in the

church," said Lady Frances, "and then the procession went back to Lady Russell's house for the banquet. The streets had all been sanded and in front of the church and in front of the house rosemary and roses were strewn."

"Was that for Mistress Anne Russell and Lord Herbert or for the Queen?"

"The Queen was carried in a litter by six knights."

"I wouldn't like to have the Queen come to my wedding," said Anne suddenly, speaking for the first time.

"Sour grapes!" said Egerton with the rudeness of friendship formed in childhood. "You probably couldn't get her."

"She probably could," said Francis Woolley. "The Queen has visited Loseley three times."

Lady Elizabeth looked impressed. "Wasn't it a fearful strain?" she said. "To have the Queen visit you? So many people—and all the gifts—and the entertainment—masques and everything."

"Yes, but all your neighbors and friends send presents to help —whole oxen and sturgeon, dozens of cygnets and quails and things like that. I can only remember one visit. I was very little. I had to give Her Majesty a gold cup with a dove on it and say a Latin poem."

"Weren't you frightened?"

"No, I don't think so. I was very proud of myself. The Queen kissed me and everybody praised my Latin."

"Then why," said John, "don't you want the Queen at your wedding?"

A nightingale in the yew tree behind them suddenly burst into song and for a moment they were all silenced, aware of beauty in the darkening garden and of a moment that could never return.

"There was a masque after the banquet today," said Anne in a voice so low that she seemed to be speaking only to John. "Eight ladies all dressed in silver danced to music made by a gentleman who was dressed as Apollo, and after they had all danced, Mistress Fitton went to the Queen and asked her to

105

dance. And then Her Majesty asked what she was intended to be, and she said, 'Affection.' And Her Majesty said, 'Affection! That's false!' "

"Affection *is* false, at some weddings," said Francis Woolley, with an air of worldliness that sat oddly on his still-angelic countenance.

"It wouldn't be at mine," said Anne, "and I don't want anybody there making cynical remarks. Besides," she added, "when the Queen's there, nobody really notices the bride."

John's eyes met hers; after a moment she looked down at the love knot in her hands, a little smile playing about her mouth. He tasted a piercing sweetness in the moment; in the midst of their friends it was as if she spoke to him alone and of her wedding, and his.

2 IT WAS AUGUST AND LONDON WAS DESERTED. The players' companies went on tour in the provinces. The Countess of Derby and her daughters had gone to the country, Francis Woolley to Pyrford. Anne returned to Loseley.

"For the first twenty years since yesterday," John wrote, "I scarce believed thou couldst be gone away."

The Court went to Nonsuch Palace and the Lord Keeper with it. John would have accompanied his master but that he was struck down with an ague. He spent most of the month in his rooms at Mother Haines's, alternately burning with fever and shivering with chill, attended by the faithful Pierre.

Christopher Brooke and his younger brother Samuel, who had recently taken orders, came to ask him to join them in an excursion up the river in search of country pleasures. Christopher's clothes proclaimed his intention to go afield. In the city and suburbs, Lincoln's Inn students must go in sober gown and round cap and carry no more than a dagger for their defense, but now he wore high black boots, bulging trunks striped purple and green and a cartwheel ruff like a platter on which rested his thin greyhound face topped by a tall, shiny hat; at his side hung a sword.

"Come with us, John," he urged. "The day is fine. Why bury yourself in this cave?"

"Alas, I can't help it. I've taken physic for my sickness and I am bound by making myself loose. Stay and talk awhile. Tell me the news. I am wholly out of the current. I long to know who and where and why does what!"

"I know only those things that you are in a position to know better. It is said abroad that John Egerton will marry Lady Frances Stanley and that his father will marry her mother."

"The Lord Keeper? Impossible. His heart is buried with Lady Egerton. Oh, he'll marry again some time, no doubt, but it's not likely in less than a year."

"Perhaps he needs a hostess for his house."

"He has his niece, Mistress Anne More."

Speaking Anne's name, he felt that his face must reveal more than he intended and he lowered his head, frowning over a rubbed place on his cuff.

"John, may I speak as a friend?"

The seriousness in Christopher's voice brought his head up quickly, like some wild animal, alert, scenting danger. "You always speak as a friend," he said defensively.

"Yes, but may I say what only the warmest friendship can absolve of meddling?"

Samuel Brooke coughed slightly and, going over to the bookshelves, took down a volume in which he became ostentatiously engrossed, his back turned.

"I cannot think of anything that you might not with propriety say to me. What is it?"

"You spoke of a certain young gentlewoman. I hope you have always in mind—forgive me if I cut too near the bone—her youth and the high place she occupies."

"You mean Mistress More?" John flung out the name defiantly, as one might throw a card upon the table. "What have you heard?"

"Nothing to distress you. Only John Egerton talking about the singing and the games that he and you and she and others have been enjoying. And the change I see in you. I know you too well, John, not to know when you are in love."

John gave a small, reluctant laugh. "But this," he said, "is altogether different."

"That is what disturbs me. A Benita Stilwell can defend herself, but Mistress More is very young and not yet versed in the ways of the world and the Court. I speak too plainly, I know, but it is only my love for you that moves me."

"If I did not know your heart, I'd throw you out. Do you suppose for one moment that I intend wrong to Anne More? Or that she would yield to me if I did?"

"Perhaps not now—though I never knew you to slip into anything unaware. As for her yielding, you have been irresistible to more experienced ladies than her."

"You mistake me utterly. Even my thoughts in no way dishonor Mistress More. Now shall we talk of something else?"

"You can't be entertaining the idea of marriage? That would be the ultimate folly! Sir George More will look higher for his son-in-law than a secretary, however brilliant and promising he may be—or whose secretary."

At this point by mutual consent the subject was dropped. Samuel Brooke emerged from his book, apparently unconscious of the heightened color and raised voices of John and Christopher, and introduced the question of whether or not the Queen would renew the Earl of Essex's monopoly of sweet wines and what he would do for money if she would not. The brothers stayed talking long enough to smooth away the discomforts of advice given but not received, the regrets on the one hand for having offered an unpalatable and possibly unnecessary truth and on the other for having rebuffed kindly meant interference.

When they had gone, Pierre brought in a supper tray with the gray gruel that he considered appropriate. John, shivering again, wrapped a blanket around his shoulders and sat, sick and miserable, his head throbbing, staring at the food he could not touch. Christopher's warning, the hard fruit of friendship, was like a plug in his throat.

He loved Anne, he knew, irreparably, irrevocably, honestly. He had never loved before. Those fevers and lusts that had sent him tiptoeing up little-used staircases and writing bitter verse to change the after-taste in his mouth were lusts and fevers, no more. In this love he had found that for which he had longed, of which he had dreamed, a love in which body and soul were joined. It had begun with no thought of the he and she but with an ecstasy of souls. They would inevitably to bodies go, but through honorable marriage. The thought of deflowering Anne in some corner was revolting. For a moment he hated Christopher for having entertained such an idea of him and of her.

He lay late awake that night, his mind aswirl with fantasies of Anne and of a course of their love that every wind would favor, wafting them at last to a wedding blessed by the Queen's absence, with Anne tossing love knots to all their friends before they were escorted with music and song to the marriage bed.

Though he thought he could not sleep, he was to his surprise awakened from slumber by a tolling of bells from St. Mary-le-Savoy. The deep, full sounds fell upon the night air slowly, heavily, solemnly. He missed the first notes but began to count as soon as he was fully awake. Twenty-three, twenty-four, twenty-five. Some poor devil of about his own age had died and gone out of this world. He slipped out of bed to his knees, to pray for the soul of the unknown person, but thought, as he prayed, only of his own state. Death walked ever at one's back and no one could know when he would feel the tap upon the shoulder. He had taken his own sickness lightly enough; now the sound of the passing bell in the night's loneliness reminded him of the account that at any moment God might demand of him.

Christopher had been right, speaking as he did out of the integrity of his friendship and with difficulty. He must not let Anne love him. Not now, at any rate. Not till he had something to offer her, something to show Sir George More besides a vague promise and a few scattered verses.

X

꒤ꆢꆢꆢꆢꆢꆢꆢꆢꆢꆢꆢꆢꆢꆢꆢꆢꆢꆢꆢꆢꆢꆢꆢꆢꆢ

"TAKE HEED OF LOVING ME," he wrote. "At least remember, I forbade it thee."

As if love could be forbidden, any more than it could be summoned by command. Nor could it, he found, be dissolved by all the arguments of a worldly mind. Anne's love for him, his love for her, remained a rock of fact which, if they could not manage to circumnavigate it, they must climb or be wrecked upon.

As far as he could, he kept himself at a distance. He could not turn her out when she appeared in his closet, perched on his desk, played with his pens, borrowed his books, but he could—he did—spend his time, when his work was done, away from York House, going to plays, talking late with Christopher at Lincoln's Inn, sitting long in the tavern over pipes of tobacco with other young men, hearing news of explorations and discoveries, arguing about poetry.

Caution in love was a new role and one that did not suit his temperament or his habits. He threw himself with all his energy into his work and was drawn closely to Sir Thomas, as the Lord Keeper gave more and more into his hands. Writing letters, bearing confidential messages, seeing and handling the suitors, the intriguers, the beggars of all kinds who pressed for attention, getting an insight into the workings of government, sharing the worries and annoyances and occasionally the satisfactions of a powerful and incorruptible man like his master, he realized that he was being prepared and groomed for future responsibility of his own.

Already, indeed, in some quarters, he was himself being sought out as one who, having the Lord Keeper's confidence, had favors to give. There were frightened, greedy, harassed or ambitious men who came directly to him to ask for influence, for introductions, for interventions. He came to know the smell of bribes and to detect them in all their ingenious disguises. He found, too, that occasionally, in the midst of the suits that he must evade or pass along to someone else or reject outright, there were times when he could actually give assistance to an honest man, and in such cases he felt a glow that he hoped— but did not inquire too closely—was satisfaction in the poor man's relief and not pride in his own power.

Sir: The little business which you left in my hands is now dispatched; if it has hung longer than you thought, it might serve for just excuse that these small things make as many steps to their end and need as many motions for the warrant, as much writing of the clerks, as long expectation of a seal, as greater.

He was sorry when he remembered that letter afterwards, for the "small thing" of which he wrote so condescendingly was large indeed to his protégé, whom he had, in fact, managed to get released from prison. But the man had pelted him with letters as if he were being dilatory in the business when in reality he had been assiduously knocking at doors and nagging at clerks, and he had at length grown testy.

Sir Thomas Egerton, he found, had in his keeping not only the Great Seal but in a sense the law itself. Recently he had set himself to weed out the abuses that he found—the sale of justice—or worse, injustice—for fees. John's admiration for his master grew as he saw the unwavering righteousness of the man; he respected him even to the point of veneration, but the immense dignity that was never relaxed even in his home and a certain inner rigidity made affection seem presumptuous.

One morning in late October, when wet yellow leaves lay

plastered on the cobbles of the courtyard and the cries of rooks filled the gusty air, John found the Lord Keeper waiting for him in a most uncharacteristic state of nerves. He was standing by the window of his study—that room where John felt that the whole direction of his life had been changed—wearing a suit of dark satin with a new lace collar and drumming with his fingers on the window pane.

"I am going to be married this morning, John," he said without preliminary.

John found no words to answer. He opened his mouth and shut it again. After an awkward pause, during which a frown gathered on Sir Thomas's brow, he said feebly, "I am afraid I don't understand, my lord."

"I believe I spoke plainly. My lady Derby and I shall be married in the chapel here. We do not intend to publish it for some time yet. I depend on you to say nothing to anyone until I give you leave, but I should be glad if you were present at the ceremony."

"Thank you. I shall be honored. I—I wish you happiness, my lord."

"There will be no changes here for the present. But we shall be happier, both of us, to be made secure of each other. Marriage is a sacrament, not a show. We are agreed that a private ceremony with only our nearest relatives present suits us best." His large and somewhat heavy face lightened in a rare smile. "I count you as a son," he said.

With an effort John masked his surprise and unease with an air of congratulation. But this sudden intention did not fit with his idea of Sir Thomas—neither the marriage itself, less than a year after the former Lady Egerton's death, nor the secrecy of it, without published banns or announcement.

The arrival of Lady Derby and her daughters brought as always a stir and a gaiety into the great house. John Egerton joined his father, Anne came floating down the stairs dressed in green and, after greeting the others, came to stand beside John.

"You avoid me," she said to him under the cover of all the high-voiced talk and laughter. "Why?"

"I am busy."

"You make yourself busy."

"Must we quarrel—on such a happy occasion?"

"Happy? Could *you* marry again so soon? He loved my aunt—or so he said. At any rate he cried when she died. I did not know men cried so. And now look at him! I think men have thin, flimsy hearts."

"Are women so constant?"

"I would be."

He regretted his bantering tone as he looked down into her serious, troubled little face. She had loved her aunt, he knew.

"I think you would be," he said gently.

Her mood changed swiftly. "When I said *men,* I didn't mean you!"

John was prevented from answering by the high, imperious voice—it was the only thing about her that was unattractive—of Lady Elizabeth behind them.

"Come, Anne, you must share Mr. Donne with me. I have no escort to the wedding."

He gave one arm to Lady Elizabeth, the other to Anne, squeezing her hand against his side as they followed the rest of the party to the chapel. They met an unusual number of servants along the way, standing in doorways, bowing in corridors. They all know, thought John; how long can he keep the secret?

Dr. King in his surplice stood before the altar, the great velvet-covered, gold-encrusted service-book open in his hands. His thin face had the kind of radiance, John thought, that ministers of the gospel ought always to have and so seldom did. It must have been a true vocation that led John King into the ministry, for he came of a family that could have helped him to anything else he wanted; it was not need that sent him to a profession that the world secretly scorned while pretending to reverence it.

The Lord Keeper, solemn to the point of grimness, towered above his chaplain; Lady Derby, wearing pale blue, pearl-sewn silk oddly unsuited to her brown face, stood small and expectant, her dark eyes twinkling.

The ceremony was a short one, even though it combined the

de futuro and the *de praesenti* rites, which sometimes made two separate ceremonies on two different days. John's sister and William Lyly had said their "I will's" a full year before the final "I do's." John Egerton, looking very young and a trifle embarrassed, gave Lady Derby away. They knelt. There being no sermon, the benediction kiss came swiftly. Anne dabbed at her eyes with her handkerchief.

Afterwards there was a bride cup with sweet wine and a sprig of rosemary, tasted by everyone. John managed to walk with Anne behind the others on the way to the dining room and what must do for a wedding feast. They were both stirred in the same way by what they had seen and the ideas it had aroused; he felt her hand tremble a little on his arm. He longed to talk with her alone, but he had no opportunity.

2   Street musicians, red-nosed and shivering, blew a skirl on their pipes as John, followed by Pierre, came through the gate of York House. He made a sign to Pierre to give them something. Their breaths smoked in the cold December air as they thanked him with exaggerated bows and called down faintly mocking blessings on his honor.

He pulled his cloak around him and bent his head into the west wind that came knifing along the Strand. It was a cheerless day but he felt buoyed and a little excited by the mission that was taking him to Northumberland House in the precinct of St. Martin-in-the-Fields.

He had never met the Earl of Northumberland, whom he was on his way to see, though he knew him well by reputation. The "Wizard Earl" he was nicknamed, for his preoccupation with alchemy and astrology. He was a notable eccentric and, perhaps, a secret Catholic. His uncle the seventh earl had been executed for complicity in a plot to put the Queen of Scots on the throne of England, and his father, imprisoned on suspicion in the Tower, had killed himself there, or been murdered. Yet the ninth earl had been reared as a Protestant and he enjoyed the title of general in the army now in the Low Countries, where, when he was not quarreling with the other generals, he from time to time fought, and from where he had recently re-turned to his London house.

Seeing him at Whitehall a day or two earlier, Sir Thomas had conceived a plan for reaching Lord Essex which John was now on his way up St. Martin's Lane to put into effect. "Try it," the Lord Keeper had said. "If it comes to nothing, there's no harm done."

Entering the red brick mansion with the urns and stone flowers under the cloak of the Lord Keeper's name, John was passed along from porter to gentleman usher to secretary—who, he was surprised to find, was an old acquaintance of his and a great friend of Christopher Brooke's, George Gerrard, a moon-faced young man with a passionate interest in other people and all their smallest affairs.

"I'll see if his lordship is disengaged, but I've no doubt he'll receive any emissary of the Lord Keeper."

He was back in a few minutes to lead John up a staircase and along a corridor, talking as he went. "I heard that you were at the Mermaid not a week since, but you had left when I got there. Here we are. Mr. Donne, my lord."

A door was opened into a small, hot room billowing with acrid smoke.

"Come in! Come in! And shut the door."

Half expecting to see his lordship crouched over a pot of snails or tending an alembic, John stepped, choking, into the stifling little room. A fire of sea-coals on the hearth sent out a furious blast of heat. Northumberland sat smoking a long clay pipe, with his feet on the brass fender.

He was a younger man than John had expected, no more than thirty-five or six. He had a long, rather melancholy face, a long nose, a light beard, which, like his teeth and the fingers of his right hand, was stained deep yellow by tobacco.

"Sit down, sit down. D'you smoke? No? A pity. It's a great benefit to one's nerves. Well, what does the Lord Keeper want of me? No, wait. Tell me who you are first."

"I am the Lord Keeper's secretary, John Donne, at your service, my lord."

"The same John Donne who wrote that witty poem about a flea?"

"I was very young when I wrote that, sir."

"No need to be ashamed. It's a very good conceit. Sucks his blood, sucks hers, marries them. No loss of maidenhead for her. Very ingenious. Are you married, Mr. Donne?"

"No, my lord."

"Sensible of you. Very much overrated custom, matrimony. I know whereof I speak. Singed dog."

John hoped that his amusement did not betray itself in his eyes. It was well known that the lord of Northumberland and his lady, who had been Dorothy Devereux, Essex's sister, were not always friends, but since the birth of a daughter earlier in the year they had been reported reconciled.

"The Lord Keeper," began John carefully, "has sent me here on a mission of some delicacy which he did not care to commit to paper. I do not know how to go about it, however, but by plainness and directness. Your lordship, I know, prefers honesty to flattering circumlocutions."

"Don't mumble. I couldn't hear more than half of that, but I suspect it of being itself a flattering circumlocution."

Raising his voice, John began again, but his lordship cut him short. "Yes, I understand all of that. The Lord Keeper sent you to say something to me he doesn't care to say himself. Let me hear some of this plain directness."

"The Lord Keeper was keenly aware of my lady Northumberland's efforts on behalf of her brother last winter——"

"Yes, I know. Going every day to Court dressed in black to plead for him. Didn't do a bit of good, only annoyed Her Majesty."

"It proved, nevertheless, her devotion to her noble brother— and it is that devotion that the Lord Keeper would appeal to. He would like to beg her ladyship to plead, not *for* my lord of Essex, but *to* him. To urge him, in fact, to moderate his course, which if he continues in his present way will end in alienating Her Majesty's favor beyond repair. My lady of Northumberland has not been at Court lately. If your lordship could persuade her to use her influence with her brother——"

"I have trouble in hearing you, Mr. Donne, but if you are saying what I think you are, you are doomed to disappointment. My wife and I do not persuade each other to anything. We dislike each other too thoroughly."

Startled out of an answer, John sat wondering what to say next.

"That shocks you. But it would be hypocritical of me to pretend anything else. I find that I have even some difficulty to love my own daughters because they are of that blood."

"Probably the young ladies will take after their father, not their mother. It is often the case."

"So you think that would be an improvement?"

John laughed. "I infer that you would prefer it, my lord."

"Impudent of you. Well, I like impudence. What I don't like is sycophancy. Are you a Puritan?"

"No, my lord."

"A papist?"

"Not that either."

"Nor am I. But I had rather be a papist than a Puritan, and I think the laws against recusancy are too harsh. There should be laws against the Puritans, not for heresy, but for dullness and long-windedness. Why, I wonder, do Puritans make such long sermons?"

"Perhaps they think it their duty to preach until their auditory wakes."

"Oh, that's very witty. I'll have to remember that. Sure you won't try a pipe of tobacco?"

"No, I thank you, my lord. I think I should repeat that the situation as regards my lord of Essex is urgent. The Lord Keeper is very anxious about him. That is why he sought to persuade you—through her ladyship—to influence him to be more prudent."

"What is wrong?"

"Surely your lordship must have heard the rumors. My lord of Essex, since he was disappointed of the monopoly of sweet wines, has flung himself off from the Queen. Some very ill-advised things he said about Her Majesty——"

" 'Her conditions are as crooked as her carcase,' " quoted Northumberland with a sardonic chuckle.

"I am afraid so—in his first fury at what is a very serious loss as well as a humiliation. At all events, that and other things, doubtless not all true, were repeated to Her Majesty and they have in no way sweetened her toward him. But now he has a great concourse of people coming every day to Essex House to listen—so the story is—to sermons of Puritan divines."

"Yes, I heard one of them. Very long and dull, as I said—yet perhaps not long enough to allow me time to wake up. But can anyone object to his seeking consolation in religion?"

"So many men flocking there to hear sermons causes some question whether religion is the only activity there."

"That is all I heard when I was there, and not my kind of religion. I have not been back."

"The Lord Keeper himself has said all that he can, but he is out of my lord of Essex's love since the affair last June. Sir Thomas thought that perhaps my lord's sister might be able to put in a word that he would listen to, as he would not suffer the advice of one who has already stood in judgment. Perhaps you yourself, my lord, could find means to protest to my lord of Essex the unwisdom of drawing so many people to his house in such a way as to hint of plotting."

"Oh, he won't see me. Hubris," said Northumberland somberly, "that is Essex's malady. It's the crime that the gods—and sovereigns—punish most severely. If we had not quarreled, I'd go to see him myself. I rather enjoy"—his face broke into a slightly satanic grin—"taking a hand in other people's lives. Beneficently, of course."

It was evident that there was nothing more John could usefully say. As he rose to take his leave, Lord Northumberland once again surprised him.

"You must be the young man who is causing apprehension to my friend, Sir George More."

"My lord?"

"No matter. I should have held my tongue. I like you, Mr. Donne. I'll say a good word for you if ever I have the opportunity."

3 Anne sat huddled on the window seat in her room in York House while her maid went stolidly on packing her portmanteau. Beyond the open window the high, blue, cloud-scudded sky and the mild, wet, heady taste of the air spoke of spring. But it was not spring; for all the swollen buds in the garden, it was still February, and she felt her heart crushed under a cold weight of sorrow. This morning, perhaps this very minute, the Earl of Essex was laying his head upon the block, and this afternoon Anne More would die another kind of death, being marched home by her angry father, cut ruthlessly away from all that now meant life to her.

She tried, from a sense of what was proper, to think only of Robert Devereux, thirty-five, so recently the Queen's favorite, Earl Marshal of England, the darling of the people, who had fallen so far, so fast, so fatally. He had plotted, he had gathered reckless men around him, had burst into the city of London armed and shouting, intending, so he said, only to frighten the Queen into restoring him to her love. How could he have imagined that he could prevail by force against her power and majesty, or have hoped to escape a traitor's death? But it was infinitely sad to think of one so handsome, and comparatively young, facing the ax and extinction, and in a mysterious way it was threatening to all who were young and ambitious. Anne put her hand to her own throat and wondered, shivering, how anyone could endure to lie down on the block and wait for the ax to fall. She thought of one poor lady running screaming from the executioner. But Essex was a man and a man of undaunted courage.

She left him with his courage and returned to herself. She had been so happy. Yesterday morning she and John had stolen a moment together on the terrace, secure and unclouded in their love; yesterday afternoon her father, having ridden from Loseley, was saying peremptorily, "You will make yourself ready to leave tomorrow. I have come to take you home."

And why? Because she was no longer needed here, now that Lady Derby and Sir Thomas were openly married. Because she was his daughter, and though she was silly and willful, he had plans for her. Because she saw too much of the secretary, who was well known to be a libertine. Because, and this was enough for her, he said so.

"But, Father, he is no libertine. He is my uncle's industrious and valued secretary. Ask my uncle how much he trusts him. He is a learned man and a poet."

But it was the poetry, some of which he had seen, that most angered Sir George. Only a libertine, he said, could have written those lines. Anne, who was, it appeared, at once innocent and high-minded, as Sir George's daughter, and perverse and perverted, as herself, was too ignorant and undiscriminating to recognize the marks of evil in this otherwise negligible man and his works.

Reliving this painful scene, she let a sob burst out of her, which, when her maid left the chest and came to look inquiringly at her, she changed into a cough. When the maid had gone back to her packing, Anne took a folded bit of paper out of her bosom and read it again with an occasional sniff and gulp.

It contained the latest of the poems that John had written for her, a sonnet, to add to the others that she kept hidden at the bottom of her chest.

> *Send me some token, that my hope may live,*
> *Or that my ceaseless thoughts may sleep and rest;*
> *Send me some honey to make sweet my hive,*
> *That in my passion I may hope the best.*

She drew a long, quavery sigh. He did not want a ribbon or a ring or the corals at her wrist, or even her picture or witty lines.

> *Send me not this nor that, to increase my store,*
> *But swear thou thinkst I love thee, and no more.*

Oh, she did, she did. She could no more doubt his love than her own. But she had a token for him too—a lock of her hair, braided and set in a bracelet by a goldsmith in Cheapside. It was in the purse that hung from her girdle and somehow, before she left, she must find a way to see him alone and give it to him.

There were many guests at dinner that day and some strangers. John was moved to the steward's table, where she could see him, effortlessly elegant, looking among the other men like a swan, a black swan, among the barnyard geese. She herself sat beside her father, hearing the heavy talk about that morning's dark event and thinking her own thoughts.

Reportedly at Essex's own request—though one of the gentlemen present ventured the remark that it was quite unlike him—the execution had been private, with only the Constable, the Lieutenant of the Tower and two divines present. Already the Lord Keeper had had a full account of it.

"I was afraid that he would make an attempt to justify himself at the last, and the Constable had been cautioned to cut him short if necessary," Sir Thomas was saying. "But his behavior was admirable—firm and modest. He acknowledged his errors, while maintaining that he had meant no harm to the person of the Queen."

"It is difficult to see," suggested another, "how the Queen's person could be separated from Her Majesty with no harm to her."

Sir Thomas made no answer. His next words fell heavily. "It took three strokes of the ax."

A long silence followed, filled only by the sounds the serving men made moving about, someone's noisy supping of his wine, a sudden laugh from the other table. Anne, crumbling her bread, thought now only of Anne More. How could she live, stranded at Loseley, her father perhaps pressing on her some man whose rank and fortune pleased him, John in London exposed to who knew what predatory women? There must be a way to make sure of him. Even Sir Thomas and Lady Derby, old as they were and free to do as they wished, had wanted to be bound. If she and John could be solemnly promised now, no one could force her to marry anyone else and some time they could be married. She sat staring at nothing for so long that Lady Elizabeth across the table nudged her foot with her own.

When they rose from the table, those at the steward's table stood waiting for them to pass. Anne, as she walked by John, dropped her handkerchief and in the pause when he stooped to pick it up, she whispered at him:

"I must see you. Now. In your closet."

"Anne," said her father, "you will be ready to leave in an hour."

"Yes, Father."

"We shall all miss our Anne," said the Lord Keeper, and Lady Derby—she kept the higher title, even after her marriage —seconded him warmly. "You must bring her back soon, Sir George."

Arm in arm with Elizabeth Stanley, Anne went along the corridor toward her bedroom. At the door she whirled around, clasped the other girl by the arm and said, "Stay here. Keep watch for me. I must see John."

"What shall I do if anyone comes?"

"Keep the door closed behind you and say I have to have privacy for a few moments."

"Where will you be?"

"In John's closet."

"Oh, *hurry*——"

The anxious words fell behind her as she skimmed along the corridor, around a corner into a smaller passage, up a winding stair. A groom looked at her curiously as she passed, but she met no one else.

John was in his little room waiting for her. In his arms she could feel his heart beat under her ear beneath the layers of his clothes, feel his cheek against her hair and then, lifting her face to his, his lips on hers. When her soul was all but out of her, she pushed him gently away.

"We've only a few minutes. I've thought what we must do."

"Have you, my sweet? What?" He was looking down at her, a little amused, as he sometimes for no reason was.

"We must make our solemn promises to each other. Now. If we don't, he'll make me marry someone else. Don't you see? It's binding, a betrothal."

"Not without witnesses. When my sister was betrothed, both families were present."

"Oh, that was only because they were afraid one or the other might deny the promises—if there were no witnesses. But we are not like that."

"Your father would not force you to marry against your will."

"But I want to be sure of you too."

She searched his face—surely he could see this solution to their predicament which was so clear to her?—and she saw a light leap in his eyes. She also saw him deliberately quench it with sober, cautious thoughts.

"My dearest love, I am eleven years older than you and your father dislikes and disapproves of me. Go home with him now and have faith that somehow we can find a way."

"I *am* going home. I have no choice. But if we are promised to each other now, we have already found part of the way."

She was so sure. It was incredible that he should hesitate.

"Perhaps you don't love me as I thought." But as soon as the words were out—before—she knew they were not true. "You are afraid for me," she amended quickly, "but you needn't be. I am strong—and when we are betrothed, I shall be strong enough for anything."

"You must be strong enough for me too, because I am nothing but wax." He took from his little finger a gold ring, which Anne had often seen there, engraved with the sheaf of snakes that was the crest of his family, and, lifting her right hand, placed it on her forefinger. "Later," he said, "you shall have a proper ring for your left hand, but this will serve now."

"Anne!" It was Lady Elizabeth's voice, calling, getting louder as it came nearer.

"Hurry!"

"Shall she come in to be a witness?"

"No, no, she might oppose us. Hurry."

"If I can remember the words. No matter, we'll make our own. I, John, do solemnly promise to marry thee, Anne, as soon as it becomes possible."

It was not as she had imagined it, with Elizabeth on the other side of the door, pounding. She fixed her eyes on John's and shut out everything else.

"I, Anne, do solemnly promise to be to thee, John, a faithful wife till death us do part."

The door burst open and Elizabeth bounced in. "Anne, for the love of God, come! Your father is asking for you."

"Yes, I'm coming. John, wait. I have a token for you."

She wrenched the bracelet out of her purse and put it into his hand.

"It is more than a token, it is a kind of miracle. I shall wear it all my life. My dearest love, I pray you may not have to regret this day's work."

"May I see? Oh, is it Anne's hair in the bracelet?"

Anne felt rasped by Elizabeth's eager, childish curiosity; she would have liked to slap that round red cheek. John's arm came around her, strong, steadying.

"Now we are safe," he said in a firm voice. "Lady Elizabeth, I beg you to keep silent about this. But if someday you are asked—and it may be crucial then that you know and tell—you can say that you saw us when we had just betrothed ourselves to each other, indissolubly."

Xi

HE WORE THE BRACELET clasped about his wrist under his sleeve. It was always there and whatever he was doing his awareness of it flowed like a hidden river in his mind. At night in his lodging, or alone in his closet at York House, he took it off to hold it in his fingers and look at it. Anne was gone so completely, so seldom spoken of at York House, that without this tangible proof he might have wondered if that hasty, secret, unplanned exchange of vows had really taken place.

He had no doubt of his love for her. She filled his mind with her beauty, her innocence, her tenderness, her strength; the lilt in her voice, the fire in her hair, the curve of her lips, her slender grace, plucked at his heartstrings and set all his body to vibrating.

Nor could he question her love for him, though with a new humility he wondered that she could stoop so far that she could see in him—eleven years older, stained, of mercantile birth and by her standards all but penniless—a love to whom to dedicate her life. At other times it seemed to him that they two were initiates in some arcane order of love, not Christian yet not quite pagan, to which she brought her purity, he his knowledge of love's rituals; that they served an altar known to few, where, caught in a passion that neither could resist, they still knew no more differences of sex than their guardian angels might.

When the bells rang late at night and he woke to the old dread of death, he saw himself lifeless and stiff, the bracelet clasped upon his arm. Those who came to shroud him would find it there and bury it with him, recognizing in its bright strands an emblem of a love rare and mysterious. Or years later, when men might dig up his grave to put another body in it, they would find the bracelet still bright around his fleshless wrist and take it for a relic, as religious folk not many centuries ago took bits of the saint's bodies, an arm, a tooth, and kept them in jeweled caskets, to intensify their worship or to use for making miracles. "A bracelet of bright hair about the bone:" the line leapt into his mind, and the cadence of it, the sounds of *a* and *i* and *o,* the throb of the repeated *b*'s, gave him a deep pleasure. In the end, sequestered from all the plaguing world without and the divided world within, he wrote two poems, inventing new stanza forms and flinging in rich, complicated patterns of rhymes that still spoke naturally without wrenching the sense or stumbling for the rhyme's sake.

When the writing fit was over, the promises they had made came back to accuse him. That he had not intended such a course, that he had been swept into it by the force of her love and will: this he could accept, though it showed him to himself more easily swayed than in his pride he had supposed. What troubled him was the fact itself: they were committed to a marriage that they possibly could never achieve. He who was older, who knew the world, ought to have protected her against her own impulses, but he had not, and now, here they were, separated, with no means of communication, yet bound. Then his knowledge of his own worth and of his potentialities would come sweeping back and he would think that he had only to go openly to Sir George More and declare his love for Anne and that Sir George, knowing the Lord Keeper's love and admiration for him, would forthwith give him his blessing and his daughter. But before the fantasy had run its course, he knew it for what it was, and again the difficulties loomed insurmountable.

It was a relief when, in April, the Lord Keeper sent him to York to attend to some business. Christopher Brooke, who was beginning now, after his years of study, to do some paying work in the law and found his best patrons in the city of his birth, rode north with him.

Christopher at thirty, keen-eyed, cheerful, confident, seemed to John enviably contented. He had no burning ambitions, no unmanageable emotions. He sought no more than a moderate success in the law, with enough money to live comfortably at Lincoln's Inn, enough leisure to drink and talk with his circle of poets—Drayton, Hall, Davies, Jonson and Donne—enough solitude to work on his never-finished epic poem, "The Ghost of Richard III." He was not, he said, interested in marriage yet. Perhaps later he would find himself a rich widow. At present he had a poor widow, a mistress whom he had brought back with him from York a year ago and established in a neat little house in the parish of St. Helen's. She was placid and grateful and he believed faithful; he trusted her and found ease with her. He had, for all his genial conformity, a cynicism deeper by far than that displayed in John's own flamboyant misanthropic satires and elegies. They were agreed on that, as on much else.

Between Peterborough and Lincoln, John told Christopher about his secret betrothal.

"You fool, Jack! Never say I did not warn you. What possible outcome can it have?"

"Marriage." But he wondered as he spoke what could be the source of that confidence he heard in his own voice.

"You've time to wait, of course. How old is she? Sixteen?"

"Seventeen next month."

"Then make yourself as strong as you can with the Lord Keeper before you do anything reckless. You're sure she will be staunch?"

"I know she will."

"You say that as if it suited you well—but who was it wrote that constancy in women was a vice? 'I can love any, so she be not true.'"

"Who indeed? Some other man. I think I have buried two or three Jack Donnes already."

"And the present one is a permanency?"

"Jack is gone. John, I trust, will be a stable fellow."

"I suppose Mistress Anne has a fortune of her own?"

He could not pretend that he had not thought of it. "Something from her mother, I believe."

He loved Anne deeply, disinterestedly, but without her portion, marriage would be impossible. They could scarcely live on his salary and the small remains of his patrimony, but with a wife who brought a fortune and with the favor of the Lord Keeper, an ambitious young man might rise swiftly, and high. He could not quell the thought entirely.

"I doubt if Sir George will ever yield. He married his older daughters to knights with good estates, or at least good prospects. That leaves you only a secret marriage and—as you know as well as I do—it is an offense against both civil and canon law to marry a young woman without the consent of her parents."

"The Lord Keeper at any rate has no objection to secret marriages."

"That was his own—which makes a difference. Besides, the Lady Derby was her own mistress and, to put it gently, of age. It is being said about, I grant you, that John Egerton and Lady Frances Stanley are also married, but they doubtless have the consent of their parents—if"—he cocked a questioning eye at John—"it's true?"

It was true, but it was not for John to say so. "Rumor will say anything," he replied noncommittally. "We should of course prefer to get the old gentleman's permission, but if it is necessary to present him with a *fait accompli,* can I count on your help?"

"You can always count on my help. But for God's sake, Jack, be discreet. This is fire. Fire burns."

2 He was on his way back to London alone, leaving Christopher in York. A name on a signpost leaning into the bushes at a muddy side road brought him up short with a jab

of memory. *To Applethorpe.* How long ago, it seemed, the Stilwells had buried themselves here—or Lord Stilwell had buried Benita. On an impulse that he did not pause to examine, John turned to Pierre behind him.

"We're turning off here to visit a friend," he said abruptly, and rode on, into the ruts, paying no attention to his man's scowls or to the muttered curses behind him as the horses went deeper into the mud and a cold spring shower of rain beat in their faces and trickled down their necks.

The village of Applethorpe huddled under a hill, an untidy jumble of wattle-walled, thatch-roofed cottages, piles of steaming dung and straw, and small, gaunt cattle splashed with mud. Past a squat stone church they came to a gate and a lodge, beyond which tracks in the green grass, flowing with water, led up through a little park where deer moved among the trees to a square stone house crouching under the weight of its own top-heavy battlements. By the time they reached it, the shower was over and pale, watery sunshine sprang at its windows. Pierre, who at the lodge had learned the name of the "friend," smiled slyly as he shook the wet off his frieze cloak.

John was welcomed, as he knew he would be. Country houses depended on the occasional traveler for news of the world, and he could, besides—after four years had glossed over the ambiguities of their parting—claim old friendship. The Stilwells were unquestionably glad to see him.

Benita had changed. Any unacknowledged thoughts that John might have had about reviving their relationship faded swiftly away. Thirty-five now, she looked ten years older. She had grown heavy, as Spanish women sometimes do, and somewhat coarsened. Dark hair shadowed her upper lip and there was a gap among the discolored front teeth. Though her eyes were wide and deep as ever and her rich voice ran caressingly along his bare nerves, she was withdrawn and tense, with a tightness about her mouth and a compulsive, jerky pursing of her lips, out and in, out and in.

Pity was not the emotion he had ever expected to feel for Benita, but he felt it now, and when she began to talk, he felt dismay as well. She had turned ardently, fanatically, to her religion. She told John almost at once that she had a priest concealed in the house and soon after that she sent for him. Father Didier, John found, was a Jesuit from the seminary at Rheims who knew both Father Harington, for whom Henry had died, and John's Heywood uncles. Seeing the priest's bright, tight face, John was plunged again into the old grief for Henry. In the last four years he had learned to agree with the Lord Keeper that England's unity and therefore her strength were threatened by these foreign priests who crept from great house to great house, courting martyrdom, keeping recusancy alive; but he hated the penalties visited on those who defied the law. That the Stilwells were putting themselves in jeopardy, even in this remote place, troubled him deeply. He would not betray them, nor would Pierre, but there were eyes in the village.

Alone with Benita for a little while before supper, he found that she wanted to talk only about the priest and the comfort it was, in spite of the danger, to have him there. Her beads, her crucifix, her devotions, absorbed her utterly. Only once, with an effort that set her lips to working more furiously than ever, she asked about his life.

"You are not married?"

"Not yet."

"It is time. You are thirty."

"Twenty-eight."

"As near thirty as makes no difference. You should be married."

"I am betrothed, Benita, secretly betrothed."

"Secretly? You do all things in secret." Her lips shot out and in. "Is she Catholic?"

"No. Her father——"

"Objects? Then leave it, Jack. You cannot marry a lady without her father's permission. It is wrong—and more than that, it is dangerous. That is, if he is a man of power—and I don't suppose that you"—there was a sudden malice in her smile—"would lose your heart to a nobody."

"I like beauty and distinction in all things," he said evenly. "Your ladyship should know that."

Her eyes softened. "You are impudent as ever. I've no doubt you are irresistible to her. Perhaps I am jealous, though I thought I had put all that aside. You are Catholic, Jack?"

"No. Not for many years."

"It makes me sad to think of you among the lost souls. I wish you would talk—alone—with Father Didier. He can answer your questions."

"I hate schism, Benita."

"But you are joining the schismatics!"

"In England today the Catholic Church is schismatic."

He had accepted the religion of his country, because it was the religion of his country, because he could not hope for advancement without it, because from the bottom of his heart—and he had searched it—he believed that it was God who was supremely important, not the color of the banner under which one worshiped him; and yet, when faced with martyrdom, or the voluntary risk of martyrdom, he found himself torn by a confusion of emotion in which guilt, anger and admiration battled painfully.

"Oh, you are determined to be perverse!"

He was relieved when Lord Stilwell just then came into the room, eager for all the news of London. Exile, it was soon evident, sat even less easily on him than on his wife, though for different reasons. He wanted to hear all the details of the Essex affair, all the news of plays and the theater, to know who was building and who had won or lost a fortune, who had traveled abroad, who fallen ill. New lines had bitten deep into his thin face; his eyes burned out of brown hollows; his voice was harsh, as if to speak out of long silence strained it. The punishment, John thought, that he had intended to visit on Benita fell heavier on him. Benita had found an escape, but he was caught in his own trap.

Thankful to ride away next morning, John thought of them with compassion, of himself with disgust. Benita might believe herself saved, but she lived in dread of the pursuivants; Lord

Stilwell was eating his heart out in bitterness. Whoever was responsible for their plight—himself, Edward Wenlock, Benita and her lord themselves—he, John, shared in the guilt. Out of his childhood training rose like a bitter taste the conviction of sin—and no place to find absolution.

3 He deliberately lost himself in the composition of a long poem on the subject of metempsychosis which he called "The Progress of the Soul." It gave him considerable wry pleasure, both the concept itself and the ingenuities and straightfaced indecencies with which he sprinkled it.

". . . I will bid you remember," he wrote in an erudite Preface "(for I will have no such readers as I can teach) as that the Pythagorean doctrine doth not only carry one soul from man to man or man to beast but indifferently to plants also . . . And therefore though this soul could not move when it was a melon, yet it may remember and now tell me at what lascivious banquet it was served."

This soul then, this deathless soul, began its career in infant morning in the apple that Eve ate and, progressing upward through a mandrake, a whale, a mouse, a sparrow, a swan, Abel's dog's puppy, an ape, Cain's wife, was to come to rest in its aged evening—and this was the cream of the jest—in Queen Elizabeth herself. "I launch at Paradise, and I sail towards home."

He was feeling little reverence for either the Court or the Queen. He could not forgive her for Essex's death, and when he heard that the Queen had lost her appetite and all her care for her appearance, that she frowned on her ladies, muttered alone in her chamber, starting up to slash furiously at the arras with a rusty sword, he felt that she was suffering no more than she deserved. The Court he saw as the embodiment of all that was jealous, envious, fawning on power, despising weakness, a place where a single honest man was a miracle.

His epic had been good sport in the planning and for a while in the writing, but after fifty stanzas in which the soul had got no further than Cain's wife, with all the Bible, all Roman and all English history still to come, he tired of it and wound it up abruptly in a final stanza addressed to "Whoe'er thou beest that read'st this sullen writ." Into the last lines he put the thought that nagged beneath the surface of his mind. Who had the right of it? The Court or its victims? The High Commissioners who punished Catholics for not going to church or the priests who risked their lives to urge their flock to stay away? Worldly parents or harmless lovers? Who was to say? Where did authority lie?

> *There's nothing simply good or ill alone,*
> *Of every quality comparison*
> *The only measure is, and judge, opinion.*

4 June came and the Egertons went to Harefield, the mansion on the Colne that Sir Thomas had bought after his marriage to Lady Derby. John had accompanied the great migration—the huge, squeaking coach, the line of men on horseback, the servants on foot, the carts with maids and chests and household goods—through Charing Cross and out the Uxbridge Road until they came at last to the river-encircled lawns and gardens of Harefield House. As he would not be needed there until the Lord Keeper should go to join the Court at Nonsuch, he got permission to visit Francis Woolley at Pyrford on the other side of London, in Surrey. Eight miles from Loseley.

Francis, John found, lived at nineteen in considerable state. His father, dead four years earlier, had been Latin Secretary to the Queen, his mother one of the ladies of the Privy Chamber. When he was a boy, the Queen herself had kept him up to the mark in his studies by asking him questions in French and Latin. Last New Year he had made her a present of a mantle of pink cobweb lawn striped with silver and got in return twenty-two ounces of gilt plate. Unmarried and apparently not interested in girls, he lived alone in his great house on the Wey and lavished on it all the imagination and care of a rich young man with his favorite toy. John, following him around the orchard, the magnificent deer-park, the gardens, the terraces, the acres of rooms in the house, the apartments in the wings, heard with amusement and some envy his rich man's talk. This arras was not nearly good enough, he was having his agent get something better in France; masons from Italy were building new terraces. Here were the drawings for a banqueting house but the architect had misunderstood him; this would be too small, too mean; he had ordered another plan altogether.

Patiently John drew him again and again to talk of Anne.

"Sir William—my grandfather and Anne's—died about a year ago and Sir George has come into his inheritance. Loseley is his at last; it hasn't been easy for him at his age to be only a son of the house, but now he has a free hand. You must see Loseley."

"I should like to see Anne."

Francis clapped his arm. "So you shall. She often asks me about you—what you did on the Islands Voyage, how you took care of me and so on and so forth. I find it difficult to satisfy her."

They rode at last to Loseley. John felt his heart pound as they came up the long tree-lined avenue from the gate, turned a corner suddenly by some pines and saw the great mass of the house there before them. With its gray stone brought from Waverley Abbey after the Dissolution, its clear glass in ranks of windows to the roof, the coat of arms with the rebus on the name of More over the door, it seemed to belong to the very citadel of English power and purpose that John longed to scale. That the daughter of Loseley House was promised to John Donne came afresh to him with a shock; Anne, against her background, seemed suddenly a different person from Anne sitting on the desk in his closet.

They met in the garden behind the house, where Anne and her younger sister Frances were walking before dinner. She greeted Woolley with cousinly affection, turned to welcome the stranger—and saw that it was John. She went white, then, her color flooding back, radiant. In the months since he had seen her she had become slimmer and she had actually—John saw with a rush of tenderness for her youth—grown taller. Her spirited little head was framed by a spreading collar of some white transparent stuff, her waist was smaller than ever, her breasts round and high under the embroidered bodice. On her own ground she had a new dignity and sureness, entrancing to John. The younger sister, Frances, whose childish mouth was stained with cherries, was but a pale and clumsy copy of Anne.

As the four turned toward the house, he and Anne managed to linger behind, to snatch a moment or two to speak in low voices, if not to kiss. Frances showed a disposition to hang on Anne's arm and listen to their conversation, but Anne quickly and with a cool authority that delighted John sent her scurrying ahead.

"I thought you would never come! Oh, John, have you forgotten?"

"My dearest love, how could I? You are in my mind always, and I batter my head for ways to find a path for us."

"Oh, I have thought and thought too, and whenever some new gentleman appears at the house and my father welcomes him, I cringe with dread. But it will be all right in the end, I know it will. So long as we are faithful."

"I must speak with your father and tell him honestly that I love you and want to marry you."

"He will be very angry."

"Because I am I—or because I have no title and estate to offer?"

"Because he wants to decide everything himself. Oh, why do we waste our bit of time like this! Look, John, we are alone. Kiss me and say you love me!"

At dinner John was set at the end of the table, between a small squire from the neighborhood and a fat parson who scarcely knew how to use the English language, both of whom seemed to regard an ample dinner as the sole purpose of social intercourse. He could see Anne sitting between her father and Francis Woolley and occasionally exchange a glance with her, but with no possibility of speaking to her. He sat in silence, eating little and tasting nothing, watching Anne, studying her father.

When Sir George smiled, his whole small, hot face changed,

135

and John could see the charm that won people—the Queen and others—to him; anger, he surmised, could change that face equally fast. It was the face of an emotional, impulsive, energetic man who had never had any need to control his temper. John, smarting at the lowness of his place at table, watched Sir George and made up his mind.

After dinner all the company went to the rustic pavilion in the garden for strawberries and cream. Here in the movement and shift of position John managed to come face to face with Sir George and, without waiting for a better moment that might never come, spoke out.

"A little later today, sir, might I have the privilege of speaking to you alone?"

The silence that followed seemed endless. Sir George moved his eyes slowly, coldly, from the top of John's head to his feet and up again.

"Have you a message from your master?"

"No, sir. This is a personal matter."

"I cannot think," said Sir George icily, "of anything that I care to hear from you, Mr. Donne," and turned away with insulting finality in the very curve of his shoulder.

There was an almost audible gasp in the pavilion. Surprise, pity, curiosity, showed themselves in widened eyes, in a mouth opened to speak and closed again, in an attentive stillness. Anne was white around the mouth, her hazel eyes suddenly darkened; she threw a look at John, warm, distressed, pleading. Francis was embarrassed and puzzled. The little parson drew his lips down at the corners to hide a quirk of pleasure.

John made no reply but a silent bow into which he threw all the mocking insolence of which he was capable. It was war now between him and Sir George, his youth and subtlety against the old man's heavy age, his steel against the other's iron; pride against pride; audacity against obstinacy. His self-division was over. His spirits rose, he heard a singing in his head.

They loved each other. They were betrothed. They would be married—and before the year was out.

Xii

THE PARLIAMENT OPENED on the twenty-seventh of October. Of the seats that he controlled, the Lord Keeper had given one to his son John, one to Francis Woolley and one to John Donne. To young Egerton and to Francis, who were both no more than nineteen, it was a game; to John Donne at twenty-eight it was a firm step upward on the long staircase of his ambition. He was there for the first trumpet call in the morning air, wearing a new dark suit, alive with interest and curiosity, eager to store up impressions to examine later.

He knew already what the issues would be. The Queen needed money: four thousand Spanish soldiers had landed in Ireland and she must have three hundred thousand pounds by Easter. The Commons would give her a subsidy but they would try to bargain for it, yielding money while asking for the abolition of the monopolies, such as the one on salt, that she gave as rewards or payments to her favorites. The Puritan faction would propose stricter laws on church attendance. The important questions were money and monopolies.

It was not the Parliament itself that interested John, for he had rather a low opinion of parliaments, believing firmly that monarchy was the best possible form of government and that the monarch was God's representative on earth. What he valued was the opportunity to take even a small part in his own person, not as the secretary of another, even a great, man and to watch those who wielded the Queen's power at work.

He rejoiced in feeling himself a part of a living organism as he stood crammed shoulder to shoulder with the unimportant members from here, there and the other place, watching the approach of the great procession.

Down the King's Road from Whitehall they came, the messengers, the gentlemen, the esquires, the clerks, the masters in chancery. Then came more trumpets, blaring forth from their brass throats the cries of triumph to which the unreasoning heart swells in response. Among the knights in their brilliant robes, knights of the Bath, knights banneret, knights of the Garter, John saw Sir George More, half a head shorter than anyone near him, marching along, his cheeks shaking to his tread. He followed him with his eyes as long as he could, wondering if he would encounter him in the Commons, how they could speak to each other.

When he turned again to the procession, Secretary Cecil was coming past, hump-backed, small and thin, with great lamps of eyes in his narrow face. The judges shuffled, the bishops swayed. Heralds in their tabards preceded earls, marquises, dukes. The Lord Keeper, carrying the Great Seal, tall and stern and wooden, seemed another man than the pressed, often nervous and irritable master whom John saw daily.

Where else in the world, he thought, were processions so fine as this? He had seen them in France, in Italy, in Spain, but nothing like this for splendor or for style. Each man walked as if he were an actor playing the part of himself, yet no stage procession could even suggest the drama, the majesty, of this one, the whole Court in motion, England herself on parade.

Shouts told of the coming of the climax: the sword of state, the cap royal, gilt maces, Clarenceux King of Arms (who was only Mr. Camden of Westminster School dressed up), the gentlemen pensioners carrying axes and, in the midst of them, in a gold litter swung between two white horses, with a crown at her back and a gold dragon at her feet, the Queen herself, her thin face white and still between the blazing red wig and the stiff, transparent flare of her ruff.

She looked withdrawn, John thought, and sad. There were

fewer shouts of "God save the Queen" and "God bless Your Majesty" than once there would have been. People remembered Essex, he thought. How long since that young, noble head had tumbled from the block? Eight months? Nine to the day, almost. Crowds forget quickly, but not in nine months, not an Essex. Nor had the Queen forgotten. Bitter memory looked out of her hooded eyes, spoke in her thin, compressed lips.

The ladies of the Court passed on a wave of perfume, and after them the guard, all scarlet and gold.

The great doors of the Abbey swallowed them up, the whole glittering procession who went to hear the Dean of St. Paul's preach them a sermon.

With other members of the Commons, John crossed Old Palace Yard to the Court of Requests, next St. Stephen's Hall, where they were to take the oath of allegiance. He found a crowd already gathered, waiting for the Lord Steward, who had to detach himself from the rest of the procession. When at length he came, he had two members of the Privy Council with him to help, and soon there was a steady trickle of men passing from the Hall of Requests into St. Stephen's Hall.

After the long wait, the oath itself took no more than a moment. John received it from Sir William Knollys, who did not look up and certainly did not recognize him, though John had borne many a message to him from Sir Thomas at the time of the Essex affair. It was the first time John had had occasion to take the oath acknowledging the Queen as Governor of the Church, and it marked the end of that long road he had come since he had sat down with his books and pen to search out what he could learn of truth, where he could find true religion. He was, he had been for some time now, a member of the reformed church, he attended its services, ate the bread and drank the wine of its sacrament, but not until now, when he said the actual words of the oath, did he feel finally, irrevocably, separated from the church in which he had been reared. He had wondered beforehand if he would experience some qualm, some last faint shadow of regret, but he knew only a calm satisfaction. This was England's church; he was a member of England's Parliament.

St. Stephen's Hall, built long ago as a chapel to rival the Sainte Chapelle in Paris but now filled with benches, all its popish and idolatrous wall paintings covered with wainscoting, was filling up, but John turned away. Turning, he bumped into Francis Woolley.

"Come along," he said.

"But aren't we to wait here till we are sent for?"

"Sir Thomas told me to go directly to the Parliament Chamber. There's not room for all four hundred of the Commons, and the early ones are sure of a place."

Others had the same idea. Already there was little space left behind the bar, where the Commons stood. Pressed from behind, John found himself breathing into the ruff of Sir Walter Raleigh, who, turning, recognized him.

"Ah, Mr. Donne! You here?"

"I am member for Brackley, sir."

"Indeed. I thought your interests were purely literary and philosophical."

They had both been on the Islands Voyage but Raleigh, who commanded a squadron, and John Donne, who was only one of many young gentlemen attending the Earl of Essex, had not met then; it was the Earl of Northumberland who introduced them. Since their meeting the previous December, Northumberland had gone out of his way to be friendly to John.

"And I should have expected to find you, sir, rather planning an expedition to the Antipodes or examining astrology in the light of the theories of Copernicus."

Rumor was making much of the almost daily meetings at Durham House of Northumberland, Raleigh and Cobham— nicknamed the Diabolical Triplicity—but my lord of Northumberland himself had told John that they talked, not of witchcraft nor of the forbidden subject of the succession, but of harmless mathematics and the new astronomy.

"I am here to help Her Majesty get the subsidies she requires

140

and incidentally to rescue my poor Cornish farmers from any laws that would ruin them."

And also, John thought but did not say, to protect your own monopoly on playing cards.

He saw an opening in the press and, pulling Francis behind him, he slipped through it to a place in the corner, against the bar, from which they could survey the whole brilliant scene.

The Queen was already on her throne at the far end of the chamber, under her canopy of state, with the Lord Keeper standing on her left, a little behind, and two of her ladies sitting on the steps at her feet. In the center of the room, in a hollow square, sat the judges and the masters in chancery on their red woolsacks. The lords in their plumed hats, short cloaks and padded trunks sat on polished wooden benches, row after row; most of them had fortified themselves with pomander balls or some sweeter, stronger perfume. At the end of the front bench sat the Earl of Northumberland, his bright eyes darting everywhere, his beard wagging as if he were talking, if only to himself.

The buzz of conversation in the hall stopped abruptly as the Queen began to speak. Behind the members of the Commons a gentleman usher closed the door.

"They haven't all got here," whispered Francis.

"Sh!"

The Queen's voice, speaking a few words of welcome and bidding the Lord Keeper to show the causes of the Parliament, was clear and strong and surprisingly young. Her final words were drowned out for John by thumpings on the door behind him and the voices of the irate Commons on the other side demanding to be let in. The gentleman usher, equally irate or perhaps only flustered, hissed through the crack of the door that if they were not quiet they should be set in the stocks, and by the time the commotion had ended, the Lord Keeper was on his feet, delivering the oration that John already knew almost by heart.

He had copied it from the Lord Keeper's notes and in places filled in paragraphs that Sir Thomas had merely indicated with a word or two. It was elaborately polished and still dull, but it made quite clear to the Parliament what was wanted of it: the Queen wished to dissolve Parliament before Christmas; money was needed for the war with Spain; it was desirable to make no new laws but only to revise existing ones; they were urged to be both provident and confident, provident because the enemy was provident and confident because "God hath ever and I hope ever will bless the Queen with successful fortune."

For a time John listened critically, recognizing certain phrases of his own, noting where the Lord Keeper departed, either from forgetfulness or the inspiration of the moment, from the original text, but soon his mind drifted off. He was thinking how many men in public affairs had started from no more exalted positions than his own. The Lord Keeper himself was a natural son; the Clarenceux King of Arms was the son of a painter-stainer; Dr. Andrewes, Dean of Westminister, the son of a London shipman; the Cecils themselves came, two or three generations back, from a mere yeoman. There were others he could not call to mind. Birth, undeniably, was a great advantage, but education, travel, intellect, friends, the patronage of a great man, were more important—and, of course, fortune, which was not so much chance as quickness to see an opportunity and resolution in grasping it. Ambition, he mocked at himself. My vices are not infectious or wandering. They came not yesterday nor mean to go away today. They inn not, but dwell in me.

The Lord Keeper finished his speech by enjoining the Commons to return to their own house and elect a speaker, the Queen rose and every man in the hall went down on one knee. In that moment when she turned from her throne toward the door at the back of the chamber, the weight of her robes, heavy with fur and jewels, was too much for her frail strength; she tottered and would have fallen but that two noblemen, standing near, jumped to support her. Regaining her balance, she passed on; the caught breath throughout the hall was released. The members of the Commons made their way to St. Stephen's

Hall, where those who had been shut out of the ceremony were already ensconced, buzzing angrily about the treatment they had received, about being threatened by a mere gentleman usher with the stocks.

The benches were full; there was scarcely even standing room.

"It's hardly worth staying. It's all settled who will be speaker anyhow. Shall we find a tavern before the crowd comes?"

"I could do with some oysters."

On the steps down into Westminister Hall the servants were waiting, talking, laughing, playing cards, making an unholy din. John nodded to Pierre; Francis had to shout at his boy to get him away from a game of dice.

"Shall we try the Bell?"

"It's as good as any. John, my cousin Anne is in town."

John stopped still, while Pierre behind him all but trod on his heels.

"Where?"

"She came with her father, for as long as the Parliament lasts. They are staying with Mrs. Herbert on St. Andrew's Lane in the Blackfriars. Her eldest son is my uncle's ward. Do you know her?"

"I met her in Oxford when I went on an errand for my Lord Keeper." It was two years or more ago but he had still a vivid memory of that odd household, of the lovely, earnest young widow, her sixteen-year-old son and his pale and petulant-looking wife, who was several years older than he. Sir Thomas had told him about it beforehand, in one of his rare moments of relaxation when he took pleasure in a bit of gossip. "She was determined to have a remedy for youthful lasciviousness, so she married young Edward off at fifteen. The girl is five years older, I believe, but a pack of money came with her. Then, to make sure that he kept at his studies, she went with the young pair to Oxford and took a house there."

So described, she had sounded puritanical and a trifle ridiculous; but when John actually met her, he had found her

143

touching as well as beautiful, with her seriousness and a certain innocent worldliness. Left a widow at twenty-nine with ten children to bring up, she had gone about it in her own way, to be sure; but her children—John had seen two younger boys also at Oxford—obviously held her in love and reverence. She had been charming to him that day, and now, thinking of her in London and Anne with her, he felt that a sudden, clear light had been cast upon his path. The time had come to go forward.

"I know how it is with you and Anne," Francis was saying, "and I'll help you all I can."

2   "Do you intend to ask Dr. King to marry you?"

"No. He is the Lord Keeper's chaplain. I do not propose to use anyone who owes loyalty to the Lord Keeper—or to Sir George More."

"I am afraid"—Christopher leaned forward and put another stick of wood on the fire—"I don't see the force of that scruple —when you are preparing to deceive and defy them both in a far greater matter."

They were sitting in Christopher's room at Lincoln's Inn. Already, at barely four o'clock, the dark pressed against the window; the firelight, flaring, lit up their intent faces, warmed their fronts while the chill of early December crept down their backs in runlets.

"It seems clear to me. When we are married and they are presented with the fact, if I have used Sir Thomas's chaplain or confided in his son or allowed Sir George's nephew to be a witness, they might well feel wronged and therefore all the more angrily deceived in me."

"It still appears muddled to me. But you are right in one thing—they will both be very angry."

"I believe the Lord Keeper will excuse it rather easily—if I have not involved him in Sir George's wrath by employing his chaplain. He is no foe to secret marriages. He only announced his own after several months—and it still is not generally known that John and Lady Frances are married."

"Whom then will you get to marry you?"

"That is why—one reason, at least—I have come to you. Your brother Samuel has taken orders recently. Would he do it?"

"I've no doubt he would. He longs to use his new powers—and he is as soft over lovers as any maiden aunt."

"Will you ask him for me?"

"Ask him yourself. He is lodging in one of Sir Robert Drury's new houses in Drury Lane."

"I will then. I should like it to be done in the chapel here. Can you arrange that? And will you engage to be present?"

"Why the Lincoln's Inn Chapel?"

"I have a sentiment about it. I lived here—happily, on the whole—for nearly three years. And I should like my wedding—Anne's wedding—to be dignified."

"Why not the Savoy Chapel near you? It is your own parish church."

"It has a bad name for runaway marriages."

"What on earth else is this, John? I am very uneasy about it. I wish you would refrain—or at least wait. You must know—you can't have forgotten—it is illegal to marry a minor without her parents' consent."

"It is a law, yes, but one frequently broken. It is a more serious matter to break the kind of solemn vows that we have exchanged—any moral issue is deeper than a legal one. Neither of us is free to marry elsewhere, and Anne's father is already talking about her marriage to someone else."

"Is he? To Mr. Woolley?"

"He would have liked that, even though they are first cousins—and that, too, is illegal. But it was the marriage of Pyrford and Loseley that he really had in mind. Anne and Francis are devoted to each other, but they balked at that. No, it is another neighbor."

"No matter. It is someone he wants. I think he is not a safe man to cross. You are putting all your prosperity in jeopardy. And what do you see beyond the secret ceremony? Will you take her to your lodging in the Savoy?"

For God's sake, John wanted to cry out, hold your tongue

145

and let me love! But he controlled himself, answering reasonably, "No, of course not. We shall have to part for the present. Then at a propitious moment we'll reveal our marriage, and when the explosions die down, I am confident that either the Lord Keeper will allow us to live at York House, as John and Lady Frances do, or else, with my stipend perhaps increased and Anne's dower, we can rent a house of our own, one of the new small ones that are building in the suburbs. Or, if all else fails, Francis has promised us apartments in Pyrford."

They had talked it all over, he and Anne, in the three times during the last five weeks that they had met: once at Mrs. Herbert's, when Sir George had been away at Court; once at York House, when Anne and her father had come to dinner on a Sunday and John and Anne had walked together in the garden in the shelter of the hedges; and once at the theater, when Francis had invited a party and had seen to it that Anne and John sat side by side. John had wanted to let Mrs. Herbert, for whom he had conceived a warm admiration, into the secret and ask her help, but Anne had vehemently opposed the suggestion. "She is *very* strict about the duty of children to parents. She wouldn't help at all. She might spoil everything." Anne's eagerness, her joy in their love, her confidence that everything must come out as they wished, had added fuel to his ardor and —almost—burned away his doubts. "We mustn't be afraid of my father," she had whispered under cover of an impassioned tirade by an actor in the guise of Mark Antony, "He is good, really. He gets very angry and he goes off like a squib, but he soon cools down and then he is sorry."

"Well," Christopher was saying, "I am thankful I have found myself a simpler way of life. This seems to me a madly dangerous course."

"But you will help?"

"I have told you that I would. You have a too persuasive way about you. I've no doubt, actually, that you will overcome the Lord Keeper and even Sir George himself almost as easily as you do me. Lincoln's Inn Chapel it is. Have you selected the day?"

"The fourth of December, in the morning."

"Next Wednesday."

"Yes. It is the day most probably when a bill that Sir George is promoting will be read for the second time and he is sure to be there. An act against willful absence from divine service upon the Sunday."

Christopher made a face. "I've heard about it. More work for justices of the peace. It has one feature, though, of which you should take note: husbands are to pay their wives' fines."

"It won't pass. December fourth, in the morning. You are a good friend, Christopher—not only now but always. I do not forget it."

"To you? To Anne? I don't know. But"—and he repeated Francis's words of a troubled month ago—"I will do what I can."

3   The morning sun sent a shaft of colored light through the painted windows of the chapel. Samuel Brooke in surplice and stole had put on authority with his vestments. Ordination, John thought, did indeed cloak the young and callow with a holiness not their own—fortunately, for how else could God use the odd, the flawed, the unfinished tools that came to his hand?

In the joy and certainty, the almost-exaltation, that swept through him, John felt himself separated into two people: one who, lifted high above it all, saw the scene as if he had no part in it; one who was so wholly in it and of it that he had no covering to his naked soul, no shield against the thoughts and feelings of others. He heard Samuel call for any man who knew just cause why John and Anne might not be lawfully joined together to speak now or forever after hold his peace, and he knew in the breathless pause that all of them there more than half expected Sir George More to fling open the door behind them, shouting, "Stop!"

" '. . . the dreadful day of judgment when the secrets of all hearts shall be disclosed . . .' "

He saw, ironically, that Christopher was giving away the

bride as gracefully and sincerely as if he had the right to do it. He pictured him stepping back again into the shadows behind and saw him and Pierre standing there, together as witnesses, yet divided by the distance between friend and servant. He was aware of Pierre's half-lascivious, half-loyal interest in the marriage, his admiration for Anne, his increased respect for a master who could win such a lady.

He saw, looking down at his side, the feather of Anne's hat curling against the curve of her cheek and her small hands clasped in the billows of her silken skirt.

The marriage service, he thought, taking Anne's hand in his and repeating the words as Samuel prompted him, contained more shadows than he had realized: for worse, for poorer, in sickness, till death. He heard his own voice, loud, confident, defiant; Anne's, when it came, was but a whisper.

He felt her at his side, tremulous but staunch, and his whole being melted into tenderness for her. So little, so innocent, so unutterably sweet, so desirable, headlong in outpouring of her love—and she was his. God had joined them—Samuel said it with unction—no man might put them asunder.

Kneeling, he heard the blessing, of which Samuel, yielding to nervousness now that it was almost over, his first wedding, lisped the final words. " '. . . so live together in this life that in the world to come ye may have life everlathting.' "

Samuel gave the bride-kiss on Anne's forehead and John swept her into his arms, knocking her hat askew, getting himself a mouthful of feathers. Her eyes were shining, her whole body vibrant with happiness.

Pierre brought the bride cup—a silver bowl that Christopher had borrowed somewhere, filled to the brim with sweet wine—and a tray of cakes. They drank in turn and nibbled at the saffron and raisin comfits, caught up in laughter and joy and love, uttering small trivialities as if they were gems of wit and truth.

"To your everlathting happineth!" said Christopher.

"It was a beautiful thervice—service," said Anne earnestly to Samuel. "I'd like to do it again, every year, on my anniversary!"

148

"To Mr. and Mrs. Donne! May their joy never be done!"

"Anne, we must drink to our friends. May they never regret this day's work!"

When the wine was gone, the sun vanished too, and a chill crept out of the stones of the chapel. The party was over. It was time for John and Anne to go home together, to go to bed and make sons; but he must take her instead back to Mrs. Herbert's house and leave her there.

"When will you tell Sir George?" said Christopher somberly.

"Not yet," said Anne quickly. "Not here in London. There are too many people here to support him in his grievance." She turned away from Christopher and spoke to John alone. "You must come down to Loseley, after we are home again, and tell him there."

XIII

THE PARLIAMENT LASTED TWO WEEKS LONGER, but John did not see Anne again. When he went to call on Mrs. Herbert and asked for Anne, he was told that Sir George had sent her home to Loseley.

"She is ill?"

"No, she is blooming. I think her father feared just what is happening now."

"And that is? I don't——"

"That you might come to see me and ask for her. Should you not be in St. Stephen's Hall, Mr. Donne?"

"There is not room for everybody. I think that for us who are young and negligible, the fines we pay for absenting ourselves are more useful than our presence would be."

"Sir George's bill lost by one vote. Perhaps if you had been there, the story might have been different."

"If I had been there, it would have lost by two votes."

"You are against religion?"

"No, but I am against force in religion—and against schism most of all. Was that why Sir George whisked Mistress Anne away?"

"I think you must answer that question yourself."

There was a moment's silence, and when Mrs. Herbert spoke again, it was to change the subject.

"I am told you write poetry, Mr. Donne? I should be happy if you would send me some to read."

"They are poor things, not worthy of your time or your eyesight, but I will have some copied for you."

It was not in him not to respond to a lovely woman's kindness, and for quite five minutes after he left he thought of the delicate flare of her nostrils, so full of pride and courage, and the rich timbre of her voice, but then the thought of Anne swept back to take possession of his mind and the troublesome question of what Sir George suspected or feared, and he forgot Mrs. Herbert and his promise to send her poems.

Throughout the twelve days of Christmas and their celebration at Court, which were quieter than in former years because the Queen was growing old and sad, he kept looking for Anne. He thought—he hoped desperately—that Sir George might return for the festivities and bring her with him. But he had no glimpse of either of them. He sent a note by Francis to Anne, to be secretly delivered, with a promise of a jewel for her hair.

He also found himself telling Francis of their marriage.

"Lord," said Francis, "you've picked a rare time for it. Don't tell her father now. He's just been made Chamberlain of the Receipts of the Exchequer and he thinks he's got the world in his hands. I think you should have somebody whom he respects very much intercede for you—to soften the blow a little. Why don't you ask the Lord Keeper? Or better, Lady Derby. She looks on you very warmly. I've heard her say she expects to see you in the Privy Council someday."

Christopher also was full of advice, but even more cautious.

"Wait until an opportunity presents itself that is propitious. You can afford to wait. She is young. You have her safe. You might lose everything by acting hastily and unpreparedly."

But as the days went past he began to feel it intolerable to be, as he was, married and not married. To ride boldly up to the front door of Loseley and claim his wife from Sir George seemed the honest, the manly thing to do, and more than once he was on the point of setting forth, but something, perhaps the fact that he had had no word from Anne, held him back. To confess to Sir Thomas and ask for his assistance would be easier and perhaps offered a better chance of success, but again something held him back. Might not Sir George resent Sir Thomas's knowing it first, and on the other hand, might the Lord Keeper refuse to do anything until he knew how Sir George felt about it? It was essential that he avoid antagonizing either man, for the consequences of their wrath could be fatal.

January was all but over when he went one day to Whitehall, to attend Sir Thomas on the breaking up of the Privy Council. It was a raw gray day with low clouds overhead; people went muffled in their cloaks.

Anyone who knew the Court, he thought, getting out of the wherry at Whitehall Stairs, could tell at once that the Queen was away. It was not just that her flag was not flying from the tower nor that there were fewer people about, for the Palace, which was like a city itself with a public street running through it, teemed with people, but there was missing the air of excitement, the tension that spoke of her presence in everyone's step, in the turn of a shoulder, the glance of the eyes, when there was hope of catching some glimpse of her Grace.

He passed under the Holbein Gate and into the Privy Gallery. The hall outside the Council Chamber was full of people waiting for the door to open. A noisy group of young men were playing primero at a table; other men walked up and down, back and forth; a buzz of conversation mounted to the wreaths and fruits and gilded pendants of the plaster ceiling.

John found himself a place to lean against the wainscoting, his arms folded, where he could keep his eye on the door and let his mind run off, as it did, to Anne. Did she think him a laggard? Why did she send him no word?

"Dreaming, Mr. Donne?"

He returned to the present abruptly, mortified at being caught. George Gerrard stood before him with his sidelong glance and knowing smile.

"My lord—who is yonder—has seen you and sent me to fetch you."

He appeared to be in high feather, the Lord Northumberland, laughing in the midst of a group of nobles whom he dispersed, when John approached, by the simple means of walking

through them and clapping his hand on John's shoulder. Drawing him aside into the embrasure of a window, he said with his
sly, twinkling look:

"I am ever curious, Mr. Donne, about other men's affairs."

From his expression it was evident that he meant no apology
but only to emphasize his kindly condescension. "How prospers
your courtship of Mistress More?"

John hesitated, wondering how much it was safe to say; yet
remembering his lordship's promise, a year back, to help, he
felt a sudden excitement.

"Come, come, I ask because I like you, Mr. Donne. I have
read such of your verses as Gerrard has in his possession and I
found them very fresh and honest. 'I am two fools, I know, For
loving and for saying so'. . . . Only you haven't really said so,
have you?"

John made up his mind swiftly. "We are married, my lord.
But secretly. She is with her father at Loseley and I am here,
beating my brains out over the question of how best to broach
the news and get my wife without arousing Sir George to my
destruction. I am," he added with a smile, "pregnant with the
old twins, hope and fear."

"But you must tell her father and claim her at once!" He had
that easy disregard of difficulties of the man whose title and
fortune swept away most obstacles from his path. "The longer
it goes on, the worse it will be—and why want a wife when
you could be having one? My wife and I are reconciled and I
am preaching conjugal felicity to everyone."

"I have reason to believe that Sir George regards me—and
quite rightly, of course—as entirely unworthy of his daughter.
My friends warn me that he is a dangerous man to oppose."

"If you are afraid"—Lord Northumberland's long, sardonic
face broke into an expression of impish pleasure, his pointed
beard tilting upward—"to meet Sir George yourself, I will go
to him and speak for you. No, no, don't say whatever you've
opened your mouth to say. I can't hear you anyhow."

He tapped John's chest with his long forefinger. "I will urge
on your respectable father-in-law all the fine things that your

153

modesty—are you modest? convention, then—will not allow you to say about yourself. And if I succeed, you shall give me a copy of all your poems, including the one about your mistress going to bed. Has she seen that one, your lady wife?"

This was going too far and too fast. John was not at all sure that his lordship's skill would equal his assurance.

"I humbly thank your lordship, but might not Sir George think it somewhat weak in me not to face him myself?"

"Perhaps. Well, suit yourself." He seemed to lose interest as quickly as he had kindled. "But I go to Petworth next week and I can stop at Loseley on the way. If you change your mind, send word to me by Gerrard."

The door of the Council Chamber opened and the members came streaming out. Lord Northumberland turned from John's bows and went off in a straight line to Sir Robert Cecil. Now, John thought, hastening toward the Lord Keeper, he must indeed take action of some kind, for he put no trust whatsoever in Northumberland's ability to keep a secret. Get someone whom he respects to intercede for you, Francis had said; was Lord Northumberland a heaven-sent messenger—or should he ride himself, tomorrow, to Loseley?

2 A spasm of pain clutching at his belly sent fiery tentacles through him, down his legs and up through his chest; he held his breath till it ebbed slowly away, then shouted for Pierre.

When he had been made more comfortable, had swallowed some medicine and had herbs set burning to freshen the air in the room, he had Pierre bring him paper and ink, a quill and a knife to shape it with, and set himself to composing a letter for Lord Northumberland to take to Sir George.

"Sir: If I had . . ." "Sir: If my illness, which is increased by fear of your displeasure, did not chain me here . . ." He crossed it out impatiently and began again.

Sir: If a very respective fear of your displeasure and a doubt that my Lord (whom I know out of your worthiness to love you much) would be so compassionate as to add his anger to yours did not so much increase my sickness as that I cannot

154

stir, I had taken the boldness to have done the office of this letter by waiting upon you myself to have given you truth and clearness of this matter between your daughter and me, and to show you plainly the limits of our fault, by which I know your wisdom will proportion the punishment.

Honesty would be the keynote, an uncompromising plainness of speech. There was no way by flattery or persuasion to sweeten the fact for Sir George; the most he could hope to do was to bring him to accept it as done, to appeal to his good sense and moderation in dealing with it. Sir George was by all reports a choleric man, but those who knew him best—Anne, Francis, Sir Thomas—had all said at one time or another that he cooled down quickly. During the sessions of the Parliament, John, from his perch on a back bench, had studied him as he sat, one of the inner circle loved by the Queen, down in front, or rose to speak about the bill he favored. He was eloquent and learned, upright, full of pride of family and of achievement. Once John had found him alone in one of the taverns that were plastered like swallows' nests against the outside wall of Westminster Hall and asked him to drink a glass of wine with him. After a moment's hesitation Sir George had accepted, pleasantly enough, and they talked—not of Anne, for John did not venture to mention her name, but of travel, which Sir George believed valuable. He himself, he said, had in his youth carried messages between the Queen and the great Earl of Leicester, and he had traveled all over Italy, France and Germany with Sir Philip Sidney. John let fall that he, too, knew France and Italy and he spoke of Spain as well. Summing up Sir George in his mind later, John felt that he was a man who respected honesty in others and one who, when once his initial displeasure was past, might well be a kind father-in-law.

"So long since as her being at York House," he continued, "this had foundation, and so much then of promise and contract built upon it as, without violence to conscience, might not be shaken."

He scratched this all out, rewrote it in the same words, and went on:

"At her lying in town this Parliament I found means to see her twice or thrice." One of those times, at least, Sir George knew about; the others he might have guessed, or extracted from Anne by questioning.

We both knew the obligations that lay upon us, and we adventured equally; and about three weeks before Christmas we married. And as at the doing there were not used above five persons, of which I protest to you by my salvation there was not one that had any dependence or relation to you, so in all the passage of it did I forebear to use any such person, who by furtherance of it might violate any trust or duty towards you.

He had not told Francis the date or allowed him to be a witness or asked him to be the one to broach the news; even Anne's maid had been kept ignorant of what was afoot. This scrupulosity had for Christopher no significance at all, but to John it seemed an important point in his favor. Now for the difficult part.

The reasons why I did not fore-acquaint you with it (to deal with the same plainness I have used) were these: I knew my present estate less than fit for her. I knew (yet I knew not why) that I stood not right in your opinion. I knew that to have given any intimation of it had been to impossibilitate the whole matter. And then, having these honest purposes in our hearts and these fetters in our consciences, methinks we should be pardoned if our fault be but this, that we did not, by fore-revealing of it, consent to our hindrance and torment.

Sir, I acknowledge my fault to be so great, as I dare scarce offer any other prayer to you in mine own behalf than this, to believe this truth,—that I had neither dishonest end nor means.

They had been chaste. He might, with her ardor and his own hot blood, have taken her any time that they were alone together, but he had not. Even now, married, they had not lain together.

The heat of his fever, mounting as the day wore on, made him light-headed and he was forced to put aside paper and pen for a time. As he lay there, sleeping, dreaming, waking now and then with a convulsive start that fairly shook the bed, he saw Anne come before him, almost as vividly as if she had actually been there; she was pale and distressed, the palms of her hands pressed against her cheeks, her eyes wide and dark with fright. When Lord Northumberland should have delivered John's letter and made his persuasive speech and departed, Anne would be left alone to face her father's anger. The full storm of it would break over her head and John, who was her husband, would not be there to share it or to comfort her. When he roused and took up his pen again, it was to make a plea for Anne.

But for her, whom I tender much more than my fortunes or my life (else I would, I might neither joy in this life nor enjoy the next), I humbly beg of you that she may not, to her danger, feel the terror of your sudden anger.

I know this letter shall find you full of passion; but I know no passion can alter your reason and wisdom [and God grant that this was true!] to which I adventure to commend these particulars;—that it is irremediably done; that if you incense my lord, you destroy her and me; that it is easy to give us happiness, and that my endeavors and industry, if it please you to prosper them, may soon make me somewhat worthier of her.

Exhausted, he had to give over and rest again. It was no matter, for his lordship would not ride tomorrow. The silence of the snow continued all day, till in the late afternoon the cry of the muffin man came to John's ears, louder than the ringing inside his head.

Early next morning he finished his letter.

Sir, I have truly told you this matter, and I humbly beseech you so to deal in it as the persuasions of Nature, Reason, Wisdom and Christianity shall inform you; and to accept the vows of one whom you may now raise or scatter—which are, that as my love is directed unchangeably upon her, so all my labors shall concur to her contentment, and to show my humble obedience to yourself.

He made a fair copy of the whole, subscribing it, "Yours in all duty and humbleness, J. Donne"; added the date, "From my lodging at the Savoy, 2nd February, 1602"; and addressed it, "To the Right Worshipful Sir George More, Kt."

Having sent Pierre off to deliver the letter to Lord Northumberland, he began another letter to Sir Thomas, for it seemed important that he should have the news as soon as Sir George. The day was warmer but still the air was chilly, charged with damp from the melting snow. He blew on his stiff, cramped fingers, got up to use the close-stool once again and returned, blazing and shivering at the same time, to bed.

In a corner of the room a lute-string broke with a ghostly breath of music.

XIV

SNOW STILL COVERED THE SODDEN GROUND, but it was melting fast. The white mist rising from its surface among the gray trees of the park lost itself against the low gray sky. Y-shaped rabbit tracks printed the snow in loops and curves and in the elm nearest Anne's window starlings whistled and called, creaking like rusty gates. For all the dismal bleakness of the gray day, there was a hint of spring in the sound and in the dank smell of the melting snow.

Anne's heart was beating fast. The Earl of Northumberland, who had arrived an hour before with twenty or more mounted men in attendance, was closeted with her father. She had been in the hall to greet his lordship and when she offered him refreshment after his ride, he had whispered to her, "I am here as love's Mercury," and had given her several winks and nods evidently intended to convey volumes of meaning. Puzzled but shot through with sudden wild hope, she had withdrawn at a look from her father and in the passageway had met his lordship's secretary, Mr. Gerrard, who had said:

"I bear a message for you from Mr. Donne."

"Why doesn't he come? Or write?" The cry had escaped from her in spite of herself, in spite of all she had told herself, over and over in the sleepless nights: that he was wise in policy, that he loved her, that she must be patient.

"His sickness holds him prisoner."

"Oh, he is ill?"

"He has been ill. He will be better, I think, when this day is well over."

"You have no letter for me?"

"He feared to inflame your father by any clandestine correspondence. My lord of Northumberland has consented to present his case to your father today. Mr. Donne bade me to say to you that he is confident that all will be set right very soon."

She had fled, once she was sure that she had every word from John, from the little man's bright, impudent eyes. John ill, suffering! Oh, she should be there to take care of him. She was a good nurse. Even when she was a little girl, she had liked to smooth bedclothes, stroke hot foreheads, bring cups of broth. She knew to move lightly in a sickroom and to draw the curtains against the sun, to clear away all clutter. She longed to pour herself out in service for John.

Then the thought of Lord Northumberland's errand chased John's sickness from her mind. She sat on the window seat in her bedroom with the door open behind her, so as to hear the first footfalls of anyone sent to summon her, and tried to quiet her inner turbulence. After all this time, nearly two months, something was happening at last. When Lord Northumberland broke the news and pled for John, surely her father must be moved to lenience. Surely he must think well of a man who could command such a messenger. They had been together more than an hour now. What were they saying? When would they send for her?

Her oscillating mind flew back to John, ill. He was given, Francis had told her, answering her eager, probing questions, to attacks of high fever and griping pain that rendered him helpless. It was less, Francis said, a weakness of constitution than an overorganization of mind and nerves. He thought, he felt, he suffered, with more intensity than simpler natures; his body gave way under the burden of his mind's travail. If it were no more than that, she thought, she could, once they were together, care for him and soothe him; but there was always the plague to reckon with. This was not a bad year for it, as other years had been, but it was always lurking and one never knew when it would pounce.

The sky was darkening; it would rain soon and wash the snow away.

It must be going badly downstairs. If Lord Northumberland had been successful, she would have been sent for by this time. She went out along the corridor and into the room called the "Queen's Room," where there was a window over the entrance and the drive. She was there in time to see the angular, slightly comic figure of Henry Percy, Lord Northumberland, with feathered hat askew, mount his tall roan and bounce off down the drive, followed by his troop of attendants with the Percy badge on their livery. There was a fine thudding of horses' hooves before the cavalcade disappeared around the corner behind the pines. Nothing about them told of success or failure, of satisfaction or regret. They were a score of men riding away in a hurry, no more.

A cough behind her made her turn. A servant was standing there.

"Sir George sent me to fetch you, Mistress Anne. He will see you in the library."

Her hand flew to her throat in an involuntary gesture of alarm. She returned it firmly to her side, nodded to the man and went steadily down the stairs, crossed the great hall and entered the square, paneled room with the Queen's arms on the chimney piece and the rows of books around the walls.

Her father was striding back and forth waving a letter in his hand. He was not, she saw at once, merely angry; he was beside himself with rage. His face was a dark, turgid red; his brows drawn together, the lines from nose to chin as deep and dark as if drawn with ink; the folds of skin that overflowed his collar were swollen and tremulous. She quailed as she met his furious blue eyes and saw his head twitch and the letter crumple and quiver.

"So, madam. You are married."

"Yes, Father." She was not a helpless girl, she told herself, she was a married woman. This moment now was the worst. When this was over, she and John would be together.

"Married to that libertine! That infernal, penniless fortune-hunter! That filthy, white-livered recusant!"

"Oh no, Father! He's not! Truly."

"Be quiet, madam. Hold your tongue."

He flung himself into the tall-backed chair beside the hearth and clasped its arms with both hands, the letter crackling against the wood. She stood before him, holding herself erect, her chin high. With hard, blazing eyes he looked her up and down.

"Goody Donne," he said. "Goody Donne. No, by God," he shouted, stung again to fury by his own sneer, "I'll not have my daughter—*my* daughter, Anne More—married to this scoundrel. I'll take it to the Court of High Commission. I'll have it declared void. You are too young to marry without my consent."

She made no answer, knowing that even a word now could only inflame him further. The mention of the ecclesiastical court drove a new fear into her heart. If he should act now, before his anger had time to cool . . .

"How dared you do this thing? You knew it was against the law and if you did not, this fellow Donne knew it full well. He's had training in the law."

He sprang up again to pace back and forth.

"Did you conspire with him to mock my authority and hold me up to public scorn? Well? Did you?"

"Oh no, Father. Dear sir, no. We meant nothing that was undutiful——"

"Undutiful? You knew I would oppose this marriage with all the strength that I possess! This fellow Donne says so himself. 'I knew that to have given any intimation of it would have been to impossibilitate the whole matter.' He says that to my face! The sheer, brazen impudence! Listen to this. 'I know this letter shall find you full of passion.' Passion! My God, what else should I feel? '. . . but I know no passion can alter your reason and wisdom——' Bah. He talks about his 'endeavors and industry.' What use are they without birth and fortune? This I

162

will tell you, Anne. Your lover lies when he says it is irremediably done. He will soon find out what Sir George More can do to remedy the irremediable."

He crumpled the letter in his hand and was about to throw it into the fire, but on second thought spread it out and read:

" 'I knew,' he says '(yet I knew not why) that I stood not right in your opinion.' By God, if he had come to me as a decent man should, I could have told him why so that even the meanest intelligence could grasp it. But I intend that *you* shall know why. Sit down, madam."

Trembling, she perched on the edge of a stool and waited.

"This man is a libertine. He is not fit to marry my daughter or any other respectable gentleman's daughter. I have made inquiries about him and I know. He has deceived several gentlewomen and I was told names. He is secretly a Roman Catholic. He has written indecent verse that is not fit for any honest man's ears, to say nothing of a gently nurtured girl's."

She was crying now. "He isn't! He doesn't," she sobbed, and then as her father went further into damning detail, "I don't care!"

At that, Sir George came toward her as if he was about to strike her, and she drew back, but he checked at a new thought.

"Has he had his way with you? Has he got you with child?"

"No, Father. He—we waited for your permission."

"Exactly when did this marriage take place?"

"December fourth it was."

"Where?"

"In the chapel at Lincoln's Inn. The Reverend Samuel Brooke married us."

"And afterwards?"

"We had the bride cup there and then Mr. Donne took me back to the Blackfriars."

"While I, all unsuspecting, served my country in the Parliament. My God, when I think how I have been deceived! But you say you have not slept with him. Are you telling the truth?"

"I have not even seen him since our wedding day. We married—so that it would be done irremediably." She said the word

163

firmly, defiantly, but when her father choked and swelled afresh, hurried on, "We knew our duty to you, sir. We agreed to have no joy of our marriage till we might overcome your displeasure and be truly married with your consent."

She summoned all her dignity to meet his eyes—and saw in them a contempt that struck her to the heart. He was coldly angry, as she had never seen him before, and far more dangerous.

"Go to your room, madam, and stay there till I give you permission to come out. I shall leave at once for London and go directly to the Lord Keeper. I shall first have your lover dismissed from his post and then I will have the High Court annul the marriage. Is that clear?"

"Oh no, Father! No, I beg of you, don't do that. Don't destroy him. Don't inflame the Lord Keeper. Oh, please . . ." Babbling her distress, she clutched at his arm.

He brushed her aside and strode out of the room. She heard him in the hall calling for his servant.

XV

THAT LORD NORTHUMBERLAND HAD BEEN UNSUCCESSFUL in his mission John knew gradually, reluctantly, despairingly, by the silence that spread like a slow stain from one day to the next. Before his lordship's brief, regretful note, brought by the Petworth carrier had time to reach him, he felt the extent and the force of Sir George's anger. He was dismissed from the Lord Keeper's service.

He had sent Pierre to York House to crave forgiveness for the inconvenience that John's protracted sickness must be causing Sir Thomas and to bring back any work that he might do in bed. Pierre had brought instead the letter of dismissal.

"I do this with reluctance," Sir Thomas had written. "You have served me well. But the injury you have done toward one whom I hold in respect and love gives me no other choice."

It was a bitter blow, but after the first shock of it John tried to convince himself that it was not necessarily fatal or final. Sir Thomas might still be induced, when Sir George's anger had cooled—and so quick, so hot, a rage usually cooled quickly in kindly natures, as Sir George's was said by all who knew him well to be—to take John back. He sent a humble letter to Sir George at Mrs. Herbert's house where he was again lodging, asking only the favor of an interview, but he received in reply nothing more than a word-of-mouth message referring him to the Lord Keeper.

He was sitting up in bed drafting a letter to Sir Thomas when there came an immoderate pounding on the door, as if someone outside would tear it down. He shouted for Pierre, but before the man could get there the latch gave way and the door flew open before two burly officers with the Queen's arms on their chests and halberds in their hands.

He knew them at once for what they were. He had seen pursuivants before. To anyone who had once been a Romanist the sight of ecclesiastical officers in the doorway brought an unquenchable dread. So he had seen his brother Henry led away to prison and, ultimately, death; to others whom he had known, it had meant fines, accusations of treason, years of imprisonment, disappearance from the world of men. He summoned the confidence of innocence, the authority of one who had been secretary to the Lord Keeper.

"What cause have you," he demanded coldly, "to burst in upon me like this?"

"You are Mr. John Donne?"

"I am. What do you want of me?"

Behind the men he saw Dame Haines hovering anxiously, her face ashen with terror.

"By order of His Grace the Archbishop of Canterbury and his Commissioners, you are apprehended and under arrest."

"You're to come with us to the Fleet," translated the other, a smaller man.

"Let me see your warrant."

They had one. It was as they said.

Mrs. Haines, a little of her color restored, since they had not come for her, raised a bravely quavery voice. "You can't take Mr. Donne away now. He's very ill."

"What am I charged with?"

"Offenses against both civil and canon law. Marrying a young woman without her father's consent. Marrying without calling the banns—marrying away from your own parish church."

The full extent, the determination and vindictiveness, of Sir George's anger, was now appallingly plain. His mind circling like a squirrel in a cage, John sought some way of escape from the immediate threat. When the doors of the Fleet prison closed behind him, it would be far more difficult to reach anyone who could help him.

"You can see that I am not able to be moved," he said. "You must wait till I have summoned my physician."

"You'll have to come along of us now and summon your physician later," said the one who seemed to be the leader, and he added, slowly, as if compelled by something in John's eye, "sir."

In the end, since there was nothing else for it, he made ready to go with as much dignity and comfort as he could muster. He dispatched Dame Haines to summon a litter, keeping Pierre to help him dress.

"My money belt. Good master pursuivants, while I am dressing, why do you not go to the kitchen for some ale to refresh you? No, go, I'll not run away."

When they had, protesting loudly yet moving toward the door as if they scarcely noticed what they were doing, removed themselves, John gathered his wits to the question of what he should need.

"Get me the metal box from behind the Spanish dictionary in the study." A pity to reveal the hiding-place for his strongbox, but there was no help for it. Stuffing the gold angels and the silver shillings into his money belt, he continued, "Make a bundle of bedclothes for me and follow along with it. And I shall need plenty of paper and quills and ink. I shall have to write my way out. You are to come along after me to the Fleet and when you have done what you can for me there, you must go to Mr. Brooke and tell him what has happened. Keep after him till you find him, then come back to me and report what he says."

He felt like an old man when he got onto his papery legs and, leaning on Pierre, shuffled across the room and out to the waiting litter. It was a shabby one for public use and it smelled. Which was nothing to what the Fleet would smell like, he thought, and sent Pierre back for his silver pouncet box while the litter men stood looking with interest at the pursuivants and the pursuivants grumbled at the delay.

It was a lead-colored day of penetrating cold; the last pockets of dirty snow lingered in sheltered corners and the wind at the turn of the tide was sharp. Attracted by the sight of the officers and the litter, a little knot of idlers and small boys gathered around. Pierre thrust the box of perfume into John's hand, the door of the litter was closed and he felt the first jolt as the men lifted him. The last thing he saw was Mrs. Haines's face with tears running down over her round cheeks and her hands, red and puffy with chilblains, clasping and unclasping over her stomach.

With the pursuivants stepping out in front and Pierre with his bundle trudging behind, the dreary little procession went up the hill past the chapel and turned to the right along the Strand.

In one way and another, from the talk and gossip among the students at Lincoln's Inn, from his experience with Sir Thomas Egerton, one of the great who had power over prisons, and from his own visits to the Clink to see his brother and, earlier, his uncle, John had more than the ordinary knowledge of London prisons. He was fortunate, if there could be any mitigation of disaster, that it was the Fleet. Few felons were there, mostly debtors and recusants, and many of them were of the better sort of person. There was—at a price—more comfortable accommodation for gentlemen. He remembered how callously he and Christopher and others used to jest about the way some of the prisoners lived there year after year, provided with their own furniture, waited on by their own servants, lacking only liberty. Only liberty; he had blasphemed.

The stench from the open sewer that was the Fleet ditch told him that he was nearly there. Looking out through one of the rents in the side of the litter, he saw the stone of the gateway, and a moment later he felt the litter set down and heard the porter's rough voice. It was time for the first of what he knew would be a steady flow of payments: money to the litter-bearers, money to the porter at the prison gate, a contribution to the alms box at the door, which he gave with a sudden rush of gratitude that he at least did not come here penniless with no resource against hunger and indignity.

The next hour or more was a nightmare. He struggled to keep on his feet while he waited to be taken to the warden, to keep his mind clear while he made the best arrangements he could for a room to himself in one of the messuages on the green court, and held out for permission to have Pierre attend him while he paid one after another the fees they claimed: the warden's fine of twenty-six shillings, merely for the privilege of getting in, the charge for the first week's diet, the clerk's fee, the gaoler's fee, the chamberlain's fee. This last one was the end, at least for the time being, and he was thankful to pay it, since it meant that he had finally come to a room up a twisting stone staircase, a square, dark room, icy, with an old, sour, fetid smell. It had a hearth, and fagots could be bought, but none were there now. A bed and a bucket made up the furniture; the mattress was hard and lumpy with old straw, the bedstead, as he soon discovered, a home to colonies of bed bugs. But bad as it was, he was glad to lie down. It seemed the ultimate degradation that his body should so betray him.

He sent Pierre away to find Christopher, and lay listening to the strange and sinister noises of the prison, enduring the throbbing and aching of his own body, trying to face calmly what had happened to him. The fact of prison walls, of closed doors, the blank in his knowledge of how this had happened and how long it might last, threw him into a panic of fear so shattering that for a time he could only lie there determined not to cry out, not to beat at the walls with his fists. The fit passed and his courage and his common sense reasserted themselves. Many a man was thrown into prison and got out again, to go on with his life as before. He himself as the Lord Keeper's secretary had been of assistance to more than one. He was fortunate that he had Pierre to run his errands for him, money enough to pay for elementary comforts and privacy. The first essential was not to let himself be forgotten. He must write letters, letters, letters, until he touched their sense of justice, their compassion, their self-interest or only their weariness, until they let him out again.

He would write first to Sir George. In his mind the letter took form in rolling sentences, balanced and potent; sometimes he took a phrase from an early sentence to use it to more effect in a later one, but when he tried to repair the first sentence, he forgot the later one; and so he toiled, more and more troubled, and did not know he dreamed till he felt Pierre shaking his shoulder and he woke to a new calamity.

"Mr. Brooke was not in his room, nor anybody else. The porter was not at his post when I went in, but I found him when I went out and I got it from him. Mr. Brooke is in prison too, sir. He was taken up at noon."

"Where? Is he here?"

"No, sir. In the Marshalsea. Mr. Brooke left word for you with the porter. He said to tell you—he was sure you would be inquiring—that he is in the Marshalsea. His brother has been taken up too, but where he is, Mr. Brooke does not know."

Now, it seemed, he had reached the lowest depth. He had ruined his friends as well as himself. (And Anne? What had he done to her? He thrust the thought of her away; he could not bear to think of her now.)

"You must go to the Marshalsea directly. See Mr. Brooke, if they will let you. If not, give the porter this money for him— and you must fee him well or he will keep it for himself. Mr. Brooke will need money there and he may have been surprised with little on hand. Then go home and get a pot of broth for me and bring it back. You can heat it up in the warden's kitchen, no doubt, if you pay for the privilege. Do you understand what you are to do? This for Mr. Brooke, this for the porter and this for the warden's cook."

Soon after Pierre had gone, the chamberlain came in with a dish of greasy meat and John bargained with him for a candle, a table and a stool. The chamberlain was a clumsy fellow with one eye, which gave him an ill-favored look, but he brought the things that were needed and John decided, paying him what he demanded, that greed rather than cruelty was the mainspring of his life. At the door he looked back to say that the gates were now locked, the porter had gone home to his supper and John need not think to see his servant again that day.

The smell of the prison food, added to those other smells of mustiness and old urine, sickened John's stomach and dizzied his head, so that after all he could not write his letters that day. He blew out the candle and went back to bed, where he lay shivering in his clothes, devoured by vermin.

All around him he could feel the mass of the prison, its floors and corridors, its cold, dirty stone staircases, its courts and turrets, its occupants in all their degrees, the poor crowded in the common wards, the rich in their chambers, the poor devils who rebelled in the dungeon, where they might die in their chains and nobody remember to take the bodies away, and somewhere in some pleasanter corner, the warden himself, who lived in some state, the lord of this unwholesome manor, signed himself Esquire and grew rich on the misery of other men.

He slept fitfully and some time in the night was startled out of his sleep by a sudden outburst of maniacal yells and screams coming from across the court. He started up, thinking that the prisoners must be mutinying, before he remembered that he had heard that they often broke out like this in the common wards, out of sheer wanton mischief, to disturb one another, even blowing horns when one of their number was dying.

Awake, he tried to gather his wits, to find some way to extricate himself from this intolerable situation. If his sky had fallen in upon him—and for the present it had—he had, he recognized, helped to bring it down upon himself. To marry a girl without her father's consent was against the law and a punishable offense. Yet men had done it before and fathers either yielded or cast off their daughters. It was madness to cause the dismissal of a son-in-law, however undesirable he might be, from the only work he could do to support the daughter. But if Sir George intended neither to come around nor to cast off his daughter? There was yet another possibility and the longer he thought about it, the more sure he became that this was what Sir George was set upon. He would cast off the son-in-law and keep the daughter. For that he had gone to the ecclesiastical court, to have the marriage declared void.

John heaved and turned on his pallet as if he wrestled

physically as well as mentally with the thought. The Archbishop would appoint three Commissioners to consider the case, and it would take time before they came to it. They had acted already, either through the insistence of Sir George or on their own motion, by imprisoning John, and not only John but Samuel and Christopher. But had they not, he wondered, by that very act indicated their verdict? When they imprisoned all three of them, were they not admitting implicitly that a marriage, an indissoluble marriage, had taken place? That, therefore, Anne was his, and however he might be punished for having married her as he had, no one could take her away from him? He thought of her, little and lithe inside her stiff brocades, of the tender whiteness of her skin, her purity, the truth that shone from her; with all his heart he hoped her father had not terrified her.

In the morning as soon as it was light he got up and dragged himself to the table to write to Sir George.

> Sir,—The inward accusations in my conscience, that I have offended you beyond any ability of redeeming it by me, and the feeling of my Lord's heavy displeasure following it, forceth me to write, though I know my fault makes my letters very ungracious to you . . .

He kept himself doggedly humble throughout. Only once, in a paragraph freighted with a long, involved and somewhat incoherent sentence, as he tried to reason with Sir George, did his feelings erupt.

> How little and how short the comfort and pleasure of destroying is, I know your wisdom and religion informs you. And though perchance you intend not utter destruction, yet the way through which I fall towards it is so headlong, that, being thus pushed, I shall soon be at the bottom, for it pleaseth God, from whom I acknowledge the punishment to be just, to accompany my other ills with so much sickness as I have no refuge but that of mercy, which I beg of him, my Lord, and you, which I hope you will not repent to have

afforded me, since all my endeavours and the whole course of my life shall be bent to make myself worthy of your favour and her love, whose peace of conscience and quiet I know must be much wounded and violenced if your displeasure sever us.

He added a short sentence stiff with his repentance, submission and hearty desire to do anything satisfactory to Sir George's just displeasure, and waited impatiently for Pierre, who came at length bringing soup and news.

He had got in to see Mr. Brooke, who was in a room with five others, very angry and alarmed. He was due at the York Assizes, where he had much business to do. His brother, he said, was in the Clink. He sent his love to Mr. Donne and thanked him for the money, which would be very useful, but he begged Mr. Donne to lose no time in persuading Sir Thomas to intercede for them all.

While he waited for Pierre to take the letter to Sir George and return, John applied himself to a letter to Sir Thomas. It was not easy to write so humbly to Sir Thomas. He had, after all, done nothing to dishonor his house; he had worked well and faithfully for him, and his only fault was that he had offended the Lord Keeper's brother-in-law. He could not suppress the feeling that however Sir George might rage in his first fury, it would have been the better part for Sir Thomas not to yield so quickly to his demands that the secretary be dismissed. Yet Sir Thomas held the key; he was, John had seen in his work with him, a just man: stern, self-important but on the whole just; he saw himself as a man of justice.

John drew a breath and began:

To excuse my offence, or so much to resist the just punishment for it, as to move your Lordship to withdraw it, I thought till now were to aggravate my fault. But since it hath pleased God to join with you in punishing thereof with increasing my sickness, and that He gives me now audience by prayer, it emboldeneth me also to address my humble request to your Lordship . . .

173

As if God and the Lord Keeper were equal partners. It was none too subtle, but flattery at Court must wear the brightest colors and the extremest styles if it was to be seen at all. He was at any rate desperately sincere when he signed himself, "Your Lordship's most dejected and poor servant."

When Pierre had once more departed, John sat on at the table, his heavy, hot forehead resting on his left hand, his right hand tracing idle circles and triangles with his pen. Though his mind told him that out of his persistent letters, out of the essential wisdom and compassion of those two powerful and angry gentlemen, out of the very force of his own destiny, would come, sooner or later, release and perhaps even restoration; yet from some deeper, sadder recesses of his heart another knowledge compelled his pen into forming words that developed, as he watched, into the shortest of his poems:

> *John Donne*
> *Anne Donne*
> *Undone.*

2 He was released the next day from the Fleet, permitted because of his illness to return to his lodgings and continue his imprisonment there, with a jailer to guard him.

"Whose orders were they, do you know?" he said to Pierre as the man helped him into his own clean, sweet, soft, inexpressibly comfortable bed. "Oh, this is heaven. Was it Sir George More? Or the ecclesiastical Commissioners? Or the Lord Keeper?"

Pierre looked up from busying himself with his master's discarded clothes, which he was handling disdainfully with the tips of his fingers.

"The Lord Keeper's—on Lady Derby's motion. I had it from Denis, the underfootman, you know, sir, who is a friend of mine from my own village. Her ladyship couldn't endure to think of you in prison and sick."

John lay back against the pillows, digesting this piece of information. He was indeed grateful to Lady Derby—her little crumpled face with the bright eyes shone in his imagination like an angel's—but he wished that it might have been the Lord Keeper's own impulse. His willingness to mitigate John's plight at his wife's request did not necessarily mean that he had softened toward John in his own mind or that he would do anything more for him.

Dropping the question as unanswerable, he turned to the more immediate problem of money. The amount that it had cost him for his three days in the Fleet and his return home startled him into realization of what the two Brookes were suffering on his account, and he dispatched Pierre forthwith to the Marshalsea and the Clink with purses for his friends.

It took a large part of the money he had left, and there sat the gnome-like, red-nosed jailer, alternately sighing and snoring in his armchair, who must be paid, and paid well, for the Lord knew how many days or weeks into the future.

At the end of a fortnight, as if someone had calculated to a nicety how much money John had, the jailer was called off. Giving him, for joy, a groat more than was asked of him, John was free again and very nearly penniless. He had still a little money out at loan and some valuable books that he could sell, but that was all.

XVI

🔲🔲🔲🔲🔲🔲🔲🔲🔲🔲🔲🔲🔲🔲🔲🔲🔲🔲

THE VERY WEATHER WAS YOUNG AND EXUBERANT, a few white clouds sailing high, the sun bright and warm, the wind flinging itself about from this direction and that, bending the trees along the river bank, tugging at John's cloak, sending a sudden spray of drops into his face as he stepped onto the wharf. He was a free man, a well man, and he was filled to the brim with exultation. His body, purged of its ill humors, felt light and new; not tireless, for he was conscious that his reserves of strength were small, but tremulous with fresh-springing health.

"Eastward Ho!"

He took the first wherry that came and stood, not bothering to find a seat, for he was going only to Blackfriars Stairs. The river was full of craft, the Queen's swans swimming majestically among them; people's voices were louder than usual and cheerful; a boatload of young men with lutes went singing past.

His jailer was gone: called off, paid off, vanished. Christopher and Samuel were free and his mind at ease about them, relieved of the nagging shame and grief that they had come to disgrace and loss through their friendship for him. Samuel had returned to Cambridge, Christopher had gone to York to engage in what was left of the Assizes and to face his formidable mother.

He himself was on his way to see Sir George More. It seemed as if he were coming to the end of a dark tunnel. To meet his father-in-law, to hear and answer the charges against him, was

176

at last something to take hold of, something to do. He was confident that in that actual presence, where his face could be seen, his voice heard, his honesty felt, he could shake himself of the imputations laid upon him. The mere fact that Sir George had suddenly consented to see him was encouraging. He knew that his friends had been active in his behalf, Francis Woolley, Lady Derby, Mrs. Herbert, who still felt kindly toward him, even though it was from her house that Anne had slipped away to be married. He wished that he could think that the Lord Keeper had softened toward him, but he knew that Sir Thomas had taken too firm a stand to reverse himself easily; only the man who had persuaded him into it could persuade him out of it.

He was, at all events, sure of Anne. The Commission had not yet acted officially, but Mrs. Herbert had told him that they had privately informed Sir George that they must confirm the marriage. It was inconceivable, John told himself, that those two powerful and fatherly men, Sir George More and Sir Thomas Egerton, should, when forced to acknowledge the marriage, persist in denying him the means of supporting his wife.

He paid the boatman and, getting off at Blackfriars Stairs, started up the hill by Baynard's Castle and came again to the house in the shadow of Paul's where he had met Anne that day of their wedding that now seemed so long ago. Half expecting to find her here again, he knocked at the door, was admitted by the porter and led by a footman up a shallow flight of stairs into the hall. Sweating lightly, for so much depended upon this interview, he came into the long, elegant room with its flowery tapestries and new gilded plaster ceiling.

There were several people in it, but not, he saw at once, Sir George. Out of a cluster of children, little girls in curls and long, full skirts, a small boy with a large book in his hands, Mrs. Herbert came rustling toward him.

"Good morrow, Mr. Donne. I rather thought you would come today."

He bent over her hand to kiss it. "I came at once, madam, as soon as I had your message. I scarcely know how to thank you."

"Hold your thanks for the present—until we see what is the issue of this venture. Thomas, dear boy, you be finding the place in the book and I'll come back and read to you in a few minutes. Come along into the parlor, Mr. Donne. You'll have privacy there and I'll send for Sir George."

Her voice was cheerful and warm, her manner maternal. Though she was only a few years older than John, she was a widow and the mother of ten children, the eldest three years married.

"Edward and Mary have gone hawking," she said, leading the way, "with a party of young people. I sent them off. I thought it would be good for them." Her voice clouded. "The baby died. So disappointing, after living for nearly three months. A little boy . . ."

It was good of Mrs. Herbert, John thought, to take up his cause so warmly, for she was no friend to unauthorized, improvident, passionate marriages.

"Now, you wait here for Sir George. I'll leave you here alone. Are you feeling quite well again, Mr. Donne? You look a little transparent to me."

"It must be translucent, rather, dear Mrs. Herbert. My heart feels so light, thanks in large part to you, that it must shine through."

"Don't glow too brightly too soon. Sir George has said only that he will see you. Now I am going—and I hope you will prevail."

She gave him an encouraging pat on his shoulder and rustled out, leaving him melted by her kindness and her grace. He wondered, while he waited in the little paneled room, whether she was now sending Sir George off with a pat and an exhortation to lenience. John smiled, thinking of her; a very managing lady, and how lovable.

The door opened. His smile faded and re-formed itself tentatively. He bowed low and silently.

Sir George planted himself in front of the hearth, where there was no fire because of the unseasonable warmth of the day, cleared his throat loudly but vouchsafed nothing more. He stood there drawn to his fullest height, hands clasped behind him, shoulders rigid, head thrown back; the small face with the cold blue eyes and red beard was flushed and the lips pressed firmly together. John, standing in front of him like a schoolboy before his master, tried not to look taller than Sir George.

"Well?" said Sir George testily.

"I am grateful to you, sir, for consenting to see me. As I have written you, I know my offense and I acknowledge it humbly, and I crave your pardon. But, sir, I intended no disrespect or injury to your house."

He paused. Sir George frowned and said nothing.

"Could you not put that one sin on the scales against the punishment I have received? Take off the weight of those ill reports —which I can clear myself of—and my fault will be more nearly balanced by what I have suffered for it."

"Mr. Donne, I have consented to see you, reluctantly. I ask you to be brief."

"I should not trouble you but that I fear malice has raised some ill reports of me which I could smoke away to your satisfaction, if only I had the chance. I hear that you have been told —that you believe—I have deceived some young gentlewomen——"

"I have it on good authority, Mr. Donne—your own."

"I am twenty-nine, Sir George, and I have lived in the world; my life has been by no means spotless. But I feel sure that report has doubled my debt. I give you my word, I have done nothing to dishonor any young girl of gentle blood or bring disgrace to her parents. If you will ask my friends, sir, who have observed my life, they will, I am confident, set your mind at ease."

"Your friends have already been very eloquent in your behalf and I am willing to concede that their devotion is to your credit. But you have condemned yourself out of your own mouth." He blew out his cheeks and tugged at the purse that hung from his girdle, bringing out at length a folded sheet of paper, which he flung onto the table. "What do you say to that?"

John picked it up and saw, in handwriting that he did not recognize, a copy of an elegy that he had written fully ten years earlier. "Once and but once found in thy company, All thy supposed escapes are laid on me . . ." His eye ran down it; it was a long time since he had read it.

Half exasperated by the ill chance that had raked up this bit of foolishness from his irreverent youth, half relieved by the ease with which he could prove its insignificance, he said:

"I thought it very witty when I wrote it, but I was no more than eighteen or nineteen. I sought to mock the sugared sonnets others were turning out like identical sweet cakes all with the same stamp, by writing cynical verses in unpoetic language." His eyes fell on the lines he had once thought so daring and the phrase "hydroptic father" leapt up at him. It purported to be a young lover's description of secret meetings with a very young girl, of the father's spying and the mother's mean suspicions, of the betrayal of the young man by

> A loud perfume, which at my entrance cried
> E'en at thy father's nose; so were we spied.
> When, like a tyrant king, that in his bed
> Smelt gunpowder, the pale wretch shivered.
> Had it been some bad smell, he would have thought
> That his own feet, or breath, that smell had wrought.

Unpoetic indeed. John crumpled it vigorously and threw it into the fireplace. "I intended no actual persons at all—no young gentlewoman nor parents nor myself. I beseech you not to take my youthful evaporations as history."

"Even if I accept your explanation that the characters and the incident are imaginary, there is still self-betrayal in your poem, Mr. Donne. You have read enough, I am sure, to be aware that poets reveal themselves when they are least conscious of doing so. Your lover speaks of the food of his love being the hope of the father's goods. That hope is not——"

Feeling the blood hot in his face, John stooped and retrieved the crumpled poem from the cold hearth, spread it out and found, after some fumbling, the damaging words.

Though he hath oft sworn that he would remove
Thy beauty's beauty and food of our love,
Hope of his goods, if I were with thee seen,
Yet close and secret, as our souls, we've been.

"I can only repeat, sir, that this was an wholly imaginary affair, and written long before I even saw your daughter."

"That hope is not often," said Sir George, ignoring the interruption, "expressed in poetry, but it is a common enough state of mind in suitors. I will put it very plainly to you. I have no intention of marrying my daughter to a man who, having no fortune of his own, has his eye upon her father's. Her sisters have married men of substance or of substantial prospects. I intend that Anne shall do as well."

"I have no fortune, sir, it is true; but before he dismissed me I had worthy employment with the Lord Keeper, and the hope and promise of still better and higher service later. But this storm has shaken me to the root of my lord's favor. I love your daughter deeply, Sir George. I will be faithful to her and I will devote all my endeavors and my industry to making myself worthy of her and providing for her, but I am helpless unless I am reinstated in my lord Keeper's service. I do beseech your pardon and your assistance in my suit to my lord."

"You have, as I thought, no means of your own at all."

"I had. My father, who was warden of the Worshipful Company of Ironmongers, had me bred carefully and honestly and left me a creditable fortune. I enjoyed the sweetness and security of independence—and I had understanding enough to value it. But I admit I have spent it recklessly, not on sordid amusements, but on books and travel and on gifts to some who needed help. Then by the favor of your nephew, Francis Woolley and his lordship's son Thomas, with whom I was associated on the Islands Voyage, I obtained employment with the Lord Keeper, and I was for four years his lordship's secretary, not dishonest nor greedy. I shall not wrong you by implying that you intend to destroy me, Sir George, but in being dismissed from my lord's service, I have lost all. My imprisonment, furthermore, has cost me dear in every way. My charges, and those of the friends who were also imprisoned because of me, have cost me over forty pounds. I rust dangerously unless I can recover my place." He paused.

"Are you in debt?" said Sir George abruptly.

"I have some small debts, which I can order easily. But it is the future that concerns me. I have thought ceaselessly about what I might do. To seek preferment abroad is out of the question because that would mean separation from Anne. I might continue my legal studies, but it would be several years before I could provide for my wife through the practice of the law. It would be madness to seek employment with anyone else but the Lord Keeper. If I go to some other great man, he will say, 'Would the Lord Keeper have imprisoned and dismissed him if he had not done some other great fault that we have not heard about?' So that, in addition to my true weaknesses, I shall have the further burden of a suspicion that I am very much worse than I am."

Sir George stroked his beard uneasily. John thought that he had in some measure reached him.

"I do not wish to destroy you, Mr. Donne, nor to be the cause of your disgrace. I wish to keep my daughter out of your hands."

"Our marriage is a fact, Sir George. The Commissioners have said that they will confirm it; it is only a matter of time until they act. I intend to provide for your daughter by my own efforts, not asking anything at all of you but your help in restoring me to my lord Keeper's service. I know that he will not yield to my suit, but he might to yours, if you would be so charitable as to mediate with him for me."

"No, no. I could scarcely do that. I should look ridiculous."

"Most men perhaps could not do it, but yours is a larger, more compassionate nature. Just as good laws grow out of evil manners, so out of disobedience and boldness you could—if you would—show mercy and tenderness. I beg of you. It is our only hope."

Sir George walked to the window where he stood looking

out, saying nothing. John waited. He had said what he could. Silence swelled in the room like a great bubble that must soon burst. From St. Andrew's nearby came the sound of the churchbell, sweet and mellow. Sir George turned around.

"I do not like you, Mr. Donne. I shall not accept your marriage to my daughter as long as there is the slightest hope of undoing it. But I do not wish to take away your means of livelihood. I acknowledge that I have been hasty and passionate. It is my failing. I have tried to overcome it. I will speak to Sir Thomas for you."

His blue eyes were steady and disdainful; there was no yielding in them. Yet he had promised to do something that must be both disagreeable and humiliating to him—rather, John recognized, as something he owed to his idea of himself than to any real kindness for John. Still, he had given his word and it was possible to hope again.

"I am most humbly grateful, sir, I shall——"

Sir George nodded and turned away. John interposed himself hastily between him and the door and said:

"May I ask one thing more?" Without waiting for permission he hurried on, "I know that Anne is troubled. Will you give her ease by some kind and comfortable message—and may I, sir, have leave to write to her?"

For the first time Sir George's eyes softened. John saw in them not hate and contempt but suffering. "That too," said Anne's father wearily, and went away.

Left alone, John slowly folded his crumpled elegy into a small wad and stowed it in his purse. His exultant earlier mood had vanished; soberly he could count two substantial gains, but the road ahead looked long and stony.

2 Looking at the Lord Keeper's heavy, handsome countenance, which might have been carved out of stone, John felt his heart sink. He knew all of his master's expressions well: the look of fatherly kindness that had comforted and encouraged so many young men, himself, Francis Bacon, the Earl of Essex in his day; the keen, open look of danger apprehended and

faced; the look of decision, of anger, of abstraction. Any other expression would have held out a degree of hope, but this hard, shut face was evidence that he felt some threat to his dignity or his power, and no other consideration was of importance but the protection and preservation of the figure he had created of himself.

"I told Sir George," the Lord Keeper said, "that I thought errors might be overpunished, and I advised him to wait and reconsider. But he persisted and I yielded to his demands, though it inconveniences me seriously, for I do not know where to find another who will serve me as you have done. Now he rather absurdly importunes me to take you back. I have had to reply to him that it is inconsistent with my place and credit to discharge and readmit servants at the request of passionate petitioners."

"My services never had so much worth in them as to deserve the favors with which they were paid," murmured John, "but they had always so much honesty as that only this has stained them. I know my fault well and I acknowledge it; I know your lordship's disposition too, and that it inclines naturally to kindness. I beg of you, sir, to consider what must become of me if you turn me off."

For a moment Sir Thomas looked at John as if he really saw him. "I am sorry, Mr. Donne," he said, "but I can do nothing. I have taken, at Sir George's demand, a public stand. The Queen has expressed sympathy for her old friend; she has known Sir George since he was a little boy playing the lute for her when she visited his father at Loseley. Her Majesty has little patience with secret or ill-considered marriages. You have kicked the ladder out from under your own feet, I am afraid, and you must just drop back and find some other way to climb again. You can get no more help from me. Preferment at Court," he continued, fastidiously picking a piece of fluff off his velvet knee, "is a dangerous, slippery prize to grasp at. Even men of birth and fortune overreach themselves and topple to destruction. Men without either cannot afford even one small misstep—and you have blundered egregiously. My advice to you, John, is to

184

relinquish your bride to her father and return to the study of the law. You have aptitude and it is a safe and often profitable profession."

If this sensible, old-man's solution to his difficulties had ever occurred to John, he had not even for a moment admitted it into his consideration. He who before he met Anne had publicly professed fickleness in himself and pretended to admire inconstancy in women ("I can love her and her and you and you, I can love any if she be not true"), now had fallen headlong into a love serious, humble and intense; he had committed himself irrevocably to marriage and fidelity. If the sacrifice were proving itself to be greater than he had expected, it still was not too big a price to pay for Anne.

He listened submissively but untouched while Sir Thomas talked till he ran down, and then he took his leave.

As he walked along the gallery toward the tower stairs, on his way to his old closet to bundle together his possessions for Pierre to fetch, he was aware, as he had not been so keenly since the day of his first coming here, of the greatness and the magnificence of the house around him. The portraits on the walls, the arms painted on the glass of the windows, the gardens below and the river beyond were part of a paradise from which he had been expelled as ignominiously and as finally as those original apple-eaters. He fancied that the gentleman usher whom he met greeted him coldly and the manservant at the door lacked only a flaming sword.

On his way through the small parlor beyond the gallery he saw the curtains at the window stir, and he paused. A face peered around them, cautious at first, then suddenly bright with joy. Lady Elizabeth Stanley, the book she had been reading closed over her finger, burst out of her hiding-place.

"Oh, Mr. Donne! Have you come back to us?"

Nearly fifteen, she was a tomboy still, romping, intelligent, guileless. John, who loved her as he might a younger sister, reflected with amusement that they would have to do some intensive taming if they were to marry her, as it was rumored they intended, to Henry Hastings, the future Earl of Huntingdon.

"No, my lady. I have been banished. Irrevocably."

"Then you won't be my Prophet any longer?"

It was a jest between them. For a time, before the Parliament, she had persuaded her mother that she had a consuming interest in reading the Testament in Greek, and John had been assigned to give her lessons in his free hours. She had called him her Prophet, and though it was plain enough that she was moved more by hero-worship for her instructor than by love of learning, John had made her work and she had proved to be a conscientious pupil.

"No, but you can go on with your Greek by yourself—or get Mr. Downal to teach you," he added teasingly. Downal was Sir Thomas's other secretary, narrow, tight-lipped, obstinate, middle-aged.

She made a little face. "No, if I can't have my Prophet, I shan't have anyone—and the first great female Greek scholar will be lost to the world." Her small face grew serious. "I am really sorry, Mr. Donne." With a sudden grace that gave a glimpse of the woman she would someday be, she stretched out her hand for him to kiss. "I think Anne More," she said earnestly, "is very fortunate."

"Not Anne More—Anne Donne," he said, and his longing to have his wife in his arms was a sword thrust in his body.

3 After six weeks the ecclesiastical commission still had not given their verdict on the marriage. Privately the Commissioners had said that it was valid; officially they were still, behind closed doors, discussing the question. Sir George would not let Anne go until the court forced him to.

The sun streaming through the open window of John's study, warm on his bare head, was the sun of late April. The bookshelves behind him were stripped bare. Those books that he would take with him to Pyrford were packed in boxes waiting for the carrier; the rest he had sold to put some money in his pocket. The volume lying open before him on the table was

186

one that he had borrowed from Mr. Cotton, for whom he was doing some research and abstracting. He was being paid for it, but so little that he had had to put hack writing out of his mind as a means of livelihood.

In the bedroom his clothes too, all but what he wore and what he would carry with him strapped to the saddle, were packed. He waited only for the word that would release him to ride to Loseley and claim his wife—and that, day after day, was withheld.

At first, ruined and stripped of his work, his fortune, his credit, he had felt curiously lighthearted, even cleansed and free, as a boy feels on a summer day having shed his clothes and plunged into the river, or as a man sometimes feels when his house with all its contents has burned down and he stands suddenly free of the bonds of possession. If he could have gone to Anne then, the mood might have lasted and they could have shared it, rejoicing together in their release from the stifling weight of form and consequence. But the looked-for message failed to come; he began to feel chilled without his raiment, lost without his house; to taste the bitter flavor of penury and to know that the chains of poverty to which he had delivered himself to be bound were heavier to bear and cut deeper into the flesh than all the smothering weight of possessions.

At first he used some of his new leisure to go to plays, with which in his days at Lincoln's Inn he had enjoyed losing the hours, but he soon tired of the noise, the ranting, the falseness on the stage and the smell of the groundlings beneath it, the racket they made cracking nuts throughout the performance and crunching the shells underfoot. He had joined the wits in the tavern, drinking canary and talking—but less about poetry and more about patrons and who had found one than in earlier days. His closest friends were away, Christopher still in York and Wotton in Italy; acquaintances, he fancied, looked at him askance, as if ruin were contagious and might infect them too. Or they badly concealed their pitying smiles at his married and unmarried state.

A week earlier, Pierre had left him for more respectable employment. Pierre was a city man; he would not have followed even a prosperous master into the desert of country life.

John quelled in himself a rising panic at the thought of the insipid dullness of country life. Pyrford House was beautiful and comfortable, and he was immeasurably grateful to Francis for offering him and Anne a home there, but Pyrford was nearly as far from London as Loseley itself; it lay beside the Wey surrounded by fields and woods, open to the melancholy sounds of the owl and the cow, the whistle of the wind in the trees and the long, sad stillness of country nights.

It would not be for long, he told himself. Thankfully as they accepted the haven offered, it would be a haven only, a place to shelter from the storm, and when the wind died down and the waves subsided, he would go forth again and capture some prize or find some new land to settle on. In the meantime, while he was at Pyrford, he would study and write. He had stumbled and bruised himself on the canon law; he would master it in all its intricacies.

They were full of such plans, he and Anne. Sir George allowing letters to come and go, they wrote back and forth, planning, exploring, declaring their love, growing in knowledge as well as in love of each other.

He had done everything in his power to hurry the Commissioners; had given gifts to their clerks, had written letters and paid visits, and still they did not act. Sometimes he imagined them unable to find an hour that would suit them all to meet, or saw them putting his case aside as small and unimportant in comparison with others that claimed their attention; or he envisaged a stack of cases accumulated over months or even years, and his on the bottom of the pile. Then out of his dwindling funds he bribed another clerk to bring his affair to the top, to thrust it under their noses. At other times he pictured the three old men talking and quibbling, citing precedents, splitting hairs, arguing.

"For God's sake, hold your tongues and let me love!" he cried out as he had once before, and heard in his words the accents of a poem.

Jonson, when he wrote a poem—they had been discussing it only a few days before—wrote the idea down first in a prose paragraph and afterward translated it into poetry as into a foreign language. They had laughed at him, John and Gerrard and Cotton and one or two others who were there, but Ben had stuck doggedly to it, and some of his poems, John had to concede, justified the method. But it was not his way.

He pushed Cotton's book on early British land tenure aside, found a piece of paper with notes on one side, turned it over and wrote: "For God's sake hold your tongue and let me love!"

Two more lines came flowing as if they had lain coiled, waiting.

> *Or chide my palsy or my gout,*
> *My five gray hairs or ruined fortune flout . . .*

He began to think of the stanza form. Some poets used the quatrain over and over, or a pentameter couplet, but John prided himself on the variety of meters and stanzas of which he was master. So far no two of his poems were alike in their stanza form, except, of course, the elegies and satires. He decided on a nine-line stanza, the first and last lines of each one ending with the word "love," two different rhymes within the stanza. Could he find enough rhymes for love? Prove, approve, improve, move, remove, above, dove . . .

> *With wealth your state, your mind with arts improve;*
> *Take you a course, get you a place,*
> *Observe his Honor, or his Grace . . .*

He left three lines to be filled in later, and ended the first stanza with: "So you will let me love."

The next stanza would ask and answer the question, "Alas, alas, who's injured by my love?"

Fragments came floating into his mind like bits of wood drifting down a stream, and he fished them out and fitted them together.

What merchant ships have my sighs drowned?
Who says my tears have overflowed his ground?
...   .
Soldiers find wars and lawyers find out still
  Litigious men which quarrels move,
  Though she and I do love.

He threw the pen down and went to the cupboard to pour himself a glass of wine from what was left in the jug. Leaning against the window, he looked out over the river, toward the brick walls and turrets of Lambeth Palace, where in some small, square, dusty room on an inner court the three old men might even now at this very moment be signing their names to a decree on the case of John Donne, gentleman, and Anne Donne, his wife. He was willing, he thought, to lose everything —he *had* lost everything—for love; willing to die for it and by it; to leave the world and go to the country, as to a hermitage, for love. All that he asked—and dear God, it was surely not too much—was that they let him have her.

XVII

OUT OF THE CAVERN OF SLEEP, black as velvet, bottomless as death itself, he floated slowly up to consciousness, opened his eyes on a single shaft of sunlight that came through the slit between the curtains, closed them again and sank back into that enveloping, supporting darkness. But though he could shut out the sun with a blink of his eyes, a spreading glow of felicity followed him, drew him upward again, so that, his eyes still closed, his body blank and heavy, his mind stirred to ask, Why am I so happy? And immediately he was awake and aware, feeling her small, warm, silken body folded against his own; her breasts under his arm, her scented hair against his cheek. A wave of exultation flooded him; he wanted to wake her up to pour his joy on her, but wanted still more to lie there beside her, to guard her sleep, to think about her, to savor what she was.

It was a line from one of Jonson's poems, not one of his own, that came to him: "Oh so white, oh so soft, oh so sweet is she." But he would write poems for her that would describe her better; the whiteness, the softness, the sweetness, were only the smaller part of what she was. He cupped his fingers around the little, incredibly soft breast as gently as if were holding a small bird in his hand. She stirred, breathed deeply but did not wake.

He had known lust, and the distaste and weariness that followed after. He had known passion, but passion without tenderness and joy was only a dream of this that he knew now. He had read the vaporings of poets who swore that their ladies were all soul and that the body was nothing and he had mocked at them, yet with an uneasiness in his laughter. Now he had found what he had, though blindly, been seeking, what all would seek if they had imagination and faith enough to conceive of its possibility: a love so whole that it made of them a world complete, made of this room in which they slept, with its tall-posted bed and the parted curtains, a very universe, an everywhere.

He raised himself on his elbow to look down at her sleeping face—innocent, serene, the reddish lashes on the milky white cheeks, the straight little nose with the delicately cut nostrils, the red, parted lips, so tender, so vulnerable. He kissed them lightly and her eyes opened. In their limpid depths he could see himself reflected and knew that in his own eyes her face appeared.

For a second she looked at him blankly, then recognition dawned, her lips curved into a smile.

"John!"

All of the miseries, the doubts, the disappointments, fears, resentments, hopes deferred, vanished in this moment when his very life seemed to be beginning afresh.

"I wonder what we *did* till we loved, you and I——"

The breeze that followed the sun through the chink in the curtains was country air, sweet and pure, with a hint of the stables. The unfamiliar sounds of the house that was going to be their home for who could say how long came to him faintly: a rooster's shrill cry, the whinny of a horse, the laughter of maids in the dairy. They were in the wing overlooking, on one side, the courtyard where the work of the place went on and, on the other, a knot garden. They were quite self-contained, with their own parlor and dining room, and need see Francis only when they sought him or he them. It was a generous arrangement, one usual enough for young couples starting out, and if he could only have paid for their lodging—and if it were nearer London—it would have been, John thought, quite perfect.

"The sun is high," said Anne. "We ought to get up."

He pulled her down again. "Why? Just because it's light? Did we go to bed because it was dark? What have we to do that is more important than this?"

"Write me an *aubade,* to celebrate our first morning. What good does it do me to be married to a poet if he doesn't make poems for great occasions?"

"How shall I begin?"

"The way they all begin. Great Phoebus Apollo, bringing in the day . . ."

"No, I will never write for you such worn and tattered lines. Why should I hail him as a god? Busy old fool, unruly sun! Why dost thou thus Through windows and through curtains call on us?"

"You are so irreverent——"

"Why should he think himself so strong? I could eclipse him with a wink—but that I would not lose sight of you so long."

"And then?"

"Some other time. I will write it all for you, how we are the world, all kings and all states. Nothing else is. I will write it all for you—but not now."

BOOK THREE 1603-1614

"And find
What wind
Serves to advance an honest mind."

XVIII

MOTHER DAWES, THE MIDWIFE, had been there a week, waiting.

"She's small and narrow," she told John privately, in the orchard where he had sought her out. "It comes hard with that kind. But she's high-hearted. She won't go all to pieces, like some that has it easier."

She was the first midwife he had ever met. He had pictured an old crone, full of wise saws, flaunting the mysteries of her craft, toothless and not very clean, but she was middle-aged, neat, matter-of-fact, with strong, deft hands. She lived on the outskirts of Guildford, where she had a little house of her own, and she was known and respected the country round.

The pains began early in a gray afternoon in late March. John saw Anne's eyes widen and darken, saw her catch her breath and seem to listen. He watched her anxiously, suspending his voice in the middle of a sentence until he saw her breathe easily again.

"Shall I call Mother Dawes?"

But Mother Dawes, summoned by Anne's maid, Alice, said briskly, "It will be a good time yet. Keep walking."

So they walked up and down the gallery, John and Anne together, to the end and back again. The long, narrow room ran across the full width of the front of the house, its windows looking out on the half-mile-long avenue of elms leading from the road. Among the bare tops of the trees they could see the red tile roof and tiny steeple of the church on its little hill above

197

the river. Francis was in Richmond; they had the house to themselves.

Anne had proved to be one of those women whom pregnancy made more beautiful; it smudged her eyes with shadow and spread the delicate fan of her nostrils, widened her sensitive, generous mouth. Her slender body with its living freight became not clumsy but stately, and from the depths of her clear heart welled up a carefree joy and a dreaming serenity that seemed to John, who grew more nervous and apprehensive as her time drew near, to surround her with a shining, almost a holy, aura.

"It's going to be a boy," said Anne, "and we'll call him John."

"Or, better, George?"

They were only eight miles from Loseley and still there was no sign from Anne's father. Her younger sister Frances, now fourteen, rode over to Pyrford sometimes, attended by a groom, to see Anne, but she brought no messages, even after she had taken home the news of Anne's pregnancy. All of Sir George's children—and his other sons-in-law as well—loved their fiery parent, and John had seen Anne's wistful expression as she waited for some sign from him. Fathers before this had been known to soften to grandsons named for them; John was willing to try.

"No, my first son must be John."

For a time she talked about him, till all interest was swallowed up in pain. The drops standing out on her forehead, her bitten lips and the tight clutch of her fingers alarmed John; he was relieved when Mother Dawes, before he had time to call for her again, came to take Anne away to the bedroom, where he saw, following along behind them, a kettle of water steaming on the fire and Alice knotting a folded bed sheet to the post.

"It will be some time yet, sir. Why do you not go take a walk or ride abroad? This is woman's work, sir."

He went into their parlor, where his books were lined up on shelves around the walls, and tried to concentrate on Pico della Mirandola, but his ears were cocked for every rustle of sound from the room beyond. When a moan on a rising note of terror escaped from beyond that door, he shuddered and buried his head in his hands. His was the guilt that every father knew, the worn-out joke of the unthinking, but more than that, for he had brought Anne estrangement from her father, wifehood without security, motherhood without the sure prospect of an honorable launching for her child.

The clatter of hooves took him to the window, from which he could see Francis dismounting in the courtyard below. He went down to greet him.

"What's amiss? Anything wrong with Anne?"

"She's in labor."

"Long?"

"All afternoon."

"Oh, then it will be over soon and you'll be a father before you know it. Come have some supper with me. I am starved."

While Francis went to wash, John hurried back to see how Anne was doing.

"It's slowed down," said the midwife at the crack of the door. "That often happens. No need to fret yourself, sir."

Her cap was awry and a long, lank wisp of hair hung down over her forehead.

"May I see her—just for a minute?"

The room was shadowy in the twilight, lit only by the yellow glow from the fire. Anne lay writhing and gasping on the bed, reduced to a mound of suffering flesh. "It hurts," she said piteously through swollen lips.

She was so young. He tried to remember, bending to kiss her wet forehead, what he had heard about birth; it was better, he thought they said, when the mother *was* young, her bones and muscles soft, not brittle; flexible, not stiff and set. And what of their child, struggling to be born? Where was his soul now? When did original sin enter into his purity? Only the child Zoroaster laughed at his birth; all others came weeping into the world head first into calamities.

"She'll forget all this when she has a fine boy in her arms," said Mother Dawes briskly, pushing him toward the door.

It was all through the house that Anne was in labor and that it was going slowly. A knot of maid servants whispering together broke apart and scurried away as John came down the stairs into the hall. In the dining room where Francis had already begun to eat the steward said sympathetically, "I'm the father of six myself, sir, and I can tell you after the first it's easier."

Six! The incredible callousness of some men. The thought of even a second was unendurable.

The candles in the tall silver holders had been lit. A big meat pie was brought in and in spite of feeling grossly insensitive John took some and fell on it hungrily.

"The Queen is dying," said Francis abruptly.

It had been whispered for several weeks; the rumor had sent Francis to Richmond; yet the doctors said that there was nothing really wrong, nothing from which she could not recover.

"She is only sixty-nine," said John.

"And sick of no disease that anyone can name; not even of old age. But she's dying nonetheless. All last week she sat on cushions on the floor with her finger in her mouth, saying nothing, looking into space. The only time she spoke was when Sir Robert Cecil said to her, 'Madam, you must go to bed,' and she answered, 'Little man, little man, must is a word not used to princes.'"

"How like her," murmured John, with admiration for her spirit. He had disliked her for her harshness to Catholics, resented her treatment of Essex, but now that her long reign was all but over, he could see the lonely courage, the devotion to England's good, the will to rule wisely.

"They have got her to bed now and her bedchamber is full of people waiting—the lords of the Privy Council, her ladies, my lord Archbishop praying till he sways with weariness, all standing crowded there drinking up the air. I got as far as the Presence Chamber myself." He waved his hand toward the cupboard and a serving man hastened to bring him a cup of ale. "Is this the new brew?" he said critically. "It's too light this time. I stayed at Richmond," he went on, "but I heard from John Egerton that all London is waiting in silence. It is uncanny, he says. The law courts are not sitting, the shops are closed, people move quietly, with long faces, not a bell rings, not a trumpet sounds. I suppose England has never had a sovereign who has been loved as she has been."

John thought of the times he had seen her: sailing down the river in the royal barge to the sound of music, passing through the Presence Chamber while all knelt, tottering under the weight of her robes the day that the Parliament opened. "The common people worship her. Yet there's a feeling in some quarters—you must have seen it—that the present age has turned sour and it is time for something new. Excuse me, Francis, I'll just run up and see what's happening."

Francis had lit his pipe when John came down again looking white around the mouth. "It goes on and on."

"God, I'm glad I'm not a woman, aren't you?"

John could not sit still but walked up and down the dining room, paying no attention to what Francis was saying till one sentence out of the monologue caught his attention:

"At any rate, she's indicated her successor."

"The King of Scots, of course?"

"Not so *of course* as all that. There's the lady Arabella Stuart and the Earl of Lennox——"

"I think they have no more chance of it than my lord of Northumberland, who stands eighth in line." He heard his own voice uttering words that appeared to have meaning, but his mind was not in them. It was upstairs in that dim, anguished room.

"They say he has been in correspondence with the King— along with several others, including Cecil and your friend Wotton, who, by the way, is in Edinburgh now, I hear."

"Northumberland wants mercy for the Catholics. Wotton wants an ambassadorship. What brought the Queen to acknowledge King James? Who dared to broach the subject?"

"The Archbishop. He asked her if she wished to name him her successor and she nodded. That was all, a nod. But it will be enough."

John stopped his pacing and sat down again. "There will be many changes. I wonder if he will fill all the offices with Scots."

"It is to be in the agreement that he shall not."

"They have arranged everything, have they not, while Her Majesty lies dying." *And I sit and talk of her and them. While my child is born and perhaps my wife dies.*

"It is Cecil who does everything. He has guards everywhere to ensure that there will be no disturbance, that the throne will be passed over peacefully—and his own power continued."

A candle guttered and the wax dripped onto the table.

"I wonder what he's like, the King of Scots. He must have some strength to have whipped those Scots lords into line—no mean feat for a man who started with the handicap of being a child king."

"One thing has come out. The Queen has been helping him to the tune of two thousand pounds a year or more."

When the table had been cleared of dishes and taken down, they moved their chairs in front of the fire; a flagon of sack and two Murano glasses stood on a small table between them. Insensibly, with the firelight and the wine, John's tension eased.

"There will be, surely, a new hand of cards all around. Perhaps now I can get something besides treys and deuces. What is his line, d'you think, the Scot's?"

"It's said he's scholarly, writes sonnets, has actually published over his royal name a treatise on demonology."

"Scholarly—and believes in witches?"

"And very religious. If I succeed in becoming a gentleman of the bedchamber—and that is all I want—I'll whisper in his ear about my cousin Mr. Donne, who will write him an elegy or a treatise on the law of sanctuary."

"Who will graciously accept a secretaryship or the post of ambassador to Muscovy . . ."

The wind howled around the chimneys and rattled the windows, drowning out a climactic shriek of anguish from the west wing above and a baby's first wail.

One of the young footmen brought the news, having been

pounced on and dispatched by Mother Dawes, who in her moment of triumph was too grand to come herself.

"It's a girl, Mr. Donne, and Mrs. Donne is ready to see you."

The room that had been like a battleground had been restored to peace, the kettles and knotted sheets removed, the tumbled bed in order. Barely making a ridge under the smooth coverlet, Anne lay weary and radiant, curling her arm around a small, tightly swaddled, red-faced morsel, bald and wrinkled but palpably alive, a new soul in a new body, launched by the mystery of birth onto the mysterious sea of life.

"It's a girl. Are you very disappointed?"

John knelt beside her, afraid to touch either her or the baby with his heavy, secular, masculine hand. "It's what I most wanted. We'll name her Anne."

"Not Anne, Constance. For our"—her voice came with difficulty—"constancy."

It was shortly after midnight in the early morning of March 24, 1603. An hour or two later the Queen died.

They found a wet-nurse for Constance, a young woman in the village of Pyrford whose breasts were so bursting with milk that her own surprisingly puny baby could not drink it all. She was clean and healthy and the wife of one of the Pyrford House gardeners—it was important to Anne that she was married, though John privately could not see that milk out of wedlock would be any less nourishing—and her cottage was near enough for them to walk through the park and across the meadows every day or two to gaze at their baby and see how much she had changed since the last time.

April flowed into May and still London waited for her new King. He had left Edinburgh at the end of March, as if he had been all packed up and ready, awaiting only the word, and was making a slow and stately progress southwards, delaying as long as possible the entry into London, where the plague raged, stopping at the great houses, eating and hunting and making new knights by the score, causing the rumors to fly—of his uncouth body, his fear of crowds, his love of the chase, his Scots followers, avid, shabby, actually lousy, some said.

Everybody who had the slightest excuse for doing so and many who had not went north to be in the crowd that hung about him, to see, to make themselves seen, to hunt for a toehold. Francis, scorning what he heard about the opportunists who flocked like hungry jackals, waited till the King was as near London as Theobalds, the great house that Cecil had inherited from his father, and then he, too, left.

John and Anne, left alone at Pyrford House, enjoyed a golden time suspended between the stress of childbirth and the inevitable tensions of the future, when John must find some way to support his wife and child, to make a place in the world for his talents and his potentialities. They walked warily, carrying their happiness carefully, as if it were a precious treasure that they carried in a fragile bowl. It had been bought at a great and continuing cost, and each was painfully aware of what the price had been to the other.

XIX

"KNIGHTHOODS," SAID SIR FRANCIS WOOLLEY LIGHTLY, "are a penny a dozen."

He had got his at the Charterhouse, where with several hundred others he had welcomed the new King on his approach to London. Not all of those who thronged there had been knighted, but full three hundred had, enough for the minority to feel slighted.

From the Charterhouse the King had gone to Whitehall and from there he took barge for the Tower. After shooting the Bridge, he had remained in the barge to watch the ordnance on Julius Caesar's Tower. On the Tower Wharf, twenty-one hundred pieces were shot off with a huge noise. All the bells had rung; all the people who were not sick with the plague or tending the sick came out to see the new king.

"He doesn't like to be looked at—not like the old Queen. He rides in an open carriage, but he has his gentlemen ride in closed order around him so that he cannot be seen."

"Is he afraid of the people?" said John.

"He may be. He's a timid man. If he were not a King, one would call him a coward."

Francis at twenty-one, a courtier and a land-owner of some importance, had lost the look of transparent fairness that when he was fifteen had so charmed and touched John. His thin, soft hair had turned biscuit-colored, his nose had grown larger, as noses unexpectedly do, his mouth was firmer. With an air of authority he was marking out the place where he wanted the banqueting house put. It was to be, after all, a temporary affair, a platform and roof with open sides, a place to sit after dinner, looking at the river and the church, eating nectarines, singing madrigals. He had two men following him with a hammer and stakes. Now and then he would take the hammer from one and a stake from the other and pound in the stake to mark where the banqueting house was to go.

"That apple tree will have to come down," he said, pointing and one of the men ran to tie a bit of red cloth to the apple tree.

"Do you think it will be done in time?" said Anne.

"It must be done in time. If I put enough men on it, they can finish it. But I started to tell you a story that is going the rounds about the number of knights that have been made. One man says to another, 'Is that a gentleman walking there?' The other says, 'No, it's only a knight.' "

"Who else has been created—that I know?" said John.

"John Egerton. Henry Wotton. Nick Carew. Wotton's to go ambassador to Venice, by the bye."

"How's that? I didn't know he was in England."

"It appears that he and the King are fast friends. He went to Sterling a year ago, disguised as an Italian, to carry letters from the Duke of Tuscany warning the Scot of a plot against his life."

So Harry was back on the ladder, and on a high rung, evidently.

"He's a good man," said John. "He deserves a change in fortune."

"The Lord Keeper has been made Lord Chancellor and Baron Ellesmere."

"So I heard." Sir Thomas Egerton had risen, and if John had still been his secretary, he no doubt would have risen too.

"The King went from the Tower Wharf to Westminster by barge and went on the next morning to Windsor. He's running no risk of getting the plague."

"That is understandable—with nearly thirty thousand dead of it already. My sister's husband, William Lyly, came up from Hawstead to London to see a man on business, caught the plague and died in three days."

"The Court will stay out of London all summer and Their Majesties will go on progress."

"When do they come here?"

For this was the reason for the banquet hall and all the things that were arriving from London every time the carrier came: the Turkey carpet to put on the floor in what was already being referred to as the "King's Room," the beautiful little basin and ewer of *repoussé* silver, of which Anne had said, holding it carefully in her hand and looking at it curiously:

"Isn't it rather small?"

"It's the size he likes. He has skin like silk—they say it's because he never puts water on it, only wipes the tips of his fingers with a dampened cloth."

The King would come to Pyrford House in the course of his progress and from here go on to Loseley: the King and all his gentlemen, the Queen and her ladies, and in their train earls and countesses, barons and new-made knights, officials of the Court and hangers-on of all descriptions. Now while all was new and fluid was the time of opportunity, when an introduction might mean an office, a presentation could be followed by a knighthood; when all the men whom the King met were new to him and a face, a voice, a leg, would speak for their owners unclouded by any previous knowledge or prejudice, when the King's fancy might fall on a man and make his fortune for him, or at the least set him on the way to taking a part again in the business of the world.

"When did you say he was coming here?"

"Late in the summer. August, perhaps, or early September. The date's not set. But he is assuredly coming."

Francis pounded down the last of the stakes and, delicately dusting a crumb of sawdust from his gauntlets, spoke to his foreman. "Come into the office, Hamblen, and I'll show you the plan I've had drawn up. We've no time to waste, no time at all."

Anne and John stayed in the orchard. The apple blossoms were gone and the apples had set, tiny green balls not even so big as marbles.

"By the time they're ripe, the King will be here—or will have come and gone—" said Anne, "and this place will look like a shambles—all the grass trampled down and branches broken from the trees, the park a mess, trash everywhere. You'd be amazed at the kind of thing decent people—Court people—leave around behind them."

"Can you remember when the old Queen visited Loseley?"

"I remember faintly her first visit and giving her some flowers. The second time she came, she was older and she said beforehand that all the children were to be sent away. When we came back after she'd gone, the place looked as if an army had swept over it. All there was to suggest that the Queen had been there were the cushions she had embroidered for the maid-of-honor chairs, the flowers and leaves so finely wrought, the colors so delicate and bright. It was wonderful, wasn't it, that someone with a mind so like a man's and with a man's decisions to make could do such fine, feminine embroidery?"

John scarcely heard her; he was thinking of what the King's visit might mean for him.

2 The sound of hammering began early in the mornings and continued into the long summer twilights. In the beginning of the month it had a brisk, cheerful sound, toward the end a hurried, harried sound. Already the harbingers, the gentlemen from the Court who came to arrange lodgings in the neighborhood for the people who could not be accommodated in Pyrford House, had arrived. They swept through the nearby villages, surveying the houses, listing rooms and beds. Constance's wet-nurse was to have three grooms in her cottage. The vicar would take in five yeoman ushers. And when there still were not enough places for the crowd to sleep, it was decided that tents should be set up in the park.

Every day a carrier came loaded—with borrowed plate, knives and damask from friends in London, joint stools, trestle tables, bedsteads and bedding for the sitting rooms that were to be converted into bedrooms, new curtains for the King's Room, a new coverlet of crimson damask with silver lace, new screens, new tapestries. Carts came from friends with gifts of game, of pastry, of wines. The King's Room and the dining parlor where the King and Queen would have their meals had Turkey carpets on the floors; all the other rooms would have fresh rushes: water mint, rosemary, meadow-sweet, woodruff. When the old rushes were swept away, three silver buttons supposed lost turned up, as well as a broken pipe, a seal that nobody recognized, and some pieces of marchpane, dirty and hard as rocks.

A fashionable goldsmith, attended by two apprentices, brought down from London the gift that Francis had ordered for the King. It was a gold standing cup, decorated with nymphs and garlands. While they all stood about in the hall admiring it, Sir George More came in.

He greeted Francis; his glance, passing over the gold cup, swept about the room till it found Anne. It was more than a year since he had seen her.

She hurried to kneel for his blessing as if she were still a child. He put his hand on her head and his eyes filled with the quick tears of his emotional nature. John stood hesitating, not knowing what to do; then, beside Anne, he went down on one knee.

"Get up, get up, both of you," said Sir George. "I forgive you, though you don't deserve it. And don't interrupt me. I came to talk with Sir Francis about the King's visit."

Seeing his tears, the gentleness of his hand touching Anne, the quick warmth of his smile, John for the first time understood why his children so loved their hot-tempered parent, and felt in himself the ice of his resentment beginning to melt. Whatever Sir George might profess to be the occasion of his visit, it was clear enough that his real purpose was to reconcile himself with Anne. For her sake John was thankful to have the estrangement ended, for he knew that she had felt it sorely; for his own part, he was ready to be on good terms with his father-in-law, to respect and even to like him. And if the old gentleman should so far soften as to give Anne the money that she inherited from her mother, that would be acceptable.

"I don't believe," Sir George said to Francis, "that it will be possible for us to lend each other furnishings. I might lend you plate—but you would not be able to return it before the royal visitors get to Loseley. Now, sit down, Francis, and I'll tell you what I know from experience about entertaining royalty."

When he left, just before he mounted his horse, he said to Anne and John:

"Constance, is it? When all the royal visiting is over, you must bring her to Loseley to see me."

3 John's first sight of the King was a fleeting one. He heard the trumpets of the heralds and saw the horses, the open carriage with the feathers flying from the top, the King's gentlemen riding close, just as he had been told they did, to conceal the King from curious eyes. Of the King he could see nothing till the carriage came to a stop, the gentlemen parted and the King was getting up from the red velvet seat.

He had a glimpse of an overlarge head with protruding blue eyes and a thin beard, a body lost in fantastically padded clothes, legs that did not seem to be able to hold him up, for he tottered as he descended from the carriage and was supported by his gentlemen on both sides. There was about him the unmistakable aura of royalty, which, to John's mind, was worthy of reverence in itself. Kings were God's representatives on earth and commanded awe, whatever their personal deficiencies, but he felt sorry for this one, a stranger in England and surrounded by all the thrusting self-interest of the Court, the intrigues, the hidden hatreds and ambitions.

The Queen was a plump, yellow-haired, pink-faced little Danish woman who liked entertainment; she had endured Scotland for fifteen years; now she had come to England where it was gay and she had smiles for everything.

Around her were her ladies. John looked with interest at Lady Bedford, whom he had heard about but never met, though Bedford House stood in the Strand nearly opposite the Savoy. She was famed for her beauty, her love of poetry—indeed, she wrote verse herself—and her kindness to poets. "The favorite of the Muses" they called her, those who clustered around her, enjoying her patronage, writing their pretty poems for her—Drayton, Daniel, Jonson and others. She was taller than the Queen and more slender; John saw a thin, oval face, high color, a rather long nose and brilliant eyes, before she moved to the other side of the Queen where he could no longer see her.

After a ceremony of welcome on the porch, with speeches and a song from the boy soprano, one of the singing boys of Paul's that Francis had brought down from London, they all swept inside, and that was the last that John saw of either the King or the Queen.

He and Anne had given up their apartments to the guests and were themselves tucked away in a tiny room in the attic. The King and Queen dined in the parlor that had been prepared for them, the rest of the Court in the hall, to which came crowding masses of people whom even Francis had never seen before. There was plenty of food and confusion indescribable. Lobsters, crawfish, venison, plaice, crabs, beef, lambs, hams, woodcock, partridges, trout, guineas, plovers, chicken, rabbits, ducks, pigeons, swans, appeared and vanished. Faintly from the rooms above came the silver tinkle of music and the soaring of a boy's clear, sexless voice, but it was well nigh drowned out by the din and clamor below. After dinner there was a progress to the banqueting hall, the King and Queen in the midst of their courtiers, Francis bowing along with them. Serving men followed in a procession with trays of marchpane, peaches, nectarines, apricots, comfits of all kinds, silver flagons of wine, trays of Venetian glasses winking in the sun. The chattering crowd followed after; when there was no more room in the banqueting house, they swarmed about the orchard, talking and nibbling sweetmeats, standing in groups to watch what was going on, to remark on who was there, who was not.

"Francis, when can you present John to His Majesty?" Anne tried to detain her cousin with an arm on his sleeve.

"I'll do what I can, but he has already refused to meet anyone else."

The drawing room was full of gentlemen playing primero.

After dinner the King wanted to go hawking and there was a great scurry while the horses, the hawks, the men, were assembled and the royal party at last rode out toward the meadows. It was late when they came back, and then there was supper, the King and Queen and their personal attendants again hidden away in their own apartment and downstairs confusion renewed, with tables set up out of doors for the people who could not get inside, the racing about of servants with more food, more trays, more drink. In silver cups and Murano glasses upstairs, in pewter cups downstairs, wine, sherry, ale, beer flowed in rivers.

A servant cut his hand open with a carving knife and Anne, white-faced but steady-handed, sewed it up for him and tied a bandage on it. One of the Queen's waiting ladies fainted and was slow in coming around. A page boy who attended on nobody could discover whom, ate too much and was sick in a silver basin.

It began to grow dark and servants ran with tapers lighting candles. Maids and menservants appeared and asked, endlessly, "Where?" Baggage was mislaid, the most needed things were in the wrong rooms, no one could find anything unassisted. Many of the bedrooms could be reached only by going through other bedrooms; people got lost; they had to be told again where they were to sleep. John, leading an elderly courtier through a dim room, stepped on a servant who had already curled himself up on the rushes at the foot of a bed. Passing another bed where the curtains had been tightly drawn, he heard whispers inside and a low laugh laden with love.

When the King and Queen went to bed he did not know. The primero party in the parlor sent for more candles and more wine; as far as he knew, they played all night. From the window on the stairs he could see the park and the tents there in the dimness; there were a few camp fires, as if it were a campaign in a war; men sat about them, their faces cavernous in the firelight. In the house, the rustlings and voices went on for some time. Gradually the candles went out.

John met Francis at the foot of the attic stairs.

"I'll see if I can present you in the morning," Francis said. "It's more difficult than I thought."

He looked exhausted. His voice had lost its timbre and gone flat; his ruff was wilted and askew.

"Do get some sleep," said John. "You've got tomorrow morning still to get through."

"The King talks broad Scots. Sometimes I can hardly understand what he says. But he seems pleased. I think everything is going about as well as possible."

John went up to his attic room and found Anne already in bed but not asleep.

"I thought you'd never come," she said.

She was sitting up in bed in her smock, looking incredibly young in the moonlight that came in through the tiny window.

"I'm tired," she said, "but I can't sleep. There's something very disturbing about having royalty in the house. It isn't them, it's all the people that follow along after them. I've been thinking how we polished everything. I went and polished the silver sconces on the stairs myself. Do you suppose anybody noticed? I don't believe they did."

"Francis said he would try to present me in the morning."

"He'll do it if he can. He really has it in his mind. I think he's managed all this very well on the whole, don't you? After all, he's only twenty-one."

"And you are nineteen and I am thirty-one—a patriarch. And what have I to show for my years on earth?"

"Oh, John! So much——"

"What?"

"Poems——"

"Poems."

"And learning——"

"Useless learning."

"And a beautiful little daughter——"

"For whom I can't provide."

"Oh, John! You would have had everything if it weren't for me! Are you sorry you married me?"

It was spoken at last: the question they both feared, the question they had asked each other silently with their eyes but

213

never until now had given urgency by giving it sound. John gathered her into his arms.

"We have had our love at too great a price to squander it like this."

"John, have you guessed?"

"What?" His heart beat faster. It could not be.

"I am going to have another baby. I thought—but now I'm sure."

4 When they were gone, after, lost in the crowd, he had cheered and waved farewell, John went back into the disordered house. He noticed at once the smell. It was the smell that followed the Court everywhere, that prevented it from staying long in any one place, sent it from palace to palace, from castle to castle, the simple, commonplace result of too many people in small space. The houses of office overflowed, the close-stools in all the rooms waited to be emptied. There were, too, the barrels of garbage, the food gone bad in the heat, the soiled sheets, the scratched bedpost, the cracked mirror, the scorched curtain where the candle was set too close, the broken glass, the dented silver, the spilt wine, the dregs in the glasses, the trampled rushes, the horse manure in the park, the flattened grass around the tents, the rubbish left behind.

Francis had ridden on to Loseley beside the King's coach at his invitation; he would return at night to sleep in his own bed. From now on he was to have a room of his own at Whitehall, where he could stay any time; he would belong to the Court; if he had not got a post as gentleman of the bedchamber, he still had something. It had been a success. He was twenty-one, a rich young man, and his feet were on the ladder.

Anne was pregnant. Her father was reconciled, but he had even yet said nothing about her portion. John himself was no nearer to employment in the state than he had ever been—farther, indeed, for the Lord Keeper, now the Lord Chancellor and Baron Ellesmere, had cast him aside, and he had not, even after twenty-four hours under the same roof, been made known to the new King.

XX

JOHN WALKED SLOWLY ALONG BREAD STREET, past the house with the large garden where he had been born and had lived for the first three years of his life. Of it he could remember nothing now but a rose tree and his father towering over him, very large and black, but whether angry for the rose he broke or sorry for his pricked finger, John could not tell now.

His mother, he thought, walking on, would have been young then, nearly as young as his own Anne; yet always he had thought of her as old, old as the hills are old and permanent. She had come back from Malines to live with his sister Anne in her cottage in Hawstead; he must go soon to see them both. Would his own children, he wondered, Constance and John and the new one soon to be born, see their young mother as he had seen his? He shivered a little in the sharp April breeze as he turned into the door of the Mermaid Inn.

It was warm inside from the fire on the hearth, the breath of wine and beer and tobacco, the body heat of men who sat reaching over tables to make a point, or leaning back in their chairs and tapping moodily with their fingers. John paused a moment to let his eyes adjust to the change from the leafless glare outside before he looked to see if there was anyone at the table where he used to sit with the wits and the poets.

They saw him before he saw them. Out of a billow of smoke an arm was raised to signal to him, and two other men turned around. He went over to them. Only three today and they looked, he saw at once, down in the mouth.

"What news?" he said.

"Jonson's in prison."

"Chapman too, and Marston."

"In prison? What for? Which prison?" John's memory of his own prison stay, short as it was, made his voice quick and sharp.

"That play of theirs—*Eastward Hoe.*"

Chapman had translated Homer; Marston was one of the satirists whose books had been burned in the last years of the old Queen. John had had many a glass of wine with both of them. Jonson, only a few months before, had been on top of the world with his *Masque of Blackness* at Court, in which the Queen herself had taken part, and Lady Bedford.

"Buried in the country I hear nothing. What was amiss with *Eastward Hoe?*"

"One joke too many. One of the characters says, in broad Scots, 'I ken the man weel, he's one of my thirty-pound knights.'"

John laughed. The new knights were fair game but it was folly to mock a King's Scotch accent.

"Is someone taking them food and money?" he said. He could do neither himself, but remembering the inside of a prison, he could remind others.

"It's paper they need most. They are writing letters all day long."

Jonson had powerful friends. The Earl of Pembroke gave him twenty pounds every Christmas to buy books. Lord Salisbury, who had been Robert Cecil and was now an earl and Lord Treasurer, was also a friend of his. Like Daniel and Drayton, he was one of the circle around the Countess of Bedford. No doubt he would be rescued.

John lingered a moment or two longer and then went on into the inner parlor to look for Christopher.

He found his friend sitting beside the fire, his long, narrow face pale in its light. In an age when nearly every young man

sported a beard—pointed, forked, spade-shaped or rounded—
he was still clean-shaven; he did not even, as John did, wear
a moustache.

"You're late," he said a little sharply. "I wanted you here
early so that I could tell you something about Dr. Morton
before he comes."

"I am sorry. I was talking to Daniel and Drayton in the other
room. Did you know that Ben was in prison?"

"Poor fellow, yes. For the third time too. I wanted to tell
you, John—I didn't want to write it, one never knows who
reads mail—Dr. Morton is a most excellent man—almost a
saint."

Christopher was becoming madly cautious, John reflected.
He had put on weight in the last two or three years; he looked
now exactly what he was, a barrister whom a man might trust
with his life.

"I should think that was safe enough to write of anyone," he
remarked a little dryly. "Boy, bring me a cup of canary."

Christopher smiled, with almost his old boyish grin. "Fool,"
he said mildly. "His father was an alderman in York when
my father was; the two families have been friendly ever since.
He's nine years older than we are—and he was at Cambridge
when we were there, at St. John's."

"Chaplain to the Earl of Rutland now, you said."

"Yes, and holds the rectory of Long Marston in plurality.
When he was living at Long Marston, when the plague struck
last time—it hit the north a year before it came to London—he
used to ride into the city carrying sacks of food and medicine
on the crupper of his saddle for the inmates of the pest houses.
He wouldn't have a servant, because he didn't want to spread
the infection. That's the kind of man he is. He went right into
the pest houses and ministered to the sick and the dying—to
their souls *and* their bodies."

"How can I serve such a man?"

"He wants somebody to do some writing for him. Here he
is!"

They rose as the little, dark, sprightly man came toward

them, erect and smiling. After John had been presented and they all sat down around the table, the little man's smile faded away and was succeeded by an expression both sweet and serious.

"No, no wine, thank you," he said. "I seldom drink it, and I have already had some today with my dinner."

"I have told you, sir, a good bit about Mr. Donne, but I have not yet had a chance to tell him much about you."

"Then I shall tell him myself. His majesty the King, one of whose chaplains-in-ordinary I have the honor to be, has been very much distressed by the boldness and clamor of the recusants recently. He came to the throne of England expecting to be clement to the Catholics, having—though he is himself a firm Protestant—a kindly feeling for his mother's religion. But unfortunately they have not understood his clemency and have taken it to mean weakness. As a result they are boldly publishing their disputations and arguments. The Puritans too. And Anglicans with more zeal than knowledge unfortunately are answering them."

"I have noticed, sir," John put in, "that many of the Anglicans writing of recusants lump both Catholics and Puritans together without any distinction between the two."

"Exactly. Rebellion and prejudice and ignorance have all raised their voices and the result is nothing but noise and fury. Drink your wine, gentlemen, please. Now the King has wished someone with knowledge of both sides to write and bring order into this chaos, and he has selected me."

"Have you been a Catholic yourself, sir, to have knowledge of both sides?"

"No, in some ways I could wish I had—as Mr. Brooke tells me you have, Mr. Donne. But I have had considerable experience of controversy with some of the leading Catholics on the Continent. I was in Frankfurt late in 1602 and I met and disputed with many of the leading Jesuits there. I also bought a great many books on the subject at the fair which should be useful now. But I find, Mr. Donne, that it is one thing to argue face to face with a man—his eye tells one so much and his very voice brings out considerations that one might not otherwise think of—and quite another thing to sit down alone before a large sheet of blank paper. I find that I have extreme difficulty in marshaling my own arguments and setting them down in an orderly way."

His eyes were round and bright, as if he found this circumstance to be the greatest surprise.

"Some of us, on the other hand," John murmured, "find it easier to write than to speak *ex tempore.*"

"Exactly. Now what I need is someone who likes to write and who understands the subject—as I believe you do, Mr. Donne, and what you don't know you can get from these books of mine—who will, in short, work with me in making some pamphlets and books for the King."

John thought of the hours that he had spent poring over Beza and Bellarmine, struggling to find the truth that was true for him. He had made what he had called a satire of it in the end, and had given his only copy of it to Sir Thomas. Something about Truth standing on a hill.

"I should be glad to serve you, sir, to the best of my poor ability."

"Good. I come to London from time to time, and stay at my lord's town house. Could you meet me here when it is necessary?"

John could not, for the moment, see how it was to be done—this was the first time he had come up from Pyrford in more than a year—but he assented, determined somehow to compass it.

"I brought"—Dr. Morton turned and scrabbled in the satchel that he had set on the floor by his chair—"here it is. Yes. I brought some notes. You will see how imperfect they are. I have left out most of my authorities and those I have put in are probably wrong. But you can see the line I am following. Take it home with you and see what kind of shape you can put it into. What I want to do, Mr. Donne," he said, looking up from the satchel, which he was closing, "is not just to hit them over the head with a clever argument. What I want is to

219

convert these poor, misled souls to the true religion—to persuade and not to bludgeon them."

"Yes, I see, sir. I will try." John spoke absently, absorbed in reading the notes he had been given. They were fragmentary, they were confused, but there was enough of them to show the mind behind them—deep, penetrating, mellow.

A moment later he looked up to find Dr. Morton's kindly, keen gray eyes studying him, and he felt himself transparent, from the worn places on his clothes to the shabby places in his soul.

"You have children?"

"Two and a third soon due."

"I was the sixth of nineteen myself. My poor mother died of the last one. I am a bachelor. I have more than enough for my simple needs." He took some gold pieces from the knitted purse at his belt. "Take these, Mr. Donne. As you said yourself, 'Gold is restorative.' "

His eyes twinkled meaningfully, and only after a dazed moment did John recognize the quotation from his own poem on his mistress's bracelet lost: "Gold is restorative. Restore it then." Accepting the angels, he altered the rest of the line with a smile, "I doubt if I shall ever restore them."

When he and Christopher had seen Dr. Morton to the door and come back again to the fire, he kept the coins in his hand, looking at them, thinking of that very surprising man.

"You can now get a place nearer town," said Christopher, "so that you can come up more easily to London when you need to consult Dr. Morton."

"What's that? Oh. Yes, so I can."

2 The little house in Mitcham had no still-room. Anne had to brew her herbs, concoct her salves, make her rose-petal jam in a corner of the kitchen, in the afternoon, when dinner was out of the way. Waiting for a cloudy liquid to clear, she sat down on the stool and leaned her head against the wall. She was deeply content.

She had three fine, healthy children. George, the baby, lay

sleeping in the wooden cradle by the fire. Constance, nearly three, and John, turned two, were on the green with Nurse. It was such a mild February day, with snowdrops blooming in the sheltered, sunny places, that she had insisted that Nurse bundle up the children and take them out. It was lovely to have her own faithful old Nurse to help her with the children, but it made her often feel young and helpless, and there were times when she had to call on John to support her authority.

She had nursed George herself, for an older woman had told her that so long as you nursed, you did not conceive; apparently it was true, for George was nine months old and still there was no sign of another baby. She wanted more, but not so fast as they had been coming. Three children under three were too close together. She poured her brew—cloves, nutmeg, cinnamon and peppers simmered in aque vitae—through a strainer into a bottle. It was good for John's neuralgia, and not unpleasant to take.

John was in London, but he would be home this afternoon.

He went to London two or three days every week and stayed in his old lodgings in the Savoy. She hated to have him away so much, but he had to see Dr. Morton, and it was easier to write there than at home, where the walls were so thin that a child's yell upstairs sounded in the hall downstairs as if it were in the same room. Still, here or in London, the books got written, almost entirely by John though they did not bear his name. On the hall table lay *Apologia Catholica* in both Latin and English; *Conspiracy and Rebellion,* a quarto volume in English which was about the dreadful plot of the Catholics to blow up the whole Parliament with gunpowder; and *Apologia Catholica, Secunda Pars.*

The gold pieces that Dr. Morton gave John from time to time paid the rent of the Mitcham house, the rent of the lodgings in London, paid for Nurse and Cook and John's man, Tod, and for the food they all ate. As for clothes, Anne and Nurse had made over a dress of Anne's for Constance, and Anne went without new clothes for herself. But for the new suit that John must have for London, he had had to go into debt. Anne had thought when she had her twenty-first birthday that her father would surely hand over the eight hundred pounds her mother had left her, but though he came occasionally to the house, to shower the children with sugarplums and to dandle his namesake, he had never mentioned money. He could be compelled by law to pay it, but John would not hear of going to law against his father-in-law.

The baby woke in the cradle and hiccoughed loudly. Anne flew to pick him up and pat his little back. He was a good child with large blue eyes, rather expressionless, and a radiant smile adorned with two seed-pearls of teeth. Crowing with delight, he bounced in her arms and flung himself backward with such suddenness that she had all she could do not to drop him.

"Come, lamb-baby, come, darling, shall we go look out of the window and see where the big children are?"

In spite of its deficiencies, its lack of space and paper-thin walls, she loved the house. Small as it was, it was no cottage, but a gentleman's house, with two gables, leaded windows and a chimney of twisted brick. It looked down Whiteleaf Lane to the green and across the green to the towers of Beddington among the trees. Sir Francis Carew, who was Anne's sister Mary's uncle-in-law, lived at Beddington, and it was from him that Anne and John rented their house. Mary and her husband, Nick Throckmorton, lived at Addington, only two or three miles away, and waited to inherit Sir Francis's land and name. Meanwhile, Nick—who most undeservedly, Anne thought, had been knighted—wrote to Anne's father asking for money, two hundred pounds by midsummer no less.

"I can't see why my father gives it to him," Anne had complained to John. "It's *our* money, really, he's giving away so generously."

"Some people," John had answered, "would rather give a gift than pay a debt, and would rather give to a stranger than a member of their own families."

In the other direction, where Whiteleaf Lane met the London road, was Sir Walter Raleigh's house. One of his houses.

His wife was Nick Throckmorton's sister. But he was in the Tower, poor man, and Bess Raleigh was in London, where she could batter at people in high places for his release. My lord of Northumberland was in the Tower too; his steward, who was also his cousin, had been convicted of complicity in the plot to blow up the Parliament, and Lord Northumberland, who was certainly innocent, had been cast into prison for nothing more than being related to him. As well imprison Dr. Morton because he had gone to school with Guy Fawkes!

While she stood there jiggling the baby and looking out, all of her family arrived home at once: Constance and Johnny with Nurse, John himself back early from London. He dismounted, tossing the reins to his man, who took both horses —hired horses—off to the stable, and turned to his little daughter, who went running to meet him both arms raised above her head. There was between John and Constance a deep, a special, bond; Anne feared sometimes that Johnny would see it and feel left out.

Anne opened the door and they all came in together, a child clinging to each of his hands, jumping up and down and squealing.

"Hush, both of you! Unhand me! Let me greet your mother —she is more important than all the children in Christendom."

Nurse took the baby and Anne went into John's arms. His kiss was different, now that he had grown a beard. A small, pointed beard, and a silky one, it suited him; it made his face look less long, more in proportion. He was still, to her, the handsomest man in England.

"Look, Dada, look! See my new dress!"

Anne had made it like her own; its stiff taffeta skirt of orange-tawny color stood out around her and reached to the ground; the embroidered bodice was tight over her chubbiness. Her hair, like John's, was dark and silky, curling a little over her shoulders, but to Anne's disappointment she had her eyes instead of his. Dimples went in and out in her round pink cheeks.

"You look like a bell," John said admiringly, "a little golden bell."

"Ring me!"

"Bend your arms and hold them stiff."

He lifted her by the elbows and swung her gently back and forth so that her feet, clapper-like, touched against her stiff skirts on this side and on that.

"Ding-dong bell. Ding-dong bell!"

"Do it again, Dada, do it again!"

"Wing me too, Dada. Wing me too!"

Johnny's voice was shrill. Not breeched yet, he, too, had skirts to the ground. John might have rung him too, Anne thought, but he only tweaked the child's ear and laid a finger against his scarlet cheek.

In the evening, after the children had been put to bed and finally silenced, they sat as usual before the fire and Anne knitted while John told her the news that he had gleaned during his two days in town.

"Francis won more than eight hundred pounds in a great golden play at Court!"

"Eight hundred pounds! How dreadful!"

"How wonderful. No gamester is admitted who does not bring at least three hundred pounds to the game. Harry Wotton is in trouble in Venice because his pet ape bit a child."

Sir Henry Wotton and John had been inky boys together at Hart Hall in Oxford, and now he was sent ambassador to Venice where he lived like a doge himself, with his vicious ape, while John . . . Anne bent her head over her knitting and counted stitches.

"It is said everywhere—everybody in Paul's was talking about it—that Mistress Elizabeth Southwell has followed Sir Robert Dudley to France and is traveling with him disguised as his page."

"But he's already married, isn't he?"

"Very much married, with children. But I believe he is seeking a dispensation from the Pope to become un-married."

Anne made a disapproving sound with her tongue against

her teeth. Anyone who tried to undermine a marriage was a hussy, and one who went abroad in page's trunks was shameless.

John had more news to tell. "Dr. Morton wants me to go to Frankfurt to buy books for him, and possibly on to Paris and Rome."

He spoke quietly, casually even, but his words brought her head up sharply, her heart in her mouth.

"Go where?"

"To Frankfurt, first."

"That's what I thought you said. But that's in Germany!"

"Yes. He has even got me a license to travel."

"Oh, John."

"I was afraid you would feel that way."

To travel. To cross the water. To see the Rhine and the German castles, eat strange, delicious food, move among unknown people!

"No, I don't feel 'that way.' Only take me with you."

"Take you with me? But that's impossible, dear. I can't take my wife."

"But you can take a servant. Let me go as your page—like Elizabeth Southwell. Oh, John, I could! I'm very slim still. I'm only twenty-one! I could look like a boy, I know I could!"

For that mad moment it seemed possible. She was carried away with the thought of herself, dressed as a boy, going everywhere with John, master and page in public, lovers alone together. To go adventuring in the wide world, away from all that was humdrum. The children? Nurse would take care of them.

One look at John's face brought the whole fantasy tumbling down. He was shocked.

"Do you imagine that a Frenchman would not see at once that you are a woman? How safe do you suppose you'd be among those spitals of diseases? And Italians—they might think you a page, but that would only rouse their lust to pursue you the more. No, it won't do, Anne. What a child you are to think it might!"

She rolled up her knitting with a trembling hand, stabbed the needles into the ball of wool and thrust it into her bag.

"So I'm to sit at home and worry! What if you died there? It's dangerous crossing the sea. Or what if I died here alone?"

"Oh, if you die before I do, wherever I am my soul will fly straight to you."

Now he was laughing at her. The More temper rose hot within her; she pressed her lips firmly together and kept silent with an effort.

"Lovers—when they are parted—live in one another still."

"Put that in a poem!" Now it had happened. She had blazed at him. With both her hands she pushed her hair back from her forehead and clasped her head.

He took her hands in his and drew them together, palm to palm, raised them to his lips and kissed the tips of her fingers.

"Shall I tell Dr. Morton that I can't go?"

"No, don't. I'll be good."

In the morning she slept late, waking only when Nurse brought the baby for his feeding. John was already up, but pinned to the pillow beside her was a sheet of paper. A poem. With her son, heavy and warm, at her breast, she read it.

> *By our first strange and fatal interview,*
> *By all desires, which thereof did ensue,*
> *By our long starving hopes . . .*

The paper trembled in her hand and the memory came flooding over her of that day when all those hard, arrogant, terrifying men had gathered at York House to censure Lord Essex. Much worse had been done to him later, but this she had known directly. From the threat, the pity, the unreasoning terror, she had fled into the garden—and found John. Strange interview indeed. How long they sat there, motionless, saying nothing, yet somehow lifted up and bound together, she did not ask then and could not tell now. She had known from that moment that she loved him with her very soul. Afterwards he had written her a poem about it. He was a poet, a great poet,

and she had ruined him by bringing down her father's anger
on him.

> *... by thy father's wrath,*
> *By all pains, which want and divorcement hath,*
> *I conjure thee ...*

She must not hold him back from Frankfurt and from Italy;
she had done him wrong enough already.

> *Temper O fair love, love's tempestuous rage;*
> *Be my true mistress still, not my feigned page ...*

When had he written this? After their love last night? Or
had he waked early and scribbled it off in a minute or two, as
he sometimes did, as if he were taking dictation from some
unheard voice?

Downstairs she could hear Constance admonishing Johnny
in big-sisterly fashion and his angry squeal in answer; then
John's calm, amused voice and, after that, quiet.

> *I'll go and by thy kind leave, leave behind*
> *Thee, only worthy to nurse in my mind*
> *Thirst to come back. . . .*

She shifted the baby to the other side and kissed his silky
head. Dear John, you have my leave, but how shall I bear it
while you are gone?

3   "Mr. Donne," said Dr. Morton, "I have asked you to come
here today because I wish to propose to you something that has
arisen since I last saw you."

They were in Dr. Morton's study in the Earl of Rutland's
town house, where regularly over the past two years John had
come to get assignments, to confer with his employer, to bring
his finished work. Today's summons, however, had a different
air about it; something new, possibly something important, was
impending. He leaned forward a little in his chair.

"I am going to make this proposal to you on one condition
—that you shall not give me an answer at once but take three

days to think it over, and spend some part of that time in fasting and prayer. Then, after serious consideration, come to me with your answer." Dr. Morton smiled. "Don't deny me, Mr. Donne. It comes out of my love for you."

John agreed and waited with some suspense to hear what this serious proposal might be. He hoped earnestly that it would not be something that would take him away from London. He had left Anne last year, but he could not do it again. The latest child, the fourth, coming feet first, had almost killed his mother. Even now, after three months, she was white and fragile still; he could not leave her.

"I know your education and abilities," Dr. Morton was saying. "I know that you have some expectation of a state employment. I know your fitness for that. But I know, too, the many delays and contingencies that attend Court promises."

Francis had introduced John to Lord Hay, a Scotsman at Court who had countless friends and no enemies, and his lordship had promised to recommend him for a Court post at the first opportunity. John had his father-in-law also, who had been appointed Master of the Exchequer to the young Prince Henry; his word had weight, if he would but speak it. But John's expectation of Court employment was, unfortunately, of the most tenuous kind.

"I have, out of my love for you and our friendship, made some inquiries about your temporal estate and I am no stranger to your necessities."

John smiled ruefully. "I am afraid my necessities are public knowledge."

"Your generous spirit could not endure it if you were not supported by a patience that comes from a divine source. Now, Mr. Donne, I should like to persuade you to waive your Court hopes and enter into holy orders."

John opened his mouth to speak but Dr. Morton silenced him with a lifted hand.

"I have said something like this to you before, but now I have a reason to add to my suggestion. Yesterday the King made me Dean of Gloucester, and I have already a benefice, the rectory of Long Marston, which is worth as much as the deanery. The deanery is quite enough to provide for my needs—which are simple, and I am and shall remain a single man—and so, if God should incline your heart to embrace this idea, I am ready to quit my benefice and establish you in it instead. I have already spoken to the patron—who is, by the way, the young Earl of Huntingdon—and he is quite willing that you should have it."

John felt himself full of confusion and conflict. Dr. Morton become the Dean of Gloucester! He would be going from London and with his new duties he would probably have neither time nor inclination for further writing. John's employment would soon come to an end. But how kind, how generous, to offer to share his good fortune, to give away his benefice, a full half of his income! And how impossible for John to accept it.

"Remember, Mr. Donne, no man's education or talents make him too good for this employment, which is no less than to be an ambassador for the God of glory. No, no. Make me no answer now, but remember your promise and come back in three days with your decision."

Riding home through the soft spring rain that glistened on the green buds of trees and splashed into the yellow cups of primroses by the roadside, he knew that his decision was already taken. Though he would, of course, wait three days to make it known to Dr. Morton, though he might fast and try to pray in that little house where every sound, from the cook thumping bread in the kitchen to the children crying upstairs, was heard in every corner, he would find, he knew, but one answer to the new Dean's generous offer.

Dr. Morton, who rose at four to pray and ate but one meal a day, who had gone into plague-infested houses with food and medicine, no doubt assumed a comparable goodness and innocence in others. Though he knew about the scandal of John's marriage and had read at least one of the early poems still circulating in manuscript, his unworldly mind could disregard the past and consider only John's knowledge of the writings of the Church Fathers and his skill in religious controversy; but there were many others, worldly men as well as ecclesiastics, who would be quick and hot in condemning his choice for the rectory of Long Marston.

My most dear and worthy friend, my heart is full of humility and thanks, but I cannot accept your offer.

Nor was there only humility and gratitude in his heart, he, ever self-analytical, could not but admit. He had no slightest wish either to preach or to live the life of a preacher, and especially not in a country parish in Yorkshire. Even Mitcham, so near to London, seemed to him barbarously rustic.

By the time he reached Clapham Common the rain had stopped and a wedge of pale blue sky was spreading among the tumbling lavender clouds. A lark, a high, singing speck, suddenly dropped like a slow stone toward the earth. A new thought swooped upon him as he pulled up his horse from a stumble: it was human love, essentially, that had moved his friend. Dr. Morton had thought to find for John Donne a means of livelihood sure and steady. Touched and warmed though he was, he felt the gesture to be a weakness that he did not expect in the man, the saint, whom he so much revered. And what was, he thought further, a generous weakness in Dr. Morton's offering, would be in him, accepting, an ignoble weakness. He discovered in himself a deep reluctance to use the church in this way. Quite apart from his consciousness of unworthiness, which anyone must feel, and those less respectable motives—his disinclination to give up his hope of state employment and to exile himself from London and his reluctance to expose himself to the scorn most laymen felt for the ministry—was the feeling that to embrace this calling for his maintenance first and God's glory some way after was to violate his conscience as he never in his life, with all his irregularities, had done.

But how, he asked himself bleakly, were they to live now?

XXI

THE WILD RAIN OF ANOTHER SPRING lashed against the windows and now and then plopped down the chimney to sizzle on the fire. John sat writing in the parlor of his flimsy little house. He had given up his lodging in the Savoy and dismissed his man, he and Anne both wore clothes so threadbare that they made him think wryly of his own satiric portrait of the courtier whose velvet had become tufftaffetie, and still, for all their pinching care, he owed money for the food they ate.

He wrote letters these days, not books nor poems, letters asking for employment. Lord Hay had promised him roundly, abundantly, profusely, but so far with no results; he wrote as delicately as possible recalling himself to his lordship's notice. Having heard that Mr. Fowler, the Queen's secretary, was resigning, he wrote asking his favor before he should have disappeared from the Court. He did his best to succeed Sir Geoffrey Fenton as one of the King's secretaries in Ireland. He even tried for the secretaryship of the colony in Virginia, but again without success.

A crash above his head sounded as though the ceiling itself would come through. A moment later three children came pounding down the stairs screaming, Constance in the van, Johnny on her heels, George stumping far in the rear. From the screeches that came flying his way, John gathered that they were playing Englishmen and Spaniards. They whirled into the parlor and out again, shaking the table on which John wrote and causing him to reach for the inkpot just in time.

"Don't go upstairs again," he called after them. "Let your mother sleep."

Anne was six months pregnant and feeling wretched.

They came trooping back, breathless, demanding to know where they could go, since they had already been chased from the kitchen and it was raining out of doors.

"You may stay here, but play quietly."

"May we make a house with books?"

John groaned. "Be gentle with them."

They retreated to the corner behind him and began pulling folios and quartos from the bottom shelves. Quiet settled on the room, punctuated by the thump of books, the grunts of the little boys and Constance's soft, steady murmur, "Now Johnny's the father and I'm the mother and Georgie's our little boy and this is your room, Georgie."

'Tis now Spring [John wrote to Sir Henry Wotton in Venice] and all the pleasures of it displease me; every other tree blossoms and I wither; I grow older and not better; my strength diminishes and my load grows heavier; and yet I would fain be or do something. But that I cannot tell what is no wonder in this time of my sadness; to be no part of any body is to be nothing; and so I am and shall so judge myself, unless I could be so incorporated into a part of the world as by business to contribute to some sustentation to the whole. This I made account, I began early when I understood the study of our laws; but was diverted by leaving that and embracing the worst kind of voluptuousness, an hydroptic desire of humane learning and languages: beautiful ornaments indeed to men of great fortunes, but mine was grown so low as to need an occupation; which I thought I entered well into when I subjected myself to such a service as I thought might exercise my poor abilities; and there I stumbled and fell too. Now I am become so little, or such a nothing, that I am not subject enough for one of my own letters.

A yell of fury tore the air. He turned hastily around, to see Constance and Johnny engaged in a bitter struggle for possession of a book. Each one, red-faced and roaring, clutched a part of it and pulled. Before, leaping up, he could intervene, it had parted and they fell backwards, each with a mutilated half. Johnny scrambled up and in hysterical excitement flung his part upon the fire.

"Little wretch! Why did you do that?"

Before he could retrieve it, some of the pages caught fire. He blew them out, but the edges were charred, the book ruined.

"Give me the other part," he commanded and Constance, subdued, put it in his hand.

"Why did you take this one? It wasn't on the shelves. It was on the window sill."

No answer.

"All 'poiled," pronounced George.

"Wantonly destroyed. And it is not my book, it belongs to Bishop Andrewes."

It was a volume by Pierre du Moulin which Dr. Andrewes had carried with him to Paris and to Frankfurt, a loved companion that he had lent to John. He held it in his hands, turning over the torn pieces, the charred bits.

"It wasn't my fault," whined Johnny. "Constance made me . . ."

He looked at them, standing side by side before him, Constance with lowered eyes, one large, round tear squeezing under her lashes and rolling slowly down her cheek to splash on her small, dirty hand; Johnny gazing straight at him with round gray eyes asserting his innocence. They ought to be thrashed, both of them. In most houses the rod was in daily use. Perhaps if he had been able to beat his children into fear and reverence he would not now be looking down at the Bishop's mangled book, wondering how he could replace it.

"Pick up all the books and put them back on the shelves. Then go and sit on that bench and don't move till I give you leave."

He could send it to that man in Guildford and have him copy it. He was very careful, very accurate, and his hand was clear and fine. When it was done, he would send it to the Bishop with a Latin verse of explanation and apology. But it would be costly; he would have to borrow more money from Francis.

He returned to his interrupted letter, but his thoughts were too somber to continue with it. To live was but a long prison sentence ending with death. We are conceived in a close prison, our mother's womb; when we are born we have only the liberty of the house, and then all the rest of life is but a going out to the place of execution.

2   John walked the shady, midsummer lane towards Beddington, where Anne's sister, Mary Throckmorton, had come with her husband, Sir Nicholas, to visit his uncle, Sir Francis Carew. He was taking to Mary the news that Anne had been safely delivered yesterday of a daughter.

The second daughter, the fifth child, this little one had come easily; John loved her for that. While Anne lay with her baby beside her, trying to decide whether to name her Mary for her sister or Bridget because she had a fancy for the name, John stepped along the country road through air fragrant with ripe wheat and loud with the buzz of bees. His heart was light. The baby was safely here and only a week before, Sir George More had sent word that he was ready to pay interest on Anne's inheritance, at the rate of twenty pounds a quarter, until it was convenient for him to give her the principal. He had built a wing on his house, got his son Robert employed as equerry to Prince Henry, married his youngest daughter Frances to Sir John Oglander of Nunwell, on the Isle of Wight—all of which achievements were expensive. When he recovered from those, perhaps he could pay Anne her money. Meanwhile, the interest, though late in coming, was welcome. It would not pay John's debts, but it would feed his family.

A small humped bridge over the Wandle suddenly appeared and beyond it, among the trees, the spire of a church; beyond the church, the roofs of the Hall, dovecote, banqueting house, orangery, huddled and bunched, peered over one another, half hidden by trees. Eight or ten years before, Sir Francis Carew had enlarged the hall and added to it, to entertain the Queen for three days. It was a notable house, even in this part of England where many houses were fine enough to entertain royalty. In time Sir Nicholas and Lady Throckmorton would inherit it.

Sir Francis Carew, like other country gentlemen, kept open house. Usually in his great room there were three tables, for his family and guests, for strangers, for the servants. Today John found that dinner had already begun, in the banqueting hall with the great hammer-beam roof. There were, then, guests of importance.

He greeted Sir Francis and Lady Carew, spoke to Nick, to Mary, found his eyes straying to the place of honor where a lady sat, older than Anne yet still young, beautiful, with lively, intelligent eyes and a mouth that combined sweetness and humor; she wore something blue and silver, and in her cloudy hair were jewels: my lady Bedford, favorite of the Muses, lady of the bedchamber to Queen Anne. . . .

"Sit down, Mr. Donne, sit down. Find yourself a place." Sir Francis, cordial, loud-voiced, gestured with his knife.

John found a seat near the end of the table, washed his hands, smiled at the boy who held the silver basin—should he, he wondered fleetingly, find a place as page for Johnny or should he try to get him into Westminster School?—and helped himself to roast swan before he realized who it was that he had sat down beside.

"George Gerrard!" he exclaimed.

He had not seen or heard of Gerrard in nearly three years, not since, in fact, Lord Northumberland had been suspected of complicity in the Gunpowder Plot and clapped into the Tower. Gerrard had disappeared then, dropped out of sight altogether. Now here he was at Sir Francis's table, plumper than ever, complacent and smiling. Unlike John, when he fell, he bounced.

"I am attached to the household of my lady Bedford," he said softly.

"You are fortunate indeed."

"Shall I present you to her ladyship?"

The opportunity came when all the party walked in the orchard after dinner. Lady Bedford said:

"I have often heard of you, Mr. Donne. You have many devoted friends. They have told me of your poems, but no one so far has shown me any of them."

Her voice was deep and rich; she looked at him with kindness in her eyes.

"They are not worth your notice. But I have heard that your ladyship writes poetry yourself."

"Shall we walk a little? If you will give me your arm . . ."

The sun was warm. They took the path into the knot garden, where summer flowers were bright in the patterned beds.

She was almost as tall as he was; her dress whispered on the path.

"I used to write verse sometimes, but lately I have been too much occupied. My mother and father, perhaps you know, have the care of the Princess Elizabeth's household; they have established her recently at Kew. They want me near them—and so we are getting ourselves, my husband and I, a large house at Twickenham. There is much to do. I shall have a garden there. Do you like gardens, Mr. Donne?"

"As a setting for the ladies who walk in them, very much. For themselves, I am afraid, no. I scarcely know a primrose from a gillyflower."

"But you have children. You do not need to comfort yourself with a garden."

"I have been blessed with five. The latest born but yesterday."

"I had a little son who was taken from me some years since."

"All our joys are fantastical—but pain is real."

"I wrote a poem about him, the only poem of mine I think of any worth at all. If I send it to you, will you in return send me some of yours?"

John promised to write a poem especially for her, they circled around the garden a second time before her husband came looking for her. Her hand outstretched, she said:

"Your new baby, Mr. Donne. Is it a boy or girl?"

"It is a girl, my lady."

"Has she been baptized?"

"Not yet—she was born but yesterday."

"Shall I be her godmother? I am here for several days. If you can have the ceremony soon—and all babies must be baptized without delay—I should be glad to stand godmother for her."

"I should be more than honored—my wife and I—and our daughter will start her little life fortunate beyond all expectation. You are too gracious and kind. May we—if you will crown your kindness—give her your name?"

"But of course. That is exactly what I intended. If I am to renounce the devil in her name, surely we should have the same name. She shall be another Lucy."

She extended her slender, fragrant hand to him and he took it in his fingers and kissed it.

"Lucy is a beautiful name; if she can but receive along with her name only a little of her godmother's beauty and goodness, she will be blessed indeed."

3   When the christening was over, John wrote a poem to Lady Bedford.

The christening with Lady Throckmorton's help had gone well, for all John's nervousness beforehand. The weather had been perfect—sunny and warm with a light breeze—the little church, plain though it was with its sacred frescoes whitewashed over and its carved rood screen gone, had been decorated with flowers. Lady Bedford had made her vows for the baby, who had wailed properly when the devil went out of her; the wine and cakes at the church door had been good; the baby in her borrowed robes had been borne on a pillow in procession back to the house; and a dinner had been served to all the guests—twenty of them—on the lawn under the trees. Afterwards Lady Bedford had gone upstairs to see Anne, who lay in bed with her red-gold hair spread out on the white pillow, and had greeted the other children, Constance, Johnny, George and Francis, newly come from his wet-nurse, a handsome child now, with chin enough and lovely fair curls.

Lady Bedford had, moreover, when they were alone together, asked John if he, like most poets, had debts, and offered to pay them for him.

When she had gone back to Twickenham—which he was invited now, warmly, to visit—all his delight in her, his reverence, his gratitude, gushed up and poured itself out in a poem.

When he—foolishly—showed it to Anne and she read it, her hair now screwed up tight for the night, she was, to his alarm, not pleased. He could see a red flush creeping up her cheeks, and her hands holding the paper began to twitch angrily. She read it through once and then a second time.

"Well!" she cried indignantly. In a high-pitched voice she began to read aloud the parts repugnant to her:

> *"Reason is our soul's left hand, Faith her right,*
> *By these we reach divinity, that's you.*

Divinity! Well!"

"It means, not Godhead, dear idiot, theology."

"Oh. But that's not all.

> *"But soon the reasons why you are loved by all*
> *Grow infinite . . .*

Indeed."

"My lady Bedford *is* loved by all."

"Including you, I suppose.

> *". . . For you are here*
> *The first good angel since the world's frame stood*
> *That ever did in woman's shape appear.*

The first good angel! But *that's* not all. 'Since you are then God's masterpiece . . .'" Her voice rose to an angry squeal. "'*God's masterpiece!*'"

John laughed and kissed her eyes, her little nose, her red, pouting lips. "It would be hard to live with a masterpiece in one's home, however pleasant it may be to see one in others' houses."

But she continued to look at him darkly under her lashes.

238

4   In his bedroom at Lady Danvers's house in Chelsea, John was dressing with care. His new suit—hose, doublet, cloak —was of the plainest black damask, with no embroidery, no silver, no lace, and yet it had cost him twenty pounds, money that he had had to borrow. Whatever it had cost, it was a necessity; he could not go before the King in rags.

He glanced out of the window to assure himself that the weather was maintaining the promise of the early morning. At the foot of the garden the Thames flowed silver; from the half-bare trees a yellow leaf now and then detached itself and twirled lazily through the blue air to the surface of the water. Across the river the sun was laying long swathes of gold over the Battersea meadows. The ground looked dry; he could walk to Whitehall without dirtying his shoes.

At last, after so many years—more than six—he was to be presented to the King. The King, in fact, had summoned him. His friends had been active in his behalf, Dr. Morton, Bishop Andrewes and his three kind ladies who so much disturbed Anne: the Countess of Bedford, the Countess of Huntingdon, who was little Elizabeth Stanley grown up, married and powerful and still loyal to "her Prophet," and Mrs. Herbert, who to everyone's astonishment had a few months earlier married Sir John Danvers, half her age. Among them they had succeeded in interesting the King in John Donne.

Without his three ladies, he thought, drawing on the pair of fine doeskin gloves that Lady Danvers had given him, he would be forlorn indeed. They encouraged him, they kept his name alive in quarters where it was important that he be remembered, they offered him hospitality—he was always welcome here in Chelsea or at Twickenham—and from time to time they paid his debts. More than that, by their warmth, their gaiety, their pretended deference to his learning and their concern for his welfare, they kept at bay the melancholy that was ever ready to seep into his thoughts like water into a cellar, that hidden, sickly inclination for death that had all but overcome him in the days of his recent illness and worst discouragement, that indeed had set him to writing a treatise that he called

Biathanatos, in which he set forth the dark doctrine that suicide was not without exception a sin. "... Whensoever any affliction assails me," he had written, "methinks I have the keys of my prison in my own hand, and no remedy presents itself so soon to my heart as mine own sword." They had not seen it, of course; it lay unpublished, in manuscript—it would never be safe to publish it, and he hardly knew why he did not burn it—but as if they sensed the dangerous cloud about him, they had all three gone about to disperse it with the sunshine of their favor.

He had expressed his gratitude and devotion in verse letters to all three, in some holy hymns for Lady Danvers and in an elaborate and elegant elegy for two much loved cousins of Lady Bedford's who had died. He went to dance attendance on them whenever he felt that he could be away from home.

The poems and compliments threw Anne into turmoil. So far as he could, he concealed them from her, but she found first drafts or demanded to see the finished poems. "No spring nor summer beauty hath such grace," he had written to Lady Danvers, "As I have seen in one autumnal face."

"That removes spring, summer and autumn," said Anne. "What am I? Just an old winter rag? And how," she added spitefully, "does God's masterpiece like *that?*"

Lady Danvers herself had received it somewhat coolly, possibly because she considered "autumnal" too strong a word for one still in her early forties. Yet Anne had kept the smudged copy and put it carefully away with her hoard of John's verses. "It's one of your best poems," she said with a hint of tears at the back of her eyes.

She cried a great deal these days. It was natural enough, he told himself, always guilt-conscious because he had taken her from her father, who kept fifty liveries, had his steward's table and used every week an ox and twelve sheep, to bring her down to hard work and poverty and grinding anxiety. Soon there would be six children to be tended, fed and clothed, to be somehow educated and provided with dowries. The noise of five children in that thin-walled house was all but unendurable.

When he could no longer bear the din, he could fling himself on a borrowed horse and ride out of earshot—but Anne was bound fast. If he sometimes in rebellion signed his letters "from my prison at Mitcham," how much more of a prisoner must Anne feel herself to be. Yet sometimes it was her very tears that sent him galloping off to Twickenham, where were peace and elegance, stimulating conversation and the pleasant game of compliments.

> *Blasted with sighs and surrounded with tears,*
> *Hither I come to seek the spring,*
> *And at mine eyes and at mine ears*
> *Receive such balms as else cure everything . . .*

He had successfully kept that one from Anne's eyes, but that he often fled to Twickenham for relief he could not conceal from her.

He hung his cloak with careful casualness over one shoulder and went down the stairs. In the hall Lady Danvers was waiting for him.

"How splendid you look, Mr. Donne! His Majesty cannot fail to be moved." She spoke jestingly but there was admiration in her large, wide-set brown eyes, warmth in her voice.

He made a leg and lifted her hand to his lips.

"If His Majesty will but judge me by the quality of my friends, I shall ask no more."

"I have told Higgins to attend you," she said.

To walk on the street without at least one servant in attendance was almost to walk naked, yet Higgins must have his reward, and there would be gatemen at the Palace to fee besides out of his thin purse. He gave no sign of his discomfiture as he thanked Lady Danvers and set out through the moist morning that smelled of wet leaves here and burning leaves there.

Passing Westminster Hall, he felt a pang, remembering the days of his youth and confidence, when the Lord Keeper had seemed to him not only all-powerful but fatherly and his own destiny had been a plum that he had only to stretch out his hand to pick from the tree. Whitehall Palace, he thought, walking up King Street toward it, was not so much a palace as a busy city where fifteen hundred people lived and struggled and pursued their fortunes. Here officials and courtiers had their apartments and lived in state, some of them keeping tables for themselves, served by their own men. And here, too, were all the host of people who made it possible for the great to live, the cooks, scullerymen, dairy maids, launderers, wood-cutters, gardeners, carpenters, barbers and all the rest. Even when the King was away—and most of the time, it was said, he was at Theobalds or Royston or Oatlands, hunting—an immense and complicated life continued to flourish here.

It was here that Francis Woolley had won in a single night's play a sum equal to the whole of Anne's inheritance, not yet paid. But Francis, their generous cousin and dear friend, was dead. Death had cut him down almost casually, with a cold that had seemed nothing, and Pyrford House, which had been a haven to which they could go if all else failed, belonged to distant cousins and strangers.

He went through the King Street Gate, along the public road between the wall of the Privy Garden on one side and the tennis courts on the other, passed under the Roman emperors on the three-storied Holbein Gate, and paid the gatekeeper to allow him entrance into the great hall. Having told his errand to one of the lackeys that crowded there, he was led through a guard room and transferred to the care of a gentleman usher, a young man with a yellow beard and a soft, childish face above it, who escorted him to the Presence Chamber, which he found looking much as it used to in the old Queen's day when he had followed the Lord Keeper there: full of color and movement, crowded with ladies, lords and gentlemen, guarded by the motionless figures of the king's yeomen in their scarlet and gold.

He saw the King at once, in a group of gentlemen. John looked for Lord Hay but he was not there. He saw a handsome, rather stupid-looking boy of eighteen or nineteen leaning intimately over the King's shoulder, and supposed that he must be the favorite of whom there was so much talk, Sir Robert Carr. But it was the King himself who held his attention. In the moment before John's name was pronounced and he knelt, he saw again the man of whom he had had so fleeting a glimpse at Pyrford years before: the big head, thin beard, prominent blue eyes and strangely padded doublet. Before any words were said, while he waited for the King to speak, a hand twitched his sleeve and a voice whispered in his ear, "Come this way please, sir." Looking up, he saw the usher beckoning to him. The King had already turned away to someone else and did not cast him a glance. Discomfited, he stepped back into the crowd and followed the man who had beckoned. "His Majesty wishes you to wait. He will see you later."

He followed the man down a corridor to a small chamber where he was left alone.

It was chillier in this small room than it had been out of doors. John drew his cloak around him and went to the window, which looked out on a court, across which he could see the brick and stone bulk of the new banqueting hall, the place, he thought, where Jonson had had another triumph with his *Masque of Queens* last Candlemas Day. Two of John's own ladies had taken part in it, the Countess of Bedford and the Countess of Huntingdon, as well as Lord Ellesmere's wife, who still called herself the Countess of Derby and who had once been kind to John.

He was alone in the little room for what must have been nearly an hour, wondering if he had been forgotten, whether he should stay or go away. Finally the same usher appeared and led him along another passage to another small room, where there was a table with a good supply of paper, ink and pens, a chair with arms and a stool with an embroidered cushion. Almost before he had time to look around, there was a sound outside in the corridor and that swift, perceptible quickening of the atmosphere that accompanies royalty. The King appeared in the doorway. The usher who had accompanied John bowed low and vanished; another gentleman followed the King into the room and stood against the wall behind him. John went down on one knee and was told to get up.

King James appeared to be in a very good humor. He smiled and nodded as he settled himself into the high-backed chair. His eyes had a look of kindness and indubitable intelligence. They had wronged him, those people who talked so freely and scornfully of his uncouthness, his slobbering, his hysterical love of hunting, his silly adulation of a green boy. It might all be true, but out of proportion. They left out his intellect and that kindly look in his eyes.

When the King spoke, recalling John's work with Dr. Morton, he showed the pale, overlarge tongue that thickened his speech and caused a little trickle of moisture to ooze from the corners of his mouth.

"Mr. Donne, doesna the country entertain a very good opinion of my learning and wisdom?"

Surprised, John hastened to assure him that it did.

"It is well for a country when its king is among its best scholars. You have read my book, *Apology for the Oath of Allegiance*? You knew that I wrote it, though it was not signed? Now I am going to have another edition published with my name attached. There have been answers to it and answers to the answers. Have you read the Bishop of Lincoln's answer to Robert Parsons?"

"I have, sir."

"A very poor answer. He leaves the Jesuit with all the advantages. It is sometimes not our adversaries but our friends who do us the most harm."

"Indeed, sir, it has renewed my complaint that the divines of these days have become mere advocates, as though religion were a temporal inheritance. They plead for it with sophistications and illusions and forgeries. They write for religion without it. But I had thought better of Bishop Barlow." He checked himself, fearing that he had gone too far.

"I am looking for a scholar, and one who has skill with words as well as learning, to write a true answer to the Jesuit attacks on the oath. The Jesuits, as of course you know, Mr. Donne, have proclaimed that anyone who suffers for refusing the oath is a martyr and entitled to a martyr's crown; what I need is someone to prove to them that it is treason, not heroism, to refuse to yield the normal respect to the King."

"Not martyrdom but suicide," murmured John.

"Precisely. If a man refuses to take the oath, he is inviting punishment. His crime is a political one and receives political retribution. I desire peace in my realm; I don't want to hang these people for treason. Write me a book that will convince them, Mr. Donne."

The audience was at an end. The King gave his hand to be kissed and withdrew, saying over his shoulder, "Write it as fast as you can. There is no time to lose."

He walked, John noticed, without leaning on anyone. It was true then that his legs were stronger than they had been when he first came to England; some said that it was from bathing them in the warm blood of the stag freshly slain in the hunt.

At the Palace gate Higgins detached himself from the crowd of servants and followed John down King Street. He thought that even Higgins must be able to see the black crow of disappointment riding on his shoulder. A book, not employment. More religious controversy, when he was already wearied to death of it. Englishmen owed their allegiance to their king, not to a foreign pope, but beyond that he considered their religion to be their own affair. He could not, himself, fetter religion in a Rome, a Wittenberg or a Geneva. All three, Catholicism, Protestantism, Puritanism, were to him virtual beams of one sun, and where they found clay hearts, they hardened them, and where they found wax, they melted them. Christianity was all one circle. That was what he would have said if he could have spoken his mind to the King. But how much could anyone say to kings—and especially to one whose sport and passion, second only to hunting, was the new religion?

He began nevertheless to plot out a book. It should be reasoned and moderate, not hot with fury like so many. He would attack directly those morbid desires for martyrdom that lurked in some souls; Henry had had a tinge of it. He would define and weigh true martyrdom in all its dignity, and contrast with it this sickly desire of the recusants for needless suffering, which led rather to suicide than to martyrdom. *Pseudo-Martyr* he would call it, and it might be that the King, thus made aware of him, would find him other employment more to his liking.

5 *Pseudo-Martyr,* with a long dedicatory epistle to the King, was published early in the next year, a handsome quarto volume of over four hundred pages, studded with authorities. In his Preface to the Reader, John emphasized that he sought in this book not to convince Catholics of theological errors in their faith but to persuade them that they "may and ought to take the oath of allegiance." The unity and peace of the church was his "principal and direct scope and purpose." He traced the course of his own passage from the Church of Rome to the Church of England.

They who have descended so low as to take knowledge of me [he wrote] and to admit me into their consideration, know well that I used no inordinate haste nor precipitation in binding my conscience to any local religion. I had a longer work to do than many other men; for I was first to blot out certain impressions of the Roman religion and to wrastle both against the examples and against the reasons by which some hold was taken, and some anticipations early laid upon my conscience, both by persons who by nature had a power and superiority over my will, and others who by their learning and good life seemed to me justly to claim an interest for the guiding and rectifying of my understanding in these matters. And although I apprehended well enough, that this irresolution not only retarded my fortune, but also bred some scandal and endangered my spiritual reputation by laying me open to many mis-interpretations; yet all these respects did not transport me to any violent and sudden determination till I had, to the measure of my poor wit and judgment, surveyed and digested the whole body of Divinity controverted between ours and the Roman Church.

This long and prayerful study, he continued, might excuse his forwardness in seeming to write about divinity and spiritual points without any "ordinary calling to that function," although in truth, it was not of divinity but "merely of temporal matters" that he wrote.

"You might have had 'a calling to that function,' " said Anne when he read this part of his preface to her. "You might, if you had accepted Dr. Morton's offer, be now three years a minister. Oh, John, sometimes I wonder if you were right to decline it! You have studied far more about divinity than most ministers—most bishops, I daresay—and I think it may really be your deepest interest after all."

"My love, I still have hope of secular employment. The King commanded this book, and if he is pleased he may well find some place for me."

Pseudo-Martyr was read and praised for its learning and its moderation—by those who agreed with its arguments. In April the University of Oxford conferred on John the honorary degree of Master of Arts, without requiring the preliminary Bachelor of Arts, which he had never taken. He did not know whether he owed this honor to his book, to the King or to Lord Ellesmere, who was now chancellor of the university and might conceivably feel some slight regret for his harshness at the time of John's marriage.

There was no further sign from the King.

As distraction from the pressure of anxiety and frustration, John plunged into the new learning, which fascinated and excited him. Years before, he had read Copernicus's *De Revolutionibus Orbium Coelestium,* in which the Polish churchman had ascribed motion to the earth, but he had regarded it purely as a mathematical theory without concrete evidence to support it. Now Harry Wotton sent him from Venice a book, *Sidereus Nuncius,* in which a professor of mathematics at the University of Padua, a man named Galileo, through an instrument he had invented that brought the heavens close and showed new, unsuspected stars, proved what Copernicus had written. With mounting excitement John read other new books along the same line, Kepler's *De Stella Nova* and *De Motibus Stellae*

Martis, and a book called *De Magnete* by a man of Colchester, and found all his ideas of the universe shaken and changed.

"You're always reading," Anne complained. "We sit in the garden to enjoy the air, and you have your nose in a book."

"I am being convinced of an extraordinary fact! The sun, it is evident, does not move about the earth. It stands still and the earth runs around *it.*"

"What nonsense! Of course it moves. I see it move. What about sunrise—and sunset?"

"You think—and almost everybody thinks, and I thought —that the earth is the solid center of the universe, but it is not."

"But that unsettles everything—or it would if it were true."

"It is true, and it does unsettle everything. All astronomy is overthrown. The world we live in is just one atom among countless other atoms, and man, who was once the crown of the whole scheme of things, has become irrelevant."

All around them the garden glowed and shimmered in the summer sun. Bees buzzed about the gillyflowers, a bird sang, the breeze brought the sharp, sweet fragrance of lavender from Mitcham Green. While they talked, the shadow of the house moved across the grass.

"It is against all religion too," pursued Anne.

"No, I think it is applicable that we, who are a little earth, should rather move towards God than that He should move towards us."

Anne, her universe overthrown and she herself become a negligible atom, went on placidly knitting. John reread a passage in *Sidereus Nuncius* and in the turning of a page was struck by an idea for one more book against the Jesuits, not ordered by the King this time, but one that he might enjoy writing for its own sake, a satire full of conceits and ironies, in which he would make use of the new philosophy for the point of the jest.

He wrote it swiftly, first in Latin, then in English; the words came pouring out; it was the reverse of *Pseudo-Martyr,* immoderate, scurrilous, hilarious. Like many of the medieval romances, it purported to be a dream.

248

I was in an ecstasy and

> *My little wandering sorrowful soul,*
> *Guest and companion of my body,*

had liberty to wander through all places and to survey and reckon all the rooms and all the volumes of the heavens, and to comprehend the situation, the dimensions, the nature, the people and the policy, both of the swimming islands, the planets, and of all those which are fixed in the firmament. . . .

He saw the heavens where Galileo and Kepler had discovered new things, and he descended into hell, where Lucifer, with his favorite, Ignatius Loyola, the founder of the Jesuit Order, on his arm, held a court to decide which of the great innovators was the greatest. Copernicus, Paracelsus, Machiavelli, Aretino, Columbus, Philip Neri and others came before him and were rejected by Loyola. Finally the Devil, to get rid of his officious favorite, suggested that he withdraw with the rest of his order to the moon and start a new hell of his own there. The book ended with a great uproar in hell when the news came that the Pope intended to canonize Ignatius.

He called it *Ignatius His Conclave,* and he published it the following year, in Latin and in English, with an Epistle from the Printer to the Reader:

"Dost thou seek after the author? It is in vain; for he is harder to be found than the parents of popes were in the old days . . ."

XXII

<hr />

AFTER THEIR FOURTH DAUGHTER and seventh child was born and christened Mary, John set out doggedly to find himself a patron. He induced Lord Hay to present him to the King's favorite, Sir Robert Carr, just recently made Viscount Rochester, a rising star in the Court, whose patronage everybody wanted. He was the handsome, curly-headed young man with the blank eyes whom John had seen, two years before, hanging over the King's shoulder, and his chief interest at the moment, it was rumored, was his pursuit of the little yellow-haired Countess of Essex, who was at leisure since her husband, whom she had married at thirteen, had not yet returned from his education on the Continent. John had presented Lord Rochester with a copy of his *Pseudo-Martyr,* not because he thought it would delight the young man but because it was the only thing he had, at thirty-eight, to show for his life.

When it was becoming evident that nothing would result from his meeting with Lord Rochester, John happened to run across his old acquaintance, the poet and satirist Joseph Hall, in Paul's and had from him one of those casual suggestions that prove to be fuses to set far distant objects on fire.

The March sunshine was hard and brilliant and he stopped for a moment inside the west door of the vast, dim cathedral to let his eyes adjust to the sudden change. He stood there, seeing nothing but moving shapes and hearing that inimitable sound of Paul's, the clatter of voices and the steady scrape of hundreds of feet as Londoners went about transacting their business and exchanging news. It was then that Joseph Hall, unconscious of his mission, joined him.

He had known Mr. Hall slightly for more than ten years, for Hall had been chaplain to Sir Robert Drury when John's brother-in-law, Will Lyly, had been Drury's agent. Before Will had introduced them, John had known Hall by hearsay, for he was a writer of satires at the time that all the young men were trying their hands at the form. There had been a great burning of satires in the Stationers' Hall on the order of the Archbishop of Canterbury, which only his and Hall's had escaped, his because they were not published and Hall's because his *Virgidemiarum* was reprieved at the last minute on the grounds that it attacked only vices, not persons or policies.

Looking now at Hall with mild interest—and still keeping himself alert in case he should catch sight of someone of possible importance to him—he saw a trim little man with a Puritan haircut, clean-shaven, with a soft, pendulous little secondary chin beneath his first one. John noted the signs of middle age, the sagging jaw-line, the deep creases in the forehead, the gray in the close-cropped hair, until the thought that Hall was a year or two younger than himself sent his hand protectively to his own beard.

"I read your book—*Pseudo-Martyr,* was it?"

John assented modestly.

Mr. Hall dropped *Pseudo-Martyr* without comment. "I am interested in the controversy with the Jesuits. Several years ago I went with Sir Edmund Bacon to the States when he disputed with Jesuits there."

"You are not at Hawstead now?"

"No, I left there some time ago. I was too ill paid. I had actually to write books in order to buy books. Fortunately, Lord Denny offered me the living of Waltham Abbey—a fine old church, built in the Norman style before the Normans came. Nothing left now, of course, but the nave."

They were walking slowly up the aisle. At the transept, John thought, he would say good-by and they would part. Meanwhile he kept the conversation going.

"Have you time for poetry these days?"

"No, I have put that behind me. I write more serious things. My *Two Centuries of Meditations* I dedicated to Sir Robert Drury. I have kept in touch with the Drurys, though I am no longer of his family. I rather wish I wrote verse now. Somebody ought to write an elegy on Mistress Elizabeth Drury, who died some months ago."

"Was she Sir Robert's daughter?"

"His only daughter since the first child died. Very beautiful, very virtuous. Her parents fairly worshiped her, and their hopes and expectations were high—they destined her for Prince Henry. That is to say, her parents did—not, so far as I know, his! But we shall never know, for she died last December, at fourteen. Sir Robert and Lady Drury have been prostrated with grief. Why don't you write an elegy for her?"

"What was she like?"

"Small and exquisite, fair almost to the point of transparency, slender, delicate hands, good eyes. Unusually in command of herself for a girl her age."

"Perhaps I shall. Thank you."

"I think part of Sir Robert's grief is that he thinks that this brilliant creature has died untimely and that nobody thinks of her or remembers what she was. If you could write something that would give him comfort, I've no doubt he would be generous."

"Are they in Hawstead now?"

"No, they're at their house in Drury Lane—I've just come from there. I took them a little gift of honey from my wife. Did you know I was married?"

Before they parted, John had heard about his wife, how she had been selected for him by a friend and how well this practical arrangement had answered, about his children, of whom he had five, all with biblical names. He had a good deal to say about the importance of his position as rector of Waltham, but much of that John did not hear, his mind being busy with the

252

thought of Elizabeth Drury and the question of how one who had not known her might write an elegy on her.

On the way home, as he was jogging along the eight miles to Mitcham, the lines began to come to him, as other poems had come on this same road. He would write it in rhymed iambic pentameter couplets; he would assure Sir Robert Drury that the world had been changed and impoverished by the loss of his beloved daughter.

> *. . . we may well allow*
> *Verse to live so long as the world will now,*
> *For her death wounded it. The world contains*
> *Princes for arms, and counsellors for brains,*
> *Lawyers for tongues, divines for hearts, and more,*
> *The rich for stomachs, and for backs, the poor;*
> *The officers for hands, merchants for feet,*
> *By which remote and distant countries meet.*
> *But those fine spirits which do tune and set*
> *This organ, are those pieces which beget*
> *Wonder and love; and these were she; and she*
> *Being spent, the world must needs decrepit be . . .*

Strong words; too strong for a girl of fourteen whom he had never seen; but he forgot the girl in the exhilaration of writing, carried away by his own eloquence. When he finished the poem at home and read it over, the final couplet—

> *And 'tis in heaven part of spiritual mirth*
> *To see how well the good play her, on earth*

—made him feel suddenly nauseated; but he did not strike out the lines. Extravagant compliment, he told himself, was a necessary art in his world; if tribute paid to a dead girl was more pleasing to the bereaved parents than any flattery to themselves, was he not to make use of it, in his need, in his determination to find a patron?

A conflicting impulse set him rummaging through his papers for some stanzas of a "Litany" that he had written two years earlier, when a tedious illness had kept him long in bed. He wrote down notes for new lines.

> *When want, sent but to tame, doth war,*
> *And work despair a breach to enter in;*
> *When plenty, God's image and seal,*
> *Makes us idolatrous,*
> *And love it, not Him, whom it should reveal . . .*

Very pious, he thought sardonically; but how seriously did he mean it? If he were sincere, would he not tear up the whole elegy? He finished the stanza.

> *When we are moved to seem religious*
> *Only to vent wit, Lord, deliver us.*

2 Not so long ago Drury Lane, which ran from the Strand northwest of Temple Bar, had been but some grassy tracks, and Drury House had sat surrounded by fields and woods. Now, with the new buildings springing up everywhere, the lane was a muddy road deeply rutted by the endless carts bringing brick and timber, and Drury House itself was hidden by a fringe of fine new tenements much in demand by fashionable people.

The gate house was a handsome one, built of the same brick as the rows of houses on each side of it, two-storied, with the Drury arms in stained glass above the entrance. John walked through it one June morning and came to a somewhat littered courtyard beyond, with houses of office on the right and wood and coal yards on the left, with the stables beyond. Straight across the courtyard was the house itself, massive and ugly, with branching steps up to the front door and over the heavy roof a pattern of gauzy trees in the garden behind. Besides this house, they had, John had learned, Hawstead Place in Suffolk, Hardwick House and two or three other manors.

John went in without hesitation; he knew the porter now, he knew some of the footmen. The stairs were familiar; he stopped on the landing to look at the yellow roses on the garden wall. The uncertainty, the almost startled awareness of his first visits, when every impression had bit into his nerves, was over; he moved accustomed and easy in this house. The young footman who preceded him was named Hobbin; he came from the village of Hawstead and his mother worked for John's sister Anne.

In the green parlor—where the furniture was upholstered in green leather, piped with gilt—he found Lady Drury with Sir Robert. They both turned to greet him as if they had just been talking about him. Lady Drury was a niece of Francis Bacon—now Sir Francis, a knight like everyone else but John Donne. She was a thin, faded, sentimental woman with an untiring interest in people and their relationships. She had early discovered that John was a friend of Henry Wotton, who was a friend, indeed the uncle-in-law, of her brother Edmund. This circumstance added value to John's poem on her daughter, which in itself brought tears to her eyes whenever she thought of it.

"Oh, Mr. Donne, have you written anything more on the new verses for Elizabeth?"

"Nothing to show yet, madam, but I shall have them ready for the anniversary of her death, I promise you."

"Never mind. You can work on them in France."

"My dear." Her husband shook his head at her.

"No, don't frown at me. I haven't said anything. It is all yours to tell."

John sat, then moved his chair slightly to get it out of the shaft of morning sun that struck his eye.

Sir Robert was nearly three years younger than his wife, and looked it. He was a florid, hearty man, warm and impulsive in both friendship and enmity. He had, John realized, taken a great liking to him, partly because of the elegy on his daughter and partly because they both had been followers of the Earl of Essex. Sir Robert, indeed, had been knighted at seventeen by Essex in the Low Countries, and had been with him in France. The only reason why he had not been involved in Essex's downfall was that he had been imprisoned in the house of Alderman Saltonstall on suspicion, and therefore was under surveillance at the time of the Essex Rebellion, even though the conspirators had used his house for a meeting-place. They had talked it over together often.

"He was too popular with the people," John had said. "The

Queen could not allow a subject to be so much loved—and my lord of Essex courted popularity instead of discouraging it. It is too great a price for hats thrown in the air when one pays for it with one's head."

"He was too sure of himself. Sovereigns—and the Queen, though a woman, was a sovereign after all—can't stand that. He ruled her—or tried to and for a time he did—with his sulks. But he was a great man in his way, and if she had handled him differently, we might have had him in the state today. You and I might both have been ambassadors somewhere."

This was another bond between them: both had sought for state employment and both had failed. It was, John thought, extraordinary that Sir Robert, who had every advantage, should have done no better than he had himself. He had been a member of Parliament in 1606—as had John in 1601—but nothing more had come of it. He was in regular attendance at the Court. He was energetic, impulsive, impatient—and indiscreet.

"I have sent for you this morning, Mr. Donne, because I have a proposal to put to you."

"I am at your service, sir."

"I and my wife are going to France. There are people whom I want to see there, things I want to learn. It is possible that the King someday may want a new ambassador in Paris and I should like to be prepared. My thought is that you accompany us as my secretary. What do you think of that?"

"I am honored, sir, and most grateful. I should like it enormously, but——"

"In that case, I see no occasion for but's."

"I can scarcely leave my wife, sir, with seven small children and another on the way."

"Oh yes, of course you are married. I had forgotten that."

"Has your wife, Mr. Donne," put in Lady Drury, "no relatives she could go to?"

"Her sister Lady Oglander has been begging her for a visit, but the Oglanders are in the Isle of Wight. Moreover, as I said, she is pregnant."

"When is the baby expected?"

"In February."

"Oh, but we'll be back by then—long before then. I plan to go for only two or three months, and we'll start in August." Sir Robert swept away all difficulties with a gesture of his arm. "Send her to Wight. It will be a pleasant change for her—good for the children. What's the matter. Doesn't that suit?"

John smiled faintly. "I would not know how to transport an ailing wife and seven small children so far—the eldest is only eight, sir."

"Oh, if that's all, I'll lend you my coach. Send them right away, so that we'll have it back in time to rest the horses and get ready for our own journey. We shall be in London till we start. We shan't need it. Yes, yes, that's it. Send them to Wight by my coach. Go with them yourself and then come back here. And furthermore, this is another thing I wanted to say to you. When we return from France, you must have one of my houses in Drury Lane. They're very comfortable, you know. The best ones rent for eighty pounds a year, but you can have whichever is empty at the time—and no cost to you at all. We shall be glad to have you so near us, and you no doubt will be glad to come back to London."

"I must consult my wife, sir."

"Very well, but tell her, don't ask her. A man must be master in his own house. Isn't that so, my dear?"

Lady Drury did not commit herself to that. "Mrs. Donne will want whatever is to her husband's best interests," she said primly, adding with more life in her voice, "I believe your wife is the daughter of Sir George More?"

"Yes, madam, and we did not have each other so cheaply that we can now afford to be much parted."

"When we return," said Sir Robert, "and you are settled in London, I shall use whatever influence I have toward finding you a post in the government. There it is, Mr. Donne. I have said all I intend to say to persuade you. Will you come or won't you?"

There could be but one answer. On one side of the scales were a rich patron, a trip to France, a house in Drury Lane and the prospect of employment of the kind he wanted; on the other, Anne's probable feelings. He thanked Sir Robert and said he would go.

3   Anne was not happy about it.

"Don't go, John, don't go! I can't bear it."

"But, dearest, you will be safe and happy at Nunwell. You have been grieving—have you forgotten?—because you never see your little sister?"

"Oh, I shall be well enough. I'm not thinking about myself. It's you I am worrying about. France is full of Catholics—and Jesuits too, which is worse. Why, only a year ago they killed their king! And you have written so much against the Jesuits. It is not safe for you to go there. They are violent people."

"I am an unimportant Englishman, not a French king. And I shall be of the party of Sir Robert Drury, who is respected everywhere. When I come home, things will be very much better for us—a house in London, sure employment."

"But what is that, if you are killed? My divining heart sees danger to you."

He laughed and kissed her. "You are only teaching fate how to harm us when you foretell such things. I shall be gone only two or three months and then we shall be together in London."

"Two or three months! I don't believe it. There are always delays, and then no doubt they will change their minds and want to go to Rome or Venice or Turkey or God knows where. And what will you do? Say, 'I think I'll go home now'? You know you wouldn't. And it wouldn't be safe for you to travel alone if you did."

"Don't cry, love, don't cry. You can't love me as you say you do if you waste yourself—and you are the best of me—in sighs and tears."

They had been married more than nine years, years filled with sickness, with continual childbearing, with hope deferred, with failure. He had been faithful to her—though he recognized that his spiritual flirtations with his great ladies might have hurt her as much as physical infidelity would have done;

he might have kept it secret, but his lovemaking and his languishing were all written out in poems. But that was a love of foam and spume, while his love for Anne was the very depth of the river itself.

"It is not for weariness of you I go, dear love. I go because it is our only hope. But we shall not really be separated—think that we are like two people who have just turned aside to sleep. We are together still, alive in one another."

"That is too metaphysical for me," she said wearily. "I need to hear and see and touch."

4   Sir Robert Drury was as good as his word. He sent his coach —not the new one that he had got to take to France but the old one that he kept for use in the country—to take Anne and the children to the Isle of Wight. The coach being filled to the roof with Anne, seven small children and faithful Nurse, John rode a horse that he had borrowed from Anne's brother Robert. A cart followed with their baggage.

The trip was a nightmare. They went no more than twenty miles a day and slept at night at inns, some of which were good and clean, but others abominably dirty and ill-managed. Just to care for the physical needs of seven small children was an unrelenting task for the three adults. All of them had to be dressed and undressed, fed, washed and put to sleep. Some of them got sick from the motion of the coach and vomited; others developed diarrhea from the questionable food at the inns. Those who were quiet in the daytime howled at night. Constance at eight had learned to be motherly with the younger ones. It was touching to John to see her with an enormous armful of baby, offering it sugar-tits and jiggling it to keep it quiet.

His happiest times on the endless trip were when he had Constance on the saddle in front of him. He liked the feel of her small, slender body, the feminine cast of her mind; he was delighted by her obvious admiration and affection for him.

She took a great interest in what she saw along the way, the villages with their little church towers, a crown of trees on the top of a hill, the loopings of a river, the endless green of field and wood and hill.

"Why is the grass green, do you think, Dada?"

"I cannot tell you, Constance. We know what Caesar did and what Cicero said, but why grass is green and blood red is a mystery."

But then Johnny would clamor for his turn, and he was much less comfortable to have on the saddle. He squirmed and whined and wanted to get down.

"Will there be any other children, do you think, at Aunt Oglander's?"

"A boy. Same age as Bridget." He thought of Wotton's cynical saying: "Next to no wife and children, your own wife and children are best; another's wife and your children worse, your wife and another's children worst of all." Fortunately the Oglander child was young—and in any case he would not himself be there to suffer.

"Just one more day," said Anne, in bed in the inn at Portsmouth. "We'll be there early tomorrow. This has been terrible for you, John. All this puling and puking, and nowhere for you to retreat to. You have been forced to be too domestic."

"I have dragged you into this as into so many other difficulties and distresses."

But she put her hand, gropingly in the dark, over his mouth. "Sh," she said. "It has been worth everything—all but your going away."

They reached Nunwell at last, the last quarter-mile with the coach swaying on a ferry, on a sky-blue day when the sun sparkled on the sea and the air was fragrant of salt and drying hay, and were welcomed with reassuring warmth by the Oglanders, John and Frances. Nunwell House was a great pile of stone and chimney stacks, roofs of different levels, all clustered around a large central court; there was room in it for the coach and horses, for the coachman and groom, for Nurse and all the children, for Anne and John.

Sir John Oglander, who was twenty-six and looked younger and who bore the stamp of Winchester, Balliol and the Middle Temple, took John Donne at once on a tour of the place. He had plunged himself, it was plain, with enthusiasm into the life of a country gentleman.

"Oglanders have kept this ground for five hundred years," he said. "This house, of course, is not much more than a hundred years old—and as you can see, it is shabby. My father has lived in Winchester as long as I can remember, and now he has turned Nunwell over to me to restore to its former state."

Frances, who was four years younger than Anne, was filled with joy to see her sister. Like Anne, she was pregnant, but she was farther along. She would be brought to bed in October.

"It is so wonderful to have Anne here," she said. She can help me so much. And she will be here when my time comes."

Anne had brought her a present—a new French invention that had but lately come to London, a pair of clogs called "pattens," with high ridges that kept one's feet dry out of the mud. Frances was delighted. "I can wear these when I cross the courtyard to oversee the dairy maids," she cried in genuine pleasure.

She was much simpler—both the Oglanders were much simpler—than John had expected. It was a rare sight to see two so well-placed young people, whose wedding had been one of London's great occasions, so much in love with each other, so united in their determination to make a success of Nunwell, so hard-working. He felt satisfied and happy about leaving Anne here—and the children would be in heaven.

"Now you must write to me," he said to her when he was leaving. "Every time the carter goes to London, you must send me a letter. Send it to Mr. John Brewer at the Queen's Arms in Cheapside—and he will convey it directly to me. He is Sir Robert's man of business. You promise, Anne?"

But her eyes were dark and she turned them away. For all her joy in being with Frances, she was in bitter rebellion against his going away. "If you care so little for me as to leave me," she said, "why should I write to you?" But then she repented, and cried, "Oh, John, I will. I will."

The coach had already gone back; he was riding alone. She clung to him, begging him to be careful, to be cautious, not to ride after dark.

"I left something for you," he murmured into her hair, "on the pillow of the bed."

"A Valediction," he had called it, "Forbidding Mourning."

> Dull sublunary lovers' love
>   (*Whose soul is sense*) *cannot admit*
> *Of absence, because it doth remove*
>   *Those things which elemented it.*
>
> *But we by a love so much refined,*
>   *That ourselves know not what it is,*
> *Inter-assured of the mind*
>   *Care less eyes, lips and hands to miss.*
>
> *Our two souls therefore, which are one,*
>   *Though I must go, endure not yet*
> *A breach, but an expansion,*
>   *Like gold to airy thinness beat.*
>
> *If they be two, they are two so*
>   *As stiff twin-compasses are two;*
> *Thy soul, the fixed foot, makes no show*
>   *To move, but doth if th'other do.*
>
> *And though it in the center sit,*
>   *Yet when the other far doth roam*
> *It leans and hearkens after it*
>   *And grows erect as that comes home.*
>
> *Such wilt thou be to me, who must*
>   *Like th'other foot, obliquely run;*
> *Thy firmness makes my circle just,*
>   *And makes me end where I begun.*

5   He returned to Mitcham, sold everything in the little house on Whiteleaf Lane except his books, which he stored in London, and went to stay at Drury House until they should leave. The days lengthened themselves out as Anne had foreseen they would; one delay succeeded another. It was not the license to travel that kept them—Sir Robert had already got that before

he invited John to go with them—but business affairs of Sir Robert's, elaborate leave-takings and especially the purchase of a new manor, Snareshill, to use as a hunting lodge.

While he waited, John became once again a bachelor in London, and for a time he enjoyed it. He spent hours with Christopher, drinking canary and talking about the state of law, of poetry, of England. He and Christopher went to Oxford, to what they called a "philosophical feast" celebrating the return of their old friend Tom Coryat from five months' travel in Europe. He went frequently to see Lady Bedford, who at Bedford House in the Strand was awaiting the birth of a child, her first attempt since the little son who died ten years earlier. She had great hopes of this child, who should be one day, if it were a boy, the fourth Earl of Bedford, and she could talk of nothing else. He visited Sir Henry Wotton in his lodgings in King Street, Westminster. Wotton had come home from Venice nearly a year before, high in the King's favor, had been talked of as the next ambassador to Spain, as Secretary of State to succeed Lord Salisbury, who was in bad health.

"Yet here I remain," Sir Henry said cheerfully, "courting courtiers."

The four walls of his room were crowded with Italian paintings that he had bought during his six years in Venice; wearing rich, dark silk with gold embroidery, a flaring, extravagantly sheer white collar and jewels in his ears, he looked like a doge himself but for his light brown hair, his large English air of calm confidence and wise moderation. It seemed extraordinary to John—and much more frightening than comforting to him —that one so well placed, so successful, as Wotton, should have had a year as disappointing as any of his own.

"What about that affair of the ape biting the child? Did it embarrass you seriously?"

"The ape? Oh, that. There was nothing to it. The child was more frightened than hurt, and a gift to the parents assuaged all feelings. No, no. I came home in good order and when I visited Royston in March, the King was most kind, most generous. I refused the ambassadorship at Brussels, thinking I was to have Spain. There is talk now, however, of my going to Savoy to promote a marriage between the princess and our Prince Henry. She is Catholic, but Savoy itself is anti-papal. Perhaps we shall meet in Paris!"

John shook his head. "I hope to be home again before you could get there—even if you go soon."

But when the weeks dragged through September into October, he poured out to Lady Danvers his concern about Anne. "I had expected confidently to be at home again when her time comes in February, but if we are so late in starting, we shall be late also in returning. Should I cancel the whole thing, I wonder, ask Sir Robert to release me?" (But what would they do—the Mitcham house gone and the house in Drury Lane undoubtedly withdrawn?)

She comforted him. "Never mind. She will be safe with her sister. And it is the eighth child. By that time they come more easily. I had ten myself—Job's number and Job's distribution—seven boys and three girls, you know—and by the eighth I had no trouble at all."

"I am like a merchant ship, I fear, with a fair large harbor before it, deep and open, going aside to take soundings and search for hidden rocks on which to shipwreck. I have committed myself to this enterprise. I should sail into the harbor with a merry sail and full gales."

"You must have faith," she told him.

To bolster himself up he looked at the empty houses—there were two or three of them—in Drury Lane and, having chosen the one he would like best to have, wrote to Anne about it in detail, describing their life there when he should return. For a long time he heard nothing from her, but at last there was a note. She was well, the children were well. Frances's time was very close; she was going to call her second child John, for her husband, the first one having been George. It was a flat, dull little letter; only at the end was there something that spoke with her voice. "Love," she wrote, "from your compass, who leans and longs to grow erect."

When October was half over, Lady Bedford lost the hoped-for child in a miscarriage. In all John's sorrow for her, it was uppermost in his mind that Anne, too, was pregnant and that if she miscarried he would not be there. Resisting the impulse to ride to Wight and see for himself how she was, he shut himself up in the study that the Drurys provided for him, and wrote the elegy he had promised for the first anniversary of Elizabeth's death. Elizabeth, whom he had never seen, became to him as he wrote a symbol of perfect womanhood; as he went on, mulling over in his mind the overturn of all former philosophy by the new science, which unseated the earth and divided the unity of thought into the opposites of science and faith, she became more than woman, religion itself, a religion not of dogma but of spirit. He wrote on in a kind of ecstasy, piling extravagances on conceits, saying things of her that no one should say of a mortal girl. The world might better spare both sun and moon; when she is gone, its heart is gone, and it is sick in all its parts. She, she is dead, ran his refrain, and the world without her is a monster without a soul, a cinder, a cripple, a ghost.

Sir Robert and Lady Drury were enchanted with it. "It must be published," declared Sir Robert, "so that everybody may read it. Put your other poem with it, and it will make a fine little book."

John was alarmed. "I never publish my verse," he objected.

"But verse that is only copied and passed from hand to hand has no life at all. It is soon buried, and its subject with it. No, no, you say yourself . . ." He fumbled for the place and read:

> *"Verse hath a middle nature: heaven keeps souls,*
> *The grave keeps bodies, verse the fame enrolls.*

It must be published, or where will our Elizabeth's fame be? We won't have time before we go, but I'll have Mr. Hall see to the printing of it. No, no, Mr. Donne, it is all decided, so put away your false modesty."

He could not quell the uneasiness he felt. Much of his verse he was ashamed of, but it was hidden in manuscript; he felt that in his search for serious employment, published and acknowledged verse would be a hindrance, but he could not move Sir Robert; he could only persuade him that it should be anonymous.

If he was troubled by this passage over the poem, he was cheered by one thing Sir Robert said: that there would not be time to see his poem through the press before they left. They were, it seemed, going at last.

They set off about the middle of November, a great cavalcade, the new coach drawn by four horses, eight horses besides, one of which John rode, servants, a pack of hounds and several hawks with their paraphernalia and attendants.

"Shall you be hunting in Paris, sir?" said John in some bewilderment.

"No, of course not. But before Paris, we shall be in Amiens. My friend, the Comte de St. Paul, has found me a house there, and he tells me the hunting is very fine. Later we go to Paris, for the ceremonies of the king's betrothal. What is the matter, Mr. Donne? Your eyes look quite wild."

"I had thought we would be out of England but two or three months."

"Oh no, we couldn't possibly do it in that time. If we are to send back reports to the Lord Treasurer, as he has asked me to do, we must stay longer than two or three months. But don't distress yourself. We'll be back by summer."

XXiii

AMIENS, LYING ON LOW GROUND between two rivers, was damp —and dull. From the pleasant and ample house that the Comte de St. Paul had secured for the Drurys there were views of the rivers, the cathedral and the wide, wooded hunting country beyond. Sir Robert hunted daily, going out early in the raw, gray mornings and coming back late, red-faced and glowing, sometimes blood-flecked, ravenously hungry; after a meal and a good deal to drink, he would sit by the fire and go to sleep. Lady Drury was engaged in embroidering a pair of bed curtains; contentedly she worked at them most of the time; she liked to have John there to talk to; she told him over and over about Elizabeth.

John, who did not hunt and who rode only to get somewhere, spent his days indoors writing and studying. He wrote letters, both for Sir Robert and himself, letters reminding the great with whom they wished to keep in touch of Sir Robert's existence. He wrote letters to Christopher Brooke, to George Gerrard, to Dr. Morton, to his ladies, to Anne—letter after letter to Anne, and no answers at all. He returned to the study of civil law and wrote to Dr. Morton suggesting that he might qualify himself to practice in the Court of Arches and asking his opinion about that course. At length, spurred on by Lady Drury, he wrote, nearly a year ahead of time, a poem for the second anniversary of Elizabeth Drury. He called it "The Progress of the Soul," using an old title over again.

"O my insatiate soul . . . Forget this rotten world, This world is but a carcase . . . She, she is gone; . . . when thou knowest this, What fragmentary rubbidge this world is Thou knowest . . . Think then, my soul, that death is but a groom Which brings a taper to the outward room . . . My body . . . Think when 'twas grown to most, 'twas a poor inn, A province packed up in two yards of skin . . ."

Dr. Morton, now Dean of Winchester, wrote back to him that in his judgment he thought the ministry in the church of God would be safer and fitter for him. He thrust the idea away, and wove into the poem a reference to the kind of minister he scorned, who decorated his sermons with unacknowledged quotations from others' writings.

> *Shalt thou not find a spungy sleek divine*
> *Drink and suck in the instructions of great men*
> *And for the word of God, vent them again?*

From Lady Drury's description of Elizabeth's transparent skin and the swift color coming and going, he wrote of her:

> *. . . her pure and eloquent blood*
> *Spoke in her cheeks, and so distinctly wrought*
> *That one might almost say her body thought.*

He made no protest this time when they talked of publishing it, and it was sent to Mr. Hall to take to his printer.

When it had gone, suddenly a little sickened by it, he returned to his studies, telling himself that he would write no more verse to order. But soon after that, Sir Robert Rich stopped in Amiens on his way to join Sir Harry Wotton's embassy in Savoy, and asked John to write complimentary verses for his sisters, Miss Essex Rich and Lady Cary, neither of whom he knew except by reputation. Outwardly compliant, inwardly weary, he brought himself like a rebellious horse to the hurdle and produced a poem stiff with ornament and studded with conceits: a verse letter to them both in one, speaking of things "which by faith alone I see." Having discoursed elaborately upon their beauty and virtue, he wound up with

May therefore this be enough to testify
My true devotion, free from flattery;
He that believes himself doth never lie.

The taste of that was sour in his mouth afterwards; was his life to be spent in flattering ladies—and in persuading himself while he wrote that he believed what he said?

Except for that one note in London, he had heard nothing at all from Anne. Even in the other letters that came, even in the one from Robert More, Anne's brother, there was no mention at all of Anne. Anxiety within him mounted, corkscrewing, until it became anguish.

"Is there no word yet from Mrs. Donne?" said Lady Drury sympathetically.

"Nothing at all, and her time draws near."

"Perhaps you ought not to have left her," said Lady Drury placidly.

John made no attempt to comment on what was now so obvious a truth to him.

"One would think that the only way for letters to come from Wight was by the Northwest Passage! This troubles me more than I thought anything in this world could have done." He buried his head in his hands and groaned.

2 In late January the days suddenly were longer. Two weeks ago it would have been dark at this hour, but now the sky behind the bare trees was yellow and the room in which John sat alone was only slightly drifted with shadow. He had been writing but he had laid his work aside to look out at the garden, pinched and hard with cold but patterned with the dark green of yews and box. When he turned back to the room, a little more of the light had gone, but the shadows were not dark enough to hide the figure coming toward him from the door.

It was a girl dressed in some pale color, with her hair loose on her shoulders, carrying something in her arms. When she came abreast of him, he saw that it was Anne, and that it was a dead baby that she carried. He sat there, frozen, unable to move or speak. She went to the end of the room and then came back. As she reached him the second time, she stopped and looked into his face. The next instant she was gone.

He jumped up, released from the stupefaction that had bound him, and went to the door from which she had seemed to come. There was no sign of her and he had expected none. He sat down again and buried his head in his shaking hands. He had no doubt that it was Anne he had seen and that she was in trouble. The baby was due about this time; was that the dead child whom she carried, or was it one of the little ones, Mary or Bridget? Was Anne herself dead? What was the meaning of this thing that had happened?

He heard a footstep—Anne had made no noise at all—and one of the footmen brought two tapers into the room, which was now dark. In the candlelight the colors of furniture and tapestry bloomed suddenly. The footman, having drawn the curtains and revived the fire, withdrew, and Sir Robert Drury came in, bringing a little cloud of cold air with him.

"Ah, you here, Mr. Donne?" He went to the fireplace and stood in front of it, toasting his back. "Your excellent French was very useful to me at the dinner table today. I can talk about horses and hawks and I can buy jewels in the language, but that learned gentleman with his philosophical chatter was too much for me. What's the matter? You look very pale. Are you ill?"

"I have seen a dreadful vision just now. I have seen my wife, with her hair hanging about her shoulders and a dead child in her arms, pass twice through this room."

"Oh surely, sir, you have been asleep. This was no more than a melancholy dream. You are awake now. Put it out of your mind."

"I am as sure that I saw her as I am that I am alive. As she came back she stopped and looked me in the face—and vanished."

"But that's preposterous! That sort of thing doesn't happen

these days. You must have a good night's sleep, and then you'll feel different."

"She is in trouble of some kind. I must leave you tomorrow, sir, and go to her."

"My dear man, you can't do that. We go to Paris next month, and I shall need you there much more than I do here. I'll send a messenger to Drury House to find out if she is alive and how she is."

"But she is on the Isle of Wight."

"Everything is known in London. I shall tell him not to come back until he finds out—if there is anything to find out, which I doubt. Come, sir, pull yourself together. The time of visions and miracles is past."

He was so vigorous and hearty, so down to earth and matter of fact, that John smiled faintly at the thought of having put to him an experience so unreasonable as the one he had just had.

"I think it is no miracle, sir, but only a sort of sympathy of souls, so that when serious misfortune comes to one, the other knows it. If two lutes, as you know, are strung and tuned to the same pitch, when one is played, the other—though lying untouched on a table—will sound faintly the same tune. Anne and I are two such lutes. I must go to her."

"We'll talk it over in the morning—if you still feel the same way after a night's sleep."

Lady Drury, when she heard the story, was more inclined than her husband to take it seriously. In fact, she promptly found supporting instances in history and in Holy Writ, reminding them that the ghost of Julius Caesar appeared to Brutus, and that Samuel appeared to Saul after his death, neither of which instances was as comforting to John as she seemed to expect.

In the morning, when John, gaunt after a sleepless night, remained firm in his conviction and determined to start at once for England, Sir Robert refused outright to let him go. And it was one of the bitterest things he had had yet to face that he did not have the money to break with Sir Robert and start off alone.

3   They had very elegant lodgings in a tall house in Paris, looking out on the Louvre on one side and on the other on the Ile-de-France and the great cathedral, with a filagree of bare branches between, which during the month they were there swelled into little nobs and then into a foam of green buds. Whenever a procession came out of the gates of the Louvre, with trumpets and outriders, and then a great coach containing the Queen Regent, or little King Louis XIII scowling through the window, they could look down from their windows upon it, and speculate and gossip.

Sir Robert Drury was in almost daily attendance on his friend of several years, the Duc de Bouillon, and he was very well up on the currents and cross currents of the court.

"The little King," he told John one day, "is very tyrannical and inclined to be cruel."

"There was talk of it when I was here before—in '06. He was a small child then, but very headstrong, people said, and determined to have his own way."

What primarily had brought them to Paris was the announcement, and the festivities attendant on it, of a double betrothal: of Louis XIII, then eleven, to Anne of Austria, and of his sister Elizabeth to the son of Philip III of Spain. Paris was crowded for the occasion; all the princes and nobles came up from their estates to the capital, bringing with them their entourages. The Duc d'Espernon had six hundred liveries in attendance on him. The streets were jammed, tempers and spirits were high and fights were frequent. The Edict against Duels was reissued, but dueling went on in spite of it.

The celebrations themselves, John thought, were not what they might have been. There were, it was true, eight hundred caparisoned horses, but there were no knightly encounters, only running at the quintain. Accustomed to the English gift for pageantry and ceremonial, he felt the French effort to be meager.

"If they tell you of any other stuff than copper," he wrote to George Gerrard, "of any other exercise of arms than running at the quintain and the ring, you may be bold to say, Pardonnez-moi."

He missed the last day of it because of an attack of dysentery, and by the time he recovered, he was faced with the London reaction to his "Anniversaries."

Joseph Hall had seen to the publishing of them. The first, "An Anatomy of the World," with the "Funeral Elegy" that had started the whole thing, appeared in December in a little book with an introductory poem by Hall himself entitled "To the Praise of the Dead and the Anatomy." When "The Second Anniversary" reached him, he wrote a poem called "The Harbinger to the Progress" and published all five poems in a book. The printer was his own, Samuel Macham, and though there was no author's name on the title page, it was soon known to everyone that the author was John Donne.

People did not like his extravagant praise of Elizabeth Drury, and they did not hesitate to write and tell him, if not what they thought of it themselves, then what they had heard others say about it. Ben Jonson was reported to have said that it was profane and full of blasphemies, that "if it had been written of the Virgin Mary it had been something." John's ladies, Lady Bedford, Lady Danvers, Lady Huntingdon, were highly offended, and there were plenty of friends to report that to John. He wrote defending himself: that he described the idea of a woman, not Elizabeth Drury as she really was; that since he never saw the gentlewoman, he could not be supposed to have spoken just truth, but that he never would have gone about to praise anybody in rhyme unless he took a person who might be capable of being all that he said; and finally, in a burst of irritation, that "if any of those ladies think that Mistress Drury was not so, let that lady make herself fit for all those praises in the book and it shall be hers." The only fault he acknowledged was that he had descended so low as to print his verse—even though several serious and high-minded men had set the example by publishing theirs.

That he had, in "The Progress of the Soul," forgotten Elizabeth Drury for a time and written of the soul itself, of its journey and its ecstasy, nobody was keen enough to see, and he would never point it out to them.

He was, swiftly, sorry for his harshness about the critical ladies, and especially for his apparent defection from that loveliest lady, the Countess of Bedford. He sought to make amends by writing his apology in a poem for her.

> *This season, as 'tis Easter, as 'tis spring*
> *Must both to growth and to confession bring*
> *My thoughts disposed unto your influence; so*
> *These verses bud, so these confessions grow.*
> *First I confess I have to others lent*
> *Your stock, and over prodigally spent*
> *Your treasure, for since I had never known*
> *Virtue or beauty but as they are grown*
> *In you, I should not think or say they shine*
> *(So as I have) in any other mine.*

But he never finished it, for in that verse, what was he doing, when he said he had never known virtue or beauty anywhere but in Lady Bedford, but spending Anne's treasure and prodigally indeed?

Whatever he did, wherever he went, however he thought, that month in Paris, in the spring of 1612, his mind came back to Anne.

To George Gerrard he wrote:

> I am in the same perplexity which I mentioned before, which is, that I have received no syllable, neither from herself nor by any other, how my wife hath passed her danger, nor do I know whether I be increased by a child or diminished by the loss of a wife.
>
> I hear from England of many censures of my book of Mistress Drury. . . .

4 Heidelberg in May was foaming with fruit blossom and musical with bird song. John walked out to the middle of the bridge over the Neckar and stood looking down at the water, then back at the town. The church spires, the solid red brick

buildings with their round gables, and over all, towering into the blue sky, the great bulk of the castle, all looked bright and new and clean in the dazzling air. He had been here before, once, in his youth when he had just left Lincoln's Inn, but he had never seen it in the glory of spring and the spring sunshine, though he had walked here with lighter heart when he had walked under the rainy skies and dark clouds of November. Then he had been young, healthy, possessed of what he erroneously believed to be an endless fortune, and he had held, so he had seemed to believe, the world in his hands.

I died ten years ago, he thought, in the worldly sense, when the Lord Keeper threw me out. Still, I have had a long funeral —and I have managed to keep myself above ground without putrefaction. He smiled wryly and went on across the bridge to the other side of the river, where he took a path along the river's edge. Not ordinarily a walker for pleasure, he was glad to get away today by himself.

They had been traveling steadily, from Paris back to Amiens, to Maastricht and to Frankfurt, where they were crowded into very small quarters, the whole town being filled with the suites of the German princes who had come to choose the new Elector Palatine. From all over Europe, too, had come people to observe, to take the news back to their governments or just to be there, where something important was going on. They had elected, as everyone had known they would, the younger brother of Rudolph II, who had died childless. This new Elector, Frederick, a gay, handsome young man of eighteen, would be, it was widely said, the husband of England's Princess Elizabeth.

In Heidelberg they had very pleasant lodgings in a tall, well-built house with round gables on the chief street near the Holy Ghost Church and the market, but Sir Robert had felt insulted because he had not been invited to stay at the castle.

The new Elector was still in Maastricht, but his sister-in-law was there, and Sir Robert had a letter of introduction to her. He felt that he should have been invited to stay at the castle where his Princess would no doubt soon be chatelaine and he felt, illogically but firmly, that it was somehow young Frederick's fault that he had been slighted.

When John returned to their despised lodgings after a long walk up the Neckar, he found Sir Robert in excellent spirits impatiently waiting for him.

"I can't think why you've been so long," he declared. "Here is news—three letters full of it. Important news."

"Not—anything of my wife, sir?"

"No, no, no. I've told you she's all right. No, this is public news. In the first place, it is all set and decided that the Princess Elizabeth will marry the young Elector. It was evidently decided even before the actual election."

"That was the Lord Salisbury's doing, I am sure, sir. It will strengthen the Protestant alliance. But quite apart from that, the two young people are handsome and gay and will make a good pair."

"Yes, yes, that's all very true, but my next two letters have more news. About my lord of Salisbury himself. He has been very ill. In fact, this letter tells me about his illness—and this one, which came at the same time, tells of his death."

"So? I am sorry to hear it. In important business between nations, he was a very good patriot."

He remembered the Lord Treasurer vividly, the little crooked man, with the great brilliant eyes, the hollow cheeks, the look of suffering. As Sir Robert Cecil, he had been the old Queen's secretary. John remembered him at York House the day of the Essex scolding, standing at the long table, delivering his clear, cold words. He had never had the greatness of his father, Lord Burghley, but he had been tenacious, scheming, loyal and hardworking. Under the very eyes of the dying Elizabeth he had worked to get James onto the throne—James, who called him his little black pygmy. He had added the post of Lord Treasurer to his secretaryship of State, and more than anyone else he had worked to keep England on an even keel, writing dispatches late into the night, since his royal master hunted all day and could not talk to his ministers till evening. He had had honors, but he had had to pay for them. The King had taken a fancy

276

to his manor of Theobalds and the great lovely house that his father had built there and Salisbury had improved, and he had had to give it to him in exchange for Hatfield, which the King did not like.

"The point is," Sir Robert broke in on his thought, "who is to succeed him?"

"There will be changes. I wonder. Has Wotton a chance, do you think?"

"More likely Sir Walter Cope, my great friend. I have a letter from him here. He has been very close to Salisbury. It's very likely he might be chosen. Though, of course, there's always Rochester."

"But he is very young—he's only twenty-two or so."

"Yes, I think too young for this, though the King dotes on him. No, I think it will be Sir Walter Cope. Now let me read you his letter—or parts of it, for it is very long. He gives a full account of the Lord Treasurer's illness first—Mr. Mayerne was in attendance and bled him, of course; then they thought it was scurvy—and then dropsy—and then they took him to Bath, and he began to improve." He scanned the letter, reading bits and phrases: " 'With diet, physic and the bath together we hope to carry him back again'—this was written only two or three days before his death. Strange, is it not, how suddenly men are mortal? And now listen to this:

"I marvel that my Lord Treasurer never receives any letters from you. Although Mr. Donne and you have no place of ambassadors, yet I trust that you have, that can and do, observe as much as the best that have employment from the States, and it will be no ill introduction towards the setting such idle persons on work. But I presume your silence hath grown rather from my Lord's long sickness, which in me (I must confess) has bred such a dullness as I have been careless of all writing or compliment; and this I assure you has been the cause that my Lord Treasurer wrote not according to his appointment his letters unto my noble friend, Sir Robert Drury, unto whom with his noble lady I commend my service; not forgetting my best commendation to Mr. Donne, who is enriching his treasury for his country's better service, toward the which, if I be not able to add a mite, yet I shall be ever ready to cry Amen.

"Then he signs himself, 'Your loving friend.'"

So they had been in the Lord Treasurer's mind—not only Sir Robert Drury but John Donne as well.

"I always said," exulted Sir Robert, "that going abroad and meeting people and becoming known, not only among Englishmen, but among men of other countries too, was the path toward preferment."

"Unfortunately, Lord Salisbury is dead."

"Yes, of course, but don't you see, if Sir Walter Cope should succeed him, I am—and you too, Mr. Donne—already firmly in his good graces and his liking."

"Should we not then go home, to be on hand when decisions are made?"

"We should, no doubt. And we will. We will just return to Maastricht to see the young Elector, and we mustn't miss Louvain, of course, and we ought to present ourselves at the Archduke's court at Brussels—but we will go home, Mr. Donne, we will indeed."

XXIV

IT WAS A WARM, SUNNY AUGUST MORNING and Anne had promised to take the older children up on the down to play. She was in the cool, dim buttery, packing a basket for their dinner, assisted, or perhaps watched over, by the massive Mrs. Muggins, the cook.

"Here's the cold beef, Mistress Donne, and there's part of a cold veal pasty. Would they like that, do you think?"

Anne hastened to decline the veal pasty. They had had it at supper the night before and she had thought it was high then.

"It's too warm a day for so much meat. Just the beef and plenty of bread—and cheese of course. And something fresh—is there fruit?" She stood chipping bits of ash and cinder from a loaf of bread.

There was always plenty of cheese, and good cheese. It was made right here at Nunwell by the dairy maids, directed by Frances. It was still, after a year—dear God, they had been here a year!—amazing to Anne to find her little sister so capable and responsible a housekeeper. Every morning early she was up and out, stepping across the courtyard—high on her pattens, if it was rainy—to oversee the maids in the dairy. She sold her cheeses at the market in Newport and the profits were hers to keep. Nor did she skimp the household on her milk and cheese in order to have more to sell; there was always cream for syllabubs and puddings, milk to drink, always plenty of cheese for the family.

The gardener's boy came in at that moment with a basket of lettuces and cabbages and in one corner a golden mound of apricots.

Muggins unloaded the lot and gave him back the basket with a friendly clout on the head. He was a small, knobby boy, all over freckles, with a grin that broke his face in half. He was very knowledgeable about the woods and fields, and in May he had taken Johnny and George bird's-nesting; they had come home rapturous but with such additions to their vocabulary that Sir John, who had strict ideas about bringing up children, declared they must not go again.

"Would you like some of the apricots?" suggested Muggins, but without very much conviction in her voice. Anne hesitated, for they were ripe and fragrant and the children loved them; but remembering that they grew against the wall of the garden and that Sir John took the most possessive pride in them, that Johnny had stolen some when they first began to be ripe, with a great row afterwards, she declined the apricots and said she would take gooseberries instead.

She was covering the basket with a white napkin when Frances came in, fresh and neat in her gown of gray linen, which had been grown and spun and woven and stitched right here on the place, with her curls twisted up on top of her head and her little, preoccupied frown creasing her forehead.

"Anne, it's going to be dreadfully hot today. Do you really think you ought to take the children out in the sunshine? Wouldn't they be better here in the house where it's cool, sitting quietly with their horn books and their lessons?" She was all of twenty-two but she knew, Anne thought with a spurt of rebellion, all there was to know.

"I promised them," she said.

"A parent sometimes has to break promises when it is best for the children—but of course it is better not to make rash promises at all. And you look so thin and pale, Anne. The children run wild when they get out of doors and you have no control over them. I'm just thinking how to spare you, you know."

She had two children of her own, George, twenty months old, and John, nine months old, both still with their wet-nurses. Anne, gripping her temper tight, hoped silently that the young Oglanders, when they came home to their mother, would be as noisy and disobedient and altogether troublesome as it was possible for children to be.

"They play quite happily up there, and I shall rest under the tree," she said stubbornly.

"Oh, apricots! Have you taken some for your dinner?"

"No, but we've got plenty of gooseberries."

Frances carefully picked out six of the ripest and best of the fruit and tucked them into the basket under the napkin, adding some comfits from a box on the shelf. "There, that's better," she said with a loving smile, and Anne, not for the first time, inwardly berated herself for a sour, ungrateful guest. But to be a guest for a year, for a whole year! And still no word when John would be home. Suppose he was ill. Suppose he was wounded—set upon in a dark street by some foreign ruffian! Suppose he was dead. What would they do, she and her seven children?

She stopped in the orchard to see Nurse and the two smallest ones before going away from the house. Nurse had aged during the past year; she was small and withered; her hair, strained back into a tiny knob, lay in separate strings over her bald scalp; she had become a great grumbler, nothing was right, there was no slightest disorder or inconvenience that she did not tell Anne about. The five older children drove her frantic, but she still could handle the two little ones, Bridget, three, and Mary, two.

"When Mr. Donne comes back," said Nurse, giving Anne an expert stab, "I'll have to have a nursemaid to help me. I really can't carry Mary up and down the stairs much longer. She's getting too heavy."

"But I've told you and told you not to carry her. It's good for her to use her own legs."

In the courtyard Anne met the older children coming away from the dairy, their mouths ringed with white.

"Are you ready, Mother? Can we go now?"

Sir John Oglander, in a wide hat and boots, came out from the house on his way to the stable. Anne thought him good-looking but only in an insignificant sort of way; so different from her John with his brown eyes under the high, arched brows, dark hair, full but flexible and sensitive mouth, his ardor, his humor, his elegance. Still, she had to admit to herself that John Oglander was hard-working and successful. When he and Frances—whom he called "Frank"—came to Nunwell, it had been neglected and poor. Together they were bringing it back to prosperity. He had planted two orchards, learned what crops to grow; Frances managed the dairy, tended the knot garden. They were planning to put in raspberries next year.

"I couldn't have done it without Frank," he was fond of saying. "She is so careful—no spender—up every day before me. Doesn't leave things to her women. Doesn't even wear a silk gown—except for her credit when she goes abroad."

Anne now saw him looking at her gown, and remembered his strictures on silk. She was wearing an old one of green taffeta that she and Nurse had just washed and turned and made over; now that farthingales had gone out of fashion, it was easy to make over a gown, for less silk was needed; you could cut out the worn pieces and discard them. It had never occurred to Anne not to wear silk—even if the money must be borrowed to buy it. But she thought Sir John must disapprove—a woman come to visit for two months who stayed a year, eating other people's bread and dressed in silk when the lady of the house wore homespun.

"Good morning, sir," and as she said it she knew that her smile was more deprecating than she intended it to be—"we are going up on the down to play and have our dinner."

She seized the children whom she could reach and wiped the milk off their faces with her handkerchief; the others licked their mouths hastily. They lined up in a row as Constance had taught them to do—she was, she had explained to Anne, preparing for the day when their father would come home—and in concert, as if they were in a masque or a play, the boys bowed, the girls curtseyed.

He laughed and returned the bow, then picked up Lucy and swung her high in the air while she squealed with delight and kicked her feet. Lucy was a favorite; she was such a chubby bundle of joy, with dancing brown eyes and orange hair in unmanageable spikes around her small, pointed face.

"I am going to Newport," said Sir John, setting Lucy down again. "Is there anything that I can do for you?"

Anne caught her breath. If she had known in time she would have written a letter to John. There was more opportunity to send a letter from Newport than from Brading, though neither place was good. There was no regular carrier to London, and few of the Oglanders' friends, who might have taken letters, ever left the island. Anne had written several times in the autumn and once in January after the baby was born dead, but none of her letters seemed to have reached John. In the few that she had had from him—and none for more than two months now—he complained that he had not heard from her. For a moment she thought of asking Sir John to wait while she scratched out a note, but second thoughts told her that it would not do.

"No, I thank you, sir, but it is kind of you to offer."

She would have liked a length of white lawn to make aprons for Constance and Lucy to wear over their dresses, but she had no money to pay for it. Her father had not sent her last quarter's money. He was short himself, she suspected, for he was spending a great deal these days, repaneling the great chamber at Loseley House, and his sons were costing him a good deal. Young George was in attendance on Prince Henry and clamored for horses, for new clothes, for money for gaming.

They were on their way up the hill at last, Constance and Johnny ahead, carrying the basket between them, Francis and Lucy following, George walking beside Anne. George was beginning, at seven, to look a little like his grandfather, but he had not inherited that turbulent disposition. Of all the children he was the best-natured, calm, easy-going, unruffled. Anne smiled down at him now as he reached up to take her hand and they walked along together swinging their hands between them.

They had a favorite place on the down where a little knot of trees, old and twisted by the wind, provided the mast of a sailing ship to climb or the battlements of a castle to guard. The children were hungry the minute they reached the trees, and they proposed to eat their dinner at once, though it would be two hours yet before the dinner was ready in the hall below.

Anne betook herself with bread and cheese to her own special spot, where she could sit leaning against a rock and looking down on the road—not that it was a road, only some tracks through the grass—from Brading to Nunwell. She no longer watched it to see if John was coming, for disappointment too often had choked her like dust in the mouth, but she liked to have the road under her eyes.

The little village with its church tower, the church where the baby was buried—had she, she sometimes wondered, killed it grieving for John, raging because he did not come?—huddled among its trees under the August sun. Those trees, which had been in the spring so many different shades of green—pale, bluish, yellowish, pinkish, emerald—were now all the same dull, rather tired color and so full of leaves that they were like mounds, wide or humped or pointed but all thick and solid, except where the tower of the chimney of a house nudged its way among them.

Beyond the village were undulating fields and meadows and woods, and beyond them the silver waters of Spithead, with Portsmouth no more than a smudge on the horizon. Today it was all bleached of color by the sun and misted over with heat; the water looked metallic and a little fishing boat was a child's toy.

Now and then a light breeze stirred the hair about her forehead and cooled her cheeks. The two younger children, Francis and Lucy, were playing "house" nearby; she could hear their soft voices murmuring in the game. Francis, with his fair hair and chiseled features, was a small reproduction of Francis

Woolley, a shy, sensitive child, gentler than the other boys, more affectionate. The memory of his difficult birth and his fragility as a baby, the long fear that they might lose him, made him especially precious to Anne. The three older children were up in the tree. Constance was far too old for such games now; at nine she should be beginning to be a lady. "These little men and women," Sir John was fond of saying, "should behave like their elders in all things as far as it is possible for them to do, but you encourage them, Anne, you positively encourage them to be childish."

Their life, Anne thought, leaning against her rock, would be hard enough when they got older; let them have what happiness they could now, while they were too young to understand their situation: fatherless, dependent upon the charity of relatives. If John was alive, why wasn't he here? If he loved his children, if he loved her, why did he stay away month after month without a word? She thought of how she had wept before he went, as if somehow she had foreseen the long anxiety, the pain, the despair.

> But think that we
> Are but turned aside to sleep;
> They who one another keep
> Alive, ne'er parted be.

It was all very well for him to say that, but once he would not have. Once he had written:

> Love's mysteries in souls do grow,
> But yet the body is his book.

A dull sublunary lover she might be, but what she wanted was his eyes, his voice, his lips, his arm around her, his shoulder warm and solid under her cheek, not his metaphysical soul.

The children's voices grew faint. She slept.

A long time later she heard a voice say, "Anne." Her eyes flew open. He was leaning over her; she felt his hand on her shoulder.

"John!"

He took her hands in his, pulled her up to her feet, then swept her into his arms. She clung to him, laughing and crying, scarcely knowing if she still dreamed, yet feeling his bones and flesh against her body, his lips warm and hard upon her own. At last she pushed him away, saying, "The children," and they turned, his arm still around her, to find the five lined up as Constance had taught them, as they had so often practiced. When they caught their father's eye, the three boys in the center of the line bowed, the little girls at each end curtseyed, Constance elegantly, Lucy all but upsetting herself. The next moment they flung themselves upon him. Anne stood aside to let him take the impact as they climbed his legs, jumped to fling tight arms around his neck, hung on his arms.

He looked thin, was her first impression, thin and tired, yet somehow French, with his beard cut shorter and more pointed and a Frenchified hat on his head. The horse from which he had dismounted cropped the grass, a gaunt, swaybacked, spavined creature that made Anne, who had grown up where there were good horses in the stables, cry out:

"Where did you get that nag?"

"I bought her to make the journey. When we get back to London, I'll sell her again. She's no beauty, but she brought me here." He detached himself carefully from his children, who clung like burrs, and said to them, "Why don't you take Petronella to the stable, feed her and water her and rub her down? You could do that, couldn't you? There are sugarplums in the saddle bag which you may have later."

Four of them went off importantly with the mare, but Constance lingered behind. In spite of a large three-cornered tear in the front of her gown and a streak of dirt down her cheek, she had a natural grave grace and dignity that were, Anne thought, enchanting. "I just wanted to say," Constance said to John, "we're glad you're home safe," and then, suddenly shy, she turned and ran off, her dark hair streaming behind her.

"She doesn't look at all like you," said John, "but she's more like you in mind and spirit than all the others."

286

"John, are you all right, really?"

"Only dusty—and not fit to touch you, my dearest love, until I've bathed."

"I don't mind dust," she cried, locking her hands behind his neck.

"Anne, I have been so worried—distracted—not hearing, not knowing even if you were alive. I came at once. Sir Robert wished me to go to Windsor with him, but I set out for Wight immediately."

Through her joy in seeing him the long, deep hurt forced its way up. She struggled out of his embrace. Kissing her hands, he let her go.

"Why did you stay away so long?"

"It seemed foolhardy to offend Sir Robert. I thought—I hoped—that through him I might obtain some preferment that would put an end to our troubles. I had no word at all from you, Anne, nothing, in all these months."

"I wrote three times, but it is difficult to send mail from here."

"I did not know whether you were dead or the baby or both."

"It was born dead, a girl. She's buried in Brading Church—you can see the tower in the trees. I wanted you dreadfully that day. I even cried out for you as if you could hear me."

"I saw you, Anne, with the child in your arms. I could not tell if both lived or neither. But I saw you as clearly as I see you now."

"But why didn't you come?"

"I couldn't. Sir Robert would not release me. And I had no money to leave without his help."

"And did you—are you—has it been worth it all?"

"I suppose one must say both Sir Robert and I came home disappointed. But I have the house in Drury Lane, and I am to write an epithalamium for the marriage of the Princess Elizabeth and the young Elector Palatine. I have hopes . . ."

Hopes. Was there a more discouraging word in the whole English language? He looked, she saw now, beyond the dust and fatigue, beyond the overlay of worldliness, defeated.

"So then," said Sir John Oglander when they sat in the orchard after supper, preparing to sing madrigals, as he and his Frank were fond of doing, "your year in France has brought you no material advantage at all?"

"It is difficult to estimate such things correctly; certainly no immediately evident advantage. I have at least ground under my feet and a roof over my head. Sir Robert has offered me one of his houses in Drury Lane."

"One of those new houses he has built on his land? Why, sir, those houses rent for twenty pounds a year!"

"Here are the music sheets," said Frances nervously. "Shall we sing? Do you like 'See What I Have,' Mr. Donne?"

"Very much, thank you. Sir Robert will not press me about the rent. Do you know Drury House, Frances?" He was speaking entirely to the Oglanders. Anne sat a little out of the circle and clenched her hands in her lap, suffering for John and for the crass assaults on his pride.

"Yes, I have seen it. It is more like a manor house than a city mansion, with that big court in front and the gardens and orchard behind."

"The house that we are to have"—and now he turned to smile at Anne—"has a small court of its own. There is a narrow passageway to Drury Lane, but the main entrance is on Drury Court. It is pleasant and well built—not like the Mitcham house—and Lady Drury will lend us what furniture we need."

"I only meant to say," said Sir John a little hastily, "that we should be glad, Frank and I, to have you remain here as long as it would be convenient to you."

"You are more than kind, but we have already trespassed too long on your generosity. We must return to London as soon as I can find a coach to hire."

"Oh, you may have mine and welcome—but don't hurry, don't hurry. You know, I have thought, Mr. Donne, that if all else fails, there is always the church."

"The church!" exclaimed Frances. "Can you imagine John Donne a country parson on thirteen pounds a year? That is what the rector of Brading Church gets."

"He needn't be a country parson," said her husband, nettled.

"I thought we were going to sing madrigals," said Anne.

But when they were alone together, she said slowly, "There *is* the church, John. You would not be a country parson—you would be a bishop soon. It might answer everything. You know so much about divinity already . . ."

She heard her voice trail away to silence. He looked like a stranger, so remote and distant, so pale, so still.

"Shall I go into God's house," he said, "only because I have nowhere else to go? I cannot think that He would welcome me."

XXV

"Good Friday, 1613, Riding Westward"

HE GAVE HIS POEM a title as he rode through the April country-
side, his back to the east and his face toward Montgomery-
shire, where Lady Danvers was staying with her son Edward
in the newly repurchased family stronghold of the Herberts,
Montgomery Castle.

> *. . . I am carried towards the West*
> *This day when my soul's form bends toward the East.*
> *There I should see a Sun by rising set,*
> *And by that setting endless day beget*

Anne, five months pregnant, was safe in the house in
Drury Lane, with two passably good maids; he rode attended by a French boy, Henri; they lived on Anne's eighty
pounds and borrowed money.

> *. . . Thou lookst toward me,*
> *O Savior, as Thou hangst upon the tree.*
> *I turn my back to Thee but to receive*
> *Corrections till Thy mercies bid Thee leave.*
> *O think me worth Thine anger, punish me,*
> *Burn off my rusts, and my deformity;*
> *Restore Thine image, so much, by Thy grace,*
> *That Thou mayst know me, and I'll turn my face.*

He brought back from Montgomery Castle this poem and another, "The Primrose," and a memory that did nothing to burn off the rust of unworthiness and uselessness that he felt encrusting, thick and heavy, his metal.

It had been a great refreshment to him to come to that lovely place of hills and valleys; to see the drifts of primroses, each with its drop of dew, sparkling like some terrestrial galaxy; to be again with Lady Danvers; to talk with her of the new philosophy and of the old, poetic, soon-to-be-discarded spheres and intelligences of the old; to show her his Good Friday poem and to bask in her discerning admiration. Her young husband was away, in Wiltshire, visiting his old mother, her son Edward occupied with the ordering of his property; she herself, happy in this country life, had grown young again, full of laughter and wit. His long, platonic love for her had melted suddenly into something much warmer and more importunate, and if she had at any moment in that week shown the slightest sign of declining from the intellectual heights on which she lived, he would, God help him, have been for the first time unfaithful to Anne. But—and he felt rueful as well as relieved—it was his mind alone that she had wanted.

Back in London again, he met Lord Rochester, to whom Lord Hay had once before presented him, and to his surprise and satisfaction was immediately given some work to do for him, though cautioned to keep silent about it. It appeared that Rochester had tired of the man of business and somewhat critical mentor whom he had brought with him from Scotland and who had guided his upward climb; he had induced the King to offer to Sir Thomas Overbury the post of ambassador to France. When he declined it, Sir Thomas found himself thrown summarily into the Tower for contempt. It was to John ironical that he should succeed a man ruined for refusing what he himself would have been only too happy to accept, but Court life was full of such ironies.

The business that John did for Lord Rochester was trivial enough, but the money he received for it was welcome, and even more was his lordship's promise to procure him a place in the government as soon as he could manage it. Soon, however, and most disappointingly, even the small tasks dwindled as Rochester—and all London—became absorbed in the scandalous spectacle of the divorce, or the "nullity proceedings," of the Earl and Countess of Essex.

The case began in June and went on throughout the summer. Ten Commissioners—bishops and legal lights—heard the arguments and the explicit, and to most people indecent, discussions as to whether the young Earl of Essex was impotent, whether the Countess was a virgin—both of which contentions everyone knew to be untrue—whether their marriage had been unconsummated and therefore could be dissolved. The Archbishop of Canterbury and John's old friend, Bishop Andrewes, with three others, stood staunchly against the divorce, but they were unable to prevail against those who knew what the King's favorite, and therefore the King, desired; they could only force a stalemate, a vote of five to five.

London talked of nothing else. All the details behind the details were known to everyone; who the heavily veiled young virgin was who substituted for Lady Essex when the midwives ascertained her virginity; why Lady Essex was willing to accept the uncomplimentary assertion of her husband's impotence only *ad illam,* toward her alone; who the second husband waiting to marry her was.

"Great folks will have their ends without respect of friends or followers," was the usual comment, made with a shrug.

John was incredulous at first when the word went around that Lord Rochester and Lady Essex would be married as soon as the proceedings were successfully accomplished. Anne's time came in August and he was thankful for a good excuse to stay away from the Court and Paul's and the seething talk. Their ninth child, a boy, Nicholas, was born easily and happily, and the summer days when John sat by Anne's bedside reading aloud to her were a little haven of peace and tenderness from the storm of evil and ugliness that he felt beating around the young lord whose patronage he had been so eager to win.

In October the King appointed two more judges, whose acquiescence he could depend upon, and by a vote of seven to five the divorce was won; in the same month Sir Thomas Overbury died, unmourned and alone, in the Tower; and in November, at a solemn ceremony at Whitehall, the King created Rochester Earl of Somerset. His marriage to the Countess of Essex was set for St. Stephen's Day, and he sent word to John that he expected him to write an epithalamium for it.

John was not at Whitehall to see his patron made an earl. A nagging little mist, which at first he tried to brush away with his hand, had begun to creep across his eyes. Ascribing it to some disorder of the stomach, he kept to his room and fasted rigorously, but to no avail. The mist spread and darkened. Each day he could see a little less, and what he did see became vaguer and more blurred.

He called in doctors. On his window sill a line of tumblers filled with drops and potions lengthened like some sinister blossoming vine. Sitting in the swirling dusk on a sunny December day, he felt icy fingers of fear probe and pinch his heart: if he should go blind, what then would become of his family, of his wife and eight children?

"It will pass," said Anne, but her voice trembled.

He was aware of voices as never before. He heard not only a trembling, a lack of conviction, a fading out, but a dozen subtly different shades of intended encouragement, from the casually hearty, through the defiantly hopeful, to the stoutly denied despair. He discerned impatience, withdrawal, unhappiness, in voices that the speakers obviously believed to be cheerful.

"I know it will pass," repeated Anne. "Dr. Laysmith can find nothing wrong."

"Nothing—except that I am half blind already and growing worse. I cannot see your face, Anne, when you stand across the room."

That brought her swiftly to him, swooping to kneel beside his chair and take his hand tightly in hers.

"If you would only give your poor eyes a rest. Stop writing. I can't bear to see you straining over the paper with your head tilted close to it."

"I can still see to write out of the corners of my eyes. I *must* write. Letters—and my lord's epithalamium."

Her face was a pale blur at the level of his knees, but the tear that fell on his hand was sharp as a pellet of warm hail. He drew his hand away. He could not carry her grief; he could barely manage his own paralysis of fear.

"If you could just have faith——"

"Faith? In God? In Dr. Laysmith? In my lord of Rochester —Somerset, I mean——"

"Faith in yourself." Her voice wisped away, in weariness, in a deeply buried accusation that she would indignantly deny but which he knew was there.

"Get up, my dear. What eyesight I have I shall use, and hope that it will not grow less."

The paper over which he bent his head was white, and the chain of words across it twinkled like black stars, one word vanishing while those on either side flashed almost clear. He could remember what he had written and go on, though only bits were visible.

> *If by that manly courage they be tried*
> *Which scorns unjust opinion . . .*

But was the world's opinion unjust? And was it courage to scorn it—or only reckless folly, if not wickedness?

"We have so much to be thankful for," Anne's voice went on pleadingly, "this house, and London. You so often say you only feel really alive in London. And our children—all well and handsome and intelligent. There's not one of them lacking in wits or twisted in body. We have a little money."

"A little, not enough. I must write this epithalamium that my lord has commanded."

She was standing at the window now, her back to him. Her voice came muffled, by her intervening body or by some unwillingness in her heart.

"I don't see how you can think of anything to write, so soon after the other."

He had written an epithalamium for the Princess Elizabeth and the Count Palatine, who had been married on the fourteenth of February, using the old theme of St. Valentine and the marriage of the birds. ("Tell me some birds, Anne, besides the lark." "Oh, you know more than that. Sparrow, linnet, robin redbreast, blackbird, dove, goldfinch——" "That's enough. They will do.") He had enjoyed writing that one, though in all the flood of congratulatory poems and masques it had attracted little attention. This one for Lord Rochester —Lord Somerset—was far more difficult.

"I have thought of a line to end each stanza. For the rest, these poems are all the same—the bride's apparelling, the marriage, the feast, the bride's going to bed, the bridegroom's coming——"

"What is the line?"

"Which?"

"The one to end each stanza."

He stirred restlessly in his chair, oddly reluctant to tell her, feeling churlish in his unwillingness, irritated with her for forcing him into this self-division.

" 'The fire of these inflaming eyes or of this loving heart,' " he said stiffly, thinking how abysmally false it sounded.

"How can you say she has a loving heart?"

"It could be his. I suppose we must concede that they love each other."

"I think this whole affair has made you ill," Anne said suddenly, "and blind—as if your eyes refused to see it."

She knew him so well; he felt imprisoned by her knowledge. He could not deny to her, or to himself, the deep revulsion that he felt at the thought of celebrating the marriage of Lady Essex and Lord Somerset. Without answering her, he bent his head sidewise close to the paper again. If the King and the Court and seven bishops and legal gentlemen endorsed it, who was he to disapprove? They were young— Fanny Howard but nineteen, Lord Somerset twenty-four or

295

twenty-five—and highly placed; they had the habit of getting everything they wanted; perhaps now that they had each other they might start afresh, though young Essex went off humiliated, though their happiness was built on perjury—for Lady Essex had been, as everyone knew, Prince Henry's mistress before he died, a year ago. But John could not write an acceptable epithalamium if he thought about those two young people; he must imagine an ideal couple and write about them.

Blest pair of swans, O may you interbring
Daily new joys . . .

May never age or error overthwart
With any west these radiant eyes, with any north this heart.

"Oh, John, let me write it for you. Say it to me and let me write it down."

But when she sat there, pen poised, expectant, his ideas vanished.

2   From the window of his study John could see Sir Robert Drury approaching, blown across the courtyard by the force of a cold February wind. The weeks had given him back his sight, though he shared the ague and flux that had stricken all his family and made of his house a hospital. Huddled in blankets, he sat in his big chair by the fire and worried about Anne and the sick children upstairs.

"Well, Mr. Donne, better this afternoon? It is hot and airless in here. You'd do better to open the window wide and let in some of this cold, invigorating breeze!"

Shuddering at the very thought, John felt the icy yet helpless distaste of the weak and sick for the healthy blusterer.

"Have you eaten anything yet? Some good rare beef would build up your strength."

"No, I am better to fast. A miserable distribution of mankind, is it not, where one half lacks meat and the other stomach?"

Sir Robert pulled the other chair as far away from the fire as he could get it, and sat down.

"How is Mrs. Donne today?"

"She is better, thank you—or would be, if she would only remain in bed. But the illness of her children terrifies her and she must be up and caring for them."

Less than a week ago Anne had miscarried. She had kept her pregnancy from him. It had not been difficult to do, with his threatened blindness and deep preoccupation with himself, the ashes that had drifted between them. She had lost half a child, and though he had grieved for her sake, he could only feel thankful for his own that there would not be a ninth child in the summer. They were ill provided to meet even these present expenses of physic and physicians.

"And my little pet?"

Three-year-old Mary was the darling of the whole family, even small, imperious Lucy adoring her with a motherly indulgence. John sighed. "She seems less well today, very quiet and patient, poor mite, but weak."

"I brought her a toy. It's in my pouch—here." He pulled a small rag doll, bent double, out of his purse and laid it on the table.

"It is good of you to bear my child in mind. She will be overjoyed. I'll have Henri take it up."

He tinkled the bell again. Henri arrived with a glass of ale for Sir Robert.

"I have my seat for the Parliament," said Sir Robert, sitting back and sipping the ale, "as one of two members for the borough of Eye in Suffolk. In the end I had to ask my brother-in-law to come to my aid. It is past my understanding why I find it so difficult to find means to serve the state. As you do too, of course, but in my case I should have thought there would be no question. Knighted on the battlefield, widely traveled, known abroad, money to spend. Why, I laid out two thousand pounds for the French ambassadorship and then did not get it. Any other country but England would be glad to make use of me. My wife," he added, "says I am indiscreet."

He admitted the charge with some complacence, as if indiscretion implied courage and honesty. He was indeed, John thought, indiscreet—his disparaging remarks about the Elector

Frederick had been both widespread and impolitic—but he was kind and intelligent and loyal.

"Your indiscretion is small compared with that of Sir Harry Wotton," said John, "and he is back again in the King's favor, I am happy to hear."

Ten years earlier, Wotton had lightheartedly written in a friend's album a definition of an ambassador as "one sent to lie abroad in the service on his country," a sufficiently damaging pun in English; but to make it worse, he had written it in Latin, in which the word *mentire* has but one meaning. For nine years it had lain hidden, unnoticed; then Scoppius, the controversialist, had happened to come upon it and had used it in his *Ecclesiasticus,* a bitter attack on King James's *Apologia;* if, he crowed, the King's own ambassador boasted of being sent abroad to lie, what truth could one expect to find in the King himself or in his book? The King had been understandably angry with Wotton, but after a year of disgrace and two abject apologies in the form of a Latin pamphlet addressed to the public and a private letter to the King in English, Wotton was again in good odor. John, who saw him fairly often and exchanged poems with him, rejoiced for him.

"He is to sit for Appleby, I am told," said Sir Robert. "By the bye, are you settled for the Parliament?"

"The Master of the Rolls has offered me the borough of Taunton." He had the offer of two other seats besides, a fact that he forebore to mention. He was looking forward with pleasure to the Parliament—if only he could recover his health —for to sit again in St. Stephen's Hall, and with friends beside him, would be, if not a return to his youth, at least a reminder of those days when he had been the Lord Keeper's able young secretary, full of hopes and ambitions.

"The piece of news that I came to tell you," said Sir Robert, "is that I heard in Paul's that Sir Dudley Carleton grows tired of Venice and wishes to come home. The other thing is that my lord Harington has died suddenly—of a combination of measles and smallpox—after the doctors had declared he would recover."

"Oh, oh, I am sorry to hear that. My lady Bedford will indeed be desolate—her father but a few months ago and now her brother. He was very young, not more than one-and-twenty, and promising."

"Extravagant, like all that family. Have you seen Lady Bedford since her own illness?"

"Yes, I was in Court when she first appeared—ravaged and without a touch of rouge, her hair straight. Among all the painted and frizzled ladies she looked strange indeed, but her goodness and her intelligence tower above the others'."

He spoke mechanically. He was beginning to tire of the effort of talking, and he wanted, moreover, to hear some news from the sickrooms upstairs.

"I hear your 'blest pair of swans' have begun to peck each other."

To this further proof of Sir Robert's indiscretion, John, who had already heard from George Gerrard that all was not going well with the Somersets, answered shortly:

"I have heard no word from them."

"No answer yet to your epithalamium?"

"None."

He had not finished it until the wedding was over and friends had brought him accounts of it: of Lady Essex with her hair defiantly flowing on her shoulders like a virgin's, of the masques that Ben Jonson wrote, of the Lord Mayor's dinner, of the fireworks and of all the wedding presents, the gold warming pan, silver fire tongs and all the other fantastic extravagances. He had added an eclogue to his poem, in which a character named Idios explained his absence from the wedding and offered a "poor song" in testimony of his recognition of the day—a weak device but the best he could conjure up. Whether offended by the lateness of the epithalamium or merely occupied in quarreling with his bride, Somerset had sent no word to John in two months. Much as he deplored the divorce and the wedding, John still looked to Somerset to fulfill his promises. He might try to comfort himself with the reflection that though he was poor and sick, he had learning and philosophy, that he could make his study a court with a few books supplying the conversation of many friends; but he labored still under a sense of unprofitable retiredness that declined into melancholy, a need for work to do that tended toward desperation.

After Sir Robert had left, John heard a faint wail from upstairs, a sound so full of weariness and pain that it brought him to his unsteady feet. Gripping the oak banister, he pulled himself up the stairs and made his way to the room where the little girls slept, three in one enormous bed and Mary, who was sickest, in a trundle bed by herself.

The three in the big bed, Constance, Lucy and Bridget, were whining and squabbling among themselves, complaining each one that the others usurped the cool parts of the bed; they were flushed and bright-eyed with fever, but that they were well enough to be cross was a relief to John, who tousled their heads in turn on his way to the trundle bed, where Anne, thin and pale as a wraith, knelt bathing the child's forehead with rose water.

She turned an anguished face to him. "She's worse! You must send for Dr. Laysmith at once."

He knelt beside her, putting his arm around her and drawing her close, feeling the thin shoulder blades, the rib-cage, the point of her hip-bone, and looked down at the child they both loved deeply. Her yellow hair was limp and dull, her little face pinched, the eyes unseeing, the small nose sharp, the breath rustling through the dry, parted lips. The healthy, joyous child who had kept them all rejoicing was transformed into this shrunken doll—lifeless and limp as the toy that Sir Robert had brought for her. In that moment John felt death a presence in the room, death, whom for so long he had studied, courted, feared, defied, but always in relation to himself, not to one he loved. In the cold February light he saw them all—himself, Anne, the children—as if in a painting, felt the darkness, smelled the sickroom odors, heard Anne's caught breath, felt the prickle of the rushes under his knees, tasted the bitterness of helplessness.

The children in the bed, sensing the trouble in the atmosphere, burst into loud cries, and Anne, turning, hissed fiercely, "Be quiet!"

"I'll get the doctor," said John, rising. "Never fear, dear heart!" But he felt the hollowness of his words.

Passing the big bed, he saw the little faces streaming with tears, heard the choking as they tried obediently to stifle their sobs, and remembered his own childhood, when he cried for some pain or grief and was whipped for crying. He found Henri and sent him flying for the doctor, but when he came upstairs again to Anne, she was holding the little body tight in her arms and rocking back and forth in an agony of grief. "It's too late," she said. "She's dead."

That evening they heard the passing bell from their parish church, St. Clement Danes, three long, somber strokes.

"I loved her well," said John.

"You don't understand," cried Anne. "You're not a mother."

She went to each of the children who remained, to the boys' room, where John and George and Francis slept in one bed, kissing tenderly each feverish, sleepy little face, waking them to give them physic, coaxing or scolding, whichever was necessary to get it down, drawing the covers tight around their necks; then to the girls' room, where Constance was quietly crying, and Lucy, with her hair in red spikes around her little face, and Bridget, pale and puzzled, lay like two spoons, Bridget's knees tucked into Lucy's behind. When she came to the cradle in the room that she and John shared, where the baby, Nicholas, slept, she looked into it incredulously, hot wax from the tipped candle dropping unnoticed on her hand.

"John!" she cried and then, screaming, "John!"

3 John sat again in the study window, where the glaring March sun streaming through the diamond panes warmed his shoulders and touched his heart with spring. After the babies' deaths and the bitter little funeral, he had himself, adding flux to fever, knocked at the gates of death. They had not opened, however, and now, weak as a day-old chick, he was content to be alive. The Lord Somerset, hearing of his illness, had sent a

haunch of venison from Royston and, what was more to the point, a kindly message. The relief of knowing that he was not, in spite of the long silence, out of favor with his lordship, had done more to conquer his illness, he thought, than all the bottles on his window sill.

Through the window he could see his three sons on their way to the stables, where they were sometimes permitted by Sir Robert's grooms, as a great kindness, to help clean out the stalls. Francis, trailing along behind the bigger boys, was so muffled in cloaks and scarves loaded on him by his mother that he looked nearly as wide as he was high. Always the delicate one of the children, he had made the least good recovery from his illness. When the Easter term began, Johnny would go to Westminster as a scholar, returning home only occasionally on Sunday or feast days. The other two went to a petty school in the neighborhood, but John hoped that George might in the autumn be admitted to Paul's. The little girls were being taught to read and to write—though not to cipher—by Anne.

He dipped his pen in the inkpot on the window sill and began to write on the paper balanced on his knee. The tone of extravagant compliment used in writing to great lords, especially when asking a favor, had become, by long practice, natural to him. The venison and the message from Lord Somerset made it feasible, he thought, to act now upon the information that Sir Robert had given him that day of the babies' deaths.

My most honored Lord,—Since your Lordship will not let me die but have by your favor of sending to me so much prevailed against a vehement fever that I am now in good degrees of convalescence, I was desirous that my first sacrifice to any person in the world for my beginning of health should be to your Lordship, that I might acknowledge that, as ever since I had the happiness to be in your Lordship's sight, I have lived upon your bread; so I owe unto your Lordship now all the means of my recovery and my health itself; so must all the rest of my life and means be a debt to your Lordship from whom, since I received a commandment so much to assist myself as to present to your Lordship whatsoever appears to me likely to advantage me and ease your Lordship.

So much for the preamble. Now for the meat.

I am bold now, in obedience to that commandment, to tell your Lordship that that is told me, that Sir D.C. is likely to be removed from Venice to the States. If your Lordship have no particular determination upon that place, nor upon me, I humbly beseech you to pardon me the boldness of asking you whether I may not be sent thither; all the substance and all the circumstances of this I most humbly submit to your Lordship, with a protestation as true as if I had made it six days since, when I thought myself very near an end, that I had rather be anything that arises out of your Lordship than any proposition of mine; and that I have been in possession of my fartherest ambitions ever since I had the dignity of being your Lordship's most humble and thankful servant, J. Donne.

He sealed it with the sheaf of snakes of the Donnes and sat looking at it as it lay on his knee. Venice. He had never been there. Rome, Florence, Milan, yes, but not Venice, the queen of them all. Harry Wotton's letters had filled him with a longing to see it—the canals, the palaces, the great basilica, the paintings—to meet and talk with the scholars and the artists, to enjoy the pageantry, the milder air and the endless sunshine. He spoke Italian fluently, he had experience of writing letters, of observing, he was skilled in the art of compliment. Lord Somerset, who was closer to the King than anyone, had promised him some good post. He sat there, turning the letter over and over in his long thin fingers, dreaming.

4 Even after supper the moist blanket of the August heat pressed down on the little courtyard where Anne and John

and Constance sat in the shade of the wall. The other children were all in the orchard, which when the Drurys were away became their playground, but Constance, who, being eleven, was constrained to behave like a young lady, toiled over her sampler, the rusted needle squeaking in and out, the silk tangling, while perspiration dripped down upon it from her round forehead.

London was a desert, for it was company, not houses, that distinguished between a city and a desert. The King was making a progress in one direction, the Queen in another, and those nobles who were not in attendance on one or the other had departed to their country places. The Drurys were in Suffolk. John, who had a borrowed horse pastured in Covent Garden, stayed home in hot and empty London to be with Anne.

One small expedition he had made; this morning early he had ridden to Harefield, on the Colne near Rickmansworth, to see the Lord Chancellor, returning just in time for supper.

"Tell me about it," said Anne, putting a stitch into the cambric collar that she was embroidering.

"We talked in the garden and then I dined with him. Lady Derby was away and there was very little company. What there was, was mostly at the steward's table. I think the Lord Chancellor was feeling lonely. Lord and Lady Huntingdon are in Yorkshire, Lady Frances and Sir John Egerton are at Ashridge. Did you know that John had had a fever several years ago and still walks lame from it?"

"How did my uncle look?"

"Old. His face has sagged, rather like a hound's, with long folds of skin beside his mouth, and he has lost several teeth. But still he has immense presence, even nobility is not too strong a word. He asked for you most kindly and expressed sympathy over the loss of our two little ones."

"Today Nicholas would have been just a year old."

John, sitting in the tiny courtyard where the hot breeze stirred the smells of London, imagined himself back in the garden at Harefield, under a beech tree, looking across the grass to the river and talking with that great man for whom he had had so much respect and affection and from whom he had been so long estranged. He had been filled with joy and hope when a roundabout message delivered by Christopher before he left for the north had intimated that the Lord Chancellor would be glad to see him.

"He was very kind, very fatherly, gave me good advice——"

"What kind of advice?"

"Not to lose heart, to keep my talents polished and ready for anyone who might be able to use them and"—he felt the color in his face—"he gave me a well-disguised but I thought pointed warning against attaching myself too closely to the Lord Chamberlain."

"Against Lord Somerset? But you have been working for him for over a year!"

"It is not generally known, it seems."

"Why does he dislike him?"

"He did not say—and indeed it was all so wrapped up that it was difficult to tell whom he meant. But he did remark that the Archbishop is promoting a new favorite—that extremely pretty young Villiers. But no matter about that. The important thing is that he was kind. And Anne, he expressed real distress about my fortunes, all but saying outright that he now feels remorse for his part in my downfall."

"Did you ask him if he has any work for you to do?"

"Dear love, I could not."

"I suppose that if he had had any, he would have broached the matter himself." The sudden flatness of her voice betrayed her disappointment.

"I was so content with his manner toward me and our companionship that I could not bring myself to turn it to good account. I was like an alchemist who, not finding the elixir, still rejoices in some little discoveries by the way." He spoke ruefully. The Parliament in the spring, dubbed the Addled Parliament, had been adjourned after two months. The ambassadorship for which he had applied had gone to Harry Wotton, who had naturally enough wanted to get back to Venice. While John waited for another sign from Lord Somerset, his debts mounted.

"Shall you go to Montgomery Castle?" said Anne.

The memory of his visit there sixteen months earlier came vividly to his mind, and its distillation in his poem about the primrose.

> *Upon this Primrose hill,*
> *Where if heaven would distil*
> *A shower of rain, each several drop might go*
> *To his own primrose and grow manna so;*
> *And where their form and their infinity*
> *Make a terrestrial galaxy,*
> *As the small stars do in the sky;*
> *I walk to find a true love; and I see*
> *That 'tis not a mere woman, that is she,*
> *But must or more or less than woman be.*
>
> *Yet know I not which flower*
> *I wish; a six or four;*
> *For should my true-love less than woman be,*
> *She were scarce anything; and then should she*
> *Be more than woman, she would get above*
> *All thought of sex, and think to move*
> *My heart to study her and not to love ...*
>
> *. . .   . .*
> *Live, primrose then, and thrive*
> *With thy true number, five;*
> *And, woman, whom this flower doth represent,*
> *With this mysterious number be content ...*

If Lady Danvers were a six-petaled primrose, above thought of sex rather than deficient in it, his Anne, after all, was ever the five-petaled flower, the true number, mysteriously right.

"No, I shall send the horse back to your brother tomorrow by the Guildford carrier. I won't leave you alone. So much company as I am you shall have."

5　The great rolling tones of the bell still sounding in their ears, they walked away from the Church of St. Clement Danes, where they had just heard prayers and sermon over the small, shrouded body of their son Francis and seen him buried in the churchyard. The voice of the minister, the yellow leaves drifting through the unseasonably warm November air, the sobs of the children, the stiff, silent body of Anne like a brittle wand beside him, that somber bell which seemed to catch up all their grief and roll it around in the air; all this summed up for John his failure and his guilt. At forty-one he looked back on a life of waste, the fortune his father had left him dissipated, his education and his travels useless, his gifts of mind and spirit wanted by no one. He felt empty and drained, and by nothing so much as by the loss of his children —three in so short a time and the last little boy, so fair and loving, the idol of Anne's heart.

Constance walked ahead holding Bridget's hand, Johnny, home from Westminster for the day, marching beside George; Lucy, her little face swollen and blotched, clung to Anne on the other side of John. Behind them came Jane Grimes, Anne's sister, and her husband Sir Thomas, who had come up from Camberwell to be with Anne.

They went into the house by the narrow passage from Drury Lane and found that Henri and the maids had prepared a little funeral feast—baked meats, biscuits and comfits, tankards of ale and wine. The best tankard was Lucy's, a tall silver one that Lady Bedford had given her as a god-mother's present. It would have to be pawned again, as it had had been once before, for Henri had declared his intention of going back to France (though John suspected that actually he had found better employment in London) and he would have to be paid for his last quarter's work and given a severence present. All the other debts could be put off, but he must have cash for this. He dreaded the business, summoning the gold-smith's man, weighing and appraising the tankard, wrapping it up in a linen handkerchief and pocketing the few pounds that it would bring; dreaded still more Anne's quietly rebel-lious acquiescence, and Lucy's howls if the transaction could not be kept from her. He shook his head as if to shake out such thoughts. What was a tankard when they had lost a child? And yet he knew, too, the gritty truth that grief which goes shod in velvet walks easier than that which goes barefoot on the stony ground.

He turned to his guests and poured Sir Thomas a glass of canary from the tankard soon to be sacrificed. Anne moved like a sleepwalker, gently removing Bridget's small, fat fist from a plate of comfits and offering it to Jane instead. Lady Grimes, who with her still-young painted face, her high-built frizzled hair, fashionable yellow-starched ruff and stiff silks and gleaming velvets seemed to John like a creature from another world than the shabby one of debts and makeshifts that had fastened itself on him, let the proper gloom lift from her face as she took a sweetmeat and popped it into Bridget's eager mouth.

"Anne looks quite dreadful," she said. "Can't you persuade her to come to Peckham for a few days and rest? It would do her good just to get away from home and the children and forget the holes in the family."

"Thank you. I'll do my best to induce her to go."

Sir Thomas was at his other elbow to confirm the invitation. A kind but rather fussy man, with a long nose over a two-pronged beard, he was respectful of grief but what he really wanted to talk about was what was happening in their world. Was it true that the Earl of Somerset was declining in the King's favor? Who was this George Villiers who had been made cup-bearer to the King? Had John heard the rumor that Sir Thomas Overbury's death in the Tower had been due to something other than natural causes?

"Times are bad," he said. "There is more wickedness now than in the old Queen's day—though we thought we were ready for a change when she was giving her friends so many monopolies. We miss Lord Salisbury too. It is my opinion that it was he who ruled England while the King hunted and wrote theology, but nobody now works the way Salisbury used to do."

The children had vanished. Lady Grimes drew on her fine embroidered gloves and announced that they really must go. John sent Henri out to call their coach, which was waiting in the stable yard of Drury House, and soon, after a final flurry of murmurs and handshakes, the Grimes departed.

Anne put her hand on John's arm. "Shall we walk in the orchard for a little? I can't bear to go upstairs and put his things away."

The Drurys were at Hawstead, for Sir Robert was ailing. Behind them the rambling stone house was empty but for a caretaker; on one side, over the wall, mounted the roofs and chimneys of Tanfield House; but as they walked in the pale sunshine under the bare, branchy apple trees, they might have been far from London in this little haven, withdrawn and cloistered.

"Jane wishes you to go to Peckham for a rest."

"And leave the children? I couldn't. I shall never feel safe to take my eyes from them. Three gone in less than a year, John. I wonder if I had put Nicholas out to nurse—as you wanted—instead of having the nurse in the house, if we might have had him still. And if I had made Francis wear his jerkin that day——"

"Dear love, you must not torture yourself. It is the fate of most parents. My own mother, too, lost three children in a year—and out of six."

As they turned at the brick wall at the far end of the orchard and started back again, Anne stopped suddenly and said with a rush:

"John, I am pregnant again."

He caught his breath in consternation. The words were like a refrain of some old, too often heard song.

"Oh," she cried, backing away from him. "Don't say anything. Don't touch me. I know how you feel. We have not enough money to feed and clothe and educate even five. But can I help it if I am fecund—and if we love each other?"

He stood paralyzed with his hands hanging at his sides, not touching her, not deserving, because of his failure, to draw her close, to comfort her and himself.

"Don't worry, Anne," he said, and even in his own ears his voice sounded dull and strained. "I will write again to Lord Somerset. He must do something to redeem his promises."

BOOK FOUR 1614–1617

"Till God's great Venite *change the song."*

XXVI

MOUNTED ON A HORSE borrowed in haste from Sir Thomas Grimes, John rode toward Theobalds to answer an urgent summons from Lord Somerset. Since the King had taken the great palace over from Salisbury, a private road had been made from Whitehall to Theobalds on the Essex border of Hertfordshire. Not very much better than the ordinary roads and deep in mud this late November morning, it still had the advantage of being free from the carts and packhorses, the bands of citizens on foot, the rogues and the footpads that cluttered highways not confined to the King and Court and those who came at his invitation or on his business.

John rode lightheartedly, enjoying the feeling of good horseflesh between his knees, the hope that surged at the tone, vague though it was, of Somerset's letter: "Come in haste, for that has happened that may prove to your advantage if we seize the moment." The sky overhead, pearl gray when he had started out in the dawn, was turning to rose in the east, and slowly, as it faded, a young, tender blue spread overhead. It was the time of day that he loved and he savored it as he rode, making no attempt to hurry, for he thought that this might be the best part of his trip, this pure morning air and the expectation that buoyed his spirits.

Nearing Waltham Holy Cross, he could see among the trees the squat tower of the Abbey, these many years a parish church, where his friend Joseph Hall lived contentedly with his homely wife and seven young children. John smiled, remembering a scurrilous piece he had written in his youth, an elegy called "The Anagram," in which he had set forth the outrageous proposition that an ugly woman would make a better wife than a young and beautiful one. Hall was apparently satisfied with the truth of it, though for John himself it was as always a travesty. If he had time, he thought, he would stop to see Hall on the way back.

At the great gate of Theobalds he dismounted, handed his horse over to a stable boy, rewarded the gatekeeper and started up the long causeway to the vast house looming on its hill, whose towers and chimneys—shaped like Greek columns —showed above the double line of trees leading to it. John had never been to Theobalds before and he looked about with interest. He had heard much about it; Lord Burghley had built it originally to entertain Queen Elizabeth; his son Robert Cecil, later Lord Salisbury, had added to it and enlarged it, had engaged the herbalist John Gerard to oversee the gardens and, when he had brought it to perfection, had entertained King James, who promptly coveted it and four years later got it. There were many reports of the huge hall with six columns on each side made of trees so lifelike that birds flew in through the open windows, of the mechanical sun that moved over the ceiling by day and the stars that shone at night, of the banqueting house supported by twelve statues of Roman emperors, of winding canals on which lords and ladies went boating and of the south garden full of rare plants and the large and intricate maze.

The trees over his head were bare now, though in the woods the oaks still kept their russet leaves; but the grass that stretched away on both sides of the raised avenue on which he walked was still green. The house, which now he saw in its great mass of rose-red brick and white marble, its twenty towers, stood so high that it must be approached by a series of terraces with flights of steps between them. Two or three gentlemen came down as John went up, and an usher in Somerset's livery, apparently recognizing John, turned and hurried before him up the steps and through the door at the top. By the time that John reached the last terrace, Lord Somerset himself came out to greet him.

"Ah, Mr. Donne, you are prompt. Come with me into the garden, where we can be private."

He turned into a path that led along the face of the house toward a garden where behind the high yew hedge they found a corner and a marble bench half hidden by tall, bare rose trees. He looked lively and even excited, his face creased in smiles and his neat, conventional beard bright in the sunshine. He wore a velvet doublet of the shade known as goose-turd green with a great deal of gold embroidery, and a saffron-colored cloak. Sitting down on the bench, he said without preliminary:

"One of the clerks of the Privy Council died night before last. That is why I have sent for you to come so quickly."

John's heart fell. So it was no more than this. A clerk had died. No doubt every member of the Council had some friend whom he was prepared to propose as successor—or the post might even be already filled.

"You have made me many promises, my lord, which have come to nothing. My situation is desperate. I must have something more substantial than the mere report of a clerk's death." He was blunt, impolitic, careless of rousing his lordship's wrath. If there was nothing now, there would never be anything. But Somerset was not offended; he continued eagerly:

"Mr. Donne, to prove the reality of my affection and my determination to find you worthy employment, stay in this garden till I go up to the King and bring you back word that you are Clerk of the Council. Have no doubts about it, for I know the King is favorable to you and *you* know that the King will not deny *me!*"

He went off at once, his cloak swinging as he turned, and John sat down on the bench, holding fast to his disappointment lest he hope again. To be Clerk of the Council had been for so long—ever since, indeed, he went to work for Sir Thomas Egerton—the post that he most desired. He had not asked, he thought, which clerk had died, but it was of little moment, for he did not know the present clerks. In the Privy Council itself, though, he had friends: the Lord Chancellor, who not long ago had been kind and remorseful; Somerset himself, who was Lord Chamberlain; Bishop Andrewes, now Bishop of Ely. And though it would be enough to be Clerk of the Council, the post was also a springboard to other things. It would put an end to his burdens and anxieties, wipe out the years of failure and hope deferred, set him afresh on the road to success.

A little bird scratched in the dirt near his feet; he did not know what kind it was, for the lark was the only bird he knew—when he had written his epithalamium for Princess Elizabeth he had had to get the names of the birds from Anne—but he felt a sudden tenderness for it. A sparrow perhaps, amorous and unambitious. He had liked that epithalamium, more than most of what he had written in the last few years, and there was no doubt that Anne's birds had given charm to it. "The lyric lark, and the grave whispering dove, The sparrow that neglects his life for love, The household bird with the red stomacher . . ."

The Lord Somerset had seemed confident enough; was it not true or did he not know the common rumor that he was slipping from the King's favor? Once indeed the King would have given him what he asked—he had wrested Sherborne from Raleigh to give to his young favorite, who then sold it back to the King for twenty thousand pounds—but would he now grant him even an appointment for a hanger-on?

He saw a movement of yellow through the hedge and the next moment the Earl of Somerset was there. John could not read his face, for though it was not crestfallen, as it might have been had he been refused, yet it bore no look of satisfaction. He bowed stiffly and waited.

"Mr. Donne, I am sorry to bring you news that the King is not willing for you to have the clerkship. He has, it appears, other ideas of your gifts. What he said to me, in fact, was, 'I know that Mr. Donne is a learned man and has the abilities of a learned divine.' He declared, in short, that he thought you would make a good preacher and that he will help you to that and nothing else."

John was stunned. The church. He had declined it at the

hands of Dr. Morton, brushed aside Sir John Oglander's suggestion, refused to hear Anne's pleas. All the other things he had tried, the army, the law, government, diplomacy, learning, had crumbled in his hands, and now there loomed before him the church, the haven for failures and for youngest sons of poor gentlemen, the peak of ambition for butchers, drapers and farmers' boys with an itch to rise in the world. He had good reasons for his dismay and bad ones; he knew them both. Fear of the scorn in which most laymen held the ministry; dread of the weekly sermons; distaste for the bleakness of the whitewashed churches raped of the beauty of painted walls, carved rood screens, gold and silver altar vessels and stately ritual that had been theirs in the days of the old church; disappointment over the cutting off forever of the hope of secular success: these were the bad reasons. On the other hand, equally—if not more—deterring was the reluctance he had felt from the first, deep and true under his self-interest and worldliness, to take refuge in the church because it was the only way open to him to support his family. And good or bad, there was the obvious fact that, for all his knowledge of theology, his life had not been suitable. He had written in his "Litany," "In churches, when the infirmity Of him who speaks diminishes the word"; was he now to prove the truth of it with his own unedifying past?

Lord Somerset appeared not to notice his silence. "The King will see you now. Come with me, Mr. Donne."

He had a glimpse of the great hall as they mounted the stairs, and stored it in his mind to tell Anne that the ceiling was as they said, painted with the signs of the zodiac and that he did indeed see a round golden sun jerking its way across it. Passing through the Great Chamber, he saw Lady Somerset surrounded by a crowd of gaily dressed courtiers and thought her beautiful, with her golden hair and great black eyes, but hard. He reminded himself that she had been married at eleven, divorced and married again at nineteen, and if she had hardened in the process, it was scarcely surprising. Then he forgot her as he followed Somerset across the Presence Chamber to where the King sat before a blazing fire.

John had seen the King often enough since that day five years earlier in Whitehall Palace, but this was the first time that the King had seen him. He went down on one knee and kissed the strange, silky fingers held out to him. There were others in the big room hung with gold and silver tapestry that winked in the moving light of the fire, but seeing the King occupied, they moved away, and when the King spoke, he and John and Somerset might have been alone.

"If you think yourself disappointed, Mr. Donne, because I do not offer you a clerkship, you must revise your thoughts, for I am offering something far better. I am proposing that you enter into sacred orders, and I promise you that the gift for preaching which I discern in you will not be hidden or wasted in obscure cures."

The King's voice had majesty and authority. John, summoning his courage to withstand him, produced from the turmoil in his mind those reasons for refusing the proffered employment which could best be spoken aloud.

"I most humbly thank Your Majesty and I am wholly grateful for your kind and indulgent opinion of my poor capacities, but I fear Your Majesty cannot realize that the kind of life I have led and all my ambitions and desires as well have not been those of one whom God calls to feed his sheep."

"And what kind of life is that?"

"I have committed no crimes, sir, but I have been worldly and cynical. There are many who would say that the manner of my marriage alone would disentitle me. I am no youth coming straight from innocence into the church; I am forty-one. Many of those who know me best could not hear me preach without being offended by what they would term hypocrisy. People would, I fear, believe Your Majesty deceived and mocked in being somehow led to recommend me."

"I was prepared to hear you say all of that, Mr. Donne. I think no less of you for it. But it does not alter my opinion. Was St. Augustine's early life a holy one? Was St. Paul himself, before his conversion, without sin?"

The King spoke with assurance. He had, John could not but recognize, a wide knowledge of religious matters and a care for them; he had brought together fifty of the best scholars and had them make a new translation of the Bible; he had fought—and had called on John to help him—theological battles of complexity and fierceness; he was, after all, the anointed head of the church.

"I am not commanding," said the King when John still could not speak. "I am persuading."

"I am overwhelmed by Your Majesty's kindness." John's voice was hoarse. "It would be an entire reversal of my thoughts and inclinations. May I beg for a little time to reflect and consider?"

"Take a fortnight if you like. Come to me the first of the month at Newmarket."

He turned his head and at once several courtiers hurried to his side. "Help me up, Robin," he said to Somerset.

The audience was over. John withdrew.

He rode straight home, not waiting for dinner or stopping to see Joseph Hall as he had intended. Though Hall was one of the King's several chaplains and might have given him useful advice, he could not face those quizzical eyes, that satirical tongue. They had all written satires at the turn of the century, he thought, he and Hall and Marston; Hall and Marston had both put aside their writing and found places in the church; was he about to follow their example?

He had the King's promise of advancement; he need not fear the country parish and the whitewashed church. But the thought of preaching sermons to those who had known him in his rakish, verse-writing youth and laughed with him in the taverns, to those who had frowned on his marriage, to the great ladies whose servant he had professed to be, to his friends, Christopher, George Gerrard, Ben Jonson and the rest, to the army of those to whom he owed money, paralyzed him. How could he suddenly rise up in spiritual and moral authority and expound to them the path of righteousness? How, knowing that they would discern, and correctly, his motives in his needs, could he in their presence read the sacred psalms, lessons, prayers, blessings, and have any thought at all in his mind of God?

On the other hand, if he refused the King's offer, there was nothing left for him. Every other door was closed. He had Anne and five—six—children to support. Even the old remedy, death, which had once been a temptation to him, was denied him now for their sakes.

His mind went back over his life. For the first time in years he thought of the hidden priest saying Mass for the family, his mother and stepfather kneeling, his own childish heart beating furiously, in a room with the curtains drawn; of his brother Henry, who had craved an imagined martyrdom and died when he might have lived; of the days and nights in his study when, exhausted with the conflict that divided him, he had almost physically wrestled with religion as Jacob had wrestled with the angel, trying to find the truth of it apart from schism and controversy. He had turned from the old to the new religion, not because he thought the old wrong, but because the new was the religion of the state; he did not then and he would not now compare the two; the channels of God's mercies ran through both fields. He thought of his work for Dr. Morton, whom he had loved, of the book he had written for the King, of his friendship with gentle Bishop Andrewes and acid Joseph Hall, both men of religion; of his endless reading and the books that lined his study walls, Beza, Bellarmine, Casaubon, du Moulin; Tertullian, Eusebius, St. John Chrysostom, the Gregories, St. Jerome, St. Ambrose, Origen, St. Augustine of whom the King had spoken. They stood in their rows and ranks and looked at him, but whether in invitation or in furious rejection he could not say. Looking back, he could see emerging, in spite of all he had said, and truthfully, to the King, a sort of pattern in his life, an apparently random assortment of lines and curves that only now began to have shape and meaning. Had he, actually, any choice at all in the matter? If all doors were closed against him but this one, had not God closed them? If this door alone was open, had not God Himself opened it, and did He not intend John Donne to enter it?

He pulled his cloak closer about him and spurred his horse.

XXVii

DR. JOHN KING, who had been the Lord Keeper's chaplain when John was his secretary, was now Bishop of London. When John went to him somewhat hesitantly and apprehensively to tell him of his intention to take orders, he was relieved to find his old friend still friendly and cordial to his purpose.

"You must be made deacon first, you know, before you can be a priest. But we'll do the second as soon as possible after the first. You must get your affairs in order, you know. How long will that take you?"

"To pay my debts, you mean?"

"Yes, just so. You must not go cumbered into the church."

"Give me six weeks." If he could not do it in six weeks, he could not do it in six years. Six weeks of humiliating himself, asking his friends for money to pay his debts; penance enough surely, if penance were required.

"Late January then."

"Might we say the twenty-fifth?"

"The feast of the Conversion of St. Paul? That will do. And the deaconate a week earlier. Can you manage it?"

"I shall have to."

His creditors had slumbered until he began to promise payment within a month; then the word went around and they all came swarming down upon him, each determined to have his share at once before the supply gave out. They knocked upon the doors and looked in at the windows. He could not go out without encountering two or three of them, antagonistic to one another and aggressive toward him, barring his way or running beside him down the street plucking at his sleeve. He had a new manservant, a sober country fellow named Fyfield, not elegant but strong and willing, who was with difficulty restrained from swatting at those buzzing flies.

"You shall be paid," said John to the tailor's man, angry now and abusive who had always been obsequious. "I promise you, but not today."

He was on his way to Bedford House in the Strand to see Lady Bedford. She had been so pleased and touched by his elegiac verses on the death of her brother that she had offered to pay his debts. He had not pursued her offer then, but he was going now to see if she remembered.

It was a bitter morning; the mud between the cobbles on the Strand was frozen and an icy wind swept out of the west and flung stinging bits of dust into his eyes. His cloak wound well around him, he leaned into the wind.

As he passed St. Mary-le-Savoy he thought of his old lodgings down by the river and wondered how Mother Haines might be. He had not seen her in several years. She had been cool to him when he left her house the last time, for he had written books against the Jesuits and she had showed that she felt him to be a renegade. She would not like it now that he was preparing himself for the ministry in the English church. She had managed somehow, with no doubt a lie here and a compromise there, through all the dangers to Roman Catholics, to practice her own religion and to keep out of trouble, and mentally he took off his hat to her; she was a good woman sorely pressed.

Bedford House, built more than fifty years before but completely rebuilt and refurbished by the present Earl, stood on the north side of the Strand nearly opposite the Savoy. The first time that John had really been aware of it, he thought, following a footman into a waiting room furnished in green silk and silver lace, was at the time of the Essex trouble, when

Lord Bedford, for his small part in it, had been imprisoned here in his own house, forbidden even to ride out. When James came to the throne, everything had changed and the Countess had become Queen Anne's favorite lady-in-waiting. Of Lady Bedford, John had at that time known nothing, nor imagined a day when he would enter Bedford House confident of its lady's friendship, hopeful of her assistance.

The window of the little room where he waited, moving about restlessly, not sitting down, looked out on an inner court, with a frozen fountain, to the north wing, beyond which, he knew, was a terrace and a formal garden. It was a beautiful city house, but nothing compared with Twickenham, which had been to him "a balm" and "a true Paradise," where garden upon garden flowed down to the river, and terrace walks and urns and balustrades surrounded a house both vast and graceful. His eye was caught by a small picture on the wall, the head and shoulders of a man of the last century, his rugged face half turned, a scholar in a dark gown against a darker background; he recognized it as a Holbein. So now she had so many of them that she could afford to hang one in a waiting room! Holbein was out of fashion now, but Lady Bedford had been collecting his paintings from wherever she could find them, getting them cheap from those who despised them for their oldness, paying what she must to people who knew their value.

"My lady wishes you to come to the gallery, sir."

"Ah, Bilson, how are you?" John feed the man, who was an old acquaintance, and followed him to the gallery above, where Lady Bedford, still fragile from her recent illness, sat in a large armchair padded with scarlet velvet, and extended a hand to him.

"Mr. Donne, you are welcome. It is a long time since I have seen you. Since, indeed, you brought the verses on my poor brother. In May, wasn't it?"

"In June, my lady," said a harsh voice behind her, and John, rising from kissing her hand, saw standing there her physician and—it was said—spiritual adviser, Dr. Burges. He was a man much talked about since he had come back from Leyden with a medical degree, after having suffered imprisonment for preaching Puritanism before the King, and had established almost at once a practice in Islington. John glanced at him with some curiosity, and finding him to be of a type that he did not like, a small, pompous man with a cold eye and a sour-sweet smile, dropped him promptly out of his attention.

"Oh yes, June," said Lady Bedford, accepting the correction. "In May, I remember, you were ill, and feared the return of the malady in your eyes. We are a pair of cracked vessels, I fear, you and I, my old friend."

"I am cracked, but mended—by your ladyship's kindness —but your ladyship is of that fine porcelain that gives out a ringing tone until it breaks. I find you looking stronger than when I last saw you—and as always lovely and gracious as the sunshine itself."

"You speak in hyperbole, Mr. Donne. What is your news? What have you been doing since I last saw you, to keep you so long away?"

"In the summer you were yourself away, far beyond the reach of a plodder such as I."

"I was in the north with my mother, who has been very forlorn and lonely since my father's death. But surely you know something interesting to tell me!"

"Of interest to me alone, I fear, but I bring it first of all to your ladyship. I have decided, upon the motion and suggestion of His Majesty himself, to enter into sacred orders. I hope that you will bestow your blessing on this new voyage of mine."

John felt a sharpness in the silence that followed. He saw Lady Bedford glance quickly at Dr. Burges.

"You have taken me by surprise, Mr. Donne," she said at length. "It is the last thing I should ever have expected you to do."

Her words, her cool tone, were to John painful and bewildering. He had not foreseen this. It was a moment before he could say quietly:

"I come to it late, it is true, but I am, I trust, not entirely ill prepared."

"Prepared? But my dear friend, it is the quality of the life, is it not, rather than the quantity of the learning, that is the preparation necessary for preaching the word of God?"

He heard and marked wryly the Puritanical tinge in her words. She had always had a Puritan leaning and her brother had been known to be so strict a Calvinist that he would not eat meat cooked on Sundays, but she had never before spoken like this. He looked at Dr. Burges, suspecting his influence, and surprised on his face what he interpreted as a satisfied smirk.

"I make no attempt to defend my life—though I have repented of my sins—when it has been lifted up and lighted by my humble devotion to your ladyship."

"Oh, my dear friend, your life has been no more irregular than the lives of many other men in the world—though, as I am sure you realize only too well yourself, your marriage and the wrong you did to your wife's father are open to grave criticism—but a minister of the gospel should be above all question."

It was what he had dreaded hearing, and one of the reasons why he had at first declined to take orders; but he had not expected to hear it from Lady Bedford, whose kind, and even admiring, patronage had for so many years warmed and delighted him.

"You speak only too much truth. I have been very hesitant, and I have not determined on this course without much self-searching——"

"And do you really think in your heart that you have been called?"

It was, whether by chance or by design, almost exactly the question that he would have to answer at his ordination as deacon. He gave now the response assigned to him in the prayer book, "I trust so." He went on after a moment, "The Bishop of London has professed himself willing to ordain me —and the King was gracious enough to remind me that both

St. Paul and St. Augustine were not perfect in their early lives."

"But even they—you must forgive me—were not writers of ribald verse. Oh, I don't mean of course the beautiful lines with which you have honored me, but those early poems, in which you virtually praise infidelity and license, and question all that is deepest and truest in a woman's heart. When you display unblushingly the most bald details of your own adventures."

"I did best when I had least truth for my subject." He spoke lightly, but he was bitterly dismayed. His pride needed, no doubt, reminders of this kind from friends as well as foes, but he wondered if it really came from Lady Bedford's own mind or from some ill impression he had taken from Dr. Burges. Wherever it started, at any rate it came through her and as such he must accept it.

"I acknowledge that there is justice in what you say—but my decision is already made. I shall be ordained in January. Before then, I am setting my house in order—in mundane as well as in spiritual ways. When your ladyship in the summer so graciously offered to pay my debts, I was deeply grateful, but I did not take advantage of your kindness then. Now, for the sake of what lies before me, I am venturing to ask if you are in the same mind still—or if your disapproval of my calling precludes any assistance in following it."

She rose and went to the window, Dr. Burges following her with a short fur cape, which he draped around her shoulders. Away from the fire it was cold, and the next moment she turned back again and came to stand in front of John.

"If I disapprove, it is not for lack of friendship to you—but from a sense of what is due the Lord. I should always wish to help you in any way I can, but I am not in funds now. My brother's estate is in confusion, I am involved in a suit in chancery, I have debts of my own, my husband complains I have spent too much on paintings, and Twickenham is a constant drain. I will do what I can for you, my poor friend, but you must not expect much."

He was aware, when he went away, after protestations of

unworthiness and of gratitude, that something had been shattered between them that could not be mended again, and he was convinced that he owed her changed attitude to that prim, silent figure that stood at her elbow throughout their meeting.

When, two or three days later, Lady Bedford sent him the small sum of thirty pounds, he was sure of it. By that time, however, the Countess of Huntingdon—little Lady Elizabeth Stanley of his York House days—had heard of his difficulties through George Gerrard and had sent him enough to pay off everything so that he could go into his new life clear.

He thanked her with a poem in which he declared that all virtues flowed from her: "If you can think these flatteries, they are, For then your judgment is below my praise" and ended by recalling the time when

> *I was your Prophet in your younger days,*
> *And now your Chaplain, God in you to praise.*

2 His debts paid, John shut himself up in his study to prepare his mind and his heart. Hour after hour his hand moved across the folio sheets as he wrote out his basic ideas of the nature and meaning of Christianity, the principles to which he could give assent. Using his favorite images of voyage and discovery, once employed in love poems, he likened men seeking God by reason to mariners who traveled before the invention of the compass and were afraid to get out of sight of land; but by the compass, faith, men have found a new world far richer than the old.

> And though [he wrote] the faithfullest heart is not ever directly and constantly upon God but that it sometimes descends also to reason; yet it is not thereby so departed from him but that it still looks towards him, though not fully to him; as the compass is ever northward, though it decline and have often variations towards East and West.

Then in sudden despondency, knowing how others thought of him—those who like Lady Bedford considered his past life too serious a barrier and those who like George Gerrard and

Christopher Brooke saw him falling back on the church as a sensible last resource—and acknowledging ruefully that most men were such as most other men thought they were, he wrote:

> Thou hast set up many candlesticks and kindled many lamps in me; but I have either blown them out or carried them to guide me in by and forbidden ways. Thou hast given me a desire of knowledge and some means to it, and some possession of it, and I have armed myself with thy weapons against thee . . .

When he had finished it, he wrote a title on it, "Essays in Divinity," and bundled it away.

As the day of his ordination drew nearer, he hoped for some mountain peak of experience, in which he might feel all his scruples and reluctances swept away by the wind of God and his dry heart watered with celestial dew, but he only grew more numb and moved at the last like a sleepwalker. When the second ceremony was over and Bishop King clasped his hand warmly, he knew that he was like a coin on which the old king's image has been erased and the new sovereign's face stamped in its place, while the metal itself remains unchanged.

So after all, what he took into the ministry, besides financial solvency, was no more than a finely tempered mind, a vast accumulation of theological learning and a determination to do his part to the uttermost of his ability.

3 He was an ordained minister for six weeks before he preached his first sermon. It loomed before him like an insuperable obstacle that he must with pain and danger surmount. He knew this nervous fear to be unreasonable, but he could not by inner argument dispel it. Though he told himself sternly that if, facing those rows of eyes that saw him for the sham he was, he should feel his mouth go dry and his voice fail, if in spite of written notes his mind should be blank and paralyzed, he must accept it as God's will, still he faced the ordeal with dread. He had selected for it a small country church, St. Catherine's at Paddington. The rector, a very old

man named Griffith Edwards, had fallen ill, and John agreed to take his place, thinking that here at any rate he would not disgrace himself before his friends and acquaintances.

When the day came, he asked Anne to go with him for support, and hired a coach so that she could get there in a degree of comfort. She was in the last months of her pregnancy and she carried herself ponderously, like a stately ship. It had rained in the night and when they set out in the morning twilight for the service at seven, the roads were so filled with sudden holes that the coach, which smelled unpleasantly of old hay and horse manure, heaved and rolled. John was so put to it trying to hold Anne and spare her the worst of the jolts that he had little time to think about what lay before him.

Paddington was a small, unprosperous village and the church was much older and more dilapidated than John had thought a church so near London could be. In the vestry where he put on the new gown and surplice that Lord Hay had given him, there was actually a puddle of water on the floor under a broken window.

The clumsy but well-intentioned young parish clerk with large red ears who was there to light the altar candles and to read the lessons, warned John about the broken place in the floor as they went into the church. Meeting but not mingling with the cold dawn light, the flames of the guttering candles, blown by drafts, sent shadows moving over the faces of the little congregation that huddled in the nave. John quickly found Anne against a pillar and exchanged a fortifying glance with her before he turned his attention to the people of St. Catherine's parish. They were country people, mostly old and work-worn; bundled in shabby frieze cloaks, men and women both, with rags tied around their feet, they lifted to him faces on which patience, or perhaps apathy, lay like a veil. Here and there he saw a younger face with a dogged look, or an old woman whose nose and chin all but met beneath bright black eyes with a gleam of malice in them. The squire's pew, red-curtained, was empty; whoever he was, he had not troubled to come out this morning.

As John led the stumbling voices in the Our Father and felt his voice roll out to the far corners of the church, it was pity that filled him, and no thought of his own inadequacy, pity for the hard lives and dim joys of this poor flock, who lived and worked so near to the great, brilliant city of London and doubtless scarcely knew it was there. As the service moved on and he knelt, rose or passed from one side to the other, speaking the hallowed words, he felt somewhat like an actor putting his best into his part before an unresponsive audience, and somewhat like a man moving through a dream.

He stood in the pulpit at last, with his notes in his fingers, looking down on those humble faces. He had to clear his throat twice before he could pronounce the text, but after that he had no difficulty. He found, as he set out the *divisio* and then the *explicatio,* that he did not need his notes, beyond an occasional glance to start a new heading.

His voice went ringing on. It was a closely reasoned sermon, with all the points fitting into one another and examples from the Scriptures and from the Fathers chosen to elucidate the thought. He had, knowing that it was a country parish, phrased it as simply as he was able; even so, he could see as he went on that it meant nothing at all to anyone there—except, of course, to Anne, who was listening in total absorption with her lips parted.

As he continued, the phrases rolling out with a sort of life of their own, while his mind ran free over the church, he saw a woman sleeping, with her chin on her breast, her knotted hands laid one on the other in her lap, the gnarled fingers curling upward; it seemed to him that he saw those fingers holding hours of work for others, caresses for lively children, tenderness for sick ones. He saw an old man with his hands clasped on his blackthorn stick, his faded blue eyes under jutting brows gazing at John as if to wrest from him some answer to a grief or a pain that he could not understand. John felt his confident, irrelevant periods falter. He discarded several headings that he had intended to elaborate, and drew what was left into a quick conclusion, which he tied up handily with his text. A final thought came to him unbidden and he spoke it without reflection.

"God makes sometimes," he said, "a plain and simple man's life more powerful than the eloquentest sermon."

If the patient bodies before him found anything more comprehensible in this than in anything else that had been said, they gave no sign.

He pronounced the final blessing, the congregation shuffled out in one direction and he retired in the other to the vestry, where he took off his robe and said farewell to the young man with the red ears.

As the coach heaved and bumped homeward, Anne remarked thoughtfully after a long silence, "I think it really doesn't matter very much what you say as long as you say it so beautifully; I never realized before how very rich and pure your voice is."

"I have made a beginning," he answered heavily. "I shall do better next time."

XXVIII

"Religion is no sullen thing," he wrote, sitting at his table in his study where a bright shaft of November sunlight came in to fall warm on his head, "it is not a melancholy; there is not so sociable a thing as the love of Christ Jesus."

He thought of the long faces that were usually presented to him in rows under the pulpit, solemn and depressed, as if put on like the correct garb for church as people put on feathers and jewels for gayer occasions.

Sociable, he had found it himself. Two years after he had made his decision in doubt and apprehension, he found himself occupied, respected, well-to-do, his life gathered—albeit, and this he regretted, superficially—about a supremely important center. He thrust his sermon notes aside and reached for another sheet of paper. He was writing verse again. Lines surged up when he was thinking of other things; he wrote them down and put them away; someday he would add, fill out, finish, revise.

> *Batter my heart, three-personed God; for you*
> *As yet but knock, breathe, shine and seek to mend;*
> *That I may rise and stand, o'erthrow me . . .*

Images of captives and of captured towns teased him. Not free until . . . unless they were imprisoned . . . overcome . . . set in thrall . . .

Take me to you, imprison me, for I,
Except you enthrall me, never shall be free.

He pulled out, from the drawer where he kept them, other scribbled-over papers.

"Why are we by all creatures waited on? . . . Why brook'st thou, ignorant horse, subjection?"

He had written that fragment coming back from Sevenoaks, where he had gone to preach after he had been presented to the living by the Earl of Dorset; he had been suddenly struck, riding home on his patron's high-spirited, silken-mouthed horse, by the extraordinary timorousness of those powerful and innocent creatures, which so meekly allowed man to enslave them. Why should a bull submit to be killed to feed man when it was obviously so much the stronger of the two? And the purer, since beasts do not sin.

"What if this present were the world's last night?" What indeed? Would he feel terror? In the face of Christ presiding over the event, there would be beauty, and beauty, as he used to say—to whom?—was, or should be, a sign of pity. Only ugliness indicated harshness. Now to whom had he said that? What was her name, so long ago, that imperious, dark beauty with the warm, sensual mouth that invited but did not yield? In Rome, when he was twenty. Married to a young count who neglected her for cards, duels, whores. And Jack Donne, finding it safe to importune—yet dangerous, too, if the husband should suddenly decide to take notice—had played with that delicious fire. He had written her one of his worldly poems. He remembered the opening couplet—

I long to talk with some old lover's ghost
Who died before the god of love was born . . .

—but the rest was gone. One wrote, often with labor, rewrote, copied, and later it might have been the work of someone else, imperfectly remembered.

Pushing it out of his thoughts, he returned to his sermon. He could write sermons now without dread. For his texts, for his inspiration, he turned usually to the Psalms or the Epistles, which he liked best because they were closest to his own life; the psalms were poetry and the writings of St. Paul but letters after all. He preached chiefly about sin, for he knew by experience sin that was like a privation or a darkness, sins bragged about and sins denied, unconsidered, unrepented, unconfessed sins, and he could preach about them without having to set himself up above his hearers. He had preached often and widely since that first timid effort at Paddington: before the King at Whitehall and at Greenwich, at Sevenoaks, at Camberwell, at Keyston, where he had been given the living nearly a year before. People were beginning to talk about the wit and ingenuity of Dr. Donne's sermons.

Doctor Donne. John Donne, D.D. The thought brought a slight glow of satisfaction and a wince of memory.

Cambridge eighteen months earlier, a fortnight in March that should have been springlike but was actually raw and cold, the roads foul. The King and Prince Charles lodging at Trinity; Lord Treasurer Suffolk, who was also chancellor of Cambridge, ensconced in even greater state at St. John's, where he kept a table costing, or so they said, a thousand pounds a day, with five tuns of wine drunk by himself and his guests each day; John Donne sleeping in the same bed with Samuel Brooke, now professor of divinity at Gresham College, and waiting for Cambridge to fulfill the King's desire to have his newest chaplain made an honorary doctor of divinity. And somewhere else in his lodgings the Vice-Chancellor and real ruler of Cambridge, Bishop Harsnett, setting his mouth in a grim line, showering masters' degrees like rose petals on courtiers, while day after day the festivities went on, with plays and disputations and ceremonies of all kinds, and not one man was made doctor.

Samuel Brooke, who had had a tremendous success with his Latin pastoral play, *Melanthe*—Samuel now slightly bent, angular, with a thin, scholarly air of beneficence—said to John as they walked back to Gresham through streets crowded with brilliantly dressed courtiers, men in bright livery with their masters' badges on their backs and scholars in black gowns to their heels:

"You won't get it now unless the King sends a mandate. The Vice-Chancellor has been much bitten by the rumor that doctorates at Cambridge are as cheap as pancakes. He's set to prove the contrary. Moreover, he says of you openly that you are a *filius noctis* who would get in at the window when there is a fair gate open. A university lives by its fees, in the end."

After two weeks the great men had gathered their trains and gone away, Prince Charles had returned to St. James's, the King to his hunting at Royston, while John, at the King's express command, had stayed behind and waited. Less than a week later the royal mandate had come and he had been made a doctor of divinity. Harsnett, however, had had the last word. Along with the King's choice he had made one other doctor, a nonentity named Cheke, as if to express his disdain for the whole affair.

Mortifying, yes, but soon forgotten even by those who knew, and most did not know. In the eyes of his world, Dr. Donne had buried Jack Donne. He who had been for so long on the low end of the seesaw had swung up—as that other one who had been so high, the Earl of Somerset, had fallen, swiftly, suddenly, wholly, so low. Accused, with his wife, beautiful little Fanny Howard, once Countess of Essex, tried and condemned for the murder of Sir Thomas Overbury in the Tower, he had been reprieved by the King but consigned to the Tower, of which Anne's father was now the Lord Lieutenant.

"I am thankful," Anne had said with a woman's cruel realism, "that he recommended you to the King before he was discovered." But when she heard that Lady Somerset had borne her baby in the Tower, she had cried.

If a preacher wanted, and many of them did, with righteous thunderings, to preach on Ezekiel 21:26—"Thus saith the Lord God: Remove the diadem and take off the crown: this shall not be the same; exalt him that is low and abase him that is high"—here was opportunity, but an opportunity that John had not taken. He had had good reason to be grateful to Somerset, and though—for with his knowledge, if not by his command, a man had died in agony—one must look on him with horror and with pity, one did not forget the gratitude.

John had gone back to his sermon when there was a tap on the door and Christopher came in. Christopher—a Bencher now at Lincoln's Inn and Lent Reader, a married man at last, having married Lady Jacob, a well-to-do widow, the year before—lived just across Drury Lane in a house with a garden that ran back to Covent Garden, and every day or so he would drop in to see John in his study and talk with him as Sir Robert Drury used to do. Drury now was dead. John had seen him last at Hawstead on his way home from Cambridge with his new degree; he had been dying then of an inflammation in his lungs. Drury House was rented to strangers, for Lady Drury lived alone and sad at Hardwick.

"Do I interrupt?" said Christopher, knowing that he did.

"No," said John, also knowing it. "Sit down. What news?"

"Real news," said Christopher, taking the other chair. He had grown portly and his hair had receded up his forehead; he was clean-shaven still; his narrow face had thickened; there were lines from nostrils to mouth; he carried an aura of impregnable well-being. He and Lady Jacob—for his wife preferred to keep her title—amused themselves by collecting paintings. He had a Gheerhaedts and a Zucchero; he had a portrait of Elizabeth Vernon, Lady Southampton, by some unknown, which he loved for its associations. Had not he and Jack Donne fluttered around Southampton in those early days before Jack attached himself to Essex? It was of some new acquisition that John expected him to speak now as he came in exuding an air of knowing something that he would reveal in his own good time and in a way to squeeze the most dramatic value out of it.

But instead of withholding it, he settled in his chair and said promptly:

"You will hear this officially very soon, but I have come to bring you word of it first. The Masters of the Bench last night elected you Divinity Reader. What do you think of it?"

John had heard some whisper of the possibility, but he had not given it credence. Now he caught his breath. Divinity Reader at Lincoln's Inn. To go back there, where he had spent two years of his youth, studied passionately, written verse, caroused, filled the place with stories, most of them not true, of his amorous exploits—"I have loved and got and told"—and then had left to travel abroad: to go back now, among those sober men who remembered Jack Donne, among young students who must know that he was less than two years in orders after many years of failure at other things, and preach to them as if he were the very trumpet of God?

"What would it involve?" he said.

"Two sermons every Sunday in term time, one on high days and holidays, one on the Sunday at the beginning and end of each term—say fifty sermons a year in all, and it is one of the best paid posts open to a London clergyman."

"My dear Christopher, how could I?"

"Quite easily, I think. We are critical about sermons, as you know, but you could give us what we like—a sound, reasoned discourse appealing to the intellect. There is not a trace of hypocrisy in you. We should respect your honesty as well as your learning."

John smiled faintly, remembering the great hall, with the smoke from the fire going up to the roof, the faces of the students pale in the rosy gloom; the high table where the Benchers sat, where the Divinity Reader would sit. Once he had sat there, when he was Master of the Winter Revels, just before he left for the Continent. They had staged a mock wedding, with one of the students dressed as a bride, a not very interesting ploy except as it made a reason for John to write an epithalamium. It had been intended to be entirely constructed of double meanings and sexual puns—and had been hailed with shouts of laughter as just that—but a certain beauty had crept in in spite of him, and in some ways with its freshness and zest it rivaled his later epithalamiums.

337

"This is why I determined to tell you first, before the official word came to you, so that you would not refuse it out of hand. Think it over seriously, John. This would set the seal on your new calling. You are a royal chaplain, you have Sevenoaks and Keyston, but this would establish you as one of London's leading divines. And you are an old Lincoln's Inn man. It is entirely appropriate."

"Thank you. You are ever a good friend. I will think it over."

When Christopher had gone, he did not return to his sermon but sat there twiddling with his pen knife and smiling faintly.

2 Christmas Eve, 1616, was the happiest that they had ever had, except perhaps that first one at Pyrford House. All the family was well; among the five older children there was not even a sniffle; the two babies, Margaret, not yet two, and three-month-old Elizabeth, named for John's own mother, were doing well out at nurse; Anne was blooming with new vigor and John himself had thrown away all the remnants of the medicines that once lined his window sill. For the first time since his brief possession of the fortune that his father had left him, he felt comfortable financially, so comfortable that he could send a substantial gift of money to the poor prisoners in the Fleet at Christmastime, and direct the servants to give ale and Yule cakes to all who came begging at the door.

After supper they lit the Yule log in the hall with a coal saved from—or so the fiction was—last year's Yule log, and Bridget as the youngest present recited the old charm against evil:

> *"Wash your hands or else the fire*
> *Will not tend to your desire:*
> *Unwashed hands, ye maidens, know*
> *Dead the fire though ye blow."*

Bridget, dark-haired, dark-eyed and pale, was the most easily overlooked of all the children, but she had, John considered, a sweet nature, as well as a stubborn will that reminded him of his mother.

The hands of all must have been very clean, for the fire flared up, shining on the cupboard where Lucy's restored flagon, the Murano bowl and two or three modest new pieces of plate were set out on the polished oak. There was a pounding at the door, suppressed squeaks and giggles and the shrill bleat of a tabor, and a few moments later a little band of mummers was ushered into the room. It was a shabby little band but there were St. George and his merry men, a lean Father Christmas bearing a holly bough, a youth with a wassail bowl and a pretty girl, all scarlet cheeks and dimples, with a cluster of mistletoe.

They performed their small parts rather shyly and awkwardly while the children looked on, Lucy and Bridget with wide-eyed delight, the boys scuffling silently with each other. Constance, whose beauty was like a candle flame, was in high spirits, exclaiming at every opportunity the popular catchword she had picked up, "O rare" this and "O rare" that. "O rare mummers!" she cried, clapping her hands softly.

When the performance ended with bows and curtseys there was frumenty for all, the wassail bowl was filled, the mummers' hands loaded with cakes and comfits, and they went away, the sound of their wassail song floating in the air behind them. The Donnes settled down to make some music of their own. John tuned his old lute; Constance, who had been having lessons on the virginals, settled herself importantly at the table; Johnny had a flute; the rest prepared to sing, joined by Fyfield and the maids, who were called in from the kitchen. When the carols and the Christmas songs were finished and John was setting his lute in the corner, there was a sudden silence with a meaningful little bustle of preparation. Constance cried out, "No, Father, don't go away. There's something more!" and Anne, with a smile that showed she was in the secret, took him gently by the sleeve and drew him down again beside her.

The servants went out and the five children standing close

together sang, softly and unevenly, with an occasional pause for a gulp or a giggle, but sweetly:

> *"Go and catch a falling star,*
> *Get with child a mandrake root,*
> *Tell me where all past years are,*
> *Or who cleft the Devil's foot,*
> *Teach me to hear mermaids singing,*
> *Or to keep off envy's stinging*
> *And find*
> *What wind*
> *Serves to advance an honest mind."*

It was a song that he had written long ago, which someone had set to music. It had gone the rounds and he had been at the time—or had pretended to be—much annoyed that someone had thus made free with his song. How the children had got hold of it he did not know, unless of course it was Anne who had instigated it, but he found as the childish voices went on with more confidence into the second and third stanzas that he was moved and pleased. They wound up with a burst of delighted laughter and he thought, putting his arm around Constance and kissing the top of her head, that such domestic happiness was sweet indeed, a most precious gift of God to a man who had once longed to put an end to his life of despair.

When the children were in bed and he and Anne in their room, he said,

"I ought to put the final touches on my sermon for to-morrow. I had expected to do it earlier in the evening. Anne, I suppose for the rest of my life I shall be saying that. I have a sermon to write. Fifty sermons a year at the very least."

"Leave this one now," she said. "It doesn't need polishing. I know it's good."

He smiled at her. After so many years, so many children, so many tears, quarrels, reconciliations, hopes, disappointments, failures, she saw him still as brilliant, wise, splendid. She was thirty-two, a little thin, a little worn, pale. But her red-gold hair curled up from her round forehead after she released it from the coif, her lips were tender, her eyes bright in the candlelight. All that was soft, uncertain, vague, had been burned away; what was left was clear, fine, strong, deep. The bones under the transparent skin had more beauty than even the fair young flesh had had; the wide-set eyes were more eloquent; they spoke of humor, passion, anger, scorn, delight, swiftly and freely as the dreaming eyes of the girl had never done. Her hands, as hands will, betrayed the years: they were sinewy, capable, compassionate hands but some time, imperceptibly, the young skin had become not young. But for all her hard-won maturity, her heart kept still the unquenchable life, the promise, the delicate excitement, of spring.

"Leave sin out of this sermon," she said.

He was startled. He had forgotten the sermon.

"I didn't intend to say much about sin at Christmas," he answered mildly.

"Oh, of course. I had forgotten for the moment. But I've thought of it before. You might sometimes say something about prayer. Most people don't understand it. I don't."

She sat on a low stool in front of the fire and let her hair down about her shoulders. It fell, red-gold and heavy, like a veil. He took a handful of it and stood playing with it, thinking of the long history of hair as a sexual symbol, of the use he had made of it in his youthful poems. She caught it back with one hand and looked up at him.

"I mean it about prayer. You could make a sermon about it. I don't pray. I can't. There must be others."

Something troubled her? He had been a minister for two years; recently people had begun to come to him with their spiritual problems. But not, of course, Anne. She knew enough of him as he really was not to come to him for help of that kind. And yet she sounded—looked, with her face turned up to him—troubled.

"There are many ways of prayer, Anne. I am sure of that. It may be mental, we think prayer—or vocal, for of course we speak prayers—or it may be actual, for we do prayers. My

341

dearest girl, as mother in this house, and wife, you pray all day long without knowing it."

"That's comforting. You see, you have a sermon on prayer already."

"I'm not sure that a sermon ought to be comforting."

"Why not? What should it be?" She had braided her hair into a thick golden plait and swung it back between her shoulder blades. Now her shoes and stockings were off and she was curling her bare toes in the warmth of the fire.

"It should bring people to repentance or rouse them to do better."

He spoke absently. His mind was all on her. He stood with his arm against the chimney piece looking down at her. She glanced up, met his eyes and rose swiftly to her feet, reading in his gaze what she was eager and ready to read.

When the last ember of the applewood logs on the hearth had crumbled with a flare and then dulled, and their own sweet, hot fire had burned itself out, he felt Anne roll over and press a kiss on his shoulder, whispering:

"I can't pray because I have no need of prayer. When I have you, I need no other god."

He tried to utter his startled thought, But that is blasphemy! but, sinking into the bliss of sleep, he could only hold her close.

XXIX

He came through the short cut from Lincoln's Inn where he had been talking with a committee of the Benchers about the need for a new chapel. The old one was not only shabby, it was structurally dangerous and beyond repair. It must be torn down and a new one built. Inigo Jones should be the architect. John had argued eloquently for the best, had declared, perhaps recklessly, that the money could be found, that he himself would undertake to solicit contributions.

As he neared his home, the busy, purposeful ideas that he had been sedulously entertaining began to fade and the thought of the little son born too soon, and dead, came back to press upon him. He had hoped for another son, for since he had lost Francis and Nicholas, the family had been overweighted with girls. This one was to have been called James. But he was fortunate to have his Anne, and gratitude, he told himself, not murmuring, should fill his heart. Childbirth was fraught with danger, even for one who appeared to take it as easily as Anne did. It had been a difficult pregnancy; in the spring it had seemed that she must lose the child. Once again the window sill had been full of glasses and jars, of betony water, syrup of roses, oil of almonds and other things. The danger had passed and she had appeared well until a week ago, when it had suddenly become obvious that something was wrong. He had not turned to the midwife but had called in his own physician, Dr. Laysmith. The baby was dead, but

Anne they had saved. She lay in bed spent and white, the tears rolling down her cheeks, but alive.

As he turned into the little court he saw the laundress preceding him into the house with a basket of clean shirts and ruffs, the narrow ruffs of the clergyman. From one of the windows above came the shrill squeal of rage of his daughter Elizabeth, recently brought home weaned but not reconciled. The moist, heavy air was laden with all the stenches of garbage and filth that made August in London nearly unbearable. He would have liked to take his family away, to Keyston in Huntingdonshire, where he had a large rectory in which the curate, a bachelor, lived with only a housekeeper, so that there was plenty of room for all the Donnes; but he had feared to take Anne so far from the midwife. Perhaps it would have been better, after all, to risk it.

The house was cool inside and there was a faint, fresh fragrance of new rushes and rosemary. On the stairs he met Constance coming down, with two-year-old Margaret clinging to her hand and stumping down, two feet on each step.

"I'm going to take her out into the orchard," said Constance. "Poor little thing. Nurse is with Mother. I think she isn't feeling well."

Her little maternal airs were very touching, John thought. Fourteen. Well, she was growing up.

"I heard Elizabeth howling," he said.

"Patty's got her in the kitchen. She's all right now."

Margaret. Elizabeth. James, if he had lived, would have been the third child under three. It was too many. He thought he had caught an accusing look in the doctor's eye.

He went up to see Anne. In the short time that he had been away from the house a change had come in her. She was flushed and restless, her eyes were too bright.

"I've bathed Mrs. Donne's face with rose water," said the nurse, whose name was Phyllis, an inappropriate name for the tall, heavy, slit-mouthed middle-aged woman that she was. "Now I tell her that if she'll just lie still and take a little nap, she'll be the better for it."

"I can't lie still. I feel as if I had ants walking down my arms. And I'm so hot."

John put his hand on her forehead and drew it away in surprise; it was fiery. He took her pulse and found it racing.

"She has a fever. I wonder if I should send Fyfield for Dr. Laysmith."

"Now don't fash yourself, sir. It's nothing unusual to have a little fever. I'll just draw the curtains, and if she'll quiet herself and sleep, I'm sure she'll be better soon."

"Shall I get a book and read to you, Anne?"

"Not St. Jerome."

"Certainly not. The Song of Songs?"

"If you like."

For a time the sound of his voice seemed to soothe her, but then she was tossing and turning again, asking for water for her parched and swollen lips, moving to find a cooler place in the bed. At length she said:

"Call Nurse for me. I have a cramp."

That afternoon and all through the night she was racked with diarrhea, tortured with alternating fever and sweats. John helped Phyllis to lift and turn and bathe and soothe, but she grew steadily worse. When the first bellman sounded in the pearly dawn light, she no longer knew John. "Sir," she begged, "where is my husband? Please send my husband to me." And then with a wail, "Oh, John, where are you?"

He routed out Fyfield from the cupboard off the kitchen where he slept and sent him hurrying to fetch Dr. Laysmith, but even before the doctor arrived, John knew it for childbed fever. He had read medicine enough in his youth to recognize the symptoms and to know that there was little that anyone could do, even to make her more comfortable.

Lady Jacobs sent over her maid Nancy, who was an excellent nurse, to help. The doctor came and shook his head; the apothecary's man brought waters and powders and ointments. A frightened little band of children gathered outside Anne's door and John, opening it, said to them gravely, "Your mother is very sick. You must all be very good and quiet and take care of yourselves." Through it all, Anne tossed in fever and delirium, calling for John.

She thought that she was back on the Isle of Wight, and she cried because he did not come.

"I am here, Anne. Right beside you, dearest. Can't you see me?"

She would reach out a thin, hot hand and clutch his arm, gasping, "I want my husband. Why doesn't he come?"

Nancy went away, to "rest me feet" and to eat something, and Phyllis took her place, but John would not stir from the bedside. A low sun shone through the slit between the curtains and the motes danced, the doctor came again and went. Still Anne could not sleep. Once, when there was a remission of the fever and she was bathed in a sweat so drenching that they had to change the sheets, he thought she must drowse a little, but her eyes, burning now deep in her head, stared wildly still, and her voice, growing weaker, continued to plead, "John, where are you? Why don't you come?"

Anguished, John sat beside her, holding her twitching hand, through the sunset of the third day and the long dusk, into the velvet night and the candlelight, feeling her moans of pain and her pleading for him as the bludgeoning of a sword upon his naked heart, knowing that her hoarse voice was growing weaker. He did not pray; there was nothing in his mind but that tortured body twisting and moaning on the bed. He did not see when Nancy replaced Phyllis or when she went to sleep sitting on the stool and leaning her head against the wall, her mouth open.

Some time after midnight, without knowing him again, Anne died.

2   After the funeral at St. Clement Danes, the fourth in three years, he called all the children, in their hastily dyed black clothes, poor young things, into the hall. "I have something to say to you," he told them. The stairs were draped with black, twined in and out among the balusters, branches of bay and yew smothered the chimney piece. It had comforted the servants, perhaps, to deck the house in this fashion.

The children, swollen-eyed and drooping, came into the room dragging their feet and, when he told them to, sat down in a circle, staring mournfully at him. They were all there. Constance held the baby in her arms, and Margaret, after vainly trying to rouse the others to play, plumped herself down on the floor and put her thumb in her mouth.

"You have all suffered an irreparable loss. You have lost a tender and devoted mother, and there is no cure, no mitigation, for your grief." He paused. Johnny, who always contrived to do something annoying, plucked at the damask upholstery of the chair with a dirty forefinger, pulling it away from the wood, apparently paying no attention at all to what John was saying. George, squeezed in the chair with him, stared at the floor, the slow tears dripping into his open mouth. Nine-year-old Lucy who, with her straight red hair and wide, pale mouth had no beauty but a certain honest charm, and Bridget, all but extinguished by her black dress, met his eyes with solemn, unwinking gaze; Margaret sat on the floor with her thumb in her mouth and Elizabeth wriggled herself out of Constance's arms and toddled across the room to fling her wet fists upon John's knees with a crow of delight startling in that heavy room. John picked her up and settled her in his arms, feeling some dim comfort in the warm, heavy body, strung with vitality as with wires. All these seven children, he thought, to educate, to rear, to dress, in time to marry.

"All that there is of a father," he went on, "you shall have. I shall be yours wholly. You will never have to fear a stepmother or a rival family of brothers and sisters. I shall not marry again. We are as a family forever lamed, but we shall limp along somehow. Constance will help me."

Constance lifted her head, her face flushed, and nodded at him seriously.

"The boys will work hard at school. You little girls will look to Constance as your guide. We shall all love one another and do our best."

They were getting restless now; he must let them go; but first he took a folded piece of paper from his pouch.

"As soon as possible I shall call in Mr. Nicholas Stone, the sculptor, to make a memorial for your dear mother in the church. There will be a statue of her, and perhaps of all of you kneeling on either side of her, with a plaque underneath, with these words that I have written." He read them slowly, aware that he was trying to comfort himself with monuments as the servants and the children had comforted themselves with bands of black linen and sprays of bay and yew; but he read on, and when he had finished, he translated the Latin for the girls:

" 'To Anne, daughter of George More of Loseley, a woman most choice, most beloved; a wife most dear, most pure; a mother most gentle, most dutiful; carried off by a cruel fever after fifteen years of marriage. Her husband, John Donne, made speechless by grief, sets up this stone to speak, pledges his ashes to hers in a new marriage under God.' "

In the silence that followed, the boys sighed loudly and Margaret burst into a long wail.

"Run out and play, all of you," said John. He gave Elizabeth into Constance's care, kissed them all and sent them out with an effort at a smile. They would remember this morning, some of them, some of it, they had been witnesses to his vows. Turning, he went into his study and closed the door behind.

3 He stayed there for days, and then for weeks. When he slept, which was but little and restlessly, he flung himself down on the couch; he could not endure the room and the bed that he and Anne had shared. When he ate, which was little, it was from the trays that they brought to him, Constance with an anxious, hopeful smile, Phyllis with manifest disapproval.

Hour after hour he sat, staring at nothing, or walked up and down, back and forth, in the small space, eating the bitter bread of his grief, drinking the black brew. Sleep brought him no respite, for he dreamed of her, racked and suffering, calling for him and not knowing him; or if he fell into a brief unconsciousness, he woke to a realization so sharp, so new, that it opened up his wound and made it bleed afresh.

His friends came to condole with him. He felt the kindly

hand on his shoulder, heard the words of sympathy—resignation, the will of God, time healing all hurts—and found them empty and without conceivable meaning. He left untouched the wine, the cakes, the books, they brought him. Gradually they stopped coming, and he returned into the dark and thorny forest of his thoughts.

He faced again the wrong that he had done to her, and to her father, in stealing her away. Just how her father had felt was clearer to him now than it had ever been, as he recognized how he would feel if someone married Constance against his will and knowledge. He lacerated himself with the realization that, having taken her away from Loseley and her father and brought her to privation and hard work, he had often been unkind, leaving her alone with sick and fretful children while he had dallied in the sunshine at Twickenham making literary love to Lady Bedford, enjoyed the companionship of Lady Danvers or engaged in a fatherly flirtation with Lady Huntingdon. He remembered the days he had spent at Court, tiresome enough, empty, disappointing, but still out in the world, among the notable. He thought with bitter remorse of the year he had spent in France with the Drurys while Anne had made the best of the charity of relatives. That in her last agony she had thought herself back at Nunwell, longing for him, was a knife twisting in his heart.

He thought of the thirteen births and miscarriages in fifteen years. Children were the fruit of love, and childbirth was a woman's fate, there was here no guilt, no cause for remorse. She had loved her children, grieved passionately over those she had lost, yet in the end it was they, and through them, John, who had killed her. "This is my body which is given for you . . ." The words throbbed through him, and it did not occur to him where they had come from. They were true of Anne and of himself. Yet would it have been better if he had been unfaithful to her? Or continent? They had loved each other with their bodies as well as their souls; "with my body I thee worship . . ." there was no divorce between the two.

Death was but a sleep, he told himself as he had told other

grieving souls. Superficial, crass, indifferent, complacent words. A sleep, yes, but a sleep an earthquake could not wake.

He heard the sounds in the house around him, the shutting of a door, the buzz of a fly, the noise of a coach in the street, the cry of a child; but they scarcely penetrated the cloak of aching loss that wrapped him round. Occasionally Constance would slip into the room, sit there quietly for a time beside him, saying nothing, with a sensitive love beyond her years; after a time he would smile at her and lay his hand gently on her dark curls and she would go away again, looking happier.

He went out once, to keep a promise, made some weeks before, to preach a sermon at St. Clement Danes. He stood in the pulpit of the church where Anne lay buried, and preached from a text in Jeremiah, "Lo I am the man that have seen affliction," but he might have been a statue speaking; his words were cold, logical, learned.

Back again in his study, he was assailed by memories of Anne, pictures of her in his mind that he hugged to him while they hurt him almost intolerably, pressing his heart against the thorn as the cherubim did in Andrea de Firenze's great frescoes of the Church Triumphant which he had seen long ago on the wall of the Spanish Chapel in Florence.

He saw her among her children, absorbed in sharing out some dainty, surrounded by the dark heads, the red ones, the fair heads. He saw her as he had first loved her, on that day when Essex was pilloried by the lords, when he had gone into the garden for a breath of relief and found Anne there, young, fresh, beautiful, and they had sat so long without speaking. He saw her furious with him, raging about "God's master-piece," and could have laughed, for she was so funny and so dear, but that his longing for her was a pain almost too much to bear. He saw her by their bedroom fire emerging from her clothes, saw her white and naked as a fish slipping into bed.

Sometimes he sat without thought at all and let the anguish wash over him, throbbing with pain; sometimes he looked into the desert of the future and tried to imagine enduring it. Once he would have soothed himself with dreams of death;

now, remembering his children, he thrust the forbidden thought aside.

He called on God, not with the daily prayers worn smooth with use, but with the rough cry of his whole being for God Himself, and was answered by silence, by absence. He, a minister, he accused himself, had no relation with God. He could preach elaborately of God's majesty and power; he could preach eloquently—who better?—of man's sin and God's pardon; but of God Himself he knew nothing. God, who spoke to Moses, a murderer, out of a burning bush, had nothing to say to John Donne. Once John had thought that He breathed, shone, sighed, sought to mend; now he knew only that in His might, majesty, power, and perhaps His anger, He had withdrawn, utterly.

Near midnight on St. Lucy's Day, when the rain lashed against the windows and the room grew penetratingly damp and cold, he knew himself at last as he was, a hollow vessel, an empty shell, drained of all grief and remorse, of hope as of despair. For an instant of time—or for the eternity that is outside time—he was suspended in the desolation of his acceptance.

Layer after layer of life was lifted from him, or he plunged beneath them, below sight or sound, beneath thought or feeling, beyond the near or the far, the up or the down. He had nothing, he was nothing. Not a nothing made of air and shadow, for that is still something, implying a vapor, a light, a body; but a very distillation of nothing. He was the epitaph of all living things. He was absence, he was darkness, he was emptiness.

Deep in the center of darkness, he found light; in the essence of emptiness, he found substance. Quietly, almost imperceptibly at first, he was filled with the knowledge of the love of God. It flowed into his hollowness, it irradiated his darkness, it filled his absence with Presence, undergirding him and lifting him up. It was ineffable, ineluctable, unquestionable.

4 In the morning, in the dawn, after a sleep so deep, so dreamless, so restoring that he knew it to be of divine provenance, he woke to find secure the knowledge that had come to him in the night, to discover himself a new man facing the new day. Batter my heart, he had written, and God, taking the poem for a prayer, had answered it with a terrible literalness; he was, as he had asked to be, broken, blown, burned and made anew. He had lost Anne and died one kind of death; dying, he had found God and lived again.

For the first time since Anne's death he could think of the future without agony. All that he had been, all that he was, he could use, he now saw, for the love and contemplation of God. There was nothing too dim, too poor, or too sinful for God to use. A man's covetousness could be turned into a spiritual covetousness for God's glory, his voltuousness find abundance in God, his anger flame in zeal for God's house. As those simple fishermen of Galilee became fishers of men, as St. Paul's vehemence in persecuting became passion for converting, so might not he, John Donne, turn his worldly pleasures into delight in God, direct his ambition to the majesty of the church, pour his love of Anne into the channel of universal love?

He rose and pulled the curtains, looking out into the clean-washed dawn, seeing a bare tree traced against the sky with golden light, a drifting cloud touched with color.

> *I will awake early; I will praise thee.*
> *Sero te amavi pulchritudo . . .*
> *O glorious beauty, infinitely reverend,*
> *infinitely fresh and young,*
> *I come late to Thy love if I consider*
> *the past days of my life, but early*
> *if Thou beest pleased to reckon with me*
> *from this hour of the shining*
> *of Thy grace upon me. . . .*